D0208747

# 31 Bond Street

# 31 BOND STREET

A NOVEL

## Ellen Horan

HARPERCOLLINS
PUBLISHERS LTD

*31 Bond Street*
Copyright © 2010 by Ellen Horan.
All rights reserved.

Published by HarperCollins Publishers Ltd.

First Canadian edition

HarperCollins books may be purchased for educational, business,
or sales promotional use through our Special Markets Department.

HarperCollins Publishers Ltd
2 Bloor Street East, 20th Floor
Toronto, Ontario, Canada
M4W 1A8

*www.harpercollins.ca*

Library and Archives Canada Cataloguing in Publication

Horan, Ellen, 1956–
31 Bond Street : a novel / Ellen Horan.

ISBN 978-1-55468-471-7

I. Title. II. Title: Thirty-one Bond Street.
PS3608.066T45 2009   813.6   C2009-905726-3

Designed by Emily Cavett Taff

Printed and bound in the United States of America
RRD 9 8 7 6 5 4 3 2 1

*For my father,*
*Hubert J. Horan III, an innate storyteller;*
*for him, stories were a search for meaning,*
*and history was his compass.*

*Beware of large adventures in railroads, niggers, wild lands, new banks, old banks, manufacturing enterprises, steamships, regular and fancy stocks, which promise no redeeming dividends this side of 1860. When the winds blow, and the rains fall, and the floods descend, all these things may be swept away as within the brief space of a single night.*

—*The New York Herald*, FEBRUARY 4, 1857

# 31 Bond Street

# Part I

# CHAPTER ONE

About three o'clock early Saturday morning, a heavy snow commenced and continued till daylight. The snow turned to rain and the wind blew for four hours, which we cannot but characterize as the worst, the very worst, wintry gale ever experienced in the city, ripping up window shutters and blowing down signs.

Along the side streets, the water and melted snow flooded the lowlands of the City, which are generally the haunts of the poor. The very rats got frightened, and ran about Washington Street, South Street, the docks and markets, as the gushing thaw, like a landlord weary of seeking arrears of rent, summarily ejected them.

*The New York Times*, FEBRUARY 2, 1857

*February 1, 1857*

For a boy who watched boats, his room was the perfect perch. He could see the wharves across a jumble of chimney tops, and beyond, a peek of the harbor. He'd count the ships at anchor, all sizes and shapes. There were three-masters and snub-nosed square-riggers and packet boats built to carry tonnage, with black balls on red flags. Pleasure steamers were loaded down with folks out for amusement, heading past the oyster flats to picnic on the islands. A boat from the Orient had a curving hull and mysterious symbols on the sail. Occasionally, in spring, a cloud descended and sat on top of the water, leaving a ghostly smoke that blocked the Narrows. Skiffs scuttled on the New York side of it, their silhouettes looking like paper cutouts, while the foghorns wailed from the Atlantic side, waiting for it to lift. On summer days, John would crawl out the window to get the widest view, grabbing onto a chimney pot to keep from slipping off the steep pitch. He'd watch for hours from the roof, sitting at a slant, with the sensation that the entire city was straining out to sea.

Winter was different. Ice stretched clear across the East River, and the ferryboats were stalled in their berths. The previous evening, the weather had turned foul. John awoke shivering in his tangled bedding. He hopped through the cold to find his trousers and a woolen vest. He lived in an attic under the eaves with his mother, who lay still on the wooden bed in the opposite corner. She was frail and spent her days in a rocking chair next to the stove. Her hands were gnarled and pained by the cold and damp. She no longer went to the seamstress' shop, for she could no longer sew.

This morning, there was nothing outside the dormer window but rain and a veil of grey. John couldn't see the harbor or the clock on the church tower, and because of the storm, no one was pulling the bells. He wrapped some pieces of wool around his trouser legs with twine, to protect himself from the bitter weather. He crept out of the room and shut the attic door gently, and hurried down the stairs of the small house on Rector Street. He did not know what time it was, but Saturday was payday, and Dr. Burdell would dock him half a day if he were late.

He hurried uptown. Along Broadway, the wind whipped a mixture of snow and freezing rain, rocking the shutters and setting gas lamps swinging on their posts. Old snow blocked the culverts, flooding the intersections, and carriages were left abandoned in water up to their hubs. He made his way to Bond Street, a long row of townhouses, and banged at a door under the stoop. The cook pulled the bolts. "Good, lord!" Hannah exclaimed, "You're wetter than a sea captain. Don't you dare drip on my floor." He followed her down the dark hallway and was careful not to drip, for the cook had hit him before, most recently with a wooden spoon.

In the kitchen, there were two fires burning: one in the brick beehive oven where she baked pies and puddings and one in the cast-iron stove. "Only a fool would come out on a day like today," muttered Hannah. She moved back and forth to the oven, an apron wrapped around her wide girth, pulling out a fresh pie on a wooden board and then sliding it into the pie cabinet. When one of the oven doors opened, the heat hit John like a furnace blast. Hannah threw some bread crusts into a simmering pot of milk. John watched the crusts swimming around in the bowl as they softened into a pulp.

"Doctor Burdell is still sleeping. I'm surprised he hasn't rung for his breakfast." The cook spoke with reverence about the owner of the house, a dentist and a bachelor. John worked as an errand boy: he lit the gas lamps in the sixteen rooms, wound the clocks with a brass key, and hauled coal up and down the broad staircase with buckets on a stick across his back.

"Yesterday, the serving girl was in the basement with a whiskey bottle and she was sent straight to the street."

"So Alice is gone, is she?" asked John, gulping down his porridge.

"She sure is. And, do you think Mrs. Cunningham has hired another girl?" asked Hannah. John guessed by shaking his head no.

"No, she has not," said Hannah emphatically, slamming a dough ball against a wooden board and rolling it flat. "So now it's my job to cook the meal, serve the table, bow and curtsy, all while my bread burns."

"Hannah!" said the housemistress, appearing in the doorway. Mrs. Cunningham often appeared, sudden and unannounced, to give orders. "Why hasn't the boy taken Dr. Burdell his breakfast?" she asked, illuminated by the lamp in the hallway. She placed a hand on the doorjamb and spoke from the doorway, as if hesitating to come in. She was dressed to go out, in a wide tailored skirt. Underneath the bodice, which was edged in delicate lace around the wrist and throat, a corset carved her figure into a tiny waist and ample bosom. She brushed away a tendril of a dark hair that had fallen into her face, loosened from its pins. Her milky skin looked paler than usual, and her eyes had a look of concern.

Hannah glanced at the iron bells that were strung along the kitchen wall, each a different size, one for every room of the house. "The doctor hasn't rung for his meal yet, Ma'am, that's why," she said.

"What time did he return home last night?" asked Mrs. Cunningham.

"I was asleep in the attic, Ma'am. I do not keep track of my master's comings and goings."

"Helen is taking the train at noon. Please tell Samuel to bring the carriage around." Mrs. Cunningham's daughter was returning to boarding school in Saratoga, and she spoke as if Dr. Burdell's carriage and driver were hers to command.

"I wouldn't send anyone out in this weather unless I expected them to swim or take a schooner," the cook retorted.

"I see that John arrived this morning without being swept away," she said curtly. "Please do as I say. Have John take Dr. Burdell's breakfast upstairs, now. And ring me when Samuel has come, so he can fetch the carriage." She gathered her skirts and departed the kitchen.

Emma Cunningham had arrived at 31 Bond Street the previous October with her two daughters and twenty trunks. It was common for a bachelor like Dr. Burdell, who lived alone without a family, to lease the upper part of his large townhouse to a widow who would oversee the housekeeping and the servants. Only thirty-six, and a recent widow, Emma Cunningham was younger and prettier than most in the position. She irritated Hannah, for she spent her mornings at her vanity, smoothing her pale skin with scented creams and pinning up her hair into fanciful arrangements. Hannah was always harping about her—she wasted gas and decorated her room with yellow roses and an eiderdown a foot high. Her teenage daughters, Helen and Augusta, sailed around the house as if they owned the place, their hoop skirts scraping against the walls.

Hannah grumbled while fixing the breakfast tray. She rushed about, adding missing items: a small spoon for the jam, an extra knife for some hard sausage.

"May I have some more?" John asked, lifting his empty bowl.

Hannah slapped him on the head. "Get upstairs with the tray. You heard the lady. If Dr. Burdell is missing his breakfast, everyone in this house will suffer."

John carried the tray out of the kitchen with the china teapot tilting and wobbling, balancing it carefully. He climbed up the narrow kitchen stairway to the front hall, passing the double parlor, ornamented with twin mantels and a high ceiling ringed with stucco designs like watchful angels. A tall clock in the hall rang eight times. Out the large window at the curve in the main staircase, the branches of the trees in the back garden scratched against the glass.

On the second floor, John placed the tray on the carpet in front of Dr. Burdell's office, which was next to his bedroom. He pressed his ear to the door to hear if he was awake. Then he spotted something curious—a key was dangling from the keyhole, about to topple onto the floor. It was odd because Dr. Burdell, an intensely private man, always locked his door at night from the inside. John wondered if perhaps he had risen early and left the house before breakfast. Hearing nothing, John turned the knob. The door cracked open and scraped along the carpet a few inches until it jammed against a heavy object. The boy pushed harder until the door burst open.

Inside, Dr. Burdell was sprawled in the center of the floor, his arms outstretched, and his head in a sticky puddle that had hardened like tar. His lips were pendant and blue. His throat was slashed with a wound so deep that it nearly detached the head from the torso, revealing a sinewy tangle of muscle and tiny pearls of spine. The doctor's eyes stared up at John, glazed, sunken into the temples. His tongue was protruding, swollen, as if choked on a last, silent scream.

John ran to the stairway and leaned over the banister. "The Doctor! The Doctor! Hannah, come quickly."

Hannah's head emerged, bobbing from below. "What are you yelling about boy?"

"He's in there. I seen him!" John cried.

"Seen what, pray tell."

"The Doctor. He's on the floor! He's dead!"

"Don't you go telling tales, boy. Are you playing me for a fool?"

"I am not telling a lie—there's blood on the floor, and all over the walls and his neck is cut."

In her floured apron, she huffed up the staircase, her grey hair flying from her cap. Hannah reached the doorway and peered in. "Oh, my God, my God," she screamed, putting her apron to her face.

Emma Cunningham, hearing the noise, rushed from the third floor, with Augusta and Helen behind her.

"Hannah, what is the commotion?"

"The master is dead!" cried Hannah.

"That's impossible," Emma said, pushing Hannah aside, craning her neck to peer into the office, her voice trailing, "I just saw him yesterday before supper. . . ." She turned away, clasping her hands to her breast.

"It's a carnage!" wailed Hannah. "A bloody murder!"

Augusta looked inside, and then dropped to the floor in a faint. Mrs. Cunningham grabbed Helen to keep her away from the gruesome sight, and the younger girl started to cry. John stood next to the pile of women, his eyes welling with tears.

"What are you standing there for, you foolish creature?" screamed Hannah. "Run down to the street and fetch the doctor that lives next door. Then go to the precinct house and look for an officer." She hit him on the side of the head, as if spurring a horse.

John turned and rushed down the stairs two at a time. In the vestibule he pulled the bolts on the heavy front door and jumped down the stoop. The street was misty and the rain had turned to snow. He paused and looked back at the house. For a moment he had the sensation that he had lost direction, not knowing which way to turn. Then he ran toward Broadway, his boyish figure, bundled in scratchy grey woolens, dissolving in the dim, snowy light.

# CHAPTER TWO

The teakettle whistled with an insistent shriek. John replenished the firewood in the stove while Hannah muttered prayers. The door under the stoop opened and men came in, bringing a gust of wind and wet snow. The coroner slammed the door shut. Edward Connery was a stocky man with a heavy stomach that protruded from his waistcoat, a rumpled shirttail trailing beneath his vest. He entered the kitchen and removed his oilskin coat, dropping his wet garments in a pile on the kitchen floor.

"The Coroner's arrived, Captain, the Coroner is here!" came a deputy's voice from the hallway.

"I could use a good cup of stew to chase this wetness from my bones," Connery said.

"It's about time someone hauled you uptown," said the Police Captain, George Dilkes, joining him in the kitchen. He had a lilt to his brogue and the doleful eyes of an Irish setter. "The errand boy came to the precinct," he said, pointing to John. "Then I sent my men to fetch you, over an hour ago."

"And how about a spike of rum, lass?" asked Connery. Hannah

brought him a cup of broth and poured some rum into it. "A good Irish wench would give a man a double shot."

Hannah turned, reddening. "This is a respectable home, not a downtown gin mill," she sputtered. "A man's been murdered in this house, and the Coroner is tanking up on rum? God, help us!"

"A dead man is just as dead on Bond Street as in the lower wards, wouldn't you say so, Captain?" said Connery, sipping the oily mixture.

"Could be," Dilkes replied, "but uptown or downtown, this man just had his head near cut off. You'd better brace yourself," he said. "I never seen anything so bad. He's got fifteen stab wounds, and his throat is cut from ear to ear."

"Oh God, dear God," lamented Hannah, crossing herself.

"Catch me up," Connery said with authority; as City Coroner, he was the elected official in charge of the crime scene: besides attending to medical matters and an autopsy, it was his job to call a coroner's jury to the house. The jury, pulled by lots, would interrogate neighbors and family members—anyone with knowledge about the victim—using testimony to piece together evidence at the scene. With a coroner's deft handling, the coroner's inquest could point a finger in the right direction, nabbing a perpetrator and solving a crime.

Dilkes led Connery out of the kitchen, passing a policeman with a shovel, stamping the snow off his boots. "The men have been digging up the backyard for the weapon," explained the Captain. "I sent them to search in the outhouse and down the latrines."

"Dirk or dagger?" asked the Coroner.

"From the depth of the cuts, I figure it was a two-sided blade." The two men climbed the small back stairway, their bulky frames bent, with Connery puffing behind. They emerged onto the first floor, with its soaring ceilings and chandeliers. A cluster of officers was lounging against a marble table.

"What are you waiting for, men?" shouted Connery. "Some politician to give you a handout? Go into the parlor and turn everything upside down. We're still looking for a weapon."

Dilkes led Connery to the main staircase and pointed to some tiny blood spots along the wallpaper, almost imperceptible, at the height of a man's hand. "There's hardly any trace of blood anywhere, except with the body. This morning, the cook didn't notice anything amiss. The doors to the house and the windows were locked tight."

Connery squatted, examining the specks, touching a blood spot to determine if it was still wet. "Who else lives here?"

"The victim is a dental surgeon, unmarried, about forty-six years old. A housemistress lives on the two upper floors, with her daughters." Dilkes flipped through a small notepad, reading from his notes. "The cook sleeps in the attic. A serving girl was dismissed yesterday, and there is a carriage driver who drove Dr. Burdell last night, but he doesn't live here."

"Does everyone have a key?"

"We are still checking to see if any keys are missing."

"Was anything taken?" asked Connery.

"There's plenty to take, but it seems nothing's been touched. It doesn't seem to be a robbery."

The two men started up the stairway. Connery leaned over the banister and gazed upward along the graceful arc as it curved to the top of the house. Forty feet above, a skylight was embedded in the roof, an oval of wood and glass that sat atop the stairwell like an elegant crown. He whistled. "This is a fine place, all right."

They entered the room where the body lay across the floor. Dr. Burdell's dental office, converted from a bedroom, was furnished like a parlor with engravings and a velvet-fringed sofa. The dentist chair sat in one corner, a torturous contraption with clamps and wooden blocks that held the patient's head still when a tooth was pulled. The body lay in the center of the floor. A pool of blood spread several feet in diameter around the corpse. The dead man's shirt had been torn open, exposing the purple knife wounds that punctured his white flesh.

"This is a bestial crime," muttered Connery.

An officer entered. "Your men have arrived, sir," he announced. In the hallway were several men from the Coroner's office, carrying microscopes and medical bags, and behind them, a crew of reporters, arching their necks to see the body. "And these reporters came from the New York dailies. They want to know if they can come in for a look."

"Get them out of here," said Dilkes, waving his arms.

"No, let them stay," countered Connery. "We'll put them to work. Send the reporters downstairs—we'll have them record the witnesses' testimony in the parlor, and the sketch illustrators can make a likeness of the scene. Besides, if I send them away, the editors will cry foul all the way to City Hall."

"We'd be most obliged to you, sir," said a newspaperman from the crowd in the hall, doffing his hat.

"Take the body to the bedroom and strip it naked for an autopsy," Connery ordered. Two coroner's deputies entered and rolled the dentist's body onto a sheet, grabbing the corners like a sling and lifting the sagging mass. Dr. Burdell's neck twisted at the open wound and his head fell sideways. His eyes remained open, as if he were following the conversation.

"He sure didn't go down without a fight," said Connery. "It's hard to think that no one heard the attack, or any cries or footsteps."

"Well," pondered Dilkes, "these ceilings are pretty high. The victim didn't come home until midnight, after everyone in the house was asleep. The attacker could have been hiding in the wardrobe passage." The coroner paced around, opening the door of the closet that formed a wardrobe passage between the office and the man's bedroom. There were cabinets with shelves of bottles and tonics, but nothing seemed out of place. The doctor's gumshoes were placed carefully in front of the fireplace, on the sofa his shawl. His desk had papers stacked on it, in an orderly fashion. A chair had been pushed away from the desk several feet, marking the spot where the skirmish began.

Connery rifled through the papers on the doctor's desk. A ledger lay open with a quill pen on top. He put on his spectacles, pushing them along his nose, squinting as he looked over the fine columns of numbered entries. A locked safe was beside the desk. He took a tangled handkerchief from his waistcoat and wiped his face. "Something smells rotten here."

"I don't know," protested Dilkes. "Everyone seems to be telling it straight—after all, the housemistress's story is backed by innocent girls."

"Innocence—in this city?" countered Connery.

"If someone in the house committed this deed, the perpetrator would be covered in blood from head to toe," said Dilkes.

"There was plenty of time to clean up after this bloody brawl, and I don't see any trace of the killer leaving the house." Connery went to the door and yelled down the staircase to one of the officers. "I want everyone detained in their rooms until they are interrogated."

"It's the weekend, sir," said Dilkes. "Maybe we should confer with the District Attorney before we put anyone in house arrest."

"The District Attorney will be here fast enough. He'll be jumping all over this one. With a murder on Bond Street, he'll want it solved quick. Pull a jury. Drag them from their Sunday suppers if you must. Now, let me speak to the woman of the house."

✧    ✧    ✧

On the third floor, Emma Cunningham sat by the window in her bedroom. She was lost in a reverie, almost a stupor. Augusta and Helen sat with her, weeping by the fire. It had been several hours since the trauma, and the wind still howled through the street. The wood of the stairway heaved, and the bedroom door opened. The Police Captain entered along with Coroner Connery and several officers. They crowded in, an imposing presence in her floral bedroom.

"Excuse me, Ma'am," said Captain Dilkes. "We need to ask you some questions. We will be placing you under detention in your room while we conduct a full inquest."

"Detention?" asked Emma. "Why?" Connery looked her over carefully. She had been described as a widow but was remarkably youthful, seeming not much older than her teenage daughters, who were huddled on an overstuffed ottoman by the fire. Her body was prone, leaning across the arm of the chair, as if the distress of the morning had left her languishing in despair. Her linen blouse was disheveled, revealing traces of her camisole and a corseted bustier. Her complexion was blotchy from tears, her lips pink, her dark hair glossy, falling wildly from her hairpins and curling across her shoulders.

"With all due respect to you and your daughters, Madame, I need to ascertain how a man came to be viciously massacred while so many people were home. You've haven't told us everything, now, have you?" asked Connery.

"I have told the officers everything," Emma replied, her voice tinged with alarm. "I was sleeping, and did not hear a thing." She tried to summon her best composure but her expression changed like a cloud movement: flashes of red emerged in sudden streaks across her face, and tears began coursing along her cheeks. Her countenance betrayed such anxiety that Connery eyed her closely. His instinct told him to remain still—emotional moments like these were often followed by a confession.

She clutched a paper in her hand. Pale and shaking, she lifted it and offered it to the Coroner. It was a scroll wrapped with a blue satin ribbon.

He slowly opened the scroll. He looked it over, his eyes darting across the words, and then to the faces of the men.

"This sheds quite a different light on matters, doesn't it?" he said. It was a certificate, dated January 14, 1857, two weeks earlier, and signed by the reverend of the Reformed Dutch Church on Greenwich Street. He passed the paper to Dilkes. "Is this yours, Ma'am?"

"Yes, it is mine . . . ," she said, barely above a whisper. "It was supposed to be a secret and not to be made public until the spring." She drew a breath, and spoke louder, with clear diction, "This is my marriage certificate and I am Harvey Burdell's wife."

# CHAPTER THREE

## MYSTERIOUS MIDNIGHT MURDER
## AN EMINENT CITIZEN ASSASSINATED
## INTENSE EXCITEMENT IN BOND STREET

An atrocity, almost unparalleled by any of the atrocities committed in this City, came to light on Saturday morning in the house at No. 31 Bond Street. Dr. Harvey Burdell was found in his office, foully murdered, and frightfully and fiendishly mutilated. Dr. Burdell was a man of considerable wealth, and respectably connected.

All the inmates of the house, which is also occupied by the family of a housemistress, Mrs. Cunningham, are prevented from leaving the premises by a body of Police, who are detailed for that purpose by the Coroner's orders.

Bond Street was visited by hundreds of persons who came out of curiosity, to look at the house.

*The New York Times*, FEBRUARY 3, 1857

*Monday, February 3, 1857*

H enry Clinton scraped the blade along his neck and then tapped the razor against the side of the china basin. He heard a newsboy crying the headlines: "Murder, Murder! Murder on Bond

Street!" As the call echoed closer, it drifted into his bedroom like a song. He continued scraping the skin and tapping the bowl without missing a beat. Bond Street was just across Broadway, a block east from his house on Bleecker Street, yet the news did not interrupt the rhythm of his shave. Clinton was a criminal lawyer and no stranger to bloodshed.

He pulled the towel from his neck and wiped away the last beads of lather. He fastened a collar to the top of his shirt, adding cuff links and a silk-lined vest. Lifting a gold watch from his dressing table, he fastened the chain to his pocket. Bond Street, he thought. That would teach her. It was his wife's idea that they move uptown from Warren Street. As the burgeoning commerce of the city spread like a fan through lower Manhattan, the fine homes downtown, once belonging to bankers and merchants, gave way to shops, and the houses along the side streets were now flanked with tradesmen. The well-to-do had long ago moved north to the quiet elegance of Bleecker Street, Bond Street, and Washington Square.

It wasn't to keep up with the wealthy that had prompted Elisabeth to insist they move. She had argued for it because their old home was walking distance to his office on Chambers Street and the courts, allowing Clinton to rush back and forth at all times of day and night, never sitting still long enough to eat a proper meal. Now his ride downtown took half an hour on the Bowery omnibus, the distance allowing, Elisabeth had hoped, for a fuller domestic life. In fact, the long commute aggravated him, and his longer absences made her nervous. Now, she was always traveling downtown to visit him and to deliver him food.

Putting on his jacket and fixing his cravat, he entered the breakfast room. Out the high windows, wisteria vines hung bare with icicles and snow drifted deep across the garden from the weekend storm. The aroma of fresh muffins came from the kitchen below. The cook was at it again, making batches of baked goods for his office. His wife fretted about his nourishment and believed that if pies and cakes accompanied him downtown, they would buffer him from the harsh world of the prison and the courts.

The *New York Times* was folded next to his plate. Elisabeth entered, and as she passed his chair, she kissed him on the head. She sat down at the opposite end of the table, fluttering her napkin to her lap. She had a blooming complexion even in the deep of winter.

"Did you sleep well?" he asked, snapping his newspaper open.

Elisabeth eyed him warily. "Just fine. I dreamt that newsboys entered the bedroom and wouldn't leave until I got my purse."

"That wasn't a dream, dear, it is the spectral presence of the press." Just an hour earlier her auburn hair had been a tousle of silk, curling across her pillow as she slept; now it was expertly pinned and caught the morning light. He had met his wife after he had finished his law degree at Harvard and come to New York to work as a junior counsel for a pair of septuagenarians on Battery Place. A classmate, a New Yorker, invited him to meet some girls. Unfamiliar with the social rites of ambitious mothers and their unmarried daughters, Clinton was pulled along to an afternoon tea, which featured a roster of pretty girls taking turns at a piano, each attempting to play music that was beyond their reach. Elisabeth sat on a chair at the edge of the parlor, the loveliest in the room. Irritated by the music, he eyed the chair next to her, and whispered, "How do you do, I am Henry Clinton. I am afraid I am a bit tin-eared."

"I am, too," she whispered back.

"Tin-eared?" he asked,

"No, a Clinton," she replied. "Elisabeth Clinton." It turned out that she was indeed a Clinton, but unlike his family, who were from a small town in Connecticut, she was descended from the illustrious Clintons of New York. Her grandfather DeWitt, a Mayor, a Governor, and a candidate for President, had used political office to plow through the end of the eighteenth century and reshape the continent. He had spearheaded the construction of the Erie Canal, allowing the riches of the West to flow into the ports of New York, and then forced the streets of Manhattan into a grid to absorb the backsplash of commerce. At present, the logjam of vehicles on the city streets was so fierce as to convince its inhabitants that New York was the capital of the world.

During the course of that afternoon tea, Clinton was smitten by Elisabeth, and in a matter of weeks he had fallen in love. He wooed her with his small salary, his best wit, and invitations to entertainments that they never reached, instead walking the streets of New York, lost in conversation until the moon shone through the quiet elms and it was time to take her home. She had a passion for the Romantic poets and had devoured Thomas Paine and John Stuart Mill. Without much resistance, she had married him, making her Elisabeth Clinton Clinton. Had there ever been a woman lawyer, she would have been a superior one, and he often imagined their partnership, with twin names painted on a door.

He glanced at her from across the table. Now, nearly thirty to his thirty-six, there was not a moment of their habitual domestic life that failed to suit him. They had not been blessed with children, a circumstance that had once filled them with melancholy. Sometimes he still found her alone in the sitting room, paused over a book, looking sadly out past the lilac bushes, but as the years passed, each of them seemed to have eased their own personal wound of regret.

"I see you have already read the paper," he said. The newspaper showed evidence that his wife and the maids had been picking through it in the kitchen for news of the murder.

"The cook fears that the murderer has satisfied his revenge for dentists, and lawyers are next," said Elisabeth.

"Well, if an assassin is lurking in our alley, she will take good care of him. She wields a fierce knife. I have seen her butterfly a lamb," he replied, scanning the many pages of bold headlines.

"Do you remember you visited him once?" asked Elisabeth. "You had an abscess, and he removed it,"

"Dr. Burdell?" said Clinton. "He persecuted me mercilessly, with clamps around my head and steel calipers in my jaw. It appears he had his throat sliced from ear to ear—a just retribution for a dental surgeon, I'd say."

"Henry, please," said Elisabeth. Inured to the cruelties of life, Elisabeth could be happy if only everyone would eat a full breakfast every day.

A maid entered and passed biscuits with dried apples and nut breads thick with walnuts, crocks of butter, honey, and peach preserves and a stack of corn cakes drowned in syrup. She carried a pot of tea back and forth from the sideboard.

"'Intense excitement in Bond Street!'" Clinton read from the paper, piercing a breakfast sausage with his fork and waving it for emphasis. "My dear, I know you had hoped we'd escaped the intense excitement of my profession by moving uptown, but here we have it, practically at our doorstep."

"They've locked everyone up in the house, even the cook. The police have turned the parlor into an interviewing room. No one has been permitted to speak to a lawyer," said Elisabeth.

Clinton flipped through the pages. "Do you know why the editors are trumpeting this crime, when there are murders in the poorer wards every day?"

Elisabeth said, "Because, Henry, as you like to tell me ceaselessly, our illustrious, but corrupt mayor, Fernando Wood, has so polluted our metropolis, that this city is going to hell."

"Precisely," said Clinton waving his sausage in the air and taking a bite, for he loved to spar with her at breakfast. "However, as much as I enjoy blaming everything on Mayor Wood, I sense other motives afoot. Politics and crime make comfortable bedfellows and the District Attorney is about to throw his hat into the ring. A population roused to a fearful state by a frenzied press will be easy to deliver at the next mayoral election." He stuffed the sausage in his mouth.

"Henry— "

"Don't you agree, darling," he said, interrupting her, "that if this murder had occurred in the poorer wards, we would not be supping on it for breakfast?"

"Listen to me," she urged. "There is someone in the front parlor, to see you."

"Here? Why didn't you tell me sooner?"

"I was sure he could wait until you'd finished your meal. It is a messenger with a packet from your office." Messengers were often sent from his office to deliver urgent news.

"Well, excuse me, my dear, while I attend to the man. He is, no doubt, wondering why I am dallying over sausage." He pulled his napkin from his lap and dropped it on the table.

Clinton went into the front parlor, where a man sat on the edge of a seat with his satchels and parcels on the floor beside him. "Good morning, sir," said Clinton. "I am sorry to keep you waiting. My wife has an obsession with breakfast and I regret to say, as her spouse, I am a prisoner of the meal."

"Mr. Clinton," said the man, rising. "I was sent this morning to bring these to you." He bent down to untie the elaborate laces on his satchel.

"Has Mr. Armstrong been into the office yet?"

"No, not yet, sir, just the morning clerk." Armstrong was Clinton's partner, his senior by twenty years, who had distinguished himself as one of the city's top attorneys with formidable legal skills and a permanent air of reproach. The contrasting style of the two law partners was a source of entertainment for the junior staff. James Armstrong was sober and exacting, his clients a roster of the rich and socially connected, while Clinton was impetuous and dynamic. His cases were more exciting, with dramatic consequences at the eleventh hour. The firm of Armstrong and Clinton was one of the most notable criminal firms in the city, built by the reputation of both partners. Clinton had made a name for himself with a string of successes at trial, but he chose his cases differently than Armstrong. He was forward-looking and preferred cases where the principle of the law was at stake, championing the wrongly accused, or the newly arrived, often representing those who could not pay.

The messenger handed Clinton a clerk's note with the address of Josiah Livingstone, a mansion on Lafayette Place, not far from Bleecker Street. The case was about property disputes, with multiple lawsuits and fractional divisions arranged around lot lines. Such cases bored Clinton, for the outcome was always the same, with the bluebloods getting richer, simply by juggling pieces of earth and air.

"Mr. Armstrong would like you to stop over to Mr. Livingstone's, sir," said the messenger, "and witness his signature on these papers. They need to be filed by noon. And here's a letter for you."

"This came from the office?"

"Yes, sir, the morning clerk said it's been at the door since Sunday." It was a thin envelope on blue paper, with his name in ink across the front, in a shaky hand. When he opened the note he could see that it was written by a woman.

> Dear Mr. Clinton,
>
> I have gotten your name from my solicitor and I hope that you might come and see me. I am in need of legal assistance, but am told I can speak to no one, and have not spoken with anyone who can counsel me. This is about a murder, occurring

*Friday night, at this house where I am sequestered, perhaps you
have heard.*

*Please respond, as I am confined to house arrest,*

Sincerely,
Mrs. Emma Cunningham, 31 Bond Street

According to the newspaper, the murder scene had been turned
over to a Coroner's inquest, whereby the Coroner and his minions occupied the crime scene until they finished interrogating all
possible witnesses, to gather facts while the crime was still fresh.
In Clinton's view, calling a jury to the scene of a murder was an
antiquated custom, descended from English law, no longer suited
to crime in modern cities. In addition, he knew that the Coroner,
Edward Connery, was a blustery blowhard with a flair for theatrics.
In Clinton's mind, there was no greater obstacle to justice than the
reckless ambition of an incompetent man.

Clinton returned to the breakfast room to find the table cleared.
It was now eight thirty and his morning was slipping away. Elisabeth appeared with his overcoat.

"I'm off," he said, distracted.

"Henry," she said, looking at the envelope. "That's not about the
Bond Street murder is it?" She met his eye, which confirmed her
guess. "There is no need for you to get involved—it sounds as if it's
turning into a Broadway melodrama."

"From the reports, I suspect it is more like a circus, and I pity the
animals in captivity," he said. "You wouldn't blame me if I stopped
by to take a look—as a concerned neighbor, that is."

"As a concerned neighbor, I fear you will try to give legal aid
to every person at the scene." There had been a recent lull in his
workload and she cherished the calm. Elisabeth followed him to
the front door, wrapping a white scarf around his neck, tenderly

fretting about the cold air. From the street, he took a last look at her, shivering at the door.

"Good-bye, my dear," he said. "Please promise me you will not make a pilgrimage downtown today to bring me lunch—it's far too cold. It's best to remain inside, in the warmth."

"I will, if you promise to stay away from that murder on Bond Street," she said blowing him a kiss.

# CHAPTER FOUR

Out on the street, Henry Clinton peered at his watch to fix the time. When he reached Broadway, it was just coming to life. Downtown, the avenue would be deep into the activity of the day, but uptown, at eight thirty in the morning, shopkeepers were still lowering the shutters and cranking the blinds. A block north, a flock of newsboys was hawking their papers to passersby who congregated, their breath mingling in the cold air. As Clinton approached, he saw that the length of Bond Street, with its stately row of residential homes, was lined with a curious crowd. In the course of the early morning, the news of the crime had rippled across the city. Ragged boys in striped mittens and woolen wrappers, idle shopgirls and respectably dressed men passing to work were standing before 31 Bond Street, staring up at the façade, as if there were no entertainment more festive than murder.

Clinton ventured down the block. Policemen were standing like sentinels before the entry, occasionally stepping away to push back the crowd. The front door opened, and a murmur went through the pack as the District Attorney, Abraham Oakey Hall, emerged and paused atop the stoop in the morning sunshine, his silk hat gleaming above the heads of the throng. Hall hoisted his cane and hurried down the steps until he was swallowed into the crowd. He wore a flowing cape, a silk cravat in fuchsia; his shirt linen was deep plum. Known by his middle name, Oakey, Hall had been given the nickname "The Elegant Oakey" by the newspapers for being one of the few dandies in the legal profession. Clinton and Hall knew each other well, for they had tried many cases from opposing sides of the bench. In the courtroom, Clinton found Hall's rainbow hues to be a distraction, where the law was written, case by case, in black and white.

"Well, well," said Hall. "If it isn't Henry Clinton, the illustrious defense attorney, searching for his next case."

"And here is the District Attorney, canvassing for votes at a homicide," said Clinton.

Hall put a hand to his breast, pretending offense. "I have come to assure the people of this fine neighborhood that the perpetrator of this abominable act will be brought to justice." Hall's voice swelled with traces of the South. As a child, his family had migrated between the North and the South, and the District Attorney could enchant a group of New York ladies at Delmonico's, speaking with the upper-crust tones of the Northern gentry, and then, chameleon-like, drawl to a visiting congregation of the Southern elite, who had suddenly become numerous at political gatherings all over town.

"I have heard that there are residents of this house, under house arrest, who are being denied counsel," stated Clinton.

"An inquest is under way, and there is no need for attorneys," replied Hall.

"A Coroner cannot refuse anyone the right to counsel if they request it," said Clinton.

"It is not my jurisdiction to interfere with the Coroner. I'd wager you rushed here fresh from reading your morning paper. As much as you may prefer to be the first, there will be time for the piling on of lawyers later."

"And I would wager that prosecuting this case in the full view of the press would warm the Mayor's seat for you," said Clinton.

"You came to elect me Mayor?" asked Hall, bowing with mock gratitude. "Or are you here to offer your calling card to the poor widow upstairs?" The district attorney slid away, leaving his insult trailing in the air. Crossing the street, Hall greeted a man in a fur-collared coat and a yellow-and-black-striped vest, and the two men strolled off, huddled together.

Clinton pushed past the bystanders and headed toward the house. That a murder would become a sensation did not surprise him, but a crime scene where people were in detention and were being denied legal counsel disturbed him. He presented his card to an officer, and as he suspected, the officer recognized his name and swung open the door. Through the gloom of the vestibule, Clinton could barely make out the group convened in the parlor. The shutters were pulled tight across the tall windows to the street, blocking out the morning light. Cigar and coal smoke hung near the ceiling, and the stale odor of tobacco, broadcloth, and damp wool permeated the room.

The double parlor had been converted into a makeshift interrogation room for the purpose of the Coroner's inquest. Extra chairs had been brought in, and every seat was filled, with men standing along the walls and leaning against the mantel. A table on one side of the room was for the stenographers, members of the press, who were recording the interviews, word for word. The *New York Times* donated this service to city proceedings, and in exchange, the newspaper was permitted to print the reports verbatim, making them "The Paper of Record."

Opposite the stenographers sat the Coroner's jury. They were a motley crew of city dwellers: retired men in fraying waistcoats, working men in faded twill, and a few poorer souls who kept their clothes from falling away with twine. In a peculiar arrangement, Dr. Burdell's dentist chair had been brought down from his office and placed in the center to be used as a witness chair. Since his murder forty-eight hours before, the doctor's home had been transformed into an instrument in the investigation of his own death.

A gavel banged against a table, accompanied by the Coroner's booming voice. Edward Connery sat framed by a gilt mirror that hung between the windows overlooking the garden.

"Order! Order!" Connery called out, his *rs* trilling: "I have a long list of witnesses to interview," said the Coroner. "I will commence with the Reverend Marvine."

Two policemen brought a confused man with oily whiskers into the room. He was led to the dentist chair, where he sat with trepidation, holding on to the arms of the iron chair as he gingerly settled himself in. He stated his name as Uriah Marvine, Reverend of the Reformed Dutch Church. The coroner got up and strutted across the room. He placed a scroll on the jury table. It was the marriage certificate, stamped into evidence by the sheriff's office, which passed from hand-to-hand among the jurors.

"Sir, did you conduct a marriage between a man calling himself Dr. Harvey Burdell and a woman named Mrs. Emma Cunning-ham, two weeks ago, on January the fourteenth?" asked Connery, pointing to the scroll.

"That is my name on the certificate," replied the Reverend.

Next, Connery presented him with a daguerreotype of Harvey Burdell, a formal portrait in silver and black tones, taken at a pho-tography studio downtown. "Do you recognize this man as the man who came before you to be married?"

Reverend Marvine held the picture close to his face, removed his spectacles, and examined it ponderously. "I believe I recall this face, but then again, I am not sure. A great many couples come to my home to be married. But I do recall the ceremony. It took place in my parlor. It only took a few minutes. The woman described herself as a widow."

"Did she now? Could it be possible that she arrived at your home with an imposter, or a man impersonating Harvey Burdell?" Connery asked, suddenly raising his voice.

The coal shifted in the fireplace, causing the flame to flare. The Reverend recoiled. "I would not know, sir. I never question the identity of the people who come to be married; it is not my business." He studied the daguerreotype again. "Now that I think of it, I wonder if perhaps the man who came had hair that was falsely applied. He whispered to me that the marriage should not be published in the newspapers."

"Is that so!" Connery exclaimed. "False whiskers?"

"The woman on the other hand, seemed eager and very fetching, and she was younger than the man."

"The marriage is a fake," someone whispered, and a ripple began to echo through the crowd.

"Silence!" bellowed Connery. "Could you describe the woman's attire?"

"She wore a cloak, I believe, and a blue dress, or maybe grey. Oh I remember now, it was not a dress at all, it was a suit with black buttons!" The Reverend beamed with satisfaction as the room erupted in laughter.

"Bring her in!" Connery shouted to officers waiting outside the parlor door. Two police matrons ushered Emma Cunningham to the entrance of the parlor as a hush fell over the room. She stood just under the parlor doorway, framed by the carved moldings that rose up to the high ceiling. Her image was reflected in the tilted pier mirror, making it possible for those in the back of the room to see. She was wearing a dark dress, expertly tailored. Her hands were clasped nervously before her. Her hair was swept up with twists, and her skin was porcelain, with high color in her lips and cheeks. Her eyes were green, darkly ringed by lashes and set at a tilt. She stood perfectly still while all faces were transfixed upon her. She had an unexpected allure, a curious blend of features not often found in the drawing rooms of New York—a beauty, thought Clinton, by any standard.

She leaned to the officer at her side to whisper a question but was cut off by the booming voice of the Coroner. "Quiet!" Connery ordered. "You may not speak! You are here to be looked at, Madame, not to speak. We will interview you before this jury at a later time, and you may speak then." Mrs. Cunningham stood before him quietly blinking back tears. "Take a look at her," the Coroner said to the Reverend. "Study her features, for we will send her away so she does not hear the testimony." He waved at the officer to take her away again, and they departed into the hall and up the stairs.

At her departure, the room erupted into excited whispers, and Connery rushed over to the table to bang the gavel, which had the effect of creating more confusion. "Is that the woman who came to you to be married?" he demanded.

The Reverend began to stutter in confusion. "Why, I am now more certain about the man," he said waving the daguerreotype. "That woman has a much larger bosom than the one who came, and that is all I can say for certain." The room erupted again, and the Coroner yelled for quiet.

"We are speaking of a matter of the utmost importance," he cried. "There was a murder under this roof, committed while that woman and her daughters were at home. We must determine if she had a role." Clinton listened for a while longer, then edged his way out of the back of the parlor. Disgusted, he could the see the wheels at work: Connery was leading the witness and molding the investigation toward a theory that the marriage certificate was faked. The reporters were transcribing every word, readying them for the press engines downtown, which would grease the wheels for an arrest and a criminal trial. Solving the murder quickly was a political expediency, which would quell the fears of the populace. And a hanging would be another feather in the cap of Oakey Hall.

As Clinton stepped from the room, two men at the parlor door were whispering. "I heard the Doctor had some business on the night he was killed with a large sum of money, and none of it was found. The detectives are looking for a servant, a Negro, who drove Dr. Burdell's carriage that evening."

"That seems to me a waste of effort," replied the other. "That woman was after his money. The lady upstairs is the culprit, if you want my opinion."

Clinton mounted the staircase, unnoticed. Upstairs, the hall was empty. The policemen guarding the rooms had been drawn to the drama in the parlor below. Clinton passed the room where the murder occurred and saw the profuse amounts of dried blood that covered the floor and the walls. Inside the next bedroom, the corpse was spread on a bed as doctors leaned over, intently measuring the lesions with calipers. A man peered into the lens of a microscope. After a murder, the poor went straight to the morgue; when the wealthy were victims, an autopsy included the latest techniques of anatomical science to allow the tissues and organs to be delicately probed and examined. A newspaper artist sat sketching the scene for one of the illustrated newspapers.

Clinton mounted the next flight to the third floor. An open door led to an attic, and through it he heard the voice of a police officer chastise a boy about cleaning out the chamber pots. There was no one guarding the bedrooms. The last door on the third floor was closed, and taking a guess, he turned the knob and stepped in.

The shutters were pulled tight and the only illumination came from the coal in the brazier. His eyes adjusted and he saw a figure in an armchair.

"Excuse me, Madame, for intruding," he said. Her chair was close to the fire. She looked up with alarm, and he could now see the fearful and tired expression in her features. She studied him with wide eyes, wary of his presence.

"Madame, please don't be frightened. I am Henry Clinton, the lawyer that you summoned. I am with the firm of Armstrong and Clinton."

"Oh, thank God, you have come. I asked to speak with counsel, but I was not permitted," she said. "The Coroner has forbidden me."

"You have a right to speak to counsel. It is the Coroner who is in error."

"What is happening?" she whispered. "I have answered so many questions and yet no one has answered mine. This is such a terrible state of affairs." Her voice was unsteady and trembling. Clinton pulled an ottoman close and sat next to her, leaning forward so that they could speak softly without being heard.

"You have the right to speak to counsel," he repeated. "There is no law that says a person under house arrest in a coroner's investigation can be denied that right. Furthermore, anything you say to me will remain in confidence."

"I have been in my room now since Saturday," she said, distraught. "How long must I remain here? Why am I being detained? I have already told them what I know."

"I believe the Coroner intends that you will testify before the assembled jury downstairs, this time under oath. They will interview many people who knew the deceased, and I am presuming he will interrogate you last, so I imagine you will be here for several more days. I would strongly advise you to refuse to testify before the Coroner's jury so that you do not incriminate yourself."

"Incriminate myself? Am I a suspect? But I have not been charged with any crime. I am innocent!" she exclaimed.

"Regardless of your guilt or innocence, I am afraid that what you say now may have grave consequences later. Your testimony will be transcribed for the record." He saw her confusion as the firelight flickered across her features revealing her dark lashes, now thickening with tears.

"It is all so terrible. I have told them everything. The last time I saw Dr. Burdell was before dinner, on Friday. He had his carriage brought around. I asked him where he was going, but he did not tell me. I stayed here in my room all evening by the fire, with my daughters, sewing. The three of us went to sleep in my bedroom, around eleven o'clock. We decided to sleep together in my room because it was my daughter's last night at home."

"Did you hear any commotion, or any noises during the night?"

"I am generally a sound sleeper and I didn't wake at all. I heard nothing. In the morning, the errand boy found him—he was dead!" She broke into sobs. She knocked a sewing basket from her chair onto the floor, spilling lace and ribbons. The room smelled faintly of perfume. Clinton handed her his handkerchief.

"I have been telling them the same thing over and over," she continued. "I do not know who killed Dr. Burdell or where he went that evening. He was gone for many hours. His carriage driver, Samuel, certainly would know."

"You told that to the Coroner and the Police Chief?"

She took a breath, trembling. It took her several seconds to compose herself and then she said, "They molested me, you know."

"Who?"

"The Coroner, and his deputies. They made me undress before them, removing everything, including my stockings," she said, her hands twisting anxiously at her handkerchief. "The men ran their fingers up and down my torso, looking for marks and bruises, but there was nothing. I was so ashamed and I cried out, 'Don't expose me so!'" she said, sobbing anew. "Sir, you must help me. I fear for my daughters—they are so young. I am so frightened for them, you must help us."

He watched and listened intently as she spoke. She had a shawl around her shoulders, gripping it tightly. Her eyes darted around the room, as if searching for familiar ballast. He heard the terror in her voice at the separation from her daughters, who were being kept away from her, sequestered in another room.

"Madame, I must ask you about something important—about the marriage certificate." Clinton spoke quickly, because he sensed that time was short. "I will be blunt. You told the Police Chief that you and Dr. Burdell were married, but no one else was aware of it. Now the Coroner is trying to establish if the certificate is a fake, which might indicate your motive toward the crime, so you would gain his property as a widow."

She gasped, as if the idea stung her. "Harvey and I met in Saratoga last summer, and shortly thereafter, he proposed. I came to live in this house and we were married privately," she insisted. "Dr. Burdell preferred that we keep the marriage a secret, until the spring, when we were to go to Europe. He needed to complete some business, and to straighten out his affairs. It was his choice to keep it a secret and I complied." Clinton strained to listen, for her voice was whispery and faint.

"I will see that you get legal representation. But first, here is my advice," he said. "For now, you must remain silent. Do not speak to anyone without a lawyer present."

Suddenly, the bedroom door burst open and a police officer entered. "What are you doing in here?" he shouted at Clinton. "The Coroner has given orders that no one may enter this room!"

Clinton stood up, reflexively. "I am a lawyer. I am having a conference with this woman with her permission, as is her right."

"These rooms are off bounds to lawyers. She has no right to speak to anyone." The policeman lunged toward him, but Clinton dodged and moved toward the door.

"There is no such requirement. No one can be denied counsel. I will speak to the Coroner myself," Clinton said, moving swiftly to the hall and toward the stairs, with the officer following behind him. He started downstairs while the officer yelled loudly after him, "A man has been in to see the witness. I tried to prevent him!"

Clinton reached the last flight, just as Coroner Connery was rushing from the parlor to see the cause of the commotion. The crowd spilled out after him: jurymen, journalists, detectives, and officers, all crowding into the hall, looking up at Clinton, who was now stopped, poised on the staircase, midway down. Clinton remained where he was and addressed the group below: "Gentleman, I have just been speaking with the lady you have in custody. She has every right to consult with me, as a member of the legal profession."

"I will not allow anyone to go stealthily into the prisoner's room for any reason whatsoever," bellowed the Coroner. "Tampering with a witness is against my orders!"

"I did not go stealthily, for there is no restriction against a member of the legal profession having a private consultation with a citizen, upon their request."

"I did not say stealthily with any design to malign you, sir," the Coroner replied, with mock deference. "I am the one in charge here, and Mrs. Cunningham and her daughters cannot elect to talk to anyone until their sworn testimony before me."

"Is this woman to be interviewed as a witness or is she a suspect?" asked Clinton. "That is what I demand to know. If she is a suspect, then the law provides that no person can be imprisoned without charges made. I will present you with a writ of habeas corpus if I must. She cannot be held under arrest unless she is charged with a crime."

"She is under arrest in her own home, which is a different matter entirely. Perhaps she is a suspect or perhaps she is a witness. I am the one to decide that."

Clinton moved down the last steps. "It will be a simple matter to test your interpretation of the law before a more competent authority than yourself. I will obtain an order from a judge, if I must."

"Go ahead," said Connery, seething like a child rebuked, "but I speak to you in the presence of the jury and the press—we do not need law here! This is my investigation." He pointed to a policeman and shouted, "Get some committals made out. I want them here, so that I can send to prison any person who interferes with my orders."

Clinton walked solidly past the officers, to the outer door, and exited the house. From atop the stoop he met a blast of bright morning light; the crowd before 31 Bond Street had grown larger. It was almost ten o'clock and downtown his clerks would be busy at their desks. It was time to get to his office—he had just come across his next case.

# CHAPTER FIVE

C linton pulled the canvas strap that ran along the floor, tied to the driver's leg. The Bowery stagecoach was known for its cut-throat drivers who could steer a team of horses through any morning crush. The horses whinnied as the coach strained to a stop. Clinton hopped off and headed toward the limestone row of law offices that faced the unadorned back side of City Hall.

He waded among the newsboys, who chanted the headlines about the murder. A ragged boy stopped before him; he had the haunted, hollow look of the very hungry and wore tattered pants that were too short by a foot. Clinton reached into his pocket to sprinkle a coin into the boy's hand when he realized that the boy was not begging but handing him an envelope with his name written on the front.

"Excuse me, sir, this is for you," the boy said, handing him the letter. "Mrs. Cunningham sent me, to give you this." Clinton had left Bond Street just thirty minutes earlier, after being ejected from the house by Coroner Connery, yet somehow this boy had intercepted him.

"How did you get to see Mrs. Cunningham?" asked Clinton.

"I work for Doctor Burdell—before he died, I mean. Now the deputies keep me busy. I fetch the coal and water for all the rooms. I was cleaning out the chamber pot in Mrs. Cunningham's bedroom when she gave me this. She said to run downtown and give it to you." Clinton took the envelope and broke open the seal.

> *Dear Mr. Clinton,*
>
> *Dr. Burdell was on a mission on the night of his death, of that I am certain. He may have been involved in a danger-ous affair. When I heard his carriage return, I looked out my window and believe I saw others inside. Perhaps he did not enter the house alone. If you find his coachman, Samuel, I am sure you will discover who killed Dr. Burdell.*
>
> *Please send me word as to what I should do, as I will be asked to testify soon.*
>
> *Emma Burdell*

Clinton refolded the note. He noticed that Emma Cunningham signed the letter as Emma Burdell. He also remembered that she had told him that she was sleeping when Dr. Burdell returned to the house; now her letter stated that she was awake and she saw him from the window. Without the advice of counsel, she might contradict herself when asked to give testimony to the Coroner at the inquest in the parlor. Reporters were recording the proceeding, and any inconsistent testimony would go on record.

Looking up from the letter, Clinton saw that the boy was ready to bolt. "Wait, son—" Clinton reached into his pocket, pulling out a bill. "Your name is . . . ?"

"John, sir."

"You work in the house?"

"I am the houseboy and do errands, sir."

"Have you spoken before the coroner's jury?"

"Yes, I told them about how I found Dr. Burdell dead on his carpet."

"And did you speak the truth?

"Yes, sir, I did." The boy started to fidget, nervously.

"John—do you know who killed Dr. Burdell?"

"No, sir, I don't know who done it! Really, I don't!" he said. Clinton slipped a dollar into the boy's hand. The haunted look on John's face deepened. Clinton suspected that he had never held a dollar bill before.

"I need you to help me," Clinton said softly, placing an arm around his shoulders and leading him toward the door to his office. "Come upstairs with me. I have some food."

Clerks and junior staff looked up from a maze of desks. Clinton took off his overcoat, and the entire staff watched the ragged boy, no more than eleven years old, with a tousled head of blond hair, cowering at his side. Clinton paused, then addressed them, in a robust voice: "Good morning! It's Monday morning, and there is work to do. I need to schedule a hearing on the house arrest of the people this past weekend at Bond Street. The names of the parties in custody are Mrs. Emma Cunningham, Augusta Cunningham, and Helen Cunningham." A legal associate began to scribble Clinton's orders, and then looked up, quill in hand.

"How do you spell that, sir?" he asked.

"Cunningham," repeated Clinton. "Like it sounds. And I want someone to look up the legal code that describes a Coroner's powers and how long a Coroner can lay siege to a crime scene. Write out a copy of the code and deliver it to the *New York Times*."

"Good morning to you, too, sir," yelled one of the clerks, in a merry tone. "May I surmise that you read today's headlines, and we are embarking on a new case?"

"At the moment, I am considering it, Mr. Snarky," Clinton replied coolly to the clerk. "And since you have such an irreverent manner, I shall assign you the task of handling the press. I want you to spend each evening at Park Row, finding out the news from the inquest at Bond Street. And you shall keep the file on all the newspaper clippings on the case."

"Yes, sir," Snarky said, subdued, not that he minded mingling with the reporters who clustered in knots along the printing house row, sitting on crates in the alleys, chomping on the stumps of wide cigars, gambling at cards, while waiting for news of fresh crime from the police precincts.

"And," said Clinton, "the next time she comes, would someone please tell my wife—we don't need any more food." Clinton took John to a shelf piled high with tins. Almost every day, Elisabeth stopped by the law office with more baked goods. With Clinton always between the jailhouse and the courts, no matter what time she came, she hardly ever found him in.

Clinton opened a tin of shortbread. "Here we go, John. These are fairly fresh. I believe she brought these over Friday." John raised a triangle of cake and jammed it into his mouth. His eyes widened, embarrassed, when he heard the laughter of the clerks.

Clinton led John into his office, away from the eyes of the curious staff. He shut the door and sat John down to finish his cake. "John, you have been at the house awhile, am I correct?"

"Yes, sir," the boy said dutifully, his mouth still full.

"And you know Mrs. Cunningham and the other servants? Do you know the carriage driver, named Samuel?" The boy began chewing faster and eyed the door without answering.

Clinton now reached into his pocket and sorted through some coins until he found a penny, shiny and new, dated 1857, with a flying eagle stamped on the copper. He offered it to the boy, and his face lit up at the sight. As he suspected, it was the bird on the shiny coin that intrigued him; paper currency had little meaning.

"I don't know where Samuel is," he protested, "I swear to it."

Clinton patted him on the back. "John, I need your help. Here's what I need you to do. I want you to go back to 31 Bond Street, and do your job, and each day, come here and fill me in on what is happening inside the house. Can you do that?" The boy nodded. "Can you leave the house without being missed?"

"The police officers send me out for food and provisions, and such. I can pass the officers at the door anytime," said John.

"Good. I want you to be my eyes and ears." Clinton opened another tin—this box was filled with taffy. He placed it before the child, who added the candy to his bulging pockets. Clinton lifted a page of stationery from a stack on his desk and started penning a note. "I am writing a letter for you to give to Mrs. Cunningham. Make sure no one sees you." The boy nodded.

Clinton led John out past the clerks, escorting him out the office door, to the hallway. "Remember, John," he whispered, "it's important to be discreet," said Clinton as the boy nodded and fled away.

Clinton stepped back inside and encountered a thin-skinned, elderly gentleman standing at the edge of the room, struggling into his coat.

"The Livingstone papers, Henry. It was a simple request," James Armstrong said as he put on his hat.

Clinton slapped his head. "I am remiss, James. I completely forgot about them. I apologize. Instead, I went to the inquest at Bond Street. It's a circus there, and in the ensuing chaos, I neglected to stop for Mr. Livingstone's signature. I'll send one of the juniors right now to take care of it."

"No need, Henry, no need." Armstrong sighed. "I'll go myself. No need to ruffle a client's feathers, especially when the feathers are as richly hued as Josiah Livingstone's." Armstrong spoke with a forced nonchalance, masking his anger, leaving the impression that running off in the downtown traffic was a pleasurable morning outing. Armstrong settled into his deep cashmere coat with a banker's collar, lined with fur. "As for this Bond Street business, I suppose you should tell me what kind of mess you're getting the firm into. I heard that this past summer, this same widow was seen around Saratoga, husband hunting."

"James, the corpse is barely cold, and rumor, not fact, are giving high color to this investigation."

"Enough," said Armstrong, with impatience, opening the door to leave. "I will be going to Dr. Burdell's funeral tomorrow to pay my respects to the family. His brothers engaged me to handle a property dispute back in '54. I imagine they are shocked by this weekend's violence, as am I. I would like you to join me in the carriage tomorrow morning. On the way to the church, you can explain to me what you are doing in the middle of this."

# CHAPTER SIX

*July 1856, New York City*

When the first heat of July settled over the city, Emma Cunningham booked one of the last staterooms on the Albany steamer for herself and her daughters. Then she telegraphed the Congress Hotel in Saratoga Springs for a suite. To economize, she dismissed the maid, struggling to move the furniture to the center of the parlor, pulling dust sheets across the upholstery and shutting off the gas, preparing to close the house on Twenty-fourth Street herself. She folded her evening dresses, packing them in sturdy trunks, and wrapped her daughters' flimsy frocks and bloomers, camisoles and muslin sleeves.

A pile of bills lay ignored upon the desk. She gathered them and pushed them into a drawer. Widowed the previous summer, she had moved twice with her daughters, and soon the lease on this house was up, with the rents everywhere getting higher. In the tall pier mirror, she caught her image surrounded by the sheeted furniture as dust motes floated around the parlor. In the silvery tableaux, she imagined she saw the indistinct images of dancing ladies and gentlemen, apparitions swirling under a chandelier.

*I am so weary of black,* she thought. If she left the city, where no one knew that her mourning period was not yet over, she could wear color again. There was no reason to spend the summer in the city while neighboring townhouses were shuttered and silent, as entire families fled the heat. Both daughters were rapidly nearing a marriageable age, and if they remained in New York, sitting in a hot parlor, the summer months would unravel aimlessly with no social visits, no parties, or suitable young men. She had drawn from her dwindling savings to buy the tickets to Saratoga where there would be concerts and tea dances and ballrooms festooned with flowers.

On the day the steamship was to depart, Emma herded her daughters into a hired cab, and the cabdriver lashed their trunks to the roof. He climbed up on the bench, and then started toward the river, the cab moving with the lurching gait of a city horse. The day was hot, and the back of the cab was close, with the three women piled in tightly, with frills and flounces and parasols at their feet.

"When we get to Saratoga, I will need a new hat," said Helen. The youngest, at fifteen, she had the same coloring as Emma, with dark hair and red lips. Older men had approached Emma, interested in a marriage arrangement with Helen, but Emma knew from experience that marriage at such an early age was not advisable. Helen fidgeted while Augusta looked wanly out the window, twisting her curls.

"Augusta, stop pulling on your curls. A beau will take a turn of fright when he sees you arrive in Saratoga with limp hair," said Emma, who sat packed between her daughters.

"Augusta doesn't have a beau, Mama," said Helen.

"And he won't appear if she doesn't take more care," said Emma, readjusting Augusta's hair.

Augusta pulled away, continuing to stare sullenly out the window. Augusta, at eighteen, was a cause for concern, for she showed no inclination toward courtship. She was forever buried in a piece of music or a book and had no aptitude for social banter. Blond, with pale skin and a swanlike neck, she had ample beauty, but she did not take advantage of it—homelier girls with more outgoing manners made all the gains, especially those from families endowed with an excess of cash and a prominent family name. Emma believed that if Augusta would only comb her hair, or tie her ribbons tighter, or smile brightly when spoken to, a handsome husband would be conjured, the way the shape of a face appears in the froth of summer clouds.

The carriage stalled while a slow mule dragged stones to a building site, setting off an upheaval of dust. Large blocks of granite stood in the middle of Washington Street. There was not an avenue in New York that was not covered with scaffolding. Wherever there had been an empty lot, holding little more than a stray goat or a few scraggly fruit trees, there was now a gaping black hole.

The open windows brought little air. Emma dabbed her forehead with a lace handkerchief as beads of perspiration snaked along the rim of her bonnet and welled in the crevices of her corset. "Driver, please hurry along, our steamer is boarding," Emma called, rapping on the partition with her parasol. "Couldn't you quicken the pace by using the whip?" she called again, when the carriage did not move. The Albany steamer departed at two, and she feared they would miss the boat.

"Ma'am, whipping the horse won't get you there faster. There's ten ships leaving every afternoon, and only one avenue to the wharf. It's not my concern if your boat sets sail without you. Happens every day," he said, without lifting the reins.

"I would hate to miss our boat because you feared striking a horse," Emma said, fanning herself. Soon, the horses began clopping forward again at an infuriatingly slow pace until they finally made their way through a snarl of wagons to the docks. The carriage swung onto a pier that was piled high with exotic goods stamped from abroad: rum and sugar from the West Indies and barrels marked with oriental symbols, fragrant with spices from the East. Emma pushed her daughters out of the carriage. Helen and Augusta popped opened their parasols against the sun.

"Hurry, and unload our trunks. We don't have a moment to spare," she commanded, pacing while the stevedores tagged their bags. The steamboat loomed at the edge of the wharf, blocking the water view. The boat's engine radiated heat, offsetting the cool breeze on the river. A whistle screamed the last call and the smoke-stack blew a thick spiral of carbon.

With a sense of urgency, Emma rushed her daughters up the gangway, the last ones to board. On deck, Emma scanned the doors for her berth. During the summer, the city became enveloped by a pestilential haze, and entire neighborhoods stewed in the heat. Inhabitants of tumbledown houses threw the contents of chamber pots out the windows, along with ashes, rotten vegetables, and rum bottles, and typhus rose up from the swamps, filling the fever sheds of Bellevue Hospital. In the fall, the lease on her house would be up, and by the end of the year, her money would be gone. Without a husband, there was no one to turn to, so she gambled on leaving the hot city for Saratoga, in search of an unattached gentleman. It was a matter of survival.

Each morning, breakfast at the Congress Hall Hotel was served on the verandah beside emerald lawns, cool with dew. Afterward, Emma and her daughters strolled along the shady lanes, lined with dainty cottages in the Gothic or Grecian style. They received at-tention from passing men, who lifted their hats in greeting. Emma took note of which ones were widowed or single, handsome or di-vorced. Augusta wandered into the fields in search of daisies. Helen wore a new straw hat studded with buds and lemon ribbons. Young boys bicycled past her, stopped and pedaled back slowly, circling like bees.

One day in early July, Emma sat on a chaise, penning correspondence. A waiter brought a silver pitcher of iced tea lined with sprigs of mint. A breeze rustled the girls' dresses. A man approached and stood before them stiffly, in formal relief against the billowing lawns. He seemed older than Emma by a decade, in his midforties, firmly built, with dark skin and a firm musculature, his black hair carefully groomed and oiled. He tipped his hat.

"How do you do. May I introduce myself?" He bowed and presented a spray of violets wrapped in yellow tissue, purchased at the hotel concession, and offered the bouquet to Emma. "I am Dr. Harvey Burdell."

She lifted her hand to accept, squinting to see him clearly against the sun. "For me? Why, thank you!" she trilled, offering her hand. "I am Emma Cunningham, and these are my daughters, Augusta and Helen." He made another bow in the direction of the girls.

"Good morning, Dr. Burdell," intoned Augusta and Helen with a schoolgirl's training, tinged with boredom. Helen was eating a berry tart and wiped the stains from her lips. Augusta faded into the landscape in a blue gingham smock and fawn-colored gloves.

"Please, sit down," Emma said gaily, waving at a bench. Dr. Burdell sat and placed his hat beside him. She noticed that it was a fashionable height: an inch higher and he would be a dandy or a ruffian, an inch shorter, a clerk.

"Are you having a pleasant start to this agreeable morning?" he asked awkwardly, as if he were grasping for an appropriate phrase to describe the shimmering day.

"It couldn't be more splendid!" said Emma. "There are such marvelously cool breezes. Do you stay here often?"

"I come to the Congress Hall Hotel every year. I have a dental practice in New York and I try to get away during the summer months, if I can." He pulled at his collar, which chafed, leaving a red rash.

"Are you the dentist on Union Square?" she inquired, recognizing the name from advertisements.

"My brother, also a dentist, had an office on Union Square. He is now deceased. My office is at 31 Bond Street, where I also live."

"Bond Street! My favorite shops are near Bond Street!" She calculated to reveal little of herself, except, perhaps, that she appreciated fine things.

"I live there with my housekeeper," he said earnestly. "I am ready to sell my house, but the commercial rents near Broadway have risen dramatically. The prices just keep going up." He blinked often. He had told her much: that he was an awkward man, that he was a bachelor, and that he was rich. "I gather you are from New York?" he asked, glancing at the girls.

"My departed husband," interjected Emma, fluttering a fan across her chest, "had a mansion in Brooklyn—on Jay Street. His illness carried so many unfortunate memories that I chose to sell it after his death."

"I am so sorry," Dr. Burdell replied, gravely.

"I am looking to buy a townhouse," she continued. "I now lease a house on Twenty-fourth Street near the London Terrace. It is so difficult nowadays to find a suitable address."

"You would be foolish to part with your money in haste. Homes in the fashionable districts in Manhattan are much overpriced." Dr. Burdell continued, "Opportunities abound in the outlying areas." He dropped his voice, as if this fact was a secret, known only to insiders, and he winked, in a silly way. He had a strong jaw, a full head of black hair, a sturdy build, and intense dark eyes.

"I wish I had someone as wise as you to advise me." Emma sighed.

He appeared to be flattered by the compliment. Flustered, he patted his hands on the thighs of his dark trousers and stood, lifting his hat, ready to retreat. "Do you bet on horses?" he asked quickly. "Would you and your daughters do me the honor of joining me for a day at the racetrack?"

"We would be delighted," murmured Emma, letting her eyes convey her pleasure.

Dr. Burdell accompanied Emma and her daughters to the races, where the women paraded with parasols among the fashionable crowd. When the thoroughbreds thundered the course, a current of excitement surged through the spectators, but Dr. Burdell paid more attention to Emma than to the horses bursting from the gate. Emma bet on several and she clapped her hands with delight when her horse won and her wager yielded a small sum.

He invited them on rides through the countryside and to recitals at the gazebo in the square. On rainy days Emma and Dr. Burdell played cards in the hotel library while rain spattered the windows, and guests wandered in, looking intently for something to read. While dealing rounds of whist, he confided in her, filling her in on his occupation. He told her that his dental office catered to the teeth of a wealthy uptown clientele. He spoke of the tinctures that he concocted in his small dentistry laboratory. She nodded as she played, not listening much, until he spoke of gold—he said he had replaced gold with an amalgam for filling teeth and the technique had made him rich. He used new metals that were less expensive yet just as effective for fillings, and he could charge his patients as much as others were charging for gold.

"How clever you must be," she said. With her cards spread out before her, Emma calculated her next move and landed the winning card.

"I have created a concoction of chemical powders that I mix with various drugs in doses that have quite eliminated the pain in dental treatment."

"I have never had a tooth pulled," she said, shuddering at the thought.

"You would hardly know that it was happening. My patients remain quite happy. They experience a feeling of euphoria, a sensation of flying, accompanied by a sense of well-being. Afterward there is soreness, but there are potions to eliminate that, too." Dr. Burdell dealt again. He shuffled deftly, his surgeon's hands moving across the table with the slickness of a card shark.

"Have you thought any more about your finances?" he asked. "I might advise that you consider an investment in open land. Right now there is much activity in the areas surrounding the city."

"Well, first, I must secure a new home, for my current lease expires in the fall," she said. "Augusta is almost nineteen, and I shall need a suitable address to entertain."

"I have never understood the need for ladies teas. It seems to me to be a frivolous waste of an afternoon," replied Dr. Burdell.

"The entertainment is to attract suitors," she responded.

He dealt again, with a slap of cards against the table. "In New York, it's a large checkbook that makes a man suitable, or so it seems," he said. "The rest of the courting ritual is a waste of time and money. And as for your finances, I suggest that this is not a wise time to purchase a house in town," he warned. "Manhattan is much overpriced, and even the houses in the lower wards are asking huge sums." Dr. Burdell drew a card and then leaned forward and lowered his voice. "Recently I purchased several hundred acres of marsh across the harbor, in Elizabeth, New Jersey. I believe one day the area will be as important to shipping and commerce as the port of New York. The city's wharves are rotting, and boats are lined up out to the Narrows with no place to berth."

Emma reflected upon his words, shifting the fan of her cards. She wondered if he thought that she and her daughters should move to the swamps of New Jersey. "My, I had no idea!" she said brightly. "To think that our city shall just expand forever outward, unfurling like the sails on a ship! But I am looking for a home, not a wharf, and I am afraid I do not have enough knowledge to speculate in land," she said politely, for such speculation did not include a parlor for afternoon tea.

"I only suggest this venture to those who are wealthy enough or clever enough to take such a risk. I have already seen my own money return a profit four-fold, and there is more to be had. Of course I understand if you are hesitant."

"Well," she said, deferring, "I do have a large sum at my disposal, but I reserve it for solid things."

"It was not so long ago that my house on Bond Street was a farm, and now it is in the heart of town. Those who hold on to the past do not see the future beneath their feet. I would be glad to take you one day to see the land across the river." Emma listened with courteous attention, wondering what the advantage might be of a journey to a distant marshland, instead determining, upon her return, to wander down Bond Street, her keener interest being his townhouse, at number 31.

One morning in August, Dr. Burdell did not appear on the verandah, and days went by without so much as a note. Believing he had returned to New York, Emma later spotted him at another hotel, absorbed in a business conference with another gentleman. The two men made an uncharacteristic coupling: Dr. Burdell was attired in a suit the color of flint, and the other man wore green gabardine and a yellow cravat. They sat huddled together, animated by the topic of railroads or land or rotted docks. Disturbed by his absence, she considered taking up with another escort. Other men had approached her, mostly older men, widowers, gouty, with pink flesh that rippled around their collars, and stomachs that bloated under expensive silk vests. They greeted her, bowing a little too low, and leering, as if she were a stage girl. She decided that she would only succumb to spending an evening on the arm of such a man as a last resort.

After Dr. Burdell became elusive, Emma began to plan. She evaluated his qualities: he was around forty-five, with a smooth complexion and thick lips. He was handsome, not classically so, but in the way that men are allowed, with features that slowly align with age, and creases that deepen the personality of the wearer. He had dark eyes that squinted often, indicating that he was judging the value of what he saw. He was tall and well built. He crossed and uncrossed his legs nervously, revealing strong muscles under his freshly pressed suit.

As Emma sat at a large looking glass in her room, mounting her hair into careful twists, she thought about her future and envisioned Dr. Burdell's townhouse on Bond Street. She imagined herself the mistress of it, smartening his surroundings with taste and flair. *The bridesmaids' dresses,* she mused, *tulle and pearls for her daughters. A May wedding, with ornamental wreaths of dogwood before the entry of Grace Church. A starched serving girl, a cook who can prepare a proper duck.*

The August days grew shorter, and with each darker nightfall, her fears returned. Augusta had failed to attract any of the single young men who strolled about the country lanes with tittering debutantes in pursuit, while Helen was followed by droves of earnest schoolboys.

Toward the end of their stay, Dr. Burdell sent an invitation to join him for dinner. Emma promptly accepted. She dressed in yellow silk, with diamonds at the rounded bodice, cut low at the neck. Helen wore a maize and grenadine dress balanced on steel hoops; Augusta's dress had flounced ruffles edged in lace, studded by bouquets of roses, terminating in white fringe. Dr. Burdell appeared with the flourish of a chrysanthemum in his lapel.

In the middle of dinner, his gaze wandered across the dining room. "There are some investors here," he said, placing his napkin on the table, "who are joining me in one of my land ventures. I shall need a moment to speak with them." He excused himself and crossed the dining room, staying at the men's table for the length of the meal. When he returned, the girls had finished dessert and were cross and bored. Mrs. Cunningham sent them to bed, and Dr. Burdell asked her to join him for a walk in the garden. They strolled, arm in arm, along brick paths that glowed in the moonlight while fireflies dotted the lawn.

"I am anxious to see you when you return to New York," he said, with a sudden seriousness.

"That would be delightful," she replied nonchalantly. A path led them inside a formal garden enclosed by boxwood. Emma stopped and fingered the blade of a sundial whose base was wound, serpent-like, with ivy. The fragrance of honeysuckle blended with the scent of rose water pressed against the white skin of her bosom. Harvey Burdell's eyes flashed seductively. He grabbed her, pressing into her with a lingering kiss. She separated after a calculated measure of time. *It is done,* she thought. But she would not press any gain too soon.

# CHAPTER SEVEN

When a man dies, who can say what deep stains may
have rested, at one time or another, upon his soul? What
crimes (untouchable, perhaps, by the laws of men or the
rules of society) has he committed, either in evil wishes,
or in reality?

Walt Whitman

*February 4, 1857*

Henry Clinton gazed across the East River at spots of sunlight
that dappled the gold-flecked steeples of Brooklyn. Bowsprits
of schooners formed an arcade across the waterfront, their hulls
bobbing at their moorings. At eight thirty in the morning, he was
waiting for James Armstrong to arrive from his home in Brooklyn
Heights. By arrangement, they would ride uptown to the funeral of
Harvey Burdell.

The Brooklyn Ferry lumbered toward Manhattan, slipping
sideways, banging against the wharf, as dock hands scrambled to
tighten the ropes against the pilings. Commuters hurried off: bankers with bowlers and working girls in gingham, sidestepping horse

manure and piles of snow. Clinton's carriage tilted on its springs as James Armstrong climbed aboard.

"Morning, Henry," grumbled Armstrong, arranging his cane, newspapers, and muffler in the small space. Armstrong began each morning in a sour mood that lasted until midday, when his dour face receded behind an inscrutable mask.

"Good morning, James," said Clinton in a robust tone. He knew that exuberance this early in the morning irritated his partner.

"Uptown, to Grace Church," called Armstrong. The driver pulled the reins, preparing the horses to lurch into motion. A newsboy ran up, pressing the headline against the glass.

### SEVENTY THOUSAND COPIES!
### OVER THIRTY THOUSAND EXTRA COPIES HAVE BEEN ORDERED,
### SEE A DRAWING OF THE BODY IN ITS CASKET!
### SEE DR. BURDELL'S WOUNDS IN DETAIL!

The carriage driver swatted at the boy with a whip, and he tumbled away into the crowd. "My God!" said Armstrong. "It takes eighty-one days for a ship to bring news of the insurrections in China, but the papers are full of this murder, as if the world beyond our shore had simply vanished." The carriage turned away from the seafront, onto Pearl Street, losing view of the harbor. In the narrow jumble of downtown streets, emporiums spilled their wares onto tables and carts on the sidewalks: wigs and cutlery, adjustable bustles and India rubber gloves. Dry goods stores piled bolts of muslin and flannel; wet good stores sold fabrics from shipwrecks, still crusty with salt.

"Henry, last night I received a visit from Dr. Burdell's brothers, Gaylord and Thomas. They called on me at home. We spoke for about two hours."

"The Burdell brothers?" asked Clinton, surprised. "Did they come to you for legal advice?"

"No, they have an attorney to advise them about the ongoing investigation and estate matters. They came because they heard you had visited that woman." Clinton heard the disapproval in his voice. "Henry, it is ill-advised—no I shall say foolhardy—for you to embark upon this case, and I am dismayed that you are considering it. There is a questionable marriage document, and Harvey Burdell left no will. He was wealthy; he had property in New York and in Elizabeth, New Jersey. His dental practice, although lucrative, had become a sideline for his real estate pursuits. It seems that the Burdell family believes that a defense of Emma Cunningham is an attempt to swindle them out of their brother's estate."

"Well, of course they do," stated Clinton. "I am sure you know, James, that there is nothing novel about a fight among family members over a dead man's estate. Mrs. Cunningham is being held as a witness and possible suspect to the murder, and she deserves a good attorney for her defense. I suppose the brothers would rather see her swing from the gallows than have her inherit his money."

"The family believes that Mrs. Cunningham's claim to be Dr. Burdell's wife is false and may be the motive for this murder."

"She is a woman under duress, and there are not yet any facts to implicate her in the murder. I am not sure when it was determined that she should be denied her legal rights, but suddenly, between the District Attorney, the Coroner, and the family, it appears to be in everyone's best interest that she hang."

"Henry, please listen," interjected Armstrong, wearily. He smoothed the carriage blanket across his legs and cleared his throat. "My meeting last night informed me of many things. According to the Burdell brothers, Harvey Burdell was a difficult man. He had quarrels with many, and lawsuits with his own family. He may have been involved in any number of illegitimate pursuits."

"There you have it; perhaps one of his family killed him."

"May I continue?" Armstrong snapped. As the senior partner, he had a habit of demanding deference, and Clinton waited for him to proceed in his long-winded manner. "Dr. Burdell had four brothers. When he was sixteen, he was ejected from his mother's farm. It is not clear what happened, but his mother demanded that he leave, so he ran away to New York. The eldest brother, John, took him in. John was married and began a dental practice here. He paid for Harvey's enrollment at the Pennsylvania Medical College. After receiving his degree, Harvey moved in with John and John's rather attractive young wife."

"I seem to remember John Burdell being involved in a scandal," interjected Clinton, trying to gauge the direction of the story.

"Yes," replied Armstrong, with his usual distaste. "The two brothers set up a practice together on Broadway and Franklin Street. There were quarrels between them: John accused Harvey of being intimate with his wife, and a divorce proceeding ensued."

"Sleeping with your brother's wife is hardly a way to show gratitude," said Clinton.

"Harvey professed innocence in the affair. It appears that a judge came up with a costly alimony settlement in favor of the wife. Harvey offered his brother an ingenious plan—he persuaded John to sign over all of his properties to be held in Harvey's name—as a way for John to hide his property from his estranged wife. Meanwhile, John was forced to move to Union Square and start a new practice. When John demanded his safeguarded assets returned, Harvey refused, saying he would report him for hiding his money from his wife, and soon after John became gravely ill."

Clinton turned, gazing out the window. "James, what is your point? How does this affect my decision to take Emma Cunningham's case?" asked Clinton, impatiently. Confined in the small space, Clinton sensed a trap. Armstrong was a shrewd lawyer. He did not engage in a lengthy discourse unless he planned to win the argument.

"Hear me out," said Armstrong. "Harvey visited his brother upon his sickbed and drew up a will, making himself the sole executor of John's estate. John signed it in a delirium. Then Harvey returned with a sheriff and a repossession notice, claiming his brother had debts to him. They removed all of John's possessions, his furniture, and even the bed under the sick man, leaving him to die alone on the floor of his barren room."

"So, you're saying that Harvey Burdell slept with his brother's wife, stole away his business, blackmailed him, and swindled him of his livelihood? Is there a moral to the story, James?" asked Clinton.

"Does this sound like a moral story, Henry? That is my point," snapped Armstrong. "This case is a quagmire," said Armstrong, wearily. "I am dismayed that you have embroiled us in it."

"So you would prefer that this woman, whom I have not even been able to properly interview, be left without a defense? You have never interfered with my choice of cases before, James, and I have never interfered with yours. I would hope you will continue to honor that," said Clinton defiantly.

"The prosecution will build the case that Emma Cunningham is an imposter and killed Burdell for his money. Whatever money she had, she has lost. If cleared of the murder, her only recourse to pay us is another sensational court battle over the murdered man's estate," said Armstrong.

"Everything we know about Emma Cunningham," Clinton replied, "is based on the ramblings of a bumbling coroner and a fevered press. When I passed by the house this morning, the crowds were more numerous than yesterday, and the newspapers are making a fortune from this ordeal. This morning's paper already has accounts of Dr. Burdell's feuds with his family and his shadowy business practices," he said, patting the newspaper on his knee. "Meanwhile, Emma Cunningham will be made a scapegoat to the District Attorney's ambitions and she will hang, unjustly, for this crime."

"Henry, wake up! There is no value in this enterprise," barked Armstrong. "You do not need to save every widow. Another lawyer will rally to her cause. This case will collapse our firm in bad publicity and crippling costs. I am asking you to drop this case."

The carriage was stalled at Houston Street. The driver reported the congestion of traffic on account of the funeral. As they made their way through the snarl of vehicles, the horses neared the intersection of Bond Street. They headed into a crowd of hundreds of people, gathered along the sidewalks, noisy as if watching a parade, the curious leaning out windows. The carriage stopped again as a wagon, draped in black, drawn by four white horses, turned from Bond Street onto Broadway. Two undertakers held the coffin, and a policeman held back the crowds. As it passed, they edged northward in the wake of the funeral cortege, toward Grace Church, its Gothic marble spire sparkling white in the morning light. Armstrong spotted Oakey Hall walking briskly toward the church, wearing spats and carrying a jeweled cane.

"This is about crossing swords with Oakey Hall, isn't it, Henry?" said Armstrong, wearily. "You want to take him down. Well, I am serious about one thing: if you remain on this case, our partnership is over."

Clinton looked at Armstrong's face long enough to absorb the seriousness of his words. They had worked together for over seven years, and although they often held opposing views, the relationship had always been one of respect. But Clinton sensed that this time was different.

Without another word, Armstrong gathered his cane and exited the carriage, which was now parked deep among the other carriages arriving at the entrance. Clinton sat, pondering the effect of Armstrong's words, and just as the service was about to begin, he entered the church alone. Each bench was marked with a brass plate engraved with a family name. The newly rich had bought their pews recently, paying a handsome sum to the rectory, while the tottering aristocracy had inherited them, all the way back to the Dutch. There was a pew marked CLINTON, reserved three generations ago by the ancestors of his wife, and he squeezed himself in.

The mourners were rustling in their seats. The casket stood before the altar. Garlands of white lilies were piled on top, and the hothouse fragrance was overpoweringly sweet. The Rector, Reverend Taylor, mounted the podium, which was raised high, ornamented with carvings in the medieval style. The organ droned, and the congregation sang a hymn. The Rector's eulogy bemoaned the passing of a member of the medical profession whose contributions would be missed. In fact, thought Clinton, the deceased had been plotting and devious, his deeds washed clean behind the façade of a fancy house.

The law has taken me to strange places, Clinton mused. What chance had he to continue this case without the backing of a wealthy firm? Alone, the defense of Emma Cunningham would be difficult. He would need to rent an office and hire a staff. He would have to wait out the inquest, try to get his client removed from house arrest, and see that she was formally charged, even if that meant her being placed in jail. Then he would need to mount a defense for a trial that would surely be the sensation of the year. For the time being, his only communication with this woman was through an errand boy at the house, not even twelve years old. A key witness, a Negro driver, was missing, most likely running for his life.

At the end of the service, Clinton stepped out into the midday glare and made his way slowly through the dense crowd. Pickpockets abounded. As the carriages were pulling away for the burial, the crowd thinned and the funeral procession receded down Broadway. The hearse, reaching the tip, would board the Hamilton Ferry; after making a journey through the ice floes of the East River, it would head up the bluffs of Brooklyn to Greenwood Cemetery, where the coffin would be placed deep in the frozen earth, facing the departed island of New York.

Clinton headed toward home. New York was a walking town, and walking allowed him time to think. Elisabeth would be surprised to see him at midday, and he would discuss with her the events of the morning. She had already argued against him taking the case on legal grounds: that the marriage between the two would be hard to prove or disprove, as marriages are not witnessed by any legal authority of the state, but only by God, or in this case, a nearsighted clergyman. The entire case would be drowned in dueling perspectives of credibility and of character. Of course, Elisabeth was right.

But he also knew she would follow his lead and that she trusted his instincts. If he were to continue this case, there were great sacrifices to be made, and she was his best ally. After he stopped by the house for lunch, he would go back to Chambers Street and remove his books and papers. His long partnership with James Armstrong was over.

# CHAPTER EIGHT

C linton entered the house, dropped his hat on the hall table, and then went to the back parlor where a fire was crackling and woodsmoke was curling from the hearth. Elisabeth was deep in her favorite chair, with a book on her lap. She had a tangled look when she was reading, far away inside a story. She looked up and brushed some hair from her face. He sank into an armchair with his coat still on.

"You're home for lunch! What a surprise. Was it a hard morning?"

"It was," he said, slumping back. Elisabeth got up and sat on the arm of his chair and started to unwrap his scarf. She put a finger across his temple and traced the lines of his forehead. He let his eyes close under the warmth of her touch. Then she lifted the coat off his shoulders, and he shifted, allowing her to gently remove each arm from a sleeve, like she was undressing a young boy. Next, she sat down on a footstool and began to unbutton his boots.

"I rode with James to the funeral. I met him at the ferry."

"Well that's enough to wear a person out—a carriage ride with James Armstrong and then a funeral. Was it very oppressive?"

"Both were quite oppressive."

"Well, at least you are done with that dentist. Too bad I can't say the same about James."

"Actually, Elisabeth, I have some rather startling news." She was still sitting on the stool by his feet and looked up, wary.

"Henry?" her tone was chiding, but he heard the tinge of alarm. She knew him too well, and this was not going to be easy.

He sat forward and took hold of her hands, holding them in his, examining them as if they were part of a strange species.

"First of all, I have decided I am taking on the case."

"Oh, Henry, I suspected you would! Are you really defending that woman?"

"Yes."

"You have decided this for sure? I hope you have thought it over—this case is a runaway train."

"I was going to discuss it with you again after I conferred with James, which I just had the chance to do, this morning."

"Is he in favor of this folly?"

"No, he isn't. Not at all. I can't say he is in favor of my taking this case."

"Well, that's something to commend him. At least he still has some sense behind that rigid façade."

"Elisabeth, we've come to an impasse." He had been rubbing her hand, and she pulled it away with a stunned look on her face. "Not you, darling," he said. "James and I. We've had a parting of the minds."

"But that's been the nature of your partnership all along. I suppose you two will always disagree."

"No—we shan't disagree again, because I am no longer with the firm." Clinton slumped back in the armchair, as if overwhelmed by the morning's events. "I have quit, or perhaps it was James that fired me."

She let out a gasp. "Henry, you are not serious? It came to that?"

"It did. But believe me, it is for the best. I was too comfortable there. I was not doing good work, and I was becoming something of a clown in the office—an affable, but righteous, defender of the oppressed. James was not happy working with a criminal lawyer who defended anyone without a substantial merchant's bankbook. So I shall strike out on my own. I didn't plan for it to happen this way, but it is for the best."

"But what about the Burdell murder? How can you keep on the case? What will you do?" Elisabeth spoke softly, bewildered. He had just sacrificed his job and a large salary and a lesser wife would lash out, or even cry. She had a look on her face now that he had seen before—concerned, but ready to listen. When they had first met he would tell her a story about defending a hardened criminal, with all of its gruesome details, and she would be moved by his passion for securing the rights of both the innocent and the guilty. She would listen quietly, letting him ramble on, until he realized that he had piqued her intellectual curiosity, and she was mulling over the legal arguments, her mind leaping to the best conclusion.

Now, he sensed an opening, and he ran with it. "Darling, this case *is* a runaway train. It's a runaway train to the gallows. Everyone who has been inside 31 Bond Street in the few days since the murder—Coroner Connery, the District Attorney, the Mayor, the Chief of Police—have a vested interest in pointing the finger at Emma Cunningham. They've found the perfect scapegoat in a bedroom upstairs. It's as if they had commissioned a newspaper artist to draw up a portrait of a fictional murderess, and pinned her name to it. They've captured Emma Cunningham in a large frame and pasted the word *guilty* at the bottom. They'll pass the illustration off to the papers, all the while hoping that mob justice will finish the job."

"But what if she actually did it? You barely had a chance to interview her. Henry, what if you are defending evil?"

"I only interviewed her for a short period, but she is a woman not unlike yourself. She is a woman whose home was turned upside down during a circumstance of violence. I saw her terror at that upheaval. Regardless of her feelings for the murdered man, I saw that her surroundings were her greatest security. A woman does not desecrate her own home. Why would she commit this violence if it put her children at jeopardy and brought about everything she feared most?"

Elisabeth dropped a moccasin from her lap, and she sat, bewildered. "You really intend to keep on it?"

"I intend to. I intend to get an office, small as it may be, and prepare a defense, and take the case to trial. It will be difficult, but I believe that I am up to the task. Perhaps only I can do it. I will need money to float us for a while. The firm owes me money, and I'll take a loan out against this house. But I promise you, darling; I will pay the loan back, every cent of it. You shall see."

She closed her eyes for a minute. He could not tell if she was going to cry or lash out at him.

The cook appeared at the open door of the salon. Seeing them sitting so still, she cleared her throat and then rapped lightly against the doorjamb. Clinton swiveled around.

"Mr. Clinton, Mrs. Clinton, there's a boy come round by the kitchen door. He comes from your office. He has some things for you."

"A boy? Oh, yes. I'll come down," said Clinton. He stood up and slipped his stocking feet into the moccasins. He helped Elisabeth up, and they followed the cook downstairs where the boy, John, was standing just inside the kitchen door with a cardboard folder wrapped in string.

"John, my boy," he said.

"I went to your office to find you, like you asked, sir, and they sent me here with a package," the boy said, offering the document case.

"John, this is Mrs. Clinton, and this is our excellent cook, Mrs. Fullerton. As you see, between the two of them and these ovens, we have an unending source of shortbread."

Elisabeth pulled out a kitchen chair for the boy.

"John is the young lad who worked at 31 Bond Street," Clinton explained, "and had the misfortune of finding his master's body. He continues on as a houseboy under the Coroner's regime." Clinton undid the string on the package.

"Are you hungry?" asked Elisabeth. John gave a shy shrug, but she was already reaching for some kitchen flatware and a napkin. "Mrs. Fullerton, pull him off a piece of the beef. And serve him some vegetables if they are ready." Clinton unwrapped the parcel and looked over the papers.

"James certainly has not wasted time. This is the formal dissolution of the partnership."

Elisabeth glanced at him as the cook placed a slab of roast beef on John's plate and served up some roasted carrots and a potato. The boy began to eat the food hungrily.

"I'll give you a basket to take with you," she said. "Are they feeding you enough there, at the inquest?" Elisabeth asked John, concerned.

"I think his meals were scarce before, and now he's just scraping by," said Clinton, placing the legal papers on the edge of a cupboard. John tried awkwardly to slice the beef, which was very rare, and he chewed it with difficulty.

"Be careful swallowing now, if you're not used to red meat," said Elisabeth. She began to cut his meat for him in small pieces. "Henry, do you remember Thayer?" she asked.

"That young lawyer, fresh out of Columbia?"

"Yes, the fellow who came to dinner with his wife. They were going to have a baby; Thayer, wasn't it?"

"Barnaby Thayer. Why do you ask?"

"He will do the work of ten James Armstrongs," Elisabeth said. "He is bright and eager and has trial experience. I was very impressed by him." Clinton was always amazed by how her mind worked. She had scarcely absorbed the news and she was jumping past him, already staffing.

"Mrs. Fullerton," continued Elisabeth, "Mr. Clinton is the head of a new law office handling the Bond Street murder," she said.

"My word!" said the cook, turning around from the stove with wide eyes. "The world will be watching this one."

"If you're going to be placing bets, keep in mind, we are the underdogs," said Clinton, putting his arm around Elisabeth and squeezing her tightly. But the worry was not gone from her eyes, and he was terrified of disappointing her. He would go to the bank in the morning for the loan. There would be a slow reduction of niceties, of the things she was accustomed to, like flowers and chocolates and jewelry he brought home as a surprise, and their trips to Hastings in the summer months, where she grew a profusion of roses that rippled along trellises around the cottage.

"You are a courageous woman to be married to me, Elisabeth Clinton Clinton."

"Brave or foolish, it is the way I want it," she said back to him.

"Let's hope our roof holds out. With a new mortgage, that nasty leak will have to wait." He had been planning to hire a workman to make repairs to the roof of the townhouse after the winter thaw.

"If the roof fails, we'll live under the stars."

# CHAPTER NINE

*September 1856, New York City*

**E**mma sat toward the back of Taylor's, a ladies saloon, facing the plate glass, watching the men assemble on the street like black figurines, checking their watches. As soon as she had returned to New York from Saratoga, Dr. Burdell had sent her a stream of invitations—to tour upper Manhattan in his carriage, to dine at Delmonico's, and this evening, to the theatre, to see the Booth brothers in a Shakespeare play. It was a glorious evening, so clear that the city was framed by an iridescent sky and the windows along Broadway shone blood red with the setting of the New Jersey sun.

She sipped from a crystal glass, tasting the raisin flavor of a strong brandy, and poked at the flakes of a crème Napoleon with the prong of a tiny gold fork as yellow cream flowed from its crevices. She lifted each forkful to her mouth carefully, without altering her posture or the balance of her enormous hat.

*I am so tired of widowhood,* she thought. She had met her deceased husband, George Cunningham, when she was only fifteen, Helen's age. He was a prosperous merchant, more than twice her age, and he had turned to watch her when she passed him on the

Brooklyn Promenade one Saturday evening. She went to the railing, looking out at the harbor, and he came over to point out the ships. He reached in his pocket and offered her a dollar. "Would you walk with me?" he asked. He was more distinguished than the mechanics and seamen that strolled along the river walk and offered local girls a trinket to hook arms for the length of the waterfront, and at the end of the walk they'd offer another trinket for a kiss. Somehow she felt safe on this gentleman's arm, his elbow at her side, in wool broadcloth, scented with fine pipe tobacco. He'd gaze far away across the milky harbor, then back at her, with a caring glance.

They sauntered arm in arm until they reached the end near the sailors' bars by the ferry slip. He bought two tickets for the boat, and they went to Manhattan, to the Broadway Hotel, which she thought to be the finest place she had ever seen, with a large room that dripped with damask, and he cuddled up against her all night, like a man would a wife.

The experience was a far cry from the weathered frame house on Myrtle Avenue near the Naval Yard, where her father reigned over his children with a wooden board from the broken picket fence. He beat her with it when she returned the following day, never asking where she'd been all night. Rigid with determination, Emma brought all her clothes in a canvas bag when she met Mr. Cunningham the next day, and she never went home again.

He put her up in the city, in nice hotels, and soon after, in a house. When Augusta was born, he rented a larger one on Irving Place, and he never failed to pay the rent. He remained with his wife in his large mansion on the Brooklyn side of the river. "Take pity on me," he would say, "she is sickly," if Emma tearfully implored him to stay longer after a short visit. His wife was an unseen specter, frail and nervous, that hovered for years until she finally passed away when Augusta was seven and his second child, Helen, a toddler. After a ten-month absence, which Emma took to be a proper mourning period, George reappeared and brought them into his Brooklyn house, a gloomy pile, filled with the odor of dust and decay and room after room of family heirlooms. She became its mistress; it was more like a mausoleum, having encased an invalid for years.

They married quietly. Afterward, George retreated into his study with a tumbler of scotch and rarely emerged. His company, Cunningham & Cunningham, bottled spirits, liquor being the family fortune and its downfall. In a short matter of time, George's drinking accelerated his own bad health, and he accumulated debts while casks of whiskey remained untended at the wharves. In 1854, he went out west to recoup his fortune and gambled the rest of his inheritance on prospects in San Francisco, returning with less than he started with, the gold rush being mostly over. He caught a feverish ailment there and died of complications from it when he returned, like a plague that claimed those who chased after gold. Her husband's decline had seemed so fast—as if a demon had foreclosed upon his soul, secretly targeting her as well.

*But Harvey Burdell is so solid. He rarely drinks.* Emma's eye was trained casually toward the restaurant window, watching for Dr. Burdell's arrival. If he came early, she would put on her gloves slowly, smoothing the soft leather on each finger, making him wait. When he did show up, he was twenty minutes late, which sobered her mood like the bitter swig of a root tea. She summoned her gaiety and joined him on the twilit street between the swaying of women's hoops as the evening traffic thinned on Broadway.

They walked to the theatre, and he told her about his day, which included a difficult dental surgery, a story that lasted halfway to Astor Place. After his story was finished, they sauntered along in silence. After a long pause, Emma ventured to ask softly, "Why is it that you have never married?"

He gazed sternly ahead. "I have no reason to marry," he answered. "At forty-six, I enjoy my solitary pursuits. I enjoy female companionship, but an independent arrangement suits me best."

"I do not know what you mean," she replied coolly, "by an 'independent arrangement.'"

"Oh, yes you do, my dear," he said dismissively. "I am not an anxious schoolboy, and you are not an ingenue. You are no doubt aware, at our age, that there is no need to hide behind convention. We can be free of the constraints that society places upon the young. There are many couples, quite prominent in New York, that remain unmarried, retaining their separate residences and who enjoy the physical side of marriage. It is a most sophisticated arrangement."

The response stung. "I am indeed aware of such independent couples," Emma said, choosing her words, carefully. "But I would have difficulty with such an arrangement myself. I have my daughters to think of. At their tender age, it is important that my actions stand as an example. They are still young, and I could not steer them toward marriage if I, myself, did not respect the vows." He wants me, she thought, but is it love? For a moment she felt a twinge of panic, as if he had seen into her past. No, she assured herself, it was more likely that he had a bachelor's dread of trespass, and she should tread lightly.

"As for your lovely daughters," he replied, forcing a light tone, "a sensible parent requires only a large bank account to snare a successful suitor. And once that is secured, the job is done." He laughed, clearly hoping to change the subject.

"It is not so simple as that," she replied, her voice edging upward. "Even with means, a parent needs to be vigilant. This city provides many traps for young ladies. Many suitors are not what they seem. Some are scoundrels, intent upon a large dowry. A parent must protect a daughter's interests."

"If a suitor cared more for the fortune than the bride, he would need to be after a hundred thousand dollars to make it worth his while," he said, looking at her, to gauge her reaction.

She hesitated, wondering if he thought she was worth that large a sum. She decided it was best not to reply, for he would guess that he had hit the number close to the mark, exposing her wealth and stature.

Dr. Burdell scratched his chin, summing her up. "We were speaking about our own situation. I am preoccupied with important business at the moment and am in no position to marry right away. I cannot press events. I have a large sum of money at stake, which, if all goes as planned, will soon see a most lucrative return."

"What is the use of money if it comes into conflict with personal happiness?"

"When speaking of your daughters, you have just implied that you consider a successful marriage to be one where money is of utmost importance. I would think you would see fit to dispense with hypocrisy."

She was startled by his abrupt turn. She was not used to a man who disregarded the dance of courtship, with its delicate art of concealment.

"Perhaps I can make a suggestion," said Dr. Burdell, more gently now. "There are often solutions when one is not blinded by convention. My housemistress, Mrs. Jones, has just departed, leaving the upper floors of my house vacant. You and your daughters could come and live at 31 Bond Street. I need a refined woman to oversee my home. It is not an uncommon arrangement, and in the eyes of the outside world, it would not compromise your integrity. You and your daughters might find my house most suitable."

Stunned, Emma was not sure whether to be insulted or pleased. A bachelor sharing the upper part of his house with a widow was not uncommon, although the widow was usually an elderly woman, with thick legs and a sagging jowl. "A housemistress? For pay?" she asked.

"You could have the rooms without rent; in exchange, you would oversee the servants. I could help you with your investments," he added gently. "I could offer the protection of a fine home, and we might consider the suitability of marriage at a convenient date, possibly by the spring."

Emma sensed a window opening where previously doors had been shut, and this sounded very much like a marriage proposal, although an unconventional one. Her lease was soon up, and her funds were perilously low, and there were few options she could afford as grand as the house on Bond Street. The term "arrangement" could mean many things. "Bond Street is a very respectable location," she said carefully. "My daughters are very active, and I should need the parlors to entertain on their behalf." She hoped to sound skeptical.

"My patients use the parlor as a waiting room during visiting hours, usually in the morning. After that, the rooms would be at your service. You shall consider my offer then?" he asked. He gazed into Emma's eyes as if he was searching for approval. "I have something to tell you if you can keep a secret," he added. "I have a great deal of money invested with a group of prominent financiers, even a politician or two. If my interests prevail, my land in New Jersey, which I have spoken about, will be very valuable. I must conclude my business by the end of the year, or nothing will be gained, for there are others with interests in opposition."

He lifted a curl from her cheek. "If you were to turn over to me, say, a sum of ten thousand dollars, your investment would help to speed the process. I will certainly see that you—no I say 'we'—shall enjoy the most handsome returns."

Startled by the sudden request for money, she stalled. "Well, sir, this seems to be a separate issue. As I have told you, I am not interested in land speculation."

"There is no need to make a hasty decision. However, I would like to invite you on a tour of my land," he said. "I can assure you that any investment will grow greatly. With my own profits, we might build a larger, more modern home on Fifth Avenue."

Mrs. Cunningham stopped abruptly. "We'd live on Fifth Avenue?" she asked, then color spread across her face when she realized that he had said "we" and she had automatically assumed possession of their next home.

"Well, why not!" he answered jovially. "Fifth Avenue has the largest lots, and plenty of room to build. Soon enough, we will need a bigger residence."

They had reached the theatre and they entered, arm in arm. Dr. Burdell encountered acquaintances and patients who nodded in greeting. He proudly made introductions. She knew she appeared attractive at his side. The curtain came up, and the actors marched across the stage spouting Shakespeare, wearing embroidered costumes, and gesturing from the turrets of cardboard castles, but she could barely concentrate on the play. She thought about his offer, and the need to maintain appearances, wary not to make any decision that might compromise her. His enthusiasm for their future plans belied his hesitation toward marriage. Her feminine instinct told her that if she were to move in with him at Bond Street, and show him the satisfaction of an intimate domestic life, they would certainly be married by spring.

The play ended with a blaze of trumpets, and the audience rose to the exits. Samuel, Dr. Burdell's driver, sat waiting atop his carriage outside the theatre. They got in and drove to her home on Twenty-fourth Street. In front of her house, Dr. Burdell engaged in a parting kiss that was more ardent than the others, and she skillfully edged out of the carriage, leaving him longing for more. *A mansion on Fifth Avenue,* she thought, *would be a brilliant place for weddings.*

# CHAPTER TEN

*October 1856*

Visiting the marshland of New Jersey on an October morning to examine real estate was an activity like going to the opera—a refined form of leisure wrapped tightly in the concept of wealth. Samuel picked her up on Twenty-fourth Street and brought her to the riverbank at the foot of Christopher Street. Emma carried an overnight bag. Samuel would ferry her across the river, and Dr. Burdell would meet her on the other side to give her a tour of his property. He would offer her a piece to buy, and she intended to accept.

After much thought and discussion, she had put aside a sum with which to purchase some land—it was money left by her husband for Augusta's dowry. Dr. Burdell had convinced her that this land investment would swiftly gain in value. Although she was taking a gamble, she felt assured that the transaction would be successful and would secure a significant gain. Instead of feeling anxious, she felt closer to her goal, as if she were a bird gliding gracefully in circles, high above her prey.

Emma sat on the deck on a canvas chair, settling herself among the crude fittings of the small craft. There were just the two of them on the boat. Samuel steered silently, like a sentinel, his dark skin outlined against the sky at the stern. The boat glided past the dockyards, glassworks, distilleries, and furnaces of Greenwich Village, following the river motion south. The city split away as the river opened into the wide mouth of the harbor, swelling like an upturned silver dish.

They sailed toward New Jersey, into the narrow strait of the Kill van Kull, and the boat seemed lost in miles of grassland. Occasionally Emma looked up from her book, squinting into the blue and green expanse. Miles away, in the distance, a southbound train left a smudge of black against the horizon. The whistle blew, setting off a flock of egrets rising on the wing, thousands of them, spreading across the reeds, like a fluttering cloud.

Emma asked Samuel questions: "How far do the marshes stretch? How far is Newark? Do any roads pass over this land?" Samuel, wary, gazed toward the horizon and answered in monosyllables, only saying what was necessary. Emma kept her hand to her brow, shielding the glare. "Which part is Dr. Burdell's land? she asked.

Samuel pointed to a promontory of discarded shells on the marsh side of New Jersey, "Past that ridge, it was the Indian's road," he said, of a faint white line shimmering into the salt marsh. All along New York harbor were small islands dotted with bone white beaches formed of shells, piled into middens and mysterious mounds. The Indians had used shells as currency, and these ancient shell paths formed bridges and roads through the lowlands, marking a path to the riches they once associated with the sea.

It was from an Indian that Samuel learned everything about the harbor—about the marsh elder, goosefoot, and sunflower, which produce edible seeds, and about the otters and giant bullfrogs, a freakish species that sing before a summer rain. He could have told her about his lazy summer days in a dugout canoe, dipping a bucket into the water, with Katuma, a Lenape, whose ancestors had once ruled this watery kingdom, and who worked the oyster barges. On lazy days, they fished together. Just below the surface was a harbor's bounty of oysters, clams, scallops, mussels, and whelk that burrow in the sandy waterbeds.

And it was the Indians who had aided him and other runaway slaves through the Maryland swamps when he fled North. Tribes still lived along the fingers of land that jutted into the eastern waterways, and when they encountered a starving Negro fugitive, they fed him, teaching him to catch and roast a duck, and to smear his body with bear grease to ward away the bugs and the smell of the dogs.

Since coming to New York, Samuel had found work at the stables and was hired to drive Dr. Burdell. He spent his days riding papers and satchels up and down the streets of New York, or ferrying him along with other men back and forth across this piece of harbor, all the while hearing mischief wrapped in deeds and schemes that had no place under God's sun.

"Where does the water end and the solid land begin?" Emma asked, dismayed, looking at the tall reeds and grasses that spread for miles.

"This swamp can swallow a man," was all he said.

They reached the shore of Elizabeth Port, a tiny hamlet with whitewashed houses and a single church. It was afternoon, and Dr. Burdell was waiting near the dock with a buggy. Samuel drove while Emma and Dr. Burdell surveyed the land. They bounced along a dirt road that bordered the sea, flanked by rich meadows that seemed to lift up out of the swamp with deeply rooted stands of trees. The horse stopped when its hooves began to sink into the sticky mud. Ahead was the watery amorphous vista: a patchwork of meadows and marsh that spread for miles inland where one could see the tips of barns on a far horizon.

"We are dividing the land into lots, one hundred acres each. Each piece starts at the water and runs inland. Where the water is shallow it will be dug deep for docks and berths," said Dr. Burdell, waving his hand along the salt marshes. "The dredged mud will be poured for higher land and roads. A railroad runs south from Hoboken, crossing this expanse of marsh, before it heads on to Philadelphia." Emma was glad he did not suggest they get out of the carriage where the mud would be sucking at their shoes. "There are only two lots left," he said. "You can see the best one from here—it ends at the Bound Creek, a freshwater stream that bisects this part of the marsh."

Since they were on a rise, she could see the shell mounds and a clear stream starting at Newark Bay, cutting into the marshland, a spiraling creek that made a demarcation going east to west. "Farther up, the Hackensack and the Passaic Rivers converge, so the coal barges pass by here as well." He spoke with such authority that one would think that all the commerce in the harbor was waiting to berth in this spot where now there were only bugs and spiny creatures and enormous fields of useless grasses, swaying for miles. "Buyers have been discreet in purchasing these lots, but it will soon result in a frenzy of speculation once the builders and financiers come on board."

"Turn around, and head back," Dr. Burdell ordered Samuel, directing him to turn back to Elizabeth Port. Samuel was familiar with the route and took little direction. They headed toward the village and stopped before a small wooden building that had a sign for a country notary. Dr. Burdell and Emma stepped inside, and the notary nodded a greeting. Dr. Burdell took papers from a satchel and spread them along a central table. He unrolled a map that had thin lines bisecting the furrows and marshes into rectangular plots. Emma studied the survey, trying to make sense of the markings. Dr. Burdell put his hand on her arm, and she felt his grip tighten as she hesitated. "That is the section I shall choose," she said, finally, pointing to a dotted line that marked a plot along the water's edge. She recognized a hook shape on the map that corresponded to a promontory she had seen from the boat ride; from the water it had looked like a bone that was raised out of the water, its dry ridge continuing like a highway through the wetland. The line of the freshwater creek was within its boundary. She hesitated again, and then nodded. "Yes, this is the one I will take."

"The lady has a large amount of money at her disposal," Dr. Burdell said to the notary, as if that oblique flattery were designed to impress the countryman. "She has chosen a gem of a property." Then he said to Emma, "You would do well to purchase the other plot to reap the most profit when we resell the land."

"One parcel will be enough for now," replied Emma with a laugh, as if land lots were casually dispensed like cards dealt at a table. The notary prepared the deed, marking her parcel by number. She bent over, dipped the pen in the ink, and carefully attached her name. Her banker would prepare a note assigned to Dr. Burdell for ten thousand dollars. She trembled at the precariousness of her action. Her own reserves were nearly gone, and this sum was the total of Augusta's dowry, but she felt strangely protected by the sense of fortune that had brought Dr. Burdell to her on that summer day in Saratoga. She felt as if she were purchasing a slice of the sky, and that profits would rain down from the heavens.

Darkness covered the countryside when the buggy arrived at Fairbanks's Public House. Dr. Burdell instructed Samuel to post the horse and to sleep in the barn. Then he engaged a room for the night, signing the inn register as Dr. and Mrs. Burdell. He ordered supper sent up to the room, and they ate at a table set beside a roaring wood fire. They drank cherry and currant wines served with fresh game.

"You will not be disappointed," he said as he tore the flesh off the bird. The firelight broke his face into patches of orange and shadow, illuminating his grinning teeth as he devoured his meal. The brisk country air, the candlelight instead of gas, and the remote howling of wolves in the woods brought on a rich, deep indolence. Relieved of the tension of respectability and the confines of the city, Emma Cunningham succumbed to the aromatic fumes of woodsmoke and to Dr. Burdell in the goose down bed.

# THE BOND-STREET MURDER.

## Thirteenth Day of the Coroner's Inquest.

### The Blood-Stains Analyzed.

### REPORT OF THE CHEMISTS AND MICROSCOPISTS.

### Science Shows Justice Some Nice Distinctions.

### The Surgeons' Report and their Theories of the Fatal Struggle.

### THE MARRIAGE CERTIFICATE.

### THE INQUEST ADJOURNED TILL SATURDAY.

### The Burdell Estate in the Surrogate's Court.

The Coroner's investigation was resumed at eleven o'clock yesterday. The Coroner again received the assistance of Judge Capron. The crowd which gathers daily across the way was on hand again, punctually; some fifty or a hundred people patiently cooling their heels in the sharp wind, and commanding a fine view of the outside of the premises. A few of the highly-favored forced their way into the front parlor, where they stood about, and gazed over each other's shoulders, envious of seven other more lucky individuals, who had appropriated the sofa and enjoyed the luxury of reserved seats. The public appetite does not seem to be at all sated, though this was the thirteenth day of a spun-out investigation.

The first witness called was Dr. Wm. Knight.

#### DR. KNIGHT'S TESTIMONY.

*Dr. Wm. Knight* sworn and examined by Judge Capron.

Q.—Were you present during the examination yesterday of Dr. Woodward? A.—I was.

Q.—Did you hear and understand his evidence? A.—Yes, Sir, perfectly.

Q.—Do you agree with or dissent from the Doctor's statements in whole or any part of them? A.—I agree with about all he has stated.

Q.—If there is any portion of his narration or of his opinions which you dissent from, you will have the kindness to state it? A.—The only thing was about

# Part II

## CHAPTER ELEVEN

Look at that city, and see her extending streets, her palatial establishments, with her vast congregation of vessels at her docks bursting forth like a crab from the shell.

President John Tyler

*February 16, 1857*

Henry Clinton's new law office was in the Mercantile Building on top of a bluff on Spruce Street, where the city sloped down to the waterfront. The Mercantile Building was brick and marble, five stories high, with an octagonal tower. It was topped with a gold dome, obscured now among the cornices of taller buildings that had crowded around it. A weather vane tipped the dome, still visible through the rooftops, of the young god Mercury, with wings on his feet and helmet, his slender body rotating in the wind.

It was the octagonal room at the top of the building that Clinton had rented. Originally used as a watchtower, ship owners went up with telescopes to spot their errant ships. With the shipping concerns now concentrated at the wharves, the garret office at the top of the building had fallen into disuse, for the scenery was too distracting for other professions. The eight windows in the cupola created a kaleidoscope of the city, with views of the avenues spilling into the watery continents of two rivers flowing into the brilliant blue harbor, whisked into a silvery sheen when the wind rippled the surface.

James Snarky sat on top of one of the window ledges, his legs dangling. Clinton had hired the brash clerk from Armstrong and Clinton, promising him a small raise. What had set him apart from the other dutiful clerks in Armstrong's office was his connection to the rough-and-tumble world of reporters. Snarky had started off as a writer for the *Tribune* but switched to a job clerking in a law office because the salary was better and he had an ailing mother to support, but his passion was for the jargon of the city beat. There was nothing that James Snarky enjoyed more than placing bets at the card games that were played on crates in alleyways between the newspaper offices along Park Row. Clinton had assigned Snarky the job of keeping abreast of the reporters and of using his nose for investigation, to get the inside scoops. Released from the moribund atmosphere at Armstrong and Clinton, Snarky came to work each day in the attire of the newspaperman: plaid pants, two-toned shoes, and a bowler hat.

Barnaby Thayer swiveled on an oak chair in front of a rolltop desk, chewing the pointed end of a pen. Thayer was a young trial lawyer who had been a junior litigator for a firm on State Street. At the death of one of the partners, the other retired, leaving Thayer out of work with a young wife and a newborn. He had contacted Henry Clinton, with an inquiry about employment. It was Elisabeth who had remembered the overture by the ambitious young man. Thayer's credentials and letters of recommendation were impressive, including high praise from a circuit judge. At Columbia Law School, he had studied under Dr. J. W. Gideon, the dean of Medical Jurisprudence, which was a newly formed discipline that applied the knowledge of anatomy and medical science to criminal law. Now employed by Clinton, Thayer had been assigned to enlist Dr. Gideon as a defense expert. Thayer also oversaw a laboratory at the Medical College of technical men skilled in the new science of forensic analysis. They could identify the corpuscles of blood by microscope, or isolate a red stain on a silk dress and determine if it came from wine, grape juice, or the blood of an ox. Thayer had also enlisted a squadron of undergraduates who buried themselves in the Columbia Law Library, doing the voluminous case research and acting as clerks for the case, preparing the motions that would be needed as the case moved to trial.

Thayer wore a wrinkled tie, hastily knotted. His jacket had been quickly brushed, most likely in a dusky room, for it showed signs of missed lint and what appeared to be stains from his baby on the right shoulder. In his late twenties, he still looked like a freshman. His hair was thick and slightly unruly, flopping forward over his face. He had a strong jaw that flashed the winning combination of a broad smile and straight teeth. Clinton did not have the means to engage a top litigator, so this promising, but slightly unkempt, young man would have to do.

Clinton paced the room, looking through legal briefs that were spread everywhere on wide tables.

"The *Herald* got the best dispatch on her," said Snarky, from his perch on the windowsill. "All the papers will be scrambling after it tomorrow."

"I dread to hear it," said Clinton.

"Begins something like this—Emma Cunningham Burdell, born Emma Hempstead, in Brooklyn—was remarkable chiefly for a well-developed bosom, and voluptuous form. She had more than ordinary powers of fascination over men and was known to give a man a favor . . ."

"I am sure such a flattering portrait has nowhere to go but down," said Thayer.

"Meekham from the *Herald* got himself over to the Surrogate's office in Brooklyn," continued Snarky. "He looked up the family will. Her father was a rope maker and didn't leave her much except a Bible and a chest of drawers."

"Totally irrelevant," said Clinton, half listening as he sorted through the papers on the table.

"She was a looker, all right," continued Snarky. "The husband, George Cunningham, was older, rich, and thought she was fetching. Meekham says Cunningham paid for a date with her, and then kept her on as a mistress. She had the daughters out of wedlock, but he put them up in fine style. He already had a wife, an invalid, who was wasting away in the family mansion. Well, happily, she died, and finally George Cunningham married Emma, making an honest woman of her."

"Now that is the touching story of a Brooklyn girl made good," said Thayer, rubbing his hand through a thick lock of dark hair. "If only her happy tale had ended there."

"Meekham looked up Cunningham's will, and Emma got the money from a life insurance policy when he died. So the *Herald* will be running a story on her first marriage—gold digger, paid woman, the girls born out of wedlock, etc, etc."

"None of this is important," repeated Clinton, his concentration never leaving the documents.

"Well, here's the relevant part," said Snarky. "The District Attorney's office calls in Meekham, Finnerty, and some guys from the *Herald*, for a visit in the hallowed office of His Elegance."

"I hope the press boys wore their most eye-popping plaids," said Thayer.

"A meeting with the District Attorney? What about?" Clinton was now facing Snarky, leaning against the table. Clinton conjured an image of Oakey Hall, his feet on his desk, his striped trousers stretching crisply before him, addressing the reporters with his languid drawl. Leather books and legal circulars would be strewn among volumes of Shakespeare and subscriptions to the theatre.

"Seems the DA wants the press boys to know that he is thinking about exhuming George Cunningham's grave. The official verdict at the time of his death was congestion of the brain, death by drinking. But now they want to look at the body again."

"Good Lord!" said Thayer. "Will he stop at nothing? Now they intend to imply she killed her first husband. None of this can be used in court. They are manipulating the press. This is unprecedented."

"Even the medical examiners are saying that the idea of exhuming the body after so long a time has elapsed is nonsense." Clinton was listening now, but with a distracted look on his face. "The other part that's relevant," Snarky continued, "is that George Cunningham ran the family's liquor business into the ground—they say he guzzled away the family fortune. After his death, his creditors got everything, including the big old house on Jay Street, but they couldn't touch the life insurance or the daughters' dowry. A life insurance payment of twenty thousand dollars went to Emma, and now the DA is implying that she may have done him in, just like she did Burdell, to get after his money."

"This is running tomorrow?" asked Thayer, agitated. "Maybe we should visit Greeley at the *Tribune* and have a little conference with him. And James Raymond at the *Times*."

"No, let it all come out all at once," said Clinton, wearily. "Just like a mudslide, the faster it exhausts itself in a pile, the better."

"I am glad you can be so sanguine," said Thayer. "Our hides are on the line."

"It is Emma Cunningham's body that hangs, not ours, something to keep in perspective." The stair creaked, and John's fair head came into view as he mounted the stairs to the garret, lugging a wicker basket covered with a checkered cloth, filled with lunch.

"Ah, my fleet-footed friend, I see you have visited my wife. Is it quince pie?" asked Clinton.

"She says to tell you, no pies on Tuesday," John said, hoisting the basket onto the long table. The smell of baked chicken and herbs emerged as John lifted the cloth and unloaded piles of biscuits and bread. Plates were laid out all around, and John handed one up to Snarky.

"Thanks, lad. You're worth your weight in gold," Snarky said, tucking a napkin under his chin. Clinton and Thayer pushed papers away from the table to make room for their meal. There was an envelope in the basket and Clinton picked it up.

> *Darling,*
> *Remember how frightened she will be,*
> *Good luck today,*
>
> *ECC*

At breakfast that morning, Elisabeth had a law book at the table when he came down. "If she is a witness at the inquest, is she compelled to testify?" she asked, flipping through for the citation. The Coroner's inquest had dragged on; it was now two weeks old, an unprecedented length of time, and Emma Cunningham was still sequestered by Connery in her bedroom upstairs.

"In essence, yes," Clinton answered. The Coroner had interviewed close to a hundred acquaintances of Dr. Burdell, medical colleagues, neighbors, shopkeepers, and servants, but he was saving Emma Cunningham and her daughters for last.

"But the statute does not say that a coroner can hold persons on suspicion of guilt, only as witnesses. If she were a suspect to the crime, that would be unlawful imprisonment."

"Exactly," he said, hastily eating his eggs and toast. He was preparing to serve Coroner Connery with a writ of habeas corpus, releasing her from the house arrest. Connery was enjoying his time in the limelight, not ready to relinquish his power. No one had ever tried to stop an inquest, or challenge the grim majesty of the Coroner.

"Are you serving the papers today?" she had asked.

"I understand that they will be signed and ready by the afternoon."

'Since you will meet all sorts of bedlam when you go to the house to release her, why don't you take the sheriff along and have his wagons waiting?" said Elisabeth. "That way you can go straight downtown with an escort."

"That's a brilliant idea," he said to Elisabeth. "I hadn't thought of that. The bedlam will mostly be of the Coroner's making, and he may even order me to be arrested. With the sheriff present, even in handcuffs, we can make it safely downtown to a hearing on the writs. Then the house arrest will certainly end."

For a short while the office was quiet except for the avid noises that surround the appreciation of fresh food. "So tell me, John, what is happening at Bond Street?" Clinton asked, between bites. "Who is being called at the inquest today?"

"I wasn't in the parlors this morning," John replied. "But neighbors are going in and out, to give testimony. I saw old Mr. Barksdale, from across the street, and the chemist's son from next door."

"The newspapers are printing page upon page on the inquest," remarked Thayer. "Each neighbor's testimony conjures up imagined scandals that went on behind the walls of that house—Emma had lovers, the daughters had lovers, there were burning smells from the chimney when she burned the bloody clothes. Rumors are breaking faster than waves in a hurricane."

"She was seen buying a dagger on Pearl Street," volunteered Snarky through a mouthful of bread, adding to the list. "You can tell a newspaper from a fishwife, by the speed with which they spread gossip. A fishwife can spread the news up and down Fulton Street in half an hour, but a newspaper reporter gets the word to City Hall before the presses have even rolled."

"What else, John?" asked Clinton.

"Well, sir, I was up in the girls' room, cleaning out the stove, and I heard the prison matron tell them they were to come down and talk to the Coroner's jury in the parlor this afternoon."

"Today!" exclaimed Thayer.

"The girls got all up in a fuss about what they were going to wear," said John.

"What frivolity!" Snarky laughed. "You'd think they were preparing for a stage review."

Clinton stood and started rifling again through the papers. "This is it boys. If the daughters are testifying today that means Connery will be springing Emma's testimony as well. Who has seen the writs?"

"The copies are all prepared, in the pile on the left," said Thayer, motioning to the far end of the table. "Shall we deliver them right away?"

"I thought we'd serve them late this afternoon, but now we had better hurry. Snarky and Thayer, I want you to go to Judge Davies right now. Get the signed writs of habeas corpus and we will deliver them to Coroner Connery and forestall the testimony altogether." Clinton found the stack of papers he was looking for and began to study them.

"Does Mrs. Cunningham go to jail?" asked John, alarmed.

"That's sure possible, son," said Snarky. "This might force them to make a criminal arrest and indict her. Locked up, she'll be protected by the Bill of Rights. As it stands now, she's a prisoner at the whims of the Coroner, King Connery, Monarch of Rumland. By tomorrow his reign at Bond Street will be over."

"What about Augusta and Helen?" John asked.

"Nothing happens to them yet. Not unless a grand jury gets some hard evidence against them," explained Thayer.

The clock struck one. "What time does the inquest resume with the daughters?"

"After lunch, right about two," John told him.

"Let's go," said Clinton, pulling on his coat. "Snarky, you go with Thayer to the courthouse, and then find a way to rush the papers to Bond Street. I'll go get the sheriff, and get him to bring a prison wagon. I'll have to convince him to move without orders, so make sure the papers are waiting at the house. Hurry, this is what we've been waiting for."

# CHAPTER TWELVE

We do not see why the press should not state, and prove its statement by facts, that in a hundred ways the wolves are after the sheep—that a hundred scoundrels are watching for a single innocent—that this is an evil world, and that we are all under a dire necessity of keeping our eyes open.

*The New York Tribune*, FEBRUARY 6, 1857

Augusta and Helen sat in their bedroom at 31 Bond Street, usually so neat, now in disarray. Trays of half-eaten food sat on tabletops, meals brought by a matron from the prison who kept watch over them and took them out to the water closets. They had been allowed to see their mother only twice. The girls had been led to her bedroom, where she started to weep when she saw them. They were ordered to say nothing about the murder and were taken away in tears after a brief meeting. From below, the house was filled with chaotic noises that burst every now and then up the staircase to their room, but mostly it was quiet, their door kept shut, sealing them inside an envelope of uncertainty.

Helen's trunks were still on the floor since that terrible day, over two weeks ago, when she was to leave for boarding school. The detectives had rifled through, pulling out her petticoats and under things, leaving clothes strewn across the floor, as they had done with the contents of every drawer and closet. Ribbons and trinkets lay about, mixed up with fashion sheets and penny jewelry. A straw hat with rice paper flowers lay trampled by the door.

Helen sat curled on one of the beds buried in a romance novel. Augusta spent her time at the window seat before the deep-set window that looked out over the garden behind the house, past a large sycamore tree and a small stable that was attached to the brick wall shielding the house from the alley. She could see across the yards to the backs of the houses that faced Bleecker Street. Since being confined, she had gazed for hours at this rear-window view of the city, seeing only occasional shadows, gaslight flickering on in the evening, a back door briefly opened by a cook—evidence that domestic life continued on, muffled and serene. The backyards were like a cloistered garden, an empty place of the imagination, sheltered from the calamity inside 31 Bond Street.

Their door banged open. It was the matron, a wide squat woman who wore a heavy wool skirt, black boots, and a white shirt with a crooked tie. "Getcher things," she announced from the door.

"Where are we going?" asked Helen. She was always the one to speak first. She could react instantly to a situation, while Augusta could never make out the circumstances fast enough to respond.

"Just the older girl, you're to stay here," replied the matron.

"I don't want Augusta to go!" said Helen defiantly. "Don't take her away!" Now her voice sounded childish and alarmed.

"You ain't got no choice in the matter. Them's the orders. Getcher things," the woman repeated. Augusta shuttled around the room confused as to what she should be getting. She picked up a cloak. The matron grabbed her by the arm and hurried her from the room.

"Mama!" Helen cried out, sobbing as Augusta was lead down the stairs.

Snarky ran with Thayer to the court offices. "Meet me right here," Thayer said as he dashed up the steps. Snarky stayed on the sidewalk for what seemed an interminable amount of time, but he knew that there was a procedure for retrieving the papers from the judge, and they would have to be shuffled from clerk to clerk, unmindful of the minutes that hung in the balance. He paced back and forth along the street in his plaid pants and spats, pulling off his hat and smoothing his hair. He didn't dare stray more than several paces from the entrance in case Thayer should suddenly emerge.

He tapped his foot and pulled out his pocket watch only to see the second hand tick loudly round the dial. A girl of about seven years old stood before a little cart at the corner. She was selling sticky buns on a stick. She dipped the buns into a vat of honey and then placed the sticks upright into holes on her stand, waiting for customers. Snarky pulled out his pocket watch again; twelve minutes had gone by when finally he saw Thayer bounding down the steps. "Here it is," said Thayer. "Signed and sealed by the Judge."

"Good going," said Snarky. "That's some speedy lawyering."

"It took awhile because there was an old gent that had to make a slow ritual of melting the wax on the Judge's seal. I had the notion to throttle him and light the place aflame." Thayer wiped his brow. He handed the rolled documents to Snarky as if handing off a baton. "Two fifteen," he said. "I am sure they have the girl on the stand by now."

Snarky looked around. There wasn't a cab in sight, and even

if there were, the route uptown would be congested and slow. He had a backup plan. He dashed off toward the Herald building. In the alley near the reporters' entrance he ran up to a horse that was always tied to a hitching post. He grabbed its reins, and a boy groom yelled, "Hey, that horse is the editor's, Mr. Bennett's, for his courier."

"Tell him I'm just borrowing it for a bit," Snarky said, undoing the tether and putting his foot in the stirrup, pulling himself onto the saddle. "I'll bring her back," he yelled, kicking the hindquarters and bending forward to get her moving. The horse trotted out of the alley, clattering along the cobblestones, and then broke into a canter. At the bend in the narrow street, he turned the corner. Snarky knew that when he reached Mulberry Street, he could ride straightaway north at a near gallop. If he didn't fall off, or rear into a pile of bricks, he'd make it to Bond Street in fifteen minutes.

Augusta stepped through the doorway of the parlor dressed in a dark brown-plaid silk dress. She had gathered her warmest cloak, a Russian sable cape, not sure if she was going to be taken away from the house. She hesitated long enough to be examined by the crowd, hushed at the sensation of her presence. Stunned, she was led to the metal chair that Dr. Burdell used for his patients, and a terrible feeling of foreboding came over her. Her expectations were suddenly askew. She recognized no one in the room; in fact she did not recognize the room at all, which no longer looked like the parlor of the house. The furniture was rearranged and the light was murky and strange. Mismatched chairs from the kitchen and dining room, even stools from the attic, were scattered all along the room, and so many men were everywhere, leaning against the walls. From the sea of bodies popped individual faces, springing toward her like jackin-the-boxes, each facial characteristic momentarily distinct, jeering, and foreign.

She sat down in the chair while two men paced around her.

"You are the oldest daughter of Mrs. Cunningham?" Coroner Connery began to interrogate her, even though he had questioned her several times in her room.

"Yes," she replied meekly.

"Please speak so that the reporters can hear," he said, more for their benefit than hers.

"I will speak as loud as I can." Augusta tried to sit straight and appear composed, but her body felt heavy and unwilling to respond.

"How long has your father been dead?"

"A year last June."

"Where were you living after his death?"

"On Twenty-fourth Street." She tried to raise her voice, but no matter how loudly she tried to speak, it came out in a murmur.

"What number on Twenty-fourth Street?"

"I cannot remember the number."

"Between what streets—do you remember that?" asked another man sharply. This man and the Coroner were alternating questions to her, like taking turns practicing at a rifle target.

"Between Eighth and Ninth Avenues?" she replied, but she could not tell if the feeling of confusion was hers or was emanating from everyone around her.

"Was your mother planning on going away from this house to Europe with Dr. Burdell?"

"I don't know. I don't know if she was planning that."

"Aren't you in the habit of talking with your mother about her affairs?"

"I never spoke to her about her plans—whether she was going to leave here or not."

"You never even asked the question?"

"No, sir, I never did." Augusta struggled for air.

"You felt no interest in whether you were going to remain here or were going away?" The Coroner appeared incredulous. Augusta could not keep her heart still. She did not know how she managed to both hear the questions and answer, and she felt as if her heart was pumping the air right out of her body, and at any moment her breath might stop altogether.

Clinton had made it to the sheriff's office and commandeered Sheriff Crombie, the constable's stagecoach, and a prison van to head up to Bond Street. The sheriff had been skeptical about heading uptown without a set of orders from the chief, but Clinton had convinced him he was obtaining judicial orders, and that they would be waiting for them at the house. "You better know your business," warned the sheriff. "If you don't have the papers, it's you who is going to prison." Clinton's goal was to keep Mrs. Cunningham and her girls from testifying inside the house, and the only hope of preventing that was by serving the papers to Coroner Connery, suddenly and by surprise.

The caravan started up Broadway, which was a mistake, and as they tried to get through the traffic the two vehicles got separated. "Hurry up, man," Clinton urged the driver from inside. Finally he stuck his head out of the coach where he sat with the sheriff and yelled, "Take Orange Street to Elm." When it appeared that the driver couldn't hear him, he opened the door and jumped out onto the carriage step and swung up onto the high driver's bench. "Let's get out of this mess," he yelled, and the driver handed him the reins.

Clinton gestured for the van behind them to follow at the next turn. When they got as far as Third Street, he hoped that none of the crowds amassing in the neighborhood, especially any of the reporters, would spot them. On Bleecker Street there was a little driveway that led to the stable alley behind Bleecker and Bond Streets. Clinton wedged the coach up the driveway, and the prison van followed down the lane. They stopped at a high wall behind 31 Bond Street and Clinton got down. "Wait here," he said to the sheriff, who was inside his coach.

"I am the New York City sheriff and I am not hiding in an alley. You said the Judge's papers were ready to go. You better have them ready now."

"Just give me two minutes," Clinton said, wondering whether he should go to the front of the house to look for Snarky. He knew there was a slim chance that the papers had made it before them.

"You said there's going to be an order and I'm taking prisoners to a hearing with the Judge. If anything's not right, you're going to get in a heap of trouble," called the sheriff. Just then, a horse leapt over the low gate at the end of the alley and bounded toward them with a man on top in a bowler and plaid pants, charging forward like a jockey. Snarky pulled the horse's reins in an abrupt tug, and the horse reared on its hind legs. He jumped down and fished in his rucksack.

"Here you go, sir, the orders from the Judge," Snarky said, handing over the papers to Clinton.

Clinton waved to the sheriff, who got out and took a look. "This is it. Orders to release," the sheriff called to the men in prison wagon, and the deputies poured out.

"What do you mean you don't know what happened that night?" the Coroner yelled. He was pacing back and forth before the witness. Augusta noticed the edges of the parlor darkening and disappearing. "Did you see your mother get out of her bed that night?"

Augusta thought she saw the Coroner raise his hand, and then that part of her vision turned black, like an aperture closing in from the edges. She heard a loud sound, like a "Whoa!" from the crowd, then darkness and silence. The next thing she knew her face was on the ground. "Get away, give her air!"

"She's fallen," screeched another, and there was calamity and footsteps.

A police officer leaned over, and the next thing she knew, he was lifting her in his arms. He looked down at her and said, "You fainted, miss." As the drowsiness subsided, it left a feeling of exposure and then she became fully conscious of where she was: back in the parlor of 31 Bond Street, in the middle of a nightmare.

Clinton banged on the kitchen door. An officer opened it, and the men rushed through. Police officers were loafing around the kitchen table; they looked up startled. "Hey, you can't come in here!" they called. Clinton and the deputies rushed past them, up the kitchen stairs to the parlor, which was packed solid with people standing or milling around in confusion. Mrs. Cunningham's daughter was sitting on an armchair surrounded by men, sipping a glass of water.

"What is this?" declared the Coroner at the sight of the sheriff's posse. He spotted Clinton and sputtered, "What is going on?"

"I have come with orders from the Court of Common Pleas," said Sheriff Crombie, reciting loudly. "This proceeding is suspended until further notice, by order of Judge Davies. I have writs of habeas corpus delivered for Emma Cunningham, Augusta Cunningham, and Helen Cunningham, to release them to appear before him, to determine the nature of their imprisonment."

"You can't do this! My investigation is not concluded!"

"Your investigation will not include these women. The people you have in custody are being removed from the house and will appear before the judge. If there are no charges against these girls, they are freed." The reporters rushed around to their table, scribbling the sheriff's words, and the jury members looked perplexed.

The group of sheriff's deputies had followed, and within a few moments, a line of six men in deputy's uniforms pounded up the stairs.

The Coroner put on his spectacles and was thrashing through the papers that the sheriff had delivered. "This is my investigation. They are not free to leave this house. Just because a judge orders . . ."

Within minutes, the deputies reappeared at the top of the stairway and were descending with Emma Cunningham. She came down slowly, looking bewildered. It was the first time she had been out of her room in weeks. A matron followed, bringing down Helen. When Helen reached her mother, Emma grabbed her and hugged her on the crowded stair.

"Mama, Mama," cried Helen, looking childlike and burying herself in her mother's embrace. Emma lifted her face and placed kisses all over her daughter's tear-stained cheeks. Then the matron intervened and continued to move them down the stairs.

Mrs. Cunningham spotted Clinton in the hall. "What is happening? Is it over?" she blurted.

"Madame, we're going downtown." Clinton said, addressing Emma when she reached the bottom where he was standing.

"These people are in contempt of my investigation," yelled Connery. "Nobody can walk out of here until I say!"

"Mr. Connery, we have orders to appear before the Judge, who will determine Mrs. Cunningham's rights under the amendments of the Constitution. No person can be detained without cause."

"Arrest her then, for contempt against my proceeding. She

cannot leave. I wish to hold her and interrogate her!" shouted the Coroner, pointing theatrically to Emma on the stair. As Elisabeth had predicted, the Coroner was reluctant to let Emma slip from his control.

The sheriff stepped up to Emma and said, "I place you under arrest."

Clinton went to her side. "I assure you, Madame, we are on our way to see a judge, who will ensure that you will be free to speak to counsel. Even if you are placed in jail afterward, I will see that you have everything you need and will be well taken care of."

When she heard the word *jail*, she looked as if she were going to swoon.

"Jail! But I am innocent!"

"Madame, trust me, I will be at your side. You will have more legal protection in confinement than you have had in this house. We will have a hearing before the Judge, and if you are charged with this crime, there must be a Grand Jury proceeding."

"My daughters! What about my daughters?"

"They will come with us now. Then they will be released to whomever you feel will take the best care of them. Have courage, this is for the best." He took her arm and led her down the last step into the crowd in the hall.

Pandemonium ensued with cries of, "She's off to the Tombs!" Reporters fled the house to spread the word. Clinton and the sheriff's men cordoned off a path back down the kitchen steps and they led Emma and her daughters out through the back door to the alley, where they were placed in the back of the prison van. Clinton sat with them. As the somber procession lurched forward, he knew that nothing was over and everything was just beginning.

# CHAPTER THIRTEEN

*November 1856*

The autumn day was warm enough for shirtsleeves. Bars of autumn light, warm as butter, filtered through the trees. Samuel waded through the back garden strewn with yellow leaves, struggling with a barrel hoisted over his shoulder. Emma pushed away a strand of hair that had fallen across her face. She stood at the kitchen door, watching that he did not drop any boxes. Samuel was carrying the last of her things into the house from a cart that had been pulled up to the gate in the alley. Over the last several days she had Samuel move all her possessions into 31 Bond Street in shifts, a wagonload a day, brought from her house on Twenty-fourth Street.

"The blanket chest goes upstairs to my room, and everything else should go to the attic," she told him as he wedged it through the door and up the rickety kitchen stair with the heavy load on his back. "If you bang the wall Dr. Burdell will charge you five dollars to fix it," she called after him. Since appearing as the mistress of the house, it was important that she establish her authority with the servants from the beginning.

Dr. Burdell was away from the city on business for several days, which was just as well, for he would have hated the turmoil. To conserve her funds, she did not hire a large van with eight men, which could do the job in single a day, but brought everything over piecemeal. By the time he returned from his trip, she would be out of her housedress and dressed in her best silk.

After the trip to Elizabeth, Emma had effectively avoided Dr. Burdell's invitations to dinner or theatre, until one morning, he sent word that he was coming by to visit her at the house on Twenty-fourth Street. When he arrived, he seemed pressed for time, brusque and nervous, and did not take off his coat. She ushered him into her parlor and gaily pointed him to the settee. He sat, listening to her banter, until he finally spoke. "I need to know if you will live in the rooms of my house as I have offered. I will rent them to a house-mistress if you have decided not to come."

"Oh dear, have I let this slip?" she said, feigning surprise. "I had no idea of the seriousness of your invitation. As you can see, I have been putting aside the thought of moving. We are so comfortable here, and the disruption would be quite total." In fact, her lease was soon over, and the owner expected the house to be vacated in a matter of weeks.

"I understood that it was pressing that you find a place, and Bond Street is a superior location, with larger rooms," said Dr. Burdell, confused.

'Well, yes, but Helen has missed school this fall, and I would like her to return to boarding school in Saratoga at the turn of the year. I have considered that I might possibly move to Saratoga in January instead. I could take a beautiful house there and keep it for the summer. Perhaps I need a rest from the city," she said, sighing, as if it was all too much to decide.

Dr. Burdell looked alarmed. "The inconvenience of moving into my house should not deter you. I can write you a check to defray the cost of your move. It would only take a day with a large horse van. As for your daughter, perhaps it is best that she boards—I also can write a banknote for the tuition and board for both of your daughters to go away, if it would make your transition easier." He leaned over and pulled out a bankbook from his satchel, which had the printed letterhead of his bank on each note.

"Oh no, Augusta is not going, she has finished her schooling," Emma explained. "She is eighteen," she said, placing a hand on her breast, as if taken aback by his mistake. "It is only Helen who is going to the Girls Seminary." Dr. Burdell started to write out the name The Girl's Seminary on one of the printed lines, and then looked up quizzically. "You can fill in the amount yourself," he said, signing his name across the tight black line and handing her the note along with another one for her move.

Emma took the banknotes and placed them on the table beside her, as if to dismiss them. "But, Harvey, there is the question of our marriage. You have not brought up the formal nature of our union. I cannot see how I can take you up on your offer to live at your house, even if I have a separate set of rooms upstairs."

"It is a respectable arrangement, and I cannot see how you would be compromised. Marriage will follow, but I would like to see you secure under my roof while I finish up my business. Once all is concluded, I hope we can take a long trip, and I propose going to Europe for the summer season. We could sail together in June."

"Europe!" she said. Paris and London, along with a mansion on Fifth Avenue were dazzling prospects, but she still had not received a proper marriage proposal. She had waited these past several months to force his hand and decided that perhaps it was only awkwardness that prevented him from following the social conventions. There was very little time left. "I suppose I could settle into Bond Street," she said. "You have made the case that it is a tidy solution."

"It is decided!" he said brightly, getting up suddenly. She followed him toward the door, where he gave her a strong embrace and then departed. As soon as he was gone, she got her coat so she could rush to the bank and send a telegraph to Saratoga that Helen would be coming back to school in January, at the turn of the year.

Emma had nearly finished arranging her new bedroom on the third floor, placing her crystal and perfume across the vanity and lace on the arms of the chairs. She hung pictures of landscapes and cottages on the rose-patterned wallpaper, using large velvet ribbons that tied in bows and hung from the ceiling molding. She had taken advantage of Dr. Burdell's absence to wander the house, deciding how she might rearrange the furniture and improve the housekeeping. The piano in the back parlor needed oil and a tuning. She asked John, the errand boy, to push it over to an alcove near the bay window, making the room look more like a conservatory. Dr. Burdell's patients used the second parlor as a waiting room, but her daughters could practice music when the patients were gone. With some concentrated effort, she would make the double parlor more elegant, suitable for social receptions and teas.

She roamed upstairs and downstairs, checking all the rooms, which had nooks and cabinets positioned in odd places. There were closets everywhere, with large keyholes and brass knobs with layers of tarnish, many locked. Alice, the chambermaid, carried keys around on a big ring while she was cleaning. Emma decided to borrow the stack of keys to look inside the closets to see which keys worked and which ones no longer had any use. She found Alice in Dr. Burdell's office, listlessly waving a feather duster along a bookshelf.

"Are you making sure to get the dust on the lower shelf?" asked Emma, coming in from the hall.

"Yea," said the girl, looking up. Alice was a rangy girl whose hair hung in stringy clumps.

"Alice, it's 'yes,' not yea. Please say 'Yes, Ma'am.' And, Alice, I would prefer that you wear a maid's cap when you work. Please tie your hair and pin it under a cap." Alice looked at her sullenly, as if she were speaking a strange language, and Emma worried that such training would be lost on her. Emma walked over and picked up the iron ring that lay next to the cleaning basket that Alice carried from room to room. "I will take these for a while," Emma said.

"You can't do that, Ma'am. I got to lock the doctor's chambers when my dusting's done," said Alice, alarmed. "The doctor don't want anyone in his rooms when he is gone."

Emma started out of the room with the ring of keys. "I shall take care of it. I will lock up, later," she said. "And, Alice, I hope you have not been drinking liquor. I don't abide by that." Alice placed a hand up to her mouth, alarmed, which told Emma that her suspicion was correct, that Alice's slovenly manner had much to do with an indulgence in spirits.

Emma tested the doors around the house and found that the keys were an odd set. Some keys slid easily into a cabinet or closet and the bolts worked smoothly, whereas others were a difficult fit, or the catches were rusty. A few of the doors remained stubbornly locked. The closets were mostly empty with some forgotten items like old china packed in straw, or a rolled-up rug. She returned to the doctor's office, and Alice had gone. The maid's absence gave her time to look about—the dental office, a large room converted from a bedroom, had a high ceiling and was furnished like a salon, with engravings and a velvet fringed sofa. By the window was the steel dentist chair where Dr. Burdell conducted his surgery. Next to the fireplace was a mahogany desk with ledgers and cubbyholes for papers, and next to it, a steel safe. On top of the fireplace mantel were two human jaws, preserved under glass.

A long wardrobe passage connected the office to Dr. Burdell's bedroom. Emma passed through the passageway, which was lined with drawers and cupboards. She opened the door to a wardrobe and saw a line of identical dark black suits of expensive wool and tailoring, evenly placed upon their hangers. Starched linen shirts and high cardboard collars were stacked on shelves and a velvet tray was filled with pairs of cuff links.

Laid out before a mirror were ointments, tonics, powders, dentifrices, and tooth wash. She picked up a silver brush, and marveled at the placement of domestic things. She ran his brush against her cheek. The silver was cool, and the bristles the finest, and she pictured these same possessions, along with hers, lined up together years from now.

She entered his bedroom, which was dimly lit, for the shutters were closed. The room was furnished as a sumptuous sanctuary with vermilion velvet curtains and nickel-plated gas burners. A fur throw covered the bed, and on the doctor's bedside table were crystal glasses and a seltzer bottle with a silver top. She crept back though the passage to the office and locked the door carefully behind her. If she had not come to Bond Street with his offer, in a short time her money would have run out. She would have been put out of her house, her possessions in crates, forced to live on credit in a hotel, slowly selling off her jewels. It would not be long before she was on the street, for she had no source of income. There was no work for a lady besides working in a shop, or sewing, and a day's pay for handiwork could barely buy a day's meals. *How close she had come.*

When Emma returned to the kitchen, Hannah was speaking with John. Hannah stopped midsentence, as she always did when Emma entered, giving the impression that whatever she was uttering, it was something she preferred Emma not to hear.

"Hannah, I would like to have you prepare a plate of crumpets as a refreshment for Dr. Burdell's patients who come to the house in the morning."

Hannah raised her eyebrows. Her tone was equally arch. "Crumpets in the parlor, Ma'am?"

"Yes, please. I think that would be a gracious touch."

"You want me to bake up a fresh batch of crumpets, every day, midmorning?"

"Well, on certain days. I will ask Doctor Burdell which mornings his patients visit."

"Who will serve and pass these crumpets round to the people waiting in the parlor?"

"No one need pass them. They could be placed on an attractive tray, and the guests can serve themselves between their appointments. We could also have a pitcher of cold drink, or a pot of tea."

Hannah shrugged, clearly skeptical, as she stirred the batter in the bowl. "The patients come to get their teeth fixed, not eat sugar crumpets," she muttered, low.

"Did you say something?" asked Emma.

"Ma'am, I was just thinking how the one's with toothaches will have a hard time chewing, that's all."

"That is not your concern, Hannah. You are a cook, not a dentist." The cook had been difficult from the start. Emma planned to ask Dr. Burdell to speak to the servants when he returned about the standards she wished to bring to the household. Just because he had been too preoccupied to notice the housekeeping in the past did not mean that the servants should not work harder to make improvements. They needed to understand that her orders were his as well.

That night, Dr. Burdell returned. It was late, and Emma was in her nightclothes, brushing out her hair when the carriage came clattering up the street and stopped before the house. She had hoped that he would come home earlier in the evening and had planned to greet him in her most fetching dress. It was past eleven o'clock and the firelight flickered in her grate when she heard him enter the house. The deep carpets on the stairs absorbed his footsteps as he ascended to the second floor, and she heard the faint click as his key unlocked his bedroom door. Brushing her hair some extra strokes so that it flowed down her back, she put on a silk and lace dressing coat over her thin nightgown. She stepped into the dark hallway. Hannah had turned off the gas jets on her way to bed, so Emma took a candle to guide her way downstairs. On the second floor, Emma saw light from the crack under Doctor Burdell's bedroom door. She tapped softly and heard his key turn from the inside. He pulled open the door and bid her to enter his bedroom.

"I am so glad you are home," said Emma, warmly. "I hope you had a successful trip. I would like to go over the housekeeping schedules with you in the morning."

"Speak to the servants about the housekeeping," he said brusquely, turning away from her. Dr. Burdell had begun undressing before she had knocked and had removed his coat and vest and was in his shirtsleeves.

"Would you like me to wake Hannah to prepare you a supper?"

"No, I am not hungry."

"Then I shall see you in the morning," she said, hesitating, turning to go.

"Stay," he said, his back still toward her. He went over to his washbasin and leaned down to a low cabinet. Inside was a brass latch, which, when pulled, sprung open a rectangular panel, revealing a recessed cubby. He reached inside and retrieved an apothecary jar that was filled with white powder and spooned some into a glass, then added some liquid from the seltzer bottle. "Laudanum and quinine," he said, stirring the liquid with a spoon, and handing her the tonic. "Drink it up."

She sat at the edge of his bed and sipped the fizzy drink. The bed was covered in fur, and the canopy was draped in dark red velvet. Everything in the room seemed padded and plush. Dr. Burdell removed his cuff links and shirt studs and placed them on the bureau. He removed his sash and shirt collar and walked toward her, the white linen of his shirt loosely flapping. He took the glass from her, and put it on his night table, then he pulled her to him. He unlashed her dressing coat and lifted it off her shoulders and let it drop to the floor. He lifted the thin film of her nightgown, exposing her, and then dropped her down onto the bed. He fell on the bed with her. He was as savage as the first night, but they no longer were in the wild countryside, but encased in a townhouse in the hard heart of the city.

Again, he seemed intoxicated, devouring. She felt herself falling into a dark hole that was lined with the smooth pelt of fur and the slippery satin sheets. As they tumbled around, her eyes would flicker open, registering her surroundings: the anthracite sputtering in the fireplace, the wallpaper with a regal pattern veining up to the high ceiling where plaster ornament knotted into hard clumps in the corner; the musk scent in his whiskers. He whispered as he moved, his voice guttural and sharp. When he was finished, he fell asleep quickly. She arranged herself comfortably inside the sheets. She tossed about, but he never stirred, and then she too fell into a deep slumber.

The room was still dark when she opened her eyes in the morning, with a trace of grey light dawning through the window slats. He had shaken her shoulder and he was sitting up on one elbow, watching her. Their clothes were strewn across the floor from the night before, as if dropped from a whirlwind.

"Leave, now, before the servants wake," he said. There were no niceties attached to his tone. She sat, alert now, sensing that he was concerned about the looming business of his day. She reached for her nightgown and pulled it over her head as her skin rippled with goose pricks from the chill of the cold morning air.

"There is a bell that rings in your room from this pull," Dr. Burdell said, reaching for a brocade strip that hung sinuously along the canopy frame, attached to wires that were behind the velvet curtain. "It rings a tiny bell next to your bed. Never come to my room at night, unless I ring for you."

# CHAPTER FOURTEEN

*December 1856*

The month of November passed. Housekeeping, preparing the menus, and tending to Augusta and Helen took up most of Emma's day. 31 Bond Street was a little less dull for the efforts of her management, with new polish on all the silver, and the brass fixtures unclogged so that the crystal globes and lamps shone brighter. Each improvement only exposed another layer that needed attention. Emma had Samuel roll up the rugs and put new wax on top of the parquet. She hoped that by the time the holiday season approached, the house would be suitable for entertaining. Because moving the sullen Alice from room to room was a slow progression, the shimmering house that Emma envisioned was always a project away.

Soon enough, December was upon them, which meant the streets were filled with sleighs, fur mufflers, and horses covered in monogrammed blankets. Dr. Burdell conducted his day as if he were on a separate clock. In the morning, patients rang the doorbell, and John led them upstairs, where the office door would close for a half an hour, then John would retrieve buckets of bloody towels and dump them in the attic on the pile of washing. In the afternoon, after the dental appointments, Dr. Burdell would dash off to a bank, or out in his carriage, taking care of other business. He ate his breakfast on a tray alone in his bedroom, and his lunch and supper at the men's dining room at the Metropolitan Hotel on Broadway. Some days she never encountered him at all. Other times, she saw him at night, when he would pull the bell, and he would use few words as he bid her to join him in his bed.

One afternoon, Emma was on the stair as Dr. Burdell passed, in a mad dash for the front door. He stopped, suddenly, and said, "Emma, Thursday, next, I have an engagement. I would like you to join me at the opera. A business associate shall join us. His name is Ambrose Wicken."

"Thursday, the opera? How delightful!"

"Please have Augusta come. The curtain is at nine." Emma was elated at the prospect of an evening on the town.

"Thursday is Verdi I believe. We'd be delighted to meet Mr. Wicken."

"I'll send word to his hotel and arrange the carriage," Dr. Burdell said as he hurried out the door.

On the morning of the opera, Mr. Wicken appeared at the house in the early afternoon to present his calling card and properly introduce himself to Emma. He had the most exquisite manners—he formally asked her permission to be Augusta's escort for the evening. He was a dashing figure in his late twenties, a Southerner, with corn-colored hair. She told him that her daughter was eighteen, and she would be delighted to have her accompany him. Emma had always pictured that the man Augusta would marry would be an outsider—a risk taker, an adventurer, a man without a New York pedigree, someone who would sweep her away and marry her for love. Ambrose Wicken was such a man, and his timing was perfect.

That evening, Emma and Augusta began the ritual of dressing in Emma's bedroom after an early supper. Emma sat on the stool before her vanity, deciding which necklace to wear with her dress. She pulled a leather case from her drawer and lifted her ruby necklace from its velvet pouch, fastening the cold jewels along her throat. Augusta pulled the strings of her mother's corset, tightening the laces of the whalebone stays, arching the rib cage upward.

Augusta sat on the edge of the bed and rolled pearl-colored stockings up her legs. Emma lifted a velvet gown off the bed and balanced it over Augusta's head. When her daughter emerged from the piles of fabric, Emma readjusted her daughter's curls and spread the fabric around her hoops. She fastened the tiny buttons at Augusta's back, her fingers working like spiders up the length of Augusta's spine.

"Keep your back straight and smile at Mr. Wicken when you curtsy. He seems like a distinguished and dashing prospect for you."

"Mother, you see possibility in every man that walks along the street."

"You are eighteen and there is no time to waste." They heard the doorbell ring and Alice's raspy voice as she greeted the visitor. The moon glowed, reflecting against the marble of the mantel. Alice came upstairs and tapped on the bedroom door. "Mrs. Cunningham, the man is waiting and the carriage is outside," she hissed. "He says the curtain goes up at nine."

"Please serve him a sherry, Alice, and ask him to sit," said Emma. Alice plodded back down the stairs. Emma turned to Augusta, who was rustling before her, anxious and radiantly pale, in her tea-colored gown. Emma stepped into her own dress, a ruby velvet that matched her necklace, and then patted the knot in her hair. She appraised Augusta. "Let me twist some more," she said, grabbing one of Augusta's coiled curls. Augusta stood, resigned to the anxious fingers in her hair.

Emma grabbed a fur. "We are done!" she said triumphantly, as if they had performed a difficult musical score. The two women descended the staircase. In the parlor, in evening dress, Ambrose Wicken was more handsome than he had appeared in daytime. Augusta stepped toward him, and then faltered, her tiny heel catching in the pile of the carpet.

"Ladies!" exclaimed Mr. Wicken, taking Augusta's hand, lingering, and then bending to kiss it. "I have the singular pleasure of escorting you to the opera." He spoke in a southern cadence that sounded exotic in the overfurnished parlor. "Dr. Burdell has left word at my hotel that he will be late. He has been detained on a business matter and will meet us at the opera house. So, my two arms shall be graced with an abundance of beauty."

"Mr. Wicken, it is our honor, isn't it Augusta?" When Augusta did not reply, Emma curtsied, aware of the effect of her low cut dress.

"Madame, you could not be more than a year older than your lovely daughter," said Wicken. "How radiant you two appear side by side."

"Oh, sir," said Emma smiling, dismissing the compliment. She had heard it often and was aware enough of its truth. A more matronly woman would stumble and blush at the comment, only reinforcing the insincerity of the remark.

"We should be off," Mr. Wicken said, bowing, "before the curtain rises."

When they arrived at the opera, the orchestra was tuning. They were led to a box in the loggia, where a card reserved seats in the name of Dr. Burdell. From her seat, Emma pulled out her opera glasses and scanned the scene. The aisles below were a circulation of taffetas and magnificent diamonds, swirling beneath an enormous gas chandelier, which slowly dimmed. A brass-buttoned porter appeared from behind the velvet curtain of their box, and Mr. Wicken ordered Champagne. "There is nothing like a fine wine to lubricate the ear," he whispered intently to Augusta, but she responded with an awkward "Yes, thank you, sir," and fixed her eyes out into the audience with an uncomfortable stare.

The curtain rose and the performers came onto the stage, launching into a throaty score that resonated up to the highest tiers. Mr. Wicken whispered intermittently into Emma's ear about the tenor or the libretto, reflecting a fine knowledge of Italian opera. Dr. Burdell's chair remained empty. He had missed the curtain. Emma fanned herself furiously. She could not imagine what had detained him, when he had a box full of guests and she had dressed in her finest gown.

At intermission, Dr. Burdell still had not arrived. Emma fidgeted anxiously. All the opera glasses in the theatre came out at once and seemed to be pointing around the opera house with their opaque circles. She was proud of her appearance in the gilt box, with the handsome man between them, but was self-conscious about the empty chair. Emma made conversation with Mr. Wicken. "Dr. Burdell so enjoys Verdi, I am surprised he missed the first act," she said. "I do apologize. It is unlike him to be late."

"I do wonder how he could put such beauty on display without arriving to claim his prize," said Mr. Wicken, with a disapproving tone. "I have the good fortune to be doing business with him and I have learned that he is a man with many keen interests. I suppose at times they are in conflict." He poured Champagne from the bucket, filling Augusta's fluted glass.

Emma attempted to divert his attentions to Augusta. Leaning toward Wicken, she said softly, "I am glad that tonight my daughter has a companion of such refined manners. My concern is that her virtue and her dowry be placed in the hands of the worthiest of gentlemen."

"She is but a half-opened bloom to your rose. Seeing you together shows where her fine cultivation will lead," he said in a low tone. He turned, now addressing Augusta, who was seated on his other side. "I imagine Miss Augusta has many interests, besides a passion for Champagne." Augusta looked up and nodded, lifting her glass to her lips.

"I do enjoy music," she said, coolly.

"She plays the piano magnificently," interjected Emma. "Why, just yesterday I heard the loveliest Bach sonata coming from the parlor. I thought I was at the Academy of Music."

"Musical gifts, to add to her beauty?" exclaimed Wicken.

"But she is too modest," said Emma. "She is artistic. She writes poetry and verse. I can only imagine how a trip to Europe would enhance her poetic sensibilities." Augusta turned scarlet and darted a look of displeasure at her mother.

"Please," she faltered, "I would rather read the poets than attempt to match them." The conversation trailed off, with no further assistance from Augusta. Mr. Wicken became distracted, glancing down at the audience, eying the crowd. Emma fluttered her fan, groping for pleasantries.

Emma leaned closer to him and raised her fan to whisper, "Augusta may seem sophisticated, but she is just shy, and very pure at heart." His glance now shifted to Augusta, whose neckline was bare of jewelry, the dusty color of her dress emphasizing the milky whiteness of her skin. Emma, still whispering, said, "Mr. Wicken, I shall be having a party at the end of January. I do hope you will attend."

Wicken narrowed his eyes, and glanced downward at Emma's chest. Emma was not sure if he was eying her rubies or her décolletage. "Why thank you, I'd be delighted," then he added, "for the singular pleasure of seeing Miss Augusta again." Emma exhaled as the curtain rose. A gain was made. She pictured Wicken on horseback, galloping under a row of mossy oaks, with Augusta on the back of the saddle, headed to a pillared plantation house. Augusta was looking at her lap, picking on the button of her glove.

The opera finished, without Dr. Burdell. After the performance, his carriage was in the pile at the curb, waiting, with Samuel dressed in britches on the perch. Emma contemplated asking Samuel why Dr. Burdell had never appeared, or if he knew where he might be, but she resisted the impropriety of engaging a servant in conversation in the presence of Mr. Wicken. As the carriage headed up Broadway, Mr. Wicken suggested they stop for a sherry at the Majestic Hotel. Emma declined, insisting instead that the carriage return her home, and that he and Augusta should continue for a drink. She saw the look of panic on Augusta's face at the suggestion but was relieved when the carriage pulled away, leaving Emma at the door of 31 Bond Street, with Augusta's soft voice trailing away in conversation.

Emma let herself into the house. The servants had dimmed the gas sconces along the hall. Upstairs, there was no light under Dr. Burdell's door. In her room, she took off her dress and left it in a puddle on the floor. What a waste of a dress and a corset, she thought, without a man to place his hand firmly along its cinched waist and guide the elaborate construction of jewels and fabric through the crowd. Why had Dr. Burdell arranged for Mr. Wicken to escort them to the opera, without coming himself? As for Mr. Wicken and Augusta, however, it was a perfect match.

# CHAPTER FIFTEEN

She had tossed and turned all night, listening for Dr. Burdell to return. When she passed down the stairs early in the morning his door was inscrutably locked, with no signs of light under the crack. She finished a small breakfast and headed out to Broadway, where the wintry streets were bustling with people wrapped in scarves and mufflers, in all colors of cashmere. She wandered past the finest shops and stopped inside to place orders for pastries and liquors and fine champagnes for her party next month. Augusta's birthday was approaching. She would order engraved invitations to send around to her old acquaintances, to Doctor Burdell's patients, and to the neighbors on Bond Street—people she had never met, prominent families that she hoped would appear with their unmarried cousins and single sons. She would make it a fine affair, and besides being for Augusta, it would serve another purpose as well: it was time she and Dr. Burdell presented themselves as a couple. It would be the perfect time to announce their engagement.

It was early afternoon when she returned to the house and let herself into the front door using her key. She untied her hat and removed the hatpin, pausing before the mirror in the hall. In the still of the afternoon, the patients were finished, so there was no sign of the errand boy, usually stationed at the front door. She pulled off her gloves and adjusted her hair in the pier mirror. Distracted, she walked into the front parlor and picked up some sewing left by Augusta on a chair. The large sliding doors separating the two parlors were pulled shut. She went back out to the hall to enter the back parlor, wanting to look over the furniture arrangement to make plans for her party, and she pulled open the door to see Dr. Burdell seated, intently talking with an elderly gentleman.

"Excuse me, gentlemen," she said startled. "I did not mean to intrude."

A cast came over Dr. Burdell's eyes, and his lip curled in disapproval. "Emma, this is Commodore Vanderkirk," he said reluctantly. The man stumbled to his feet. He had a florid face with flushed cheeks and was swaddled in expensive clothing. His midriff spilled forward, knocking him off ballast, as if he were not comfortable standing fully upright.

"So enchanted to meet your lovely wife. You're a lucky man," said the Commodore. The shadow across Dr. Burdell's eyes deepened. She expected Dr. Burdell to correct his guest's error at assuming she was his wife and introduce her properly, but he did not.

Emma took the lead. "Please, sit down, sir. I am so sorry for the interruption. I feared that Augusta left her piano music in here. My daughters are so absentminded." The man sank heavily into the stuffed armchair, like an overfed child. He twisted a large gold ring on his fat finger.

"No intrusion, my dear. I love the sight of a woman in the afternoon. It is a dull day of business that is not graced by the sight of the female sex." He grinned appreciatively at Emma.

Emma laughed. "I hope my daughters do not fly by, for then you will have a great distraction."

"Oh my, a bevy of lovelies. Unfortunately, my own have flown the coop," he said ruefully. On a low table, spread before the seated men, were long maps that she recognized to be of Elizabeth, New Jersey. Emma saw her name scrawled across one tract, a vast empty terrain. "Come look," offered the Commodore. "I'd keep a woman alongside me during all my business dealings if I could—just like at craps—they bring you luck." Dr. Burdell sat on the edge of a wooden chair, leaning forward, glowering. Emma was pleased at the attention. She attempted a charming banter that always worked favorably with men.

"I profess that I wouldn't be much of an asset if you are discussing business. I don't understand much about land or shipping," said Emma. "I only know that I can see the clipper ships backed up all the way to the Narrows, waiting to find berths."

"Shipping is no mystery," the Commodore replied, amused. "But I am done with clipper ships. Soon there will only be iron ships pulling up to iron piers that will unload cargo onto railways that will carry it straight across the continent. There won't be a piece of wood or sailcloth in sight."

"Well, then, the world will be quite unrecognizable," Emma said, rolling her eyes to the heavens. As she suspected, the gesture amused him. He laughed heartily, which made his gouty flesh jiggle like jelly.

"It is already unrecognizable, my dear. You are just living under an illusion that the world is a familiar place. Familiarity is just smoke and mirrors."

"Emma," interrupted Dr. Burdell, sternly. "Shouldn't you see to supper?" It was clear that he wanted her gone.

"Ah, domesticity calling," chuckled the Commodore. "Such a shame."

"Excuse me, but I have a meal to oversee." Emma laughed and

curtsied. Before she retreated she said, "Oh, sir, I would like to invite you to a party we are having, on January thirtieth. Just a small affair," she ventured.

"How kind, to offer an invitation! But my wife has me running all over town to engagements, so that all I do is dress and eat. Pitiful existence, I tell you. I shall have to ask you to address all such propositions to my social secretary—my wife."

Emma again gave a slight curtsy. "It was a pleasure to meet you, Commodore Vanderkirk."

The Commodore attempted to raise his posterior out of the chair but decided against the effort. "Enchanted, my dear. You are most enchanting."

Emma left and closed the heavy parlor doors behind her. Then she paused, and leaned gently against the door, and turned her head so that her ear was close to the thick wood. In the deep pile of the carpet in the hall, her footfall made no sound; she could hear the Commodore's voice clearly—he spoke with a robust baritone. Dr. Burdell mumbled, and his part of the conversation did not carry.

"I want this land to build factories for steel and iron, where I can connect to the railroad," she heard the Commodore say. "I cannot find that on the Manhattan side of the river. I'll buy the land in a simple sale. But I do not want to give you a share of any business, if that's what you are angling for." Harvey mumbled something and the Commodore continued, "I will give you a fair price. A premium." Emma dipped her head closer. Dr. Burdell spoke, again too softly to hear.

"You say you have Southern buyers?" boomed the Commodore. "Balderdash. Why would you want to go into business with them? It's Northern companies that run the South. We distill their rum, process their sugar, roll their tobacco. If the spindles and looms in Massachusetts were to go silent, the Cotton Zone would dry up overnight. The only thing the North doesn't own are the depleted cotton fields and the slaves, but we make more money insuring them."

"The Southern contingent has made me a very lucrative offer with ongoing profits as a part of the deal." Dr. Burdell made this point with a raised voice.

"Your Southern friends are looking for a Northern port because they are stuck with New Orleans. Let it sink!" the Commodore said, howling with laughter. "I could run the whole Southern economy from this armchair."

Dr. Burdell mumbled again.

"When you met with me last night at Delmonico's," said the Commodore, "I was intrigued by your proposition. But I know the men you speak of, and I understood you to propose that you join my venture, but I am only interested in the land." So he had been at Delmonico's, Emma thought, explaining his absence from the opera, detained by business, as Mr. Wicken had suggested.

Emma jumped away from the door when she heard the Commodore say, his voice perilously close to the other side, "I'm done now, I want an answer by next week, or we're off." As Emma backed away from the door, she spotted Alice, the chambermaid, on the staircase. It was clear that Alice had been watching her.

Emma hurried to the stair, and as she approached the girl, she grabbed her by the arm. "Don't you say anything," she whispered.

The servant girl looked at her askance. "You let go of my arm or I'll tell the master you been listening," she hissed.

"Do I smell whiskey on your breath? He won't abide that now, will he?" Emma replied. Alice scurried away and disappeared, descending to the kitchen stair, and Emma swiftly climbed toward the second floor but stopped at the turn on the stairwell, and waited, hidden on the landing. The door of the parlor opened, and she heard Dr. Burdell come into the hallway and lift the Commodore's coat from the peg near the vestibule.

"That northernmost tract is worth fifty thousand dollars to me. It has the high ridge in the center of the marsh and the freshwater stream. That is the plot I want," boomed the Commodore.

"The Southern party is offering me a deal of ongoing business profits from an active port and depot," repeated Dr. Burdell, with a stubborn resistance.

"I shall not offer you any profits, but I'll double my offer for the land, here and now. Make it one hundred thousand dollars."

"I shall let you know," said Harvey dryly.

"Just understand, a clean deal is the only deal I make. You hand me the deed, I pay you the money." The Commodore was squeezing himself into his coat. "You have until this time next week, and no longer." Emma heard the front door open and shut behind the Commodore, without a word of farewell. The northernmost tract with Bound Creek weaving through the salt marsh—that was her own plot. Isn't this what Dr. Burdell had been waiting for? One hundred thousand dollars was an enormous sum. She felt elation rising in her breast and wanted to rush downstairs and dance with Harvey. It didn't matter what other deal was pending, he should embrace this offer—they would be rich, plenty rich. As she turned the bend in the staircase and headed down to the hall she heard the front door close again and realized that Dr. Burdell had put on his coat and had gone.

# CHAPTER SIXTEEN

Murder after thus stalking abroad unpunished, at length, enters houses, enters them as if in defiance, while the streets are ringing with sleigh bells, the side walks full of pedestrians, and the window of our dwellings are yet bright with their evening illumination, enters and does his frightful work and departs untracked.

A murder so frightfully atrocious, committed at an hour and place which should seemingly make it easy to detect the perpetrators, will, if it goes unpunished, greatly encourage the practice of assassination.

*New York Post*, MARCH 15, 1857

*March 15, 1857*

Clinton and Thayer walked up Centre Street to the Tombs. The sky, which had been so blue earlier, now had patches of yellow light bleeding through clouds the color of greyhounds. The city prison loomed like a stone ziggurat. Designed like a mausoleum in the Egyptian style, it had high façades of granite, and a portico of four columns, topped with palm fronds.

The usual throng mixed along the street. Since the incarceration of Emma Cunningham, a thin assemblage of crime reporters and hangers-on lingered around the doorway all day. A soapbox orator had placed a carton near the crowd and was sermonizing to no one in particular: "It's the crime of the century!" he cried. "Every now and then a tremendous explosion blows off the covering and lets us look in upon the rotten heart of a certain style of city life. We have looked inside this house at 31 Bond Street with loathing. We see the bitter end of a man's career, his very life, which came about when he traded the sweet caresses of domestic purity for the polluting caresses of a 'black-hearted woman.'"

"This fellow sounds like he's been sacked from the *Herald*," said Clinton as the two headed up the granite stairs.

Thayer, who had seen Emma the day before, replied, "I'd say she's feeling black hearted. Prison life is taking its toll, now that the prison routine has set in. There has been a marked difference since the reporters' visit." Emma had been arraigned and charged, and a full indictment for murder in the first degree swiftly followed. The grand jury had found the case to be largely circumstantial, but even without physical evidence, a weapon, or an eyewitness, they determined that Emma Cunningham had the means and the motive to commit the crime.

The press had clamored for an opportunity to interview Emma in jail, and after pondering it carefully, her defense team decided to oblige them. A stream of reporters was handpicked from each newspaper, with a select group chosen to ask the questions. The most notable benefit was that at the first mention of the press, the Chief Warden, knowing that the city prison was a favorite source of journalistic condemnation, shifted Emma permanently to one of the largest and most commodious cells, then provided her with a good bed, a carpet, and a writing desk and chairs. She was permitted to have some personal effects brought in and special meals. For the day of the interview, Emma was given the advantage of her own wardrobe, some books, an embroidered pillow, and a navy blue bombazine silk dress.

Clinton had calculated that the brief personal interview would humanize her to the public, after a month of caricature and misleading reports that were being issued by the newspapers and the District Attorney's office. While Emma had been sequestered in house arrest in her bedroom, she was not seen by anyone, and her image was that of a mysterious recluse, upon whom all evil intentions could be fixed. In the interval before the jury was to be selected, it was essential to create a picture of sympathy and an antidote to the hearsay and rumor. By giving the newspaper readers a brief encounter, he hoped to present her as respectable and sympathetic, a woman in the flesh.

The public fascination with Helen and Augusta was almost as strong as with Emma. Two attractive girls, well acquainted with the art of fashion and seduction, had inspired a public curiosity usually granted a celebrated actress, even though they had done nothing more than huddle near their mother, crying, wearing the latest hat. When their mother was incarcerated they were placed with a distant relative, a stern woman who lived on Second Avenue. After a day or two, Augusta had chosen to separate and requested to stay at the home of a childhood nanny, an old lady who lived by the river on Bedford Street in Greenwich Village. On the appointed day of the press interview, the two girls were brought to the jail through a back entrance. They came well coiffed and wearing their nicest dresses.

The pressmen crowded down the stone corridor in a pack. Helen and Augusta were brought in first, for a quick visit. Under the watchful eyes of the reporters, they did not disappoint. They fell into a tearful embrace with their mother, as the scribes noted every detail. When the girls were led away, Emma stood erect, facing the reporters from behind the bars, ready to address their questions. Reporters in the back of the crowd bobbed up and down, trying to spot every item and book title in her cell. She answered their questions, one by one, holding her hands clasped before her, responding with respect and candor.

She emphatically proclaimed her innocence. She claimed that she was unaware of the horrific occurrence in the bedroom below until the following morning. She pointed out that on the night of his death, between the hours of five and midnight, the whereabouts of Dr. Burdell were unknown. She declared that surely there were others who had been with him that night, and whoever those companions were, they were highly suspicious, by the very fact that they had not stepped forward as witnesses. She spoke about her personal distress at the slanders that had been leveled toward her during the Coroner's inquest, and told the reporters that she was nothing more than a dedicated mother and a noble wife to two deceased husbands. "I was fit to be his wife," she insisted of Dr. Burdell, "despite all that is said about me," and tears sprung to her eyes. "I have suffered so by the indignity of the comments delivered by servants and others who do not even know me."

The performance went brilliantly and ended when the Warden banged on the bars and the prison officers herded the reporters away. The following morning, the *New York Times* mentioned her bombazine silk dress and the encounter with her daughters. "Her features are regular," the paper noted, "her eyes green. Her hair is a dark black and brushed plainly away from her temples. The expression of her countenance when she is speaking is amiable and prepossessing, that of a well-bred woman. She certainly bears herself with a degree of self-possession and with great composure. Whether she be ultimately found guilty or innocent, we remark here that none of the previously published newspaper portraits have given the true sense of her personal appeal and charm." Clinton was pleased at the report but knew that her performance had been nothing short of a spectacular feat of will.

A light dusting of snow began to fall on Centre Street. It was the middle of March and spring was late. When Clinton and Thayer passed through the Egyptian portal, any association to the pharaohs ended. The interior of the penitentiary was dank and foreboding, with a central court that rose upward four stories high, with occasional murky shafts of daylight entering through openings in the fortresslike walls. Tiers of balconies circled the inner courtyard in rings, and iron stairs zigzagged upward between them. From the balconies came the distant whine of prisoners, the clanking of bars, and the sharp rebukes of wardens.

The two lawyers started the climb to the top where Emma was held along a special corridor. They had to follow along the balconies, passing rows of inmates, who appeared hungrily at the bars, with thin arms holding out tin bowls for food. The first tier was for minor offenders: brawlers and knuckle-busters, pickpockets, inebriates, and gin thieves and a whole row for prostitutes, who lounged on thin cots and called back and forth to one another. The next level was for the more infamous: burglars and arsonists, ruffians, gang members, and dirk men, who made dexterous use of ropes and garrotes to accost honest people on their way home in the dark, and deprive them of their possessions.

The third tier had an aisle known as the Murderer's Block, for those who had already been sentenced to death. Each cell had a small window in full view of the prison yard where the scaffold stood. The final ceremony required a solemn roll of a drum, and then a shroud was placed over the condemned man's head. When the spring was touched, an iron weight fell toward the ground, which jerked up the other end of the rope, and the hatch lifted, launching the criminal into the air, leaving him dangling, in a fresh suit provided by a charity. The only motion was a slight kick of the feet, like a person who had lost his footing and was endeavoring to find a more secure terrain. Then whispers and cries would come up from the cell blocks below that had no view, calling, "Have they jerked him yet?"

Emma was still detained on the isolated hall reserved for special prisoners, those with well-connected families, or politicians who had been on the dole. The chief matron hurried toward them with a key, allowing them entry. Emma was pacing about. Her face was still lovely, but the prison air had left a grey cast upon her complexion and dark shadows under her eyes. In this light, it was not hard to picture her skin becoming papery and lined with age.

"My daughters were here this morning to visit," she began, "and they say they continue to overhear the most slanderous lies."

"You must put your best face forward, and try not to pay attention. You must remain strong," Clinton said.

"But the accusations still tear me up inside. They vilify me." She was agitated, walking back and forth, wringing her hands.

"The trial will be more of the same, perhaps worse. A desperate prosecution is the cruelest."

"God knows I was fit to be the wife of Dr. Burdell!" she said. "They say I was not. He need not ever have been ashamed to call me his wife!" Clinton and Thayer glanced at each other. She was caught up in the plight of prisoners—too much time alone to spin endless scenarios to their own defense.

"That brings me to our business today, Madame," said Thayer. "Can we discuss a few incidents that have come to my attention?" Thayer had a list of questions—loose ends that he was pursuing to counter the prosecution's case. Almost every person that had known the victim had been interviewed by the Coroner or discovered by the press, and it was important to prepare against testimony from future witnesses. The defense needed to close all holes, but this was going to be difficult, given her state of mind.

"First off, let's all have a seat," said Clinton. Thayer and Clinton sat in hardback chairs, and Emma sat on her cot, facing them.

Thayer hesitated, then began: "Were you aware that Dr. Burdell had a mistress?"

Emma looked taken aback. It was the look of someone who is ready to flee from danger, Thayer being the danger at hand.

Thayer quickly interjected: "This has no reflection on your own character, in our eyes as your counsel, and we have no intention of disturbing you with unpleasantness from the past. However, we have it upon good information that Dr. Burdell had a mistress and was seen with her often. I am sorry if it is painful for you, but our understanding is that if the prosecution called this woman as a witness, her existence might prove the motive of your jealousy."

Emma still looked stunned. Her eyes darted about, as if she was groping for a way to react to the news. It was never easy for a woman to listen to the details of her own debasement.

"No, I knew nothing of that," she said. As Clinton watched, he saw her pause, and wondered if she was telling the truth. "Now," said Thayer, looking down at his page, to continue. "Fortunately for us, her husband, having becoming aware of this scandal, has whisked her far from the city, where I believe she will remain. I suspect she will never testify, but we need to plan for the remote possibility."

Thayer flipped through his pages, and continued. "Do you know if there was money that Dr. Burdell owed, or any parties in particular that might have been aggrieved by his business pursuits."

Clinton watched Emma carefully. Again, Emma looked stunned, as if the probing was a personal assault. "He was a very private man, in all matters, both business and personal, he kept such information to himself. He conducted his business in his office or private rooms. As for these associates you are asking me about, I cannot tell you what went on behind closed doors."

"You lived in that house, didn't you?" asked Thayer. "We know that in the past, Dr. Burdell was engaged in certain business ventures, not all of them above board. You would have had a peek behind those doors, wouldn't you? You might have seen some of the goings-on?"

Clinton tapped his foot impatiently. It was a warning for Thayer to tread lightly. The young man had a litigator's instinct, but he needed to be trained to save it for the courtroom. Only the poorest of defense lawyers unleashed it against their own clients, and the most disreputable hoped to rattle their clients and raise their fees.

"I'm sorry, Madame," Thayer said. "With all due respect, I recognize that you trusted Dr. Burdell, and it must be distressing to learn the many ways that he was not worthy of that trust. In bringing up these difficult matters, as your counsel, we are looking for clues to other individuals or actions, all with a motive to vindicate you."

Clinton interjected, "We need you to trust us and think hard, and tell us what you might have seen or heard."

"I know there were individuals that he was meeting to do business with on the night of his death, but I do not know who they were. He did not confide that matter to me. I know that he was dealing in matters to do with land. I fell asleep and woke only briefly when I heard the carriage outside, and immediately fell asleep again. He had probably been in some improper place on Friday night, I do not know who he was with."

This was the spot when Emma's story always became the most dramatic, and sure enough, she began to sob. "I am so worried for my daughters, and the things they are hearing. My whole life has been guided by the aim to be a noble woman, to bring them up, as respectable girls. God knows I was fit to be the wife of Dr. Burdell. To slander me as they do . . . when we were going to live happily together. When we were going to go to Europe."

"The marriage was not witnessed by others, and there is no

record besides the minister. His memory is not certain. Was there any other way that the marriage was known to the public?"

"We were seen publicly all around the town and at the theatre, and his intentions to marry me were plain to everyone. As far as his intentions to my family, they were clear as well. He paid for the tuition for my daughter at her school."

"Is that so? Can we verify that?" asked Thayer eagerly.

"It was the Girl's Seminary, in Saratoga. He paid the tuition in November."

"I'll look into it," said Thayer. "I'll send word to Saratoga to find the bank check with the signature."

"I think we have accomplished enough for today," Clinton said. "We will let you rest."

Emma remained on the bed, and proceeded to dab her face with her handkerchief. "In court, will they say terrible things about me?"

"I am afraid there will be a lot of that, but I suggest you try your hardest not to listen. We will soon pull a jury, a group of decent men. Keep your hopes up, that is the best way."

"I shall try," said Emma. Her response seemed to summon an effort, calibrated to please.

The men bowed and exited with the aid of the warden, who came with the key to slide the door open for them. They hurried out to the street. "I'm off to send the telegraph to Saratoga," said Thayer.

"Meet me at seven for dinner at the Astor House," said Clinton. "We will go over everything then." The two men parted ways, and as Clinton headed toward Park Row, he saw Oakey Hall, outside his office at City Hall, about to depart in a carriage.

"Mr. Clinton, what a propitious day to see you—the Ides of March," said Hall.

"Well it must be a propitious day for you—for it appears you are feasting in tuxedo and tails. I understand tonight is the Tammany Society dinner, at Delmonico's."

They tipped hats, Hall's was the taller, and when he lifted it, he revealed his ornate hairstyle. Hall made a deep bow. "I greatly anticipate our encounter in court, but I regret that the verdict will be a sorry conclusion to your already dwindling career." He mounted the carriage. His cape swooped the air, and his elongated profile was outlined in the window as he rode away.

# CHAPTER SEVENTEEN

At the dinner hour, Clinton was at Broadway, and he cursed at the crossing. The intersection was stalled with two omnibuses facing each other, each driver holding back four rearing horses, straining at the reins. A steady procession of workers was hurrying in every direction, bent on catching the evening ferry or train. Newsboys darted under the carriage riggings. They rushed from one passenger window to another, hawking papers, grabbing a coin and dashing away before the heavy wheels of the bus lurched into motion. The press barons were stoking the demand for news of the upcoming trial, and by evening every newsboy's pocket was heavy with change.

After leaving the jail, he had spent an hour at the office and now headed to meet Thayer for dinner, as planned. He crossed to the Astor House, where twin porters in knee breeches pulled open the door. As he entered, the sounds of the street faded away to a murmur of silk brushing against silk and canes tapping across the marble floor. In the paneled library, empty at the dinner hour, newspapers were folded in an array across a table.

Barnaby Thayer entered the library in a rumpled suit, recently shaved. "I am sorry I am late. I stopped home after the jail, and my wife informed me that my son spoke his first words today. He said 'la la.' She insisted he was saying 'lawyer,'" said Thayer proudly, with his winning smile.

"Congratulations," said Clinton, folding a newspaper and placing it on the table. "We can put him to work between feedings."

"I am afraid he'll need teeth first, to work on this case," replied Thayer.

"I suspect your wife would regret losing both of you to this trial." Clinton pictured Thayer and his pretty wife, the baby crying at night, in a small set of rooms with wooden furniture, in the sparse comforts of the newly married, getting by on a junior lawyer's salary, fueled by love and air.

"Shall we eat?" Clinton stood, and the two men walked through the lobby past the telegraph office, ticking with bond salesmen making late trades. At the entrance to the dining room, a battalion of waiters in red waistcoats floated around like dancers under the tinkering chandeliers.

"Good evening, gentlemen," said the maître'd, bowing deeply at the waist. He snapped his fingers with a crack, and a server rushed away to arrange a table under the balcony. After the men were seated, the waiter deposited a tray of cocktails and a mountain of oysters on a bed of shaved ice.

Clinton draped his napkin across his lap, and then poked a fork into the soft belly of an oyster, its pearly shell filling with brine. "Order well, tonight," Clinton told Thayer. "With the trial looming and our expenses mounting, this may well be our last feast."

Thayer reviewed the menu. It featured over sixty choices of fowls and meats served in pies and puddings, roasted and broiled. There was a choice of beef, chicken, veal, ham, or tongue, calf's head, sweetbreads, pork steak, pig's feet, mutton kidney, and cutlets. Separate sauces garnished each dish: walnut catsup, Yankee sauce, horseradish, piccalilli, chowchow sauce, and mushroom catsup. A second course of game offered snipe, plover, pigeon or squab, and a third fish course offered codfish, salmon, black fish, shad, and five different types of turtle caught fresh from Turtle Bay, where snapping turtles grew to forty pounds. Each meal was served with bottles of wines chosen from the hotel's inventory of Madeiras, sherries, clarets, Burgundies, Sauternes, and Champagnes.

The waiter carried a thin tablet to take their order, and he inscribed their choices, including a soup course, an assortment of game, potatoes, and prime rib of beef.

"Bloody, sir?" asked the waiter.

"Pink, not rare," said Clinton as the waiter dashed away. "Oakey Hall is feasting tonight at Delmonico's with the ward bosses and heads of the fire brigades," said Clinton. "It appears that they are planning his move for Mayor."

"Now there's a group that prefers their beef bloody," replied Thayer. "Hall, no doubt, attired himself for the occasion. I hear that he wears green gloves on St. Patrick's Day to shake hands with the Irish."

"Beware the chameleon," said Clinton. "His changes of color are merely a distraction. His ambition may take him out of the courtroom, but as a prosecutor, he is a formidable adversary." The waiter brought terrapin soup in a giant silver bowl with a ladle that he dipped into the pungent broth, swimming with chunks of turtle meat the size of a man's knuckles. They took sips from the salty broth.

"I have received word from Dr. Gideon," said Thayer. "And he has finished the examination of the evidence. We can send the evidence to the illustrators to make the exhibits." In his mind, Clinton calculated the rising costs—costs that escalated every day—exhibits, experts, fees, salaries, rent, plus the legion of law students clerking and preparing the legal papers. That it was all moving forward was nothing short of a miracle.

"So far, according to Dr. Gideon," continued Thayer, finishing up the last of the broth, "there were many shoe impressions left in the blood by Dr. Burdell, but there are mysteriously few left by the murderer, except for a few marks by a softly padded sole. There is no appearance of a woman's shoe, which would have a sharp heel. Dr. Gideon says that a crime scene reflects the personality of the perpetrator as much as a home reflects the personality of its owner, but aside from the brutality of the act, the perpetrator left very few physical traces."

"How long until these reports are finished?"

"I suppose they are working as fast as they can. He already has two teams on the microscopes. So far, the findings reveal no blood-stains on Emma Cunningham's clothes or in her part of the house. The spot examined from a dress in her closet was wine."

"As I suspected. Science is on our side."

"But what about Burdell's business associates? It was known that he shortchanged partners in shady business ventures. Snarky has been doing some sleuthing, trying to discover who he was doing business with at the time of his death. That would be a real lead. If we can call any of those characters to the witness stand, a harsh examination would certainly clinch reasonable doubt for Emma."

"I sincerely doubt any character involved in illicit activity would come forward voluntarily. With our resources stretched, we do not have the investigative tools to chase down every possible suspect," replied Clinton. "As for putting them on the witness stand, unless we have bona fide proof against a person, we are at great risk if we attach anyone with a motive to the crime. It is a high burden, and the judge would be restrictive. If a witness committed any other crime they would be advised to plead the Fifth. Or be uncoopera-tive, or simply lie. As for as our strategy, it is a far more straightfor-ward case if we attack the paucity of the prosecution's case rather than to try to implicate a third party. The physical evidence at the murder scene, presented by our experts, will do exactly that. So, that is why we need to work fast. Speed is of the essence. I want the earliest possible trial date, which should be in early May."

Thayer looked doubtful and dabbed at his mouth with a large napkin. "Well, regardless of how fast we try the case," he said, "there is no doubt that public opinion goes strongly against her character, and that is in the prosecution's favor. By the time we pull a jury for the criminal trial, every man in New York will have his head filled with conjecture from the newspapers. Without another culprit, she's as good as hanged in every drawing room in the city in advance."

"Mr. Thayer," replied Clinton, lowering his voice, "unlike our politicians and newspaper publishers, I have the highest regard for the people of this city. Jurors take their oaths most seriously. They seek justice and will search for it to the best of their ability. If given a chance, juries respond with deep thought and earnest attention."

Stung by the rebuke, Thayer said, "I'm sorry, sir, I'm not at odds with you there." Thayer put down his fork and continued, with a deferential tone. "But certainly science is not enough. We will need to counter the charges against her character. We must establish her veracity, for there is still the confounding issue of the marriage. We certainly can't put her or her daughters on the stand, which will invite the most salacious line of questioning." Clinton observed him, wondering if he was too brash, or too unseasoned. Thayer had some prior experience examining witnesses on the stand, but he was untried in a trial of this magnitude. Clinton had seen many a promising litigator crumble under pressure on the courtroom floor.

"Agreed. The daughters shall not testify. And the defendant will not go on the stand, but plead the protection of the Fifth Amendment, as is the custom in a capital case." The men returned to their food in silence, sampling four different game birds under glass.

Thayer continued. "They'll bring forward every shopkeeper and servant that had a grudge against her. There will be a whole host of unfavorable testimonies that will insinuate all sorts of motives, that the marriage was false, that she was greedy for money or hungry for status, certainly trying to elevate herself."

After deftly handling a small-boned bird with a silver fork, Clinton replied, "With no murder weapon, no direct evidence, and no witness to the crime, their case is weak. Motive is all they have, and motive is the mercury of any case. Let them slide upon it." He glanced around the room, careful to keep the conversation at a low tone, and resumed. "As far as character, we have an opening before the trial begins to rebuild her character. I intend to draw up papers asking that as Dr. Burdell's widow, Emma receive the entire marital share of Dr. Burdell's estate."

The fork entering Thayer's mouth paused, and he stopped short. He put it down incredulous. "You can't be serious?"

"I will make application to the Surrogate's Court that Emma Cunningham Burdell is the rightful wife and heir to Dr. Burdell's estate, and entitled to his house and possessions."

"But that feeds the prosecution! That is the essence of their case—that she ensnared him falsely and then killed him for his property. Furthermore, the Surrogate's Court is separate from the criminal court, and that means we will have two cases going on simultaneously!"

"All the more reason for speed," said Clinton, dabbing his chin. "Once a petition for the estate is made, the family will counter sue, saying that she is *not* the rightful widow. The papers will be filed, but the filing will be interrupted by the criminal trial."

"Aha," said Thayer, brightening, struggling to follow the tactic. "Once we begin an estate suit, any reference to it can be disallowed in another courtroom."

"Exactly," said Clinton. "The Judge will be asked to restrict the proceeding, and give limiting instructions that the issue of the marriage is a collateral matter, and not properly resolved. If that happens it can't be mentioned at all." The waiter brought hot portions of fricassee of veal with truffles and ribs of beef with anchovy butter. Clinton sampled the food.

"So, the whole character issue surrounding her morals and what went on behind the bedroom door is eliminated," said Thayer, comprehending the strategy, "and along with a 'false' marriage, it eliminates the motive."

"And Dr. Burdell's family will act on our behalf—they will surely ask for the entirety of his estate, and by doing so, prior to the trial, they will be seen as motivated by the desire for his money. They will appear to have the same motive that the prosecution says drove Emma Cunningham to kill."

Thayer fell back against his seat. He was still a bit uncertain. "So we sow reasonable doubt in advance. But won't this effort drive us in too many directions at once?"

"Remember," said Clinton, "the public mind perceives subtleties with less confusion than it grasps bold declarations. The public has fallen prey to the 'subtle' campaign of rumor and innuendo placed against her. Anyone could have committed this crime. There were many in the household, including patients and the servants, who could have obtained keys to the house. Our task is to emphasize the circumstantial nature of the prosecution's case, so that the public will be able to entertain the idea of reasonable doubt."

"We still have the missing carriage driver," said Thayer. "I think he is a paramount witness. What he saw or heard at any point may help us enormously."

"It's possible that the carriage driver has vanished because he is scared. But remember, like the other servants, he could easily have a grudge or prejudice against our client. He could shed an unfavorable light on her actions on that night. We may not want him as our witness, but we certainly don't want the prosecution finding him first and catching us unprepared."

They ate silently, finishing the main course. The plates were cleared and brandy poured. "I'll have Snarky spread the word and put up some placards with a reward for information on Samuel," volunteered Thayer. A Swiss meringue appeared, oozing with yellow custard and topped with a wobbling white cloud. Thayer was feeling the pressure of all the work still to do, reeling under the caseload, with papers that had to be checked and run up and down to the courts, working late into the night under the glow of extra lamps while hardly seeing his son, until one day his mouth was full of teeth.

As if reading Thayer's mind, Clinton said, "No doubt, the work is hard ahead of us. We must stay focused. This case will take all of our resources and then some and we will have to work around the clock." Clinton drained his last sip and pushed his brandy glass away, indicating the meal was over. He stood up, and Thayer stood as well. They shook hands.

"Mr. Clinton, I am honored that you have chosen me to serve on this case. I hope you have faith in me," said Thayer.

"For that, you can thank my wife. She suggested that I hire you, and I trust her instincts implicitly. She has one of the top legal minds around." The two men retrieved their coats at the concierge. On the street, a few carriages clattered down Broadway. "I have one last question, if I may, sir," ventured Thayer. "If Dr. Burdell was as disreputable as we suspect, why would Emma Cunningham marry him?"

Clinton observed that Thayer, like many young lawyers, was struggling to overcome the ambiguities of his client's actions. "As for the answer," Clinton replied, "I have only one explanation— Emma Cunningham was in love with Harvey Burdell. Her need for the protection of a husband took on the powerful guise of love."

Thayer pondered his words, with the mystery of the nighttime city surrounding them in the half-light. "Good night, sir, I will see you in the morning."

"Give my best to your wife. And as for your son, he should be proud to call you a lawyer." Thayer parted, pulling his jacket around him against the night's chill and started walking home. A few carriages clattered down the darkened street. Clinton hailed a cab and settled back for the ride to Bleecker Street. What he hadn't said to Thayer was that falling in love is like a trial; if one enters blindly, one finds oneself in a slippery place where it is too late to reflect or retreat. He would prepare the petition for Emma's share of the estate, and file the papers of administration. And he made a note to himself to follow up in the morning on a hunch he had about the whereabouts of the missing witness, Samuel. The Negro servant was a wild card, and circumstances demanded that nothing be left to the unknown.

# CHAPTER EIGHTEEN

*January 30, 1857*

The morning of her party at 31 Bond Street began like all the rest. Breakfast included the habitual struggle with Hannah, for the cook resented the party encroaching on the domain of her kitchen. After breakfast, Emma returned to the quiet of her room, where her daughters appeared in curling rags, to discuss their attire for the evening. Augusta's nineteenth birthday was later in the week, and the party was in her honor, to celebrate her birthday and as a way to introduce her to potential suitors. But Augusta appeared indifferent and her input was listless, whereas Helen, who was leaving for boarding school in two days, viewed the party as her own personal farewell.

Emma reviewed the guest list that she had penned on long sheets. She had sent engraved invitations on note cards that simply said "31 Bond Street" and wrote the time and date at the bottom. Ambrose Wicken had accepted, as well as a host of others. New Yorkers were always fond of an excuse to step inside a private residence, assess the decor and the food, and judge their neighbors, so Emma was intent to put on the finest display. She had also sent an invitation to Commodore Vanderkirk, but his wife had sent back a simple card that said only "Unable to attend, with regret." Dr. Burdell had not imparted anything further on the sale of the land, nor had he made any further mention of marriage. With so much uncertainty, Emma felt the time had come to force the issue all around.

She dressed and gathered her things for a trip downtown. She put on her gloves and a fur collar around her coat. She reached into the drawer of her desk and retrieved her leather document case. She had a meeting with her solicitor and then would finish shopping for the party.

The morning was cold but clear as a bell. At Worth Street, she climbed the stairs to an office and was admitted through a creaking gate that separated the solicitors' desks from the clerks.

"How do you do, Mrs. Cunningham." Mr. Billings pulled off a pair of gold bifocals and studied her solemnly.

"Good morning, Mr. Billings." She settled herself into the hard-backed chair beside his desk. She had not seen him since the spring, before she had left for Saratoga, when he had warned her that her funds were perilously low.

Mr. Billings pulled a pile of papers from a cubby that represented her financial affairs. "Your savings are nearly depleted and there are debts mounting against your account. I have a notice from the Broadway Bank—ten thousand dollars. It appears that you have withdrawn the money from a fund that was assigned as your eldest daughter's dowry."

"Yes," she said hesitantly. "I did. As a matter of fact, I have come to discuss that with you. I was steered toward an investment that is assured to be lucrative." She pulled the deed out of her purse and placed it upon his desk. "This is the land title for a large tract in New Jersey. I am hoping that its value will increase several fold."

Mr. Billings pulled the ribbon on the rolled scroll and gingerly pulled her deed closer and put on his spectacles. "I see land titles every day," he said, "for thousands of acres across the territories, or for sand dunes in the Mojave where there are said to be veins of silver and gold. Most aren't worth the ink on the signature."

"Mr. Billings," said Emma, "Commodore Vanderkirk has expressed an interest in this land. He is interested in iron and steel factories that will connect to the railroad."

"Commodore Vanderkirk, you say?"

"I have heard him speak about it with my own ears," said Emma with authority. "He plans to build piers and iron factories all along this waterfront, for commerce."

"Lots of plans are spoken of but few become more than idle whimsy. The Congress has been plotting a Continental railroad for decades, but its route is being moved from North to South and back again every week."

"I assure you, this was not idle talk. Commodore Vanderkirk had the keenest intention upon this sale. For such a sedentary man, he is most vigorous when it comes to getting his way." She laughed, hoping to convey a close familiarity with the man. "He has made an offer, and the amount of his offer was not in the least insignificant."

Mr. Billings gazed at her thoughtfully. "If Commodore Vanderkirk is truly behind this venture, as you say, then it could be worth a bona fide fortune. Although this deed is in your name, the land belongs to your daughter, and remains her dowry. I advise you, as your solicitor, that this deed or any proceeds from the sale are hers until she is married, and you are merely the stewardess of her affairs. After her marriage, it becomes the property of her husband. Does she have any plans to marry?"

"Well, there is a suitor," said Emma, thoughtfully, and then refrained from naming Ambrose Wicken by name. "I was thinking that this alone would make a handsome offering for a dowry. Augusta is turning nineteen this week, and I am expecting that a gentleman will step forward."

"Young men are gamblers and many have squandered a young wife's nest egg. I might suggest you conclude this business yourself before she marries, rather than leaving its fate in the hands of a future son-in-law. It may even raise the value in the suitor's eyes."

"As a matter of fact," said Emma modestly, "I am engaged as well."

"Engaged! Well I suppose congratulations are in order. Two marriages! That is quite a series of developments," said Mr. Billings. "As for the men, they are very lucky gentlemen indeed." Mr. Billings paused. "As a widow, the property is yours to manage for your daughter, so if a sale is imminent, you might look for a swift conclusion which would be more advantageous. Once you are married, both your affairs and your daughters' will be overseen by the gentlemen you marry."

"That is something to think about. Thank you for your counsel." Emma stuffed the papers back into her satchel.

"I look forward to hearing the announcement of the nuptials," said Mr. Billings, bidding her farewell.

Emma stood to curtsy. "Thank you, sir, although, I assure you, in my case, the wedding shall not be a public affair. My daughter, however, shall most likely desire to fill Grace Church."

"All the more reason to fortify her dowry in advance, for such weddings carry an alarming cost." Mr. Billings stood and bowed with formality. Emma gathered her gloves and departed. Outside, she made her way up Broadway, joining the flow of pedestrians. A crowd of people climbed from the ferry to the rise of Broadway, pushing past the opposing rush of the Brooklyn bound. Two exuberant girls, walking arm in arm, jostled Emma. They were wearing cotton dresses, stuffed with extra petticoats to make their skirts appear fashionably wide. A dark-haired girl was carrying a crude basket. As they sashayed past, Emma saw herself at fifteen, with a straw hat and a basket of cherries, rushing out of her family's clapboard house, one of many that stood at the end of a rutted road that forked into the farmlands of Brooklyn, along dusty paths that ran for miles eastward, toward sandy soil, and the void of the thundering ocean. The Brooklyn ferry, only ten minutes and two cents east across the river, reminded her of how far she had come, and how determined she was never to go back.

Her next stop was the Patisserie Valbonne, where the counters were painted pale lavender. Emma inquired about her pastry order. "Six dozen French cakes, vanilla with chestnut crème," she told the sales lady, "for 31 Bond Street."

"I am boxing them now, Ma'am, and shall send them right over."

"Thank, you. Please leave them with the servant boy at the lower door." She did not need to pay directly; a yellow envelope with a bill would be delivered to the townhouse at the end of the month.

Next, Emma stopped at a florist filled with exotic hothouse blooms. Ornamental shrubs were woven into elaborate sculptural forms for the entryways of the new palaces along Fifth Avenue that had wide loggias in the Renaissance style. She once thought such grandeur lacked elegance and proportion, just as she had thought the chocolate turrets of the brownstone churches seemed dreary and mean. Now, this world held a curious thrill, and she was struck half-blind by the abundance of summer flowers in January.

After signing her name on a credit for the flowers, Emma wandered past the window of a women's haberdasher, the name of the store scripted across the glass in gold. A display of cashmere shawls was piled high in all the colors of the rainbow. She stepped inside; a woman in a cotton coat was arranging a display case with painted fans, jeweled combs, hairnets with silver pearls, card cases, and a sable muff and boa. The woman looked at up her expectantly, with an imperious tilt to her head.

"Good morning, Madame. What do you need today?"

"I'd like three pair of silk stockings, in pale colors, please," said Emma. The shop woman walked to the back of the store to pull open drawers and lift out the stockings, as if each was exquisitely precious. Emma made her choice and with newly found confidence, pointed around the store in search of other luxuries: a cameo on a velvet ribbon, purses for Augusta and Helen. She allowed items to pile on the counter and asked to have them placed on an account in her name, and to have them wrapped and sent to 31 Bond Street. There was no reason not to indulge in some extra finery. She had worked hard to lay the broad strokes on the canvas, and now she could allow the scenery its embellishments.

On the sidewalk, her pace quickened—she was several blocks from home, and she began making a list of all the things left to do for the party. A group of hired girls was coming to serve. The sherry and port needed to be poured into the decanters, and the table napkins rolled with silverware.

Ahead, she spotted a carriage pulling up to the St. Nicholas Hotel. It took a moment to register the outline of Samuel on the coachman's bench, his red driver's coat bordered with braid. She stopped short on the sidewalk, several feet away, struggling to identify why Samuel would be dressed so formally in the afternoon, and was stopping at the hotel so close to the house. Then Dr. Burdell exited the carriage, his profile bent under his top hat as he navigated the low carriage door. Emma was far enough away to remain unnoticed. If he turned and saw her, he might offer that she join him for tea, but she would have to remind him that there was much left to do for the preparations, and the evening party would not be conjured up, as if by magic.

Dr. Burdell turned back to the carriage door and a gloved hand appeared from the cab. He reached for the hand, and a foot appeared on the top step; he led a woman gingerly down the carriage steps. When she was on the ground, she laughed, and with the other hand, she lifted her veil. Emma saw the woman's pretty face, smiling and flirtatious. Dr. Burdell lifted her hand and kissed it. Their eyes met. Dr. Burdell put his hand gently on her upper arm and led her past the liveried doormen into the St. Nicholas Hotel.

Emma stood frozen at the sight. There was no mistaking the intimacy between them. It was the same intimacy Emma had enjoyed in Saratoga, and during those September days in the city after her return, but lately she had come to take for granted the businesslike nature of his habits. When he was at home, he more often rebuffed her than spoke to her. She had almost become used to his dismissive attitude and the brusqueness of his manner, but now she could see clearly how differently he acted compared with the beginning of their courtship. She could not mistake his intentions to this woman. She had seen his caress on the woman's arm, and the furtive pressure of his fingers as they brushed against her upper arm.

On top of the carriage sat Samuel, whose back was still to her. She felt a strong surge of betrayal at the sight of him, as if by doing Dr. Burdell's driving, he was personally bidding against her. She could not shake the agitation caused by the image of the woman descending from the carriage, so finely dressed at midday, like an expensive courtesan, entering the St. Nicholas, with Harvey's white glove curled around her upper arm. Samuel, his back still to her, pulled the reins and rode away.

# CHAPTER NINETEEN

When she returned to the house, she snapped at Hannah. The hired serving girls had arrived, and Hannah had allowed them to remain in the breakfast room, where they had changed their clothes and were sitting idly. No one had given them any instructions, and they had left their coats in piles all over the room. It was up to Emma to direct the waitresses, in black uniforms with white aprons, upstairs to set up the tables and lay out the tablecloths for the food. She called John to fetch a ladder, and she stood behind him as he moved it around the parlor, lighting every gas fixture and lamp, so that the flames were caught in the shimmering surfaces of the polished silver and in the reflection of the tall parlor windows, now darkening in the late afternoon. Emma ordered her daughters, still in curling rags, to finish their hair. Finally she was able to rush up to her room to change.

She pushed the boxes of new purchases aside on her bed to make room for her petticoats and her gown. She struggled with her hair, carefully dabbing white powder along her face and shoulders. A bitter lump stayed in her stomach from the sight of the woman at the hotel, but she was propelled in a rush with the guests arriving.

Her hand shook as she placed diamonds at her neck and ears. As it neared six o'clock, the carriage sounded at the front of the house. She peered out the curtain to see the flash of Harvey's cape as he dashed into the front door. She made final adjustments to her hair and jewelry, and went downstairs to his room.

The door was slightly ajar, and she saw him rummaging through a drawer, still wearing his cape, as if he were about to leave again. "Why aren't you dressing?" she asked from the doorway.

"I am going to a meeting," he said, annoyed. "Downtown."

"A meeting? But the party is about to begin!"

"My business is more important than a debutante's tea. As a matter of fact, this meeting is of the utmost importance. There has been a serious turn of events, and I must attend to them immediately."

"Are you saying that you have business needs to be attended to right this instant? As guests are arriving downstairs?"

He stopped fumbling with the papers on his desk and turned to address her directly. "Emma, I have no patience, nor time, for your feminine intrusions. I have more pressing matters to attend to."

"I want to ask you about the outcome of the land sale in New Jersey. The Commodore came to visit, and it seemed that a sale was imminent."

"As a matter of fact, I did have an offer from the Commodore, but he has reconsidered."

"What do you mean reconsidered?"

"There is no longer a deal. I can salvage only a small portion of the investment with another buyer if I act tonight. Otherwise all is lost. I suggest you get me your deed, and sign it over to me now. I am afraid I will be able to recoup only a small portion of your money."

"I don't understand. You are saying that Commodore Vanderkirk no longer has an interest?"

"No, he has passed this over. I would hate to see you lose everything. So I must act in haste. Do not hesitate. Get me your deed, and I will be off."

"I purchased this land at your insistence. Its value cannot have diminished overnight."

Dr. Burdell clenched his teeth, frustrated. "I would not be stubborn, Emma, if I were you. Rather than risk your money waiting for a sale that will never happen, I shall personally offer to pay you nearly half the price you paid for it. If you get me the deed now, I may leave."

"Harvey, I have no intention of handing you my deed," said Emma, standing, blocking the doorway. "I saw your carriage today, before the St. Nicholas Hotel. There was a woman inside. You led her into the hotel."

"You are imagining things," he said, shaking his head in disgust. "And your imagination is distorting your reason."

"Should I ask Samuel or the horse if I were imagining things?"

"You have some nerve, coming into my house and turning it upside down with social gatherings and adolescent parties, and now you have the effrontery to ask me the whereabouts of my horse and carriage? I will not tolerate your intrusions."

"There is a party downstairs that has been planned for weeks," she replied, her voice raised. "I have thrown it for my daughters to meet eligible young suitors and I have every intention that you shall attend."

"And will this party bring about miracles?" He scoffed and was buttoning his cloak.

"Did you think I desired to remain your nighttime mistress, for the sheer pleasure of battling over menus with your cook? I have been living in this house, and now I am ready to be its legitimate mistress, as you have promised. Tonight I will announce our engagement and to present myself your fiancée."

"I will not tolerate your blackmail. I made it clear to you that there were to be no public announcements—and you dare to take matters into your own hands. Now, you expect me to go downstairs and trot before strangers like a pony on your leash?"

"You had no difficulty posing as my husband, in front of Commodore Vanderkirk. Perhaps it was because you wanted him to think that my land was yours to sell?"

"How dare you accuse me of deception," he said ruefully. "You were preening in Saratoga as a rich widow, when in fact you were hunting for the bounty of a wealthy man."

"Do not insult me in that way!" she gasped. He returned to his desk in a rush and continued to pack papers into his satchel. The doorbell rang and the hired girl was letting in guests. Augusta and Helen were already in the parlor, and Emma could make out their murmurings and curtsies. The servant began carrying the coats up the stairs.

"I must go downstairs, the guests are arriving," she said urgently. "I insist you come down with me."

"Then, fetch me your deed."

Overcome with anger, Emma admonished him. "Your behavior is most reprehensible! I shall part with my land when I am ready. I intend to hold you to your promise of what our evenings in your bed imply or I shall hand you papers from a magistrate for breach of promise. You and I shall be married, before I hand over my property to you."

"Then you shall have a hard time toasting our betrothal at the party without my presence." He grabbed his satchel and rushed from the room. Stunned, she followed him to the landing and watched as he dashed down the stairs. At the bottom he slipped unnoticed through the guests, now just coming through the vestibule, and rushed to the kitchen stair, disappearing out of sight.

She heard the doorbell ring, letting in a fresh wave of guests and with them, the voice of Ambrose Wicken. Rattled, she stayed at the top of the stairs, unable to face the guests. Her eyes were near to tears, and she took a deep breath to keep them away. Finally, when her composure returned, she smoothed her gown and forced herself to start down the staircase. As she circled the half landing and reached the full view of the crowd milling in the hall below, she took each step slowly. Ambrose Wicken looked up, smiling at her. She pulled herself upright and raised her head high. She put on her broadest smile and made the last descent into the array of twinkling glasses and tittering greetings.

"You look enchanting, ravishing," whispered Wicken, taking her by the arm. Together they moved through the throng in the hall.

"How do you do?" Emma said, nodding to one guest after another. "I am so pleased that you have come." She and Wicken moved into the parlor, nodding and greeting as they went.

A broad woman sailed toward Emma, with feathers in her hair. "Mrs. Cunningham, I am Mrs. Newcastle. This is such a lovely house. But I don't see the host?"

"Dr. Burdell has been called to a medical emergency," said Emma. "To Bellevue. There has been a terrible accident and they are in need of surgeons, so he has offered his services."

"How noble. But he leaves you, my dear, to dazzle, alone, at this soiree?"

"It is my penance, I suppose, for being engaged to a man in the medical profession." In the wake of Mrs. Newcastle, Emma overheard a woman whispering to a lady companion: "I rue the poor dentist his fortune, now that she has set her eyes upon it."

"I was sure they were engaged—I have heard the woman has inherited a fortune from her deceased husband," answered her companion. "With so much of her own, she may find that toothaches quickly become rather tiresome." Mr. Wicken could overhear as well, and he ushered her away from the vicinity of the huddled women.

"Ambrose!" said Emma. "Do you see Augusta? Isn't she a beauty?" Augusta was sitting on a sofa on the opposite end of the room.

"The incarnation of it," drawled Wicken. The parlor was animated with conversing guests, and the servant girls passed silver trays with flutes of Champagne. Along the sideboards, the pastries and confections were piled high.

"So Dr. Burdell is absent? I do find it difficult to fathom how, once again, he can leave such a beautiful woman unattended. He gave me the distinct understanding when I first met him that your betrothal was imminent."

"Yes." Emma sighed. She was proficient at disguising her feelings, but she suspected that he was keenly aware of her disappointment. "It will transpire in good time," she said with a brave effort.

Wicken took her arm and walked a couple of paces to a spot where there were fewer people, but the movement drew attentive glances, and she understood that he was making a gesture. "Please be assured," he whispered, "that I can be your loyal consort and friend. A woman alone often finds that she needs a man to give her protection. Please rely on me if you need advice or counsel."

"Why, thank you," she whispered back, relieved. "Southerners have such refined manners. I wish more Northerners would take an example, here in New York." Now she felt emboldened to speak frankly with him. "Augusta's father had wonderful manners. He was most generous by taking care of her in the form of a dowry."

"I am sure that a dowry is insignificant in light of her charms," Wicken replied.

"But it is not insignificant," Emma insisted. "It has been placed most recently in a purchase of land, that is most valuable." She was leaning into him, in a conspiratorial way.

"In land you say? Would that be the land Dr. Burdell owns on the New Jersey side of the bay? It is a matter he has spoken about. She has a small interest then?"

"Why yes, but it is not small, it is a sizable portion. I have purchased it with money that was left to her. It has become, I understand, the most desirable portion."

"Aha," he said pensively. "You are a business woman, as well as a beauty. And a shrewd mother always has her child's best interests at heart."

Emma smiled. She watched him now glance appreciatively in her daughter's direction. "I may need your assistance and advice in managing the sale of this land," she said.

"Why certainly, you can come to me, as soon as you'd like. I am staying at the Broadway Hotel."

"I shall do that, thank you," she said.

"But for now," he said, "it is high time that I permitted you to return to your guests and I paid respects to Miss Augusta." Wicken released her with a bow and wandered over to Augusta, who sat on a divan, her skirt fanned around her, her hands folded demurely on her lap. Emma watched him hover, mouthing his usual flatteries. As she moved toward a crowd of guests, she overheard him extend an invitation to Augusta to join him tomorrow, on a wintry ride, north of the city, in an open carriage, bundled in furs.

Augusta hesitated, and Emma thought she was about to shake her head no, when she caught her mother's eye. Emma gave her a stern look of warning.

"Yes," said Augusta, obediently, but without emotion, looking up at him. "I shall be most happy to join you for a ride."

# CHAPTER TWENTY

*March 16, 1857*

Clinton woke up and made his way to the kitchen. With the costs of running the new office, the servants had slowly been let go, and his household was making do on less and less. The cook only came on certain days, and the roof in the attic leaked. Most mornings, Elisabeth prepared him eggs in the skillet, but this morning he had risen earlier than usual. He left Elisabeth wrapped up in the four-poster bed. Maintaining the large house left her bone tired, so he let her sleep.

At this point in a case, the only thing on his mind was the trial. While adjusting a cuff link to his cuff, he would be mentally preparing a speech or a witness examination. At night, sponging himself in his bath, he would call out to Elisabeth, trying out various legal points, and she would reply with counterpoints, all while arranging his clothes in the bedroom. Because of the lack of servants, she hauled his buckets of bathwater upstairs to the water closet, heated on the giant kitchen stove. By the time he got home late at night, the water had cooled to room temperature, but now at least, the air had warmed, for it was nearly spring.

Clinton found some crumpets and bread in the pie safe, and a pot of jam with a fresh lid of wax. The milk cart came down the back alley every morning before dawn and left a bottle of milk in the tin box by the back door. He retrieved the fresh bottle, and as he reentered the pantry he saw two little shoes inside the door of the anteroom that held tools and old furniture. He peered inside, and in the dim light saw a nest of quilts and blankets spread across the floor. In the middle was a tousle of blond hair, and buried underneath, John was fast asleep.

His clothes were folded on the floor with a book and pencil on top. Clinton bent down and examined it. The flyleaf was written upon, in a boy's scrawl, practicing penmanship with lines from the Book of Matthew. Clinton studied the sleeping boy, dismayed. When the inquest ended, Elisabeth had approached him about letting the boy move into one of the bedrooms upstairs, but Clinton had vehemently objected. It was one thing to have him perform errands at the office and help Elisabeth at home. But taking the boy to live in their house was not a wise idea. "Elisabeth, this child can still be called as a witness. The prosecution can put him on the stand to establish the crime, the *corpus delicti*, which is the finding of the body."

"But, Henry, he is so young and he needs a good home. I am sure the prosecution won't use him," she protested.

"Harboring a witness is tampering. There could be an appearance of conflict, and even having him do errands is risky." Besides, Clinton lectured, John was not an orphan. He had a mother who lived in a garret downtown. She was arthritic and could no longer work or make money by sewing, so she relied on the coins earned by her son. John appeared to be itinerant, but he had a family and places to sleep.

But now, seeing the boy in the blankets, he realized that Elisabeth's desire to have him stay was about her own isolation. While

Clinton was working long hours these last months, she was trapped in the house with few funds, no servants, and no children of her own. He should have known how attached she would become to him. He felt suddenly bereft by all the things he was failing to provide for her.

Clinton shook John awake. Startled, John sat upright, his hair sticking straight up on top of his head.

"You can't sleep here anymore, John," he said. The boy's eyes darted back and forth. "Do you have anywhere else to go?"

"I have my mum's house, but it was Mrs. Clinton's idea, not mine. I only sleep here now and then," he said.

"I know she arranged it for you, but it's not a good idea, and you should stay with your mother. But first, come into the kitchen and eat. I have some crumpets." The boy got dressed and sat at the table where Clinton set him up with a plate and a glass of milk. Like his wife, he couldn't help being charmed by the earnest manner with which John approached his food. As for the sleeping arrangements, he would straighten Elisabeth out later.

"John, tell me honestly, do you know where I can find Samuel?" he asked suddenly while the boy was filling up on the sweet bread. A look of concern passed over John's face, and he swallowed slowly without answering. "You understand that Samuel was the last man to see Dr. Burdell alive? I just need to ask him some questions. Do you know where he might be?"

As Clinton suspected, he took awhile to answer. "I heard he got another job," John said.

"Where?"

"At a stable. At a big house, on Fifth Avenue near Tenth Street, but I couldn't say, exactly."

"Let's do some detective work. I need your help. Since you know the man by sight, I want you to come with me for a ride. We will go there and see if we can find him." Now John looked alarmed, as if he regretted his words. Clinton made sure he'd had his fill of breakfast and downed his tall glass of milk when he ushered him toward the door. Outside, he hailed a cab. "To Fifth Avenue, just above Tenth Street," he said. They piled in, and the cabbie pulled away at a clip. As they rounded Washington Square, the clusters of older townhouses gave way to larger, newer homes along Fifth Avenue. They passed a row of new mansions, each one springing up as if in a spontaneous procession of growth. Instead of seeming more substantial, Clinton thought, these big homes seemed tentative: the brass was too shiny, the stoops too high, the lots absent of trees, with areas that were still under new construction. New York, a dreamscape of opportunity, often presented a flimsy mirage. Large houses rose around a sudden fortune then disappeared in half a decade, blown away like stage props.

Clinton quizzed John about the house where Samuel was employed. The boy peered out the window and seemed to have difficulty identifying which one. When they reached Twelfth Street they stopped before a large mansion and got out. A carriage-house door was open to the street. It smelled of sawdust and new leather; a row of carriages glowed with fresh lacquer. Clinton walked inside while John waited at the curb.

"I am looking for a groom named Samuel, who is said to work here," he inquired.

The man brushing the horse's flank did not look up. "No one here by that name. You must be mistaken," he muttered. Clinton believed he saw a flicker of fear pass over the eyes of the stable hand, a Negro. Many were ex-slaves, fugitives seeking asylum in New York, and they knew better than to engage in a conversation that could send them back South, in shackles. Clinton asked another question, and after receiving a hostile silence, decided to retreat. Stepping back onto the street, he realized he was getting nowhere, and suddenly regretted being away from the office, with so much to do while the morning was slipping away. Clinton turned to the boy with a look of reproach.

"This isn't the place, John."

"I guess I was wrong. Perhaps I mixed that other fellow up with Samuel," he said, his voice edging upward. "I remember now! Samuel told me he lives past the reservoir, in the shantytowns. That is what I recollect, for sure!" A few miles to the north, Fifth Avenue turned into a dirt road that blended into a dusty horizon. It passed the reservoir and the remote acres of fields where the city had built a fairgrounds and a Crystal Pavilion. Beyond that were the African shantytowns, constructed of barrel staves, where goats grazed on the granite bluffs. A Negro like Samuel could disappear, protected and hidden in the mazelike dwellings. It would not be easy to find him if he did not want to be found.

Clinton turned to look at the boy, who had the same gaunt look, no matter what the circumstance. "John?"

"Yes, sir?"

"We won't find Samuel in the shantytowns, will we?"

The boy looked startled.

"Why don't you tell me where this fellow really is?" said Clinton. John appeared to be struggling, and Clinton continued. "You are his friend, aren't you, and you know that he is in hiding. And now you are scared for him. You are scared that he will get into trouble—and maybe someone will blame this murder on him. And you don't want to be a part of that, do you?"

The boy looked up, with frightened eyes.

"Have you ever seen a hanging?" asked Clinton.

John nodded.

"Down at the Tombs? One of the public ones?"

Clinton waited. All boys had seen hangings, but not all enjoyed them as much as they pretended.

"Listen," continued Clinton. "I am not in the hanging business.

In fact, my job is to keep people off the scaffolds. And that goes for a Negro named Samuel, just the same as for Mrs. Cunningham." Clinton bent down and pulled his gold watch from the fob on his vest. He cradled the watch in his hand, with its simple roman numbering and soft dents along the filigree, and showed it to John. "Do you see this?" he asked. John nodded obediently. "It was given to me by a man who was sentenced to hang for a murder he didn't commit. One night, he came upon a dead body, lying in an alley, and he reached down and took the dead man's coin purse. He didn't kill anyone, but he got caught with the purse. He went to jail, charged with murder. It wasn't until the morning he was to hang that I got a judge to set him free. He didn't have money to pay my fee, so he gave me his watch. I keep it here in my pocket, to remind myself that every man deserves a defense, even if he has done something terribly wrong in his life."

John finally spoke: "The District Attorney told me Samuel was in trouble, that he should fear for his life."

"The District Attorney?" asked Clinton.

"The first day, at the house, the Coroner asked me questions about how I found Dr. Burdell's body, and one of the deputies took me outside, back near the outhouse. The District Attorney and another man came, too. They said they wanted to find Samuel. When they asked me if he lived in the shantytowns, the deputy said they would go and burn him out."

"Who was the other man?" Clinton asked.

"He spoke like he was from the South. The man said I should tell them quick where Samuel lived, or I would be the next one to worry about my life."

Clinton, who had been crouched low, now stood up. So Hall had been searching for the missing witness from the beginning. And it confirmed that Hall had worked fast, with the aid of his pawn, Coroner Connery, to purposefully set Emma Cunningham up as the murder suspect. Her trial would be a spectacle, but not a certain conviction. If the city prosecutor had wanted a speedy conviction, Negroes and ex-slaves were a surer bet to pin a murder on. They were easier to hang, even easier if they were runaways, for few lawyers would take on their cause. If Oakey Hall wanted to resolve the murder quickly for his own political gain, he would have the fastest success by capturing and incriminating Samuel, since the coachman was the last person to see Dr. Burdell alive. But, it now occurred to Clinton that Hall and his minions were not trying to find Samuel, they wanted to silence him. There was something Samuel knew, and the District Attorney wanted it suppressed. They didn't want him to testify. They wanted him dead.

Clinton stepped back into the carriage and told the boy to get in with him. "Lead me to where Samuel is," Clinton ordered. "He won't be out of danger until we find him."

"There! There!" said the boy as the carriage rounded the south side of Washington Square Park. "That's where he prays. He helped me get food from the pastor once, when Dr. Burdell didn't give me my pay." An iron fence enclosed Washington Square Park, and the homes around it formed an elegant quadrangle, except for the southwest corner, where the dilapidated wooden houses of the Negro quarter still burrowed into crooked lanes. Across the square, this African neighborhood had grown up around an old Indian spring named Minetta Creek. Somewhere, beneath the cobbles and the paving stones, the creek still flowed under the city, buried underground.

Clinton stopped the cab. He dismounted the carriage, and the boy popped out behind him in a jump. They entered a wooden church that was badly in need of paint. The vestry was dim; there were pegs along the scuffed woodwork. A table held a collection cup, a stack of Bibles, and a cracked copy of the Book of Psalms. Footsteps resonated from within, moving toward them from the recess of the quiet nave. A Negro minister appeared, his clergyman's skirts rustling, his skin the dusky color of the shadows around the altar. He did not seem surprised to see them in the dead quiet of a weekday morning in his empty house of worship.

"Sir." The pastor greeted Clinton without embellishment, simply stating the fact that both were gentlemen, equally.

Respect seemed to require that Clinton avoid the obsequiousness of a deep bow, so necessary among his legal peers. "I am Henry Clinton, a lawyer," he said. "I am here on an important matter."

"Those who come here, come to address important matters to the Lord," said the clergyman.

Clinton paused. "With all due respect, this is a matter concerning a member of your congregation. I am looking for a man—his name is Samuel. He is tall and strongly built and he works as a groom and a carriage driver. Do you know where I might find him?"

The Reverend's lips tensed slightly. He seemed to ponder the request, as if searching for a scriptural response. It was clear he was not at ease with the request. "Forgive me, Reverend," said Clinton, sensing the man's reluctance. "I have not introduced this boy. His name is John, and he worked as an errand boy at the same house as Samuel. It was through their friendship that you once aided this boy when he was hungry. Perhaps you remember?" The boy's serious expression elicited a sympathetic smile from the minister. Clinton eyed the man closely and saw a crease of worry cross the pastor's brow. He knows Samuel, thought Clinton, and Samuel has been here since the murder to seek his counsel.

"I cannot help you," the Reverend said simply.

Clinton pressed on, speaking gently. "Reverend, I am sure you have heard much about the murder that took place on Bond Street.

Samuel was present on the night that his employer, Dr. Burdell, was killed, and as such, he is an important witness. If Samuel has the courage to come forward, he may help us solve the crime." Clinton knew instantly that he had erred by phrasing his request as a challenge.

"Mr. Clinton, I am sure you are a most venerable member of the bar, and no doubt justice is foremost in your mind," replied the minister in a modulated voice that had the depth and resonance of an organ pipe. "But I will have you know that Samuel is a man of courage—he has placed himself in the faith of God, which takes all the courage a man can summon. He is an honest man, and he needs no other guide."

"Please, sir, I intended no disrespect to yourself or to Samuel. I do not suspect him of any crime. Samuel might know the victim's whereabouts on the night of the murder, and lead us to the perpetrator." Clinton added meekly: "Perhaps you can convince him to speak with me?"

The Reverend's brow remained furrowed; Clinton saw that he had not penetrated the pastor's resistance. "I do not sacrifice my brethren," he said with a tone of rebuke. "People come here to worship in this church, which is their haven. This is a sanctuary where my parishioners shall always be safe."

"If Samuel fears he may be wrongly accused, I assure you, I can offer him protection," countered Clinton quickly. "I will see that he is granted immunity in exchange for his testimony."

"You and your law cannot protect Samuel," said the pastor with sudden vehemence. "Times have changed—and much for the worse. As a legal man, you are, no doubt, aware of the Fugitive Slave Act? Within the first year after that law, there were more Negroes removed from the North than had been captured in the preceding sixty years. And there is the case of *Dred Scott* most recently decided by the highest court in this land. And yet, as a New York City lawyer, you still come to my church to tell me that you can offer protection to my parishioner?" The Reverend nearly spat the words "New York City lawyer," as if there were no more contemptible species on earth.

"Follow this way," said the minister. Clinton followed to an easel with a notice board that had bits of paper tagged to its surface. He realized with alarm that the snips were newspaper clips about slavery that were often sprinkled into the New York dailies like a sharp spicing of pepper. Courtesy required that Clinton lean forward to read them:

> We learn that a slave man was burned at Abbeville, in Alabama, by a mob of people numbering over four thousand. He was tied to a stake, around which was heaped a fat pine wood, so as to make a pile six feet in diameter and four feet high. Fire was then applied and the poor wretch was burned to ashes. The crime of which he was accused was murder.
>
> *The New York Times*, JANUARY 31, 1857

### WHIPPING A SLAVE TO DEATH IN SAVANNAH

> The Negro Stepney was a runaway. He was arrested on Wednesday morning and returned to Boylan Jones, who gave him some thirty lashes with a riding whip or a small cowhide. When the Negro was released, he fell to the ground, speechless and prostrate. The constable ordered him to rise, and afterwards dealt him several more blows with a wagon whip while he lay on the ground insensible. Jones then dragged him from the place into the house where he died on Thursday morning.
>
> *The New York Herald*, FEBRUARY 16, 1857

"If Samuel is to be protected, it will be by God, not by the law," said the minister, his eyes hard with determination. Clinton knew that it was not just the South that was aflame; crimes against freedmen and ex-slaves were escalating at an alarming rate in New York City, including a practice whereby Negro citizens who had never been slaves were being kidnapped and sold South, to be turned bodily into gold.

With little to lose, Clinton decided to be straightforward: "There is a woman who is accused of murder, and perhaps she will hang for it, falsely. It is for that reason that I seek Samuel; his information may exonerate her."

"This woman may be fighting for her life," replied the minister, "but a man with black skin is no less worthy. I will not trade one for the other." In a sudden flash, Clinton suspected that others had been to the church before him, inquiring about Samuel.

"Have any men from the District Attorney's office come here to see you?" asked Clinton.

The minister did not give a direct reply. "Last night, perhaps you have heard, they burnt the shantytowns," he said. "They said it was to make way for the new Central Park." The minister's mouth tightened around his sparse words.

"They burnt them?" asked John, alarmed.

"Is Samuel safe?" asked Clinton, earnestly.

"He is alive," replied the minister.

"Thank you, if that is all you can tell me, I shall be satisfied." Clinton knew that the preacher's logic was clear and irrefutable: from his perspective, giving away information on Samuel would be the equivalent of having him lynched. The law cut both ways. A man's liberty could easily be taken for granted and with a twist of the blade, could as easily be taken away.

Clinton was not accustomed to ending an encounter at a disadvantage. By way of concession, he turned toward the boy, and said,

"John, now that we know your friend is in good hands, it is time for us to get back to business. We have a murder trial to prepare, and there are innumerable things to do." He offered the clergyman his name on a card. "Reverend, you may contact me, should your thoughts on the matter change."

"Proceed carefully, when you exploit the innocent," said the clergyman, with a cryptic warning. Clinton bowed, and retreated. As he exited the church, Clinton studied the back of John's head, with its delicate blond tufts, fine as down. He was now certain that both John and the minister had seen Samuel since the murder. He made a point to assign Snarky the job of keeping an eye out, for John was in contact with him, thought Clinton—he cares about this man; they have a bond.

Outside, the hansom cab waited at the curb. Clinton opened the carriage door, and the boy scurried in. They headed downtown toward the office on Spruce Street, where a mountain of papers awaited. A man had been killed and a woman who had an uncertain relationship to the dead man was accused of the crime. But tangled up in Emma Cunningham's case was an eleven-year-old houseboy and a Negro groom, both as fragile as loose pieces of straw, blown into the path of a murder that was reaching deep into the strata of the city.

# CHAPTER TWENTY-ONE

*April 22, 1857*

In New York, March turns to April by way of its trees. Apple trees dot Orchard Street, left standing after the Dutch farms fell. St. Mark's Church is known for its gnarled old pears. Washington Square is rimmed with cherry trees, the tiny petals cover the pavement like pink snow. In spring, new leaves soften the edges of the limestone edifices, and bricks and paving stones seem a part of the earth itself, with moss, sprouts, and worms wedged between the cobblestones. Magnolias bloom in church gardens, and all around the fringes of the city are stretches of wooded riverbank, with coverings of ground pine, wood violets, oak fern, and partridge vine.

Samuel sat on a log in a clearing by the river, scraping the scales off a mackerel. An Indian sat on the opposite log, carving a piece of wood. Samuel watched Katuma, in his dusty blue work pants, whittling away at the tiny piece of willow oak, smoothed into a hollow curl, not much larger than his thumb. Katuma was as tall and broad as Samuel, with skin the color of darkened butter.

There were footsteps from behind, padding along the earth of a beaten path. It was Katuma's daughter, Quietta, in a gingham skirt with a sleek braid swinging along her back. She carried a pile of vegetables in her apron. When she reached the clearing, she emptied the vegetables into a basket and sat next to her father on the log. "Here, girl," Katuma said, handing his daughter a carved whistle. "It sounds enough like a bird. Blow it if you see any men riding past the market toward these woods."

Quietta worked at a fruiterer's stall at the Greenwich Market on Christopher Street, the westernmost market in Greenwich Village, just blocks from where they sat by the river. She came down to the riverbank in the afternoons, where her father liked to sit and fish. Between the fishing hut and the city street were two acres of brambles and high brush, and the path down to the water passed an old storage shack and a broken-down building, now derelict, which shielded this part of the woods from the street. By day Greenwich Street was busy with horse-drawn lorries and lined with brick fortresses, warehouses that were filled with barrels and crates and burlap sacks—packing houses and manufactories that had swallowed up patches of the old Village. By night, the streets were empty with the workers gone. Down the slope by the river, where Samuel slept each night in the hut, the sky was large and filled with stars.

Quietta took off her shoes, padded in and out of the hut, and got some kindling for the fire. Tall trees enclosed the clearing, and the warm sunlight from the late afternoon filtered down in columns. The aspen leaves shook softly. There was a shuffling sound as soft as the wind in the leaves. A boy appeared at the clearing, coming down the path even more quietly than Quietta.

"Here comes the fancy boy," said Quietta, teasing John about the britches and little jacket he now wore, purchased for him by the lawyer's wife.

"We have a bounty," Katuma told John. "Samuel and I caught these fish without a net." The bucket was filled with glistening fish coiled in the bucket, up to the brim. The river glinted through more trees, not far from where they sat, and a raft was bobbing in the water, tied to a tree branch at the bottom of the sharp bank.

"Will you take me fishing?" asked John.

"I will take you, Eagle, when the trial is over, and you take off those fancy clothes." Katuma called John Eagle because he always carried a flying eagle penny in his trouser pocket. Quietta called him Bird. "When the summer comes, we'll go to Rockaway. To the Lenape fishing place."

Quietta placed the basket of vegetables before John. "First the vegetables, Bird. Cut them up." Samuel tossed John a knife he had been using on the fish, a dagger that landed at the boy's feet upright, point first, in the earth. John picked it up and started stabbing at a beet.

"Father, Bird is trying to make a whistle out of the beet."

"You can't cut a beet with a double-sided blade," said Katuma, handing John another knife.

Katuma lived with his wife and daughter in a proper house on Perry Street. He earned money working as a longshoreman on the oyster barges. Come spring and summer, Katuma, along with his Indian friends, used these tiny huts for weekend pleasure, fishing for striped bass, weakfish, porgies, and bluefish from dugout canoes they kept along the banks of the Hudson. It was on this stretch, one summer day, while Dr. Burdell was still alive, that Samuel had first met Katuma. From him, Samuel gained his knowledge of the waterfowl and shellfish that were so abundant that you could catch them with a stick and a pail. Even though Katuma was a day laborer, living in the city, it was not so long ago that his people reigned over this kingdom. Katuma told Samuel and John stories about his grandfather, the son of a chief who ruled the richest oyster beds and spawning grounds in the harbor, his lands stretching from this spot, spreading fifty miles east into the marshes of New Jersey.

It is always best to hide in plain sight, Katuma had told Samuel, after the murder. He had been right. The northern shantytowns and Negro neighborhoods had been the first places the sheriff's men had gone looking for him, tearing in and out of the shacks and hideaways, and startling sleeping families. Fleeing Manhattan posed a greater danger. A lone Negro wandering through the countryside would be suspected of being a fugitive from the South. A fugitive was a boon for the bounty hunters, more so if a slaver discovered there was a link to a murder.

After the murder, Samuel had first gone to seek asylum at his church, and being told that it was not safe, he had come down to the river to Katuma's hut. Quietta brought him some food and drink, and during that stormy weekend, he slept, wrapped in furs and blankets. It was February, and when he stepped out of the hut, snowflakes swirled lightly about, falling like a light ash. The ribbon of the broad river was barely visible, shielded by a blanket of white that rolled over from the opposite shore. The bank of New Jersey disappeared under a dense curtain of snow. Looking into the flurry he could see nothing but the snow itself, the infinity of its white flakes thick as the depth of a million stars.

"Did you come from the lawyer's office?" Samuel asked John.

"Yes, they are all busy. The trial is starting soon," said John.

Katuma shook his head solemnly. "Maybe after the trial they will stop hunting for Samuel."

"You are useless with a knife, Bird," said Quietta, taking the knife from his hands. The vegetables were chopped into ragged pieces. "Here, go fetch me some water. Try to keep the minnows out." She handed John a pot that hung from a tripod, and John headed over to the bank of the river.

Samuel finished scaling the last piece of fish and Katuma placed them in a pan he had rubbed with seasoning. As he was crouching over the pan to start the fire, the Indian paused, his back braced, his head cocked to one side. All of them heard the faint distant scratch of iron scraping against iron.

"Scatter," whispered Katuma. His limbs pushed him upright. He leapt to his feet, and Quietta was instantly gone, dashing silently through the trees. Samuel worried for a second about the boy, at the waterside, but he knew that John was hidden by the high riverbank, so Samuel started to run north. In the winter months, they had all talked about routes of escape, and John could run south on the sandy stretch along the river's edge. The boy was faster than all of them.

A shot rang out like a crack. Samuel heard a bullet whiz into the trees. There were voices now, back by the hut. Samuel kept on running, the adrenaline carrying his limbs at a faster and faster pace. Down South, a manhunt was accompanied by dogs, but now there were no bloodhounds, and without the use of scent, these city men were blind, crashing through bushes without a clear direction.

Samuel kept going, pumping his legs and arms faster and faster. He jumped over a fence, cutting his hand, and he landed in a churchyard. He crept along the shelter of tombstones and then dashed down a lane, under pear trees that were in bloom. Breathless, slowing down to a walk and at other times trotting, he zigzagged through the stable alleys that ran behind the houses, past the little Village kitchen gardens, keeping off the main streets. The sun was still high, and the spring evening had not yet changed to twilight. Better that it was still light—a Negro running behind the houses in the shadows would have created alarm. He bent over, catching his breath, then started again at a saunter, walking casually like a stable hand making his way home. Finally, he reached Sixth Avenue and cautiously stepped into the traffic and crossed the street.

His heart was still beating fast. There was a milk cart standing without a driver, idle at the curb, and he moved to the other side of it. He picked up the horse's brush from its bucket and started brushing the horse, ducking behind the horse's flank, crouched low, to use the vantage to look around. His heart slowed and he regained a steady breath. Across the broad avenue, he spotted a posse of men on horseback, at the corner of Perry Street, seeming to debate which way to turn. The posse turned and headed north on the avenue, and Samuel, hidden behind the milk cart, watched their backsides recede, bouncing in their saddles.

A man hurrying by, wearing spectacles and a black suit, stopped to ask Samuel where to find the apothecary. Samuel pointed him to the apothecary sign, and the man rushed off, tossing Samuel a coin. Samuel saw that not a foot away from him was a poster on a pole: Reward: Wanted in connection to the murder of Dr. Burdell—a Negro, 30 years, tall and strong. The poster had a black face in profile, an etching that could be a caricature of any Negro, with a sloping forehead, tight curly hair, and overly large lips. It so little resembled Samuel that just about any man of color could be assigned the role. There wasn't anyone among the legions of policemen or general population that could point him out as the man who drove Dr. Burdell on the night of the murder. Hide in plain sight, thought Samuel. With the posse fanning out toward the north, he would return to where he had been hiding, close to the riverfront. Katuma and his generations of Lenape, here on this crowding island, understood how to flee. Like fledgling birds, they scattered from a familiar spot, then circled around before coming back again, calmly resettling on their terrain.

THE OPENING OF THE BURDELL MURDER TRIAL.—THE JURY.

# Part III

# CHAPTER TWENTY-TWO

The Case of the People vs. Emma Augusta Cunningham, otherwise called Burdell

*Jury List*

Gilbert Oakley: *Merchant*
Gilbert Barnes: *Iron railing Manufacturer*
David Doughty: *Pickler*
Chauncey Norton: *Bank President*
Francis Gahagan: *Paper business*
William Lockwood: *Produce Dealer*
Luke Coe: *Silk merchant*
John Green: *Builder*
George Tugnot: *Forge worker*
John Archibald: *Fancy Goods*
Charles Hunter: *Merchant*
Frederick Goetze: *Tobacconist*

*May 5, 1857*

The May morning was shot through with a blast of chilled air. Henry Clinton had spent the hours before sunrise at home studying his speech, and then at seven had gone to the jail to visit with Emma and then to his office to review his speech again while the officers brought Emma and her daughters over to the courthouse for the first day of the trial.

He was now heading back to the courthouse. At the courthouse plaza, a congestion of wagons and skittish horses were reined to the hitching posts. It was nearing nine, and from around each corner, pedestrians were streaming toward the building, heading toward the steps in a frantic commotion, some breaking into a run, anxious to get inside—it was like passing through Rome on the morning of a gladiator game.

The plaza emptied except for the last stragglers, and the courthouse was full. From inside the outer rotunda, Clinton could see into the open doors that the courtroom was packed. At the distant end of a corridor, a mob was pushing and jockeying, and the prison officers were leading Emma from the room where she had been held. A group of newspapermen, with bulging eyes and thrusting chins, had somehow gotten into the restricted area. From Clinton's vantage, Emma appeared to be moving with perfect posture and purpose amid the preying scribes, inches from her face, hissing her name. Helen twisted against the horde, her skirts thrashing like the feathers of a bird being toyed with by a cat. Augusta's head flowed along passively in the slipstream. The officers muscled back the reporters, ushering the women into a rear door nearest the defendant's box.

Clinton rounded the corridor to another discreet entrance that the marshals used, and he paused at the doorway to the courtroom before entering. Two tiers of raised balconies curved in a semicircle. The spectators' seating on the upper level was full, with bodies crushed together and hands and arms dangling forward over the rails. Heads bobbed in the back, where there was standing room only. On the bottom level, seats with paneled railings and small swinging gates, led to the prosecution and defense tables. Legal aides darted back and forth among the lawyers, delivering papers and carrying the documents.

Clinton entered and headed to the defense table. No one paid him notice, for all eyes were on Emma and her daughters, now being led in through the opposite entrance. The women were taken to the defendant's box, which was on the right side of the judge, slightly raised, as was the jury box. There was a loud buzz. The spectators whispered and gasped at the sight of her. Clinton's worst fears were confirmed—it was the sound that accompanies a public hanging.

Clinton slipped into his place next to Thayer, who nodded with a glance that said: "Have faith," but there was also a twitch of concern. Clinton kept his facial muscles inscrutably still.

The prosecution's table was across from that of the defense. Hall was seated, scribbling notes, intent on the page. Clinton could tell by his posture that he was deep in the study of his speech. Hall would deliver his opening statement first.

The door behind the judge's dais opened, and the jury stumbled in, as if stunned by the impact of a full courtroom. Clinton made sure not to watch them but kept his eyes on the jury list. By following the sound of their footfalls and placement, he could tell who was moving into which place as they shifted into their arranged seats. The tobacconist wheezed, depositing his body heavily into his chair; he was farthest on the right.

Soon all twelve were seated, and Clinton ventured a glance, not letting his gaze linger for more than a few seconds. He had studied the jury carefully when each man was chosen during the voir dire, and now he burned a picture of them in his mind, lined up in their seats, the way acid burns a quicksilver image on a daguerreotype glass. They sat in two rows of six. The fancy goods merchant was tall and wiry. The bank president sprouted wild whiskers. The pickler looked a little green. From experience, Clinton knew that no matter how swiftly he glanced at a jury, several always caught his eye, reminding him to keep his study of them short.

Clinton stared at the notes on the table in front of him, yet his attention was focused on every sound. A good trial attorney perceives the courtroom through its sounds and never relies on his eyes—coughs and rustles of fabric are cues and signposts in the course of a trial. The scrape of the large chair on the dais meant that the courtroom guard was adjusting the judge's pulpit. Clinton glanced again at Oakey Hall. He was sitting upright with his long legs still crossed, watching Emma and her daughters with a defiant look, as if by their very presence in the defendant's box, he had won the case. Hall's coat was tapered, and the handkerchief that fanned out of his breast pocket was peacock blue. With the gaze of the entire courtroom upon Emma, Clinton studied the jury again. Then he ventured to look at the Cunningham women, seated. Emma was entirely in black, hidden behind an elaborate lace veil that covered her face all the way down to her waist. Augusta wore a modest dress, but her blond hair flowed all around, a little wildly, attracting attention to her like a beacon. She grasped a fan, folded demurely, and fingered it anxiously in her lap. Helen was coiffed with bits of jewelry and bows. Her rosy lips were flushed and defiant. Clinton had told the girls to dress plainly—he had wanted them to look like parish ladies, but Augusta had a strange unearthly glow, and Helen could not help but primp for the crowd.

The clerk issued the sonorous "All rise" as Judge Davies climbed onto the dais, his bony hands grasping for support as he climbed into his pulpit. There was a milling of fabric as the judge adjusted his robes, and the scrape of wood settling against wood. The gavel dropped. All sounds intensified briefly before they began to ripple toward silence.

"Members of the jury, learned counsel, defendant, I bring this court to order." He nodded in each direction. "I hereby commence the Case of the *People versus Emma Hempstead Cunningham*, otherwise called Burdell. I shall call Mr. Abraham Oakey Hall to make the opening statements for the State."

The shuffling in the room raised to a high pitch, then fell silent almost as quickly, for the faster they were silent, the faster the spectacle would begin. Hall stood and sauntered forward, then positioned himself a little off center, keeping his eyes fixed at a point in front of his feet. He scratched his chin and pulled his tie, waiting for the spectators to turn their full attention upon him. The courtroom rippled and flurried with the last twitches of anticipation, and then the last phlegmatic cough came from the far corner of the room. It was a prosecutor's drum roll. Hall began:

"May it please the court." He turned and nodded at the jury box. "Gentlemen of the jury. It is my honorable duty to serve you in this most grave, but important matter.

"My duty today is to prepare your minds to receive the evidence that will be presented to you. You already know that one of your fellow citizens, Dr. Harvey Burdell, was murdered in this very city, in his own house, and it is my role to prove to you that the deed was premeditated, and that someone in his own house did the deed. I propose to prove by the evidence that among the inmates of that house there was one, greater than any other, who had a motive to perpetrate that horrible deed. And that person was a woman, and that woman is this defendant."

His voice had risen to a pitch and he pointed theatrically to Emma, who was covered in the black lace veil. Her fingers gripped the rail, her knuckles white.

"She alone," he continued, "committed as bold, as daring and desperate a crime as we in this city, have ever seen.

"Who was the victim? He was an upright member of the medical profession, a dentist and a man of the Episcopal faith. He was said to have enemies—but, so far as the prosecution has been able to discover, he had no enemy as great as this woman," he said, again pointing. "Dr. Burdell is dead, but the woman who was his deadly enemy sits before you, a veiled picture of sorrow. But I ask the jurors to remember one thing: crime has no sex. A crime is not different whether it strikes from the hand of a man or the hand of a woman."

At this pause, Clinton heard a grunt from the jury box, a reflexive noise indicating assent, like that of a churchgoer responding to a sermon. Clinton did not turn to see who made it, but judging by the direction, it was the forge worker, a stump of a man named George Tugnot.

"You ask," Hall continued, now moving toward Tugnot, "can it be possible that one of the fair sex, upon whom God has placed his seal of purity, should become a midnight assassin and embrace hate, revenge, and jealousy? I answer you, yes—it is possible. When we open the page of history, we perceive that crime knows no sex. In Ancient Rome we read of the daughter of Servius, who drove her chariot over the dead body of her father. And Jezebel and Fulvia, who, when the head of Cicero was brought to her, she spat upon it, and drawing from her bosom a deadly bodkin, thrust it again and again through his tongue. And history recounts to us how Queen Agnes of Hungary bathed her feet in the blood of sixty-three knights, exclaiming, as she did, 'It seems as if I were wading in May dew.'

"This woman, Emma Cunningham, pursued Dr. Burdell with a fiendish hate, jealousy, and revenge until her knife found repose in his heart. And yet should we, the prosecution, or you, the jury, labor under a disability called sympathy?"

Hall paced back and forth in his colorful garb, wound up in a Shakespearean lather.

"The domestics of the house will go upon the stand. We will

take the roof off that dwelling at 31 Bond Street and allow you to gaze into the depths of moral degradation. This woman, the mother of daughters, fastened her greedy, lustful eyes upon Dr. Burdell. We shall show you that Dr. Burdell had made up his mind that life to him was useless so long as he had this shadow at his side. He had made up his mind to put her out of the house of which he was the landlord. And she would have none of it and plotted her revenge.

"She had the motive to murder him: he had spurned her advances and showed interests in other females, fairer and more genteel than herself. He had money and a beautiful home, and she saw an opportunity to affix those for herself, and to that end, she engaged in murder.

"She had the opportunity to murder him. Why, gentlemen, in the whole annals of crime, wherever you place your finger upon a bloody and malicious murder, you will never find an opportunity so carefully provided as that contrived by this woman upon this night. The Doctor was a regular man. She knew his habits. When the cook comes upon the stand she will tell you that the prisoner came down into the kitchen and ordered her to bed, although there was only one servant in the house, with many duties left to perform.

"We shall show to you that the doors and windows of the house were shut tight; the facts utterly exclude the idea of intrusion or interference by any outside person. We shall show that when the errand boy came in the morning to the basement door, it was locked, as well as the back door. We shall prove that the street door had a lock of peculiar construction; that no key was missing. The learned counsel for the defense may argue that when Dr. Burdell came home, some enemy from the outside followed him at his heels upstairs, stabbed him to the heart, and then, bloodstained, rushed from the house. No, gentlemen, Dr. Burdell came in alone. His room was secured and locked up. She had a passkey to his room and she was waiting there for him.

"She sits before you today, a veiled picture of sorrow, hiding behind a widow's black lace, but it is a role, it is a disguise, for she has no sorrow at the death of this man. Was her revenge against him enough of a motive? What is it that she wanted above all? Why it was his property, the fruits of his labor, and most of all his beautiful home. She knew the house was worth a princely sum. She eyed his possessions with greed and set her sights upon him with a plan, not to serve him, but to enter that dwelling at 31 Bond Street and insinuate herself into it. She put him at her mercy. Instead of the mistress of his house, she became his shadow, his persecutor, and his tormentor.

"Now physicians may testify here to tell you that the mortal injury inflicted on that man happened in the briefest possible space of time. And wherever he was struck, the facts will prove that the blow was given by a left-handed person. And she, gentlemen, is a left-handed woman.

"The facts will show that even when the man was dead, and the life-tide flowing rapidly from his heart, that again and again the stabs were inflicted into the unconscious corpse, to make doubly sure that this victim was disposed of.

"Whoever did that deed was in all probability covered from head to foot with blood—blood upon the wall, upon the door, and blood upon the different articles of furniture—blood upon the carpet, drops that had fallen from the bloody dagger. She had the opportunity to burn the bloody clothing in that house that night and she had time before the discovery of the body in the morning to remove all clues. She is alone in the wee hours of the morning, taking her time, feeding her clothes into the stove, while her victim lies dead upon his carpet.

"You will hear from servants, who will testify to the questionable character of the woman before you. We will present a respectable witness, who will testify that she was to take a lease and that Dr. Burdell wanted this 'housemistress' out of his house, and was taking actions to evict her.

"Now gentlemen, I will conclude my brief history of this case. Emma Cunningham was his mistress, with claims to be his wife. If I show you the facts as they relate to this defendant and prove to you that she deserves no sympathy and no respect, then, I have done my duty."

# CHAPTER TWENTY-THREE

The spectators remained hushed in anticipation as Oakey Hall returned to his seat. Clinton pushed his chair back and stepped forward to address the assembly. Listen for your cues, he told himself. Avoid all eyes. "May it please the court." He then took a breath, held the air for several seconds, and began:

"Gentlemen of the jury. We are here on a most sacred mission. We are here to honor our system of justice, whereby, in a capital case, the accused party, if found guilty, is sentenced to death. Your judicial duty is always sacred, but when the crime and punishment are equally grave, the jury must take steps to rid themselves of all prejudice, they must deliberate on the evidence, and be just and generous. Although I am accustomed to addressing juries in capital cases, I have never before risen to address a jury where the prosecution—the District Attorney—has given such an unjust and ungenerous opening beyond all conscience and tact."

He took a few steps and then stopped before the prosecution table, hovering a foot away from Oakey Hall. Hall shuffled in his seat and settled into a position with his arms crossed that was not unlike a physical sneer. Clinton gazed past him and continued: "The District Attorney—in opening this case to you, gentlemen—supposes that this defendant, Mrs. Cunningham, also known as Mrs. Harvey Burdell, is, in advance of all evidence, already proved to be the worst woman that God ever created." Again he paced and then stood still again before Oakey Hall, just inches away from the defense table.

"The abuse heaped upon this defendant by the District Attorney is so outrageous that it would render me unworthy not to mention it. Our District Attorney has overstepped all bounds of decency by ransacking the classics, both sacred and profane, with a view to selecting demons—female fiends if you will. According to Mr. Hall's account, this woman is the agent of the monarch of hell himself, the Devil's special vice-regent upon this earth, and by inference a murderess, none other than Lady Macbeth."

Clinton walked briskly over to the jury box, then half-turned, so that he was still addressing the entire room. "And yet the District Attorney knows that when it comes to the evidence to prove this charge of murder, no such evidence exists. There is no proof that she planned and schemed this murder, or that her motives toward this man were anything but pure. We are barred here from discussing the connections by marriage of this couple, for that is being litigated in another court, but I can attest that her actions were at all times consistent with a woman who was devoted to the needs of her children and to the man of the house. Her actions were consistent with the role of mistress of the house, and she believed her role to be both noble and fulfilling, a role that enriched and benefited everyone in the household.

"On the evening of Doctor Burdell's death, she was in her own bedroom, having instructed the servants at their tasks. She had ordered the cook to bring his water basin for his nighttime wash, and was sewing in preparation for her daughter's return to boarding school. What woman would perform these acts of housewifery at the very same time that she was plotting a vengeful murder, and would be able to carry out such a mortal deed with her children, unaware, in the room above?

"There is no proof that she was waiting for him in his chamber that night, nor that she emerged covered in blood, or burned any clothes in the stove inside the house. In fact, the scientific evidence proves otherwise, that she did not commit this act.

"The District Attorney told you that Mrs. Burdell is a 'veiled picture of sorrow,' and that all the sufferings which she exhibits are entirely feigned." Clinton gestured directly toward Emma. "She comes before you, gentlemen, a 'picture of sorrow' and she comes before you with the weeds of widowhood. It is not the first time she has grieved the loss of a husband. She has faced affliction before, but, unfortunately, the star of her destiny drew her to an ill-fated union with a man who had many adversaries—Dr. Harvey Burdell." Clinton heard a sharp sigh from the back of the room. Such noises were audible tics that signified disagreement or disbelief.

Turning, he took a step closer and looked directly into the faces in the jury box. As was the habit of juries during opening remarks, they directed their gaze back with the keen intensity of students. "As you are fair, intelligent, thinking men, I say you will put aside these stories of infamous females, and not allow them to prejudice your thinking in this case. The District Attorney stated to you that this defendant haunted Dr. Burdell, that she dogged him—that she was his shadow, his persecutor, and his tormentor." He lowered his head and scratched his chin, then glanced quizzically at Hall. "Gentlemen, will the counsel prove any such facts?"

He now gestured toward Hall whose long legs were stretched out, crossed. "I believe that you will agree with me, that the District

Attorney is in error. He neglected to tell you that Harvey Burdell sought Emma Cunningham's favor—which he pursued with all of his attention; that he courted her—he paid her every courtesy that an honorable suitor would pay to an honorable and high-minded woman. Why did he say she hunted him for his fortune?"

Clinton shook his head. "Does he expect to prove anything of the sort? Does he expect that intelligent men would base their judgment in a capital case on gossip from servants? Why would he open this trial with a case that builds upon biblical allusion and in-nuendo? Is it to distract you from your ability to perceive the truth? And does the District Attorney think that twelve intelligent men will be diverted so shamelessly?"

Clinton paused here to gather his breath and made a quick glance around to gauge the effects of his words. His crinkled lips pursed together like a stern headmaster, Judge Davies was look-ing at Oakey Hall, who was staring at his notes, his usual cocky posture deflated, scornful as a schoolboy. The court stenographers paused when Clinton paused, their pens held in the air midsen-tence. A sign of a captivated audience was the amount of white he could detect in eyes of the crowd; drooping lids were a sign of suspicion or disengagement. The eyes across the room were wide and alert.

"I will not now outline all of the evidence of this case," he re-sumed, raising his voice to the back of the balcony, "but I will say that we shall prove by evidence and rules of law that Emma Burdell could not and did not commit this murder. We shall prove with scientific certainty that this is so. We shall prove that someone with ten times the brute strength of this woman entered the chamber on that night and fought the victim. We will show you that the victim fought back with all his strength, up to his last bloody and desper-ate moment."

Clinton raised his voice, now to a pitch. "We shall scientifically prove that no evidence from that bloody battle was found upon this defendant, or in any other portion of the house. This woman did not murder Dr. Burdell. Someone entered that room with vicious and malicious intent, and if you have any reasonable doubt of this woman's guilt, or any idea that there were others who may be guilty, you must acquit. For certainly there were many who held this man in deep contempt—for he was a man with many enemies, including several members of the victim's own family."

Clinton walked slowly away from the jury, and then circled back again, as if he remembered another point. "The rule of law which governs you in this case, gentlemen, is simply this: if the circumstances include any other hypothesis than guilt, it is your bounden duty to acquit. As reasonable men, you must give all your weight to any reasonable doubt that this woman committed this vicious crime. I do not regret putting this case to you, for I wish not only that Mrs. Burdell should be acquitted; I wish that she be vindicated.

"Let me remind you, that an error in judgment, hastily made, on superficial grounds in this verdict brings a penalty of death. It would not rest upon good men's souls to make such a judgment of guilt when there is no evidence of such, no direct witnesses, no motive, and no weapon recovered."

He took a deep breath, and hardened his tone. "I say you will render an acquittal in this case. I know that for certain, because I am convinced that you will act upon the evidence, that you will act upon the law, you will act with your conscience—in other words, gentlemen, you will act as men."

He turned to walk to his chair. He might have elaborated upon the technical details or the virtues of the defendant. He had taken a gamble by keeping it short and chancing a plea to the jury's honor. He sat at his table, pulled in his chair, and waited for the judge to make his next order. A glance at the jury framed them in a tableau: wide eyed, with mouths hung open, still wrapped up in his words. The spectators were just beginning to shuffle in recognition that the speech was finished. By the delayed reaction, he sensed that his gambit had had its desired effect. He had lifted his bow, drawn the arrow, and hit the mark.

# CHAPTER TWENTY-FOUR

*January 31, 1857*

E mma woke before dawn, then fell back to sleep. When she next awoke, it was almost seven, and she was in a cold sweat, frightened by a vivid dream. In the dream, she stood on the stoop of an elegant home. Harvey Burdell appeared at the door and handed her a bundle. The bundle was an infant, wrapped tight—an exchange for something that was not clear. Below at the curb, a carriage waited, and Samuel beckoned, from the top seat. She saw that he was waving a bloody knife. She looked down, and there was blood on her hands and on the baby's blanket. Samuel had cut the umbilical cord, and the baby was bleeding through the blanket. Shaking, she woke, and shook off the strange dream.

From her bed, she could hear the servant boy banging the coal buckets as he carried them down the stairs. She got up and pushed hairpins into the places where it had come loose during the night, tucking strands into the folds of her twist while new strands fell forward, as if nothing was willing to hold.

She had stayed up past midnight the night before, saying goodbye to her straggling guests and directing the maids to clean up after the party. She had been satisfied with the level of gaiety in the parlor and of Ambrose Wicken's charming interlude with Augusta, but the memory of Dr. Burdell's departure had left her feeling weary. As she'd prepared for bed she'd listened for Dr. Burdell—he had never returned, and she suspected he was spending the night out of the house. She had gone to the fireplace and torn a bristle from the small hearth broom and made her way down the tall stairway to his door. There was only the faintest flame left in the hall lamp, lowered by Hannah. Emma had placed the bristle of the broom in the lower crack of door, down low, where it sat in the pile of the carpet. If it were unmoved in the morning, she would know that he had stayed out the entire night.

On her way downstairs now, she saw the bristle still on the door, unmoved. He had not come home—and the knowledge instilled a hard feeling of resolve.

She returned to her room and began to dress slowly, putting on her best suit. It was Friday. Today was the day that Augusta was riding with Ambrose Wicken, and Helen was leaving for school the following day. Emma determined that it was time that she took matters into her own hands.

In the kitchen, she asked, "Has Dr. Burdell rung for his breakfast?"

"He has not rung, this morning, Ma'am," said Hannah. Alice was at the kitchen table slurping some porridge. Both of them seemed to be mocking her, for certainly they knew from the bed linens that he was often sleeping out of the house at night.

"Hannah, would you send John to bring Samuel around. I would like to use the carriage."

"I don't know if I should tell Samuel to come around unless that's the orders from the master," replied Hannah, making herself an obstacle.

Emma did not have the patience to bicker. "Very well, then I shall see to it myself," she said firmly. She gathered her coat and headed out of the house, pulling on her gloves. The stable was at the end of the street, near the Bowery, and she found Samuel inside.

"I will be taking the carriage now," she said.

"I am waiting for my orders for the day, as I usually do," he replied.

"I believe Dr. Burdell is occupied and will not need the carriage this morning."

He gazed at her with a quizzical expression.

"Have you ever driven Dr. Burdell to the home of Commodore Vanderkirk?" she asked.

"I have been to many a home, Ma'am."

"I want you to drive me there."

"To Mr. Vanderkirk?"

"Yes, now. I am taking the carriage. You need not wait for any other orders. My own orders will suffice. Do as I say. Hitch up the horse. And put on your livery." Samuel stiffened, as if confused. He started moving to ready the horse. Emma marched out of the stable to wait on the sidewalk while the carriage was readied, and soon Samuel led the carriage out to meet her. He had put on his red jacket and his tan boots. He opened the door for her, and then he climbed onto the driver's seat.

They rode slowly north on Broadway. The morning had a wintry pall, with deep clouds that hung low in the sky, sooty as smoke. They turned onto Fourteenth Street and then onto Fifth Avenue. A few blocks farther, at Sixteenth Street, Samuel stopped before an enormous limestone residence, ablaze with light. Emma stepped down and hesitated before the door. Atop the doorway was a carving of a seafaring ship, as if it were a coat of arms. She pulled a brass bell and heard distant footsteps echo across the marble floor. A butler, in formal attire, pulled the heavy door open and said dryly, "Good morning, Madame."

Emma curtsied, but before she could speak, the butler said, "I regret to inform you that Madame Vanderkirk will not be seeing anyone today. If you leave your card, she will be most obliged to have you return when she is receiving visitors."

"I am here to see Commodore Vanderkirk," stated Emma, without preamble. "It is a matter of importance." The butler faltered, which indicated to her that the Commodore was most likely at home.

"May I ask who is calling?" he said. Emma reached into her purse and handed the butler one of the cards that she had ordered for the party that said only "31 Bond Street." The butler looked at it skeptically, and Emma said, "He will know who I am, and he will know my business."

"I shall inquire," the butler said, admitting her into the front hall, which had a black and white marble floor. The butler slowly mounted a tall stairway with her card in hand. To her left, Emma peered into the library, a vast room lined with cases of rare leather volumes. There was a writing table with a felted blotter, and a rack of newspapers, carefully folded, as if they were fine linens. A tray table sat readied before an armchair. It was set with fine china and crystal glassware and had a domed silver chafing dish, with a frost of steam across the top, spread for the Commodore's breakfast. It appeared that anything the man needed was brought forth to him, and when he was done, it was whisked away.

Emma remained waiting for a long while, examining the surroundings while the brass pendulum in the hall clock swung back and forth. Finally she heard the steady footsteps of the butler returning.

"Come this way," the butler said. She followed him down a long corridor to a rear wing of the house with numerous closed doors that might be closets or anterooms, used by servants. At the very end was a door, and the butler opened it to the cold air of the outdoors and a private service alley. Her carriage had been moved into this alley, where it sat waiting, and the butler stepped out and opened the door for her. He stood there imperiously in his black uniform, waiting for her to enter. Furious, Emma lifted her skirts and climbed the carriage step, ducked into the carriage, and settled on the seat.

"I am sorry, Madame," the butler said, "the Commodore is not at home."

Of course he is at home, she thought, I saw his breakfast waiting. But she could not bear to dignify the insult and manner of her dismissal with a response.

The butler shut the door of the cab, and she heard him whisper instructions to Samuel as the carriage started to move along the narrow driveway, flanked on one side by a wall and on the other side by the enormous façade of the house, which, at this close angle, loomed as large as a hotel. There was a row of kitchen windows at the lowest level, and Emma could see many cooks and servants scurrying about. Vegetables were piled by the sinks, and roasts were lined up beside the large iron ovens, and tarts laid out in rows on baking sheets, as if in preparation for a banquet or a ball. And there, standing to oversee the activity, was Mrs. Vanderkirk, a heavyset woman, recognizable not by her dress, for she was wearing ordinary attire, but by the flash and solidity of her jewelry, the gems on her hands evident, even as the carriage slid by.

The carriage moved several yards past the kitchen windows, under a portico at the corner of the mansion, and stopped. Ahead, Emma could see that the driveway forked left to the stables and right past a glass conservatory where the carriage could exit again on Fifth Avenue. Then the carriage door opened and the corpulent figure of Commodore Vanderkirk climbed in beside her.

"I do not know the reason for your visit, but you compromise me by coming to my house," he stated without greeting.

Startled by his presence and his tone, Emma faltered. "Sir, you must be mistaken by my purpose. I am here on the very same business about which you recently visited Dr. Burdell at my home."

"A woman does not come to speak privately at the home of a gentleman. It has a certain significance that would not be appreciated by my wife. She jumps to conclusions when I receive a lady behind closed doors."

"You must know I have no illicit intention. I am here to discuss the sale of land. There is no other business between us."

"That matter is between myself and Dr. Burdell. By coming alone, I suspect you are going behind his back. And furthermore I do not conduct business with women."

Emma found herself emboldened by her own transgression, now that she was cramped in the small carriage beside him. Even if she wanted to, she could not retreat. "Sir, with all due respect, you have come outside to meet me, and so I suspect you have a desire to hear what I have to say." Her voice was tenuous, and she nervously hastened to speak her message. "Dr. Burdell did not reveal to you the true ownership of the land. If you wish to buy it, I am able to sell it to you directly."

"This is most irregular," he said. "And who do you pretend to be? Are you the wife? The mistress? Perhaps it would be useful for me to instruct you that frauds are committed every day and I should have no reason to suspect anything but a ruse." The Commodore put his fingers together, tapping them impatiently.

She lifted her chin and spoke with the clipped diction of one who has been insulted. "I purchased the deed you desire with money from my daughter's dowry, left by her deceased father. The land in question is my daughter's, and I am in a position of authority with regard to her affairs. I shall handle this matter myself. It is my own property, not that of Dr. Burdell."

The Commodore, pondering her, said, "Your friend, the Doctor, has many schemes afloat. I saw him just yesterday, and once again, I made him a fair offer for the property, but he refused. He tells me he has other plans for this same plot. He told me that he intends to finish up this sale and then he is going to sail to Europe." Emma flushed, furious at the reference, for it conjured up an image of the woman from the hotel, strolling with Dr. Burdell along a ship's deck as they crossed the Atlantic.

Emma took a deep breath and spoke to him directly. "I know that you desire this land for your own ambitions, and it would be well to discuss a price."

"So now you are a financier! Isn't this all above your head? Hah," he said, "certainly, everything has a price in this city—land, political favors, female companionship—"

"I would like one hundred and fifty thousand dollars," said Emma, interrupting, surprised by her own brashness.

The commodore appeared visibly subdued, and his expression turned sour. "I see you are a profiteer! And if I turn down your sum?"

"I shall marry my daughter to her fiancé. He is from the South and would most likely desire this property to do with as he pleases. But, sir, I would prefer to finalize this deal with you."

He jostled in his seat and pulled out his gold watch. "I am wasting my time and the money is of little consequence to me. Hand over the deed, and I will give you one hundred and fifty thousand dollars. I am tired of bickering over it, I really prefer that this be done," he ordered.

Stunned, Emma quickly countered, "I will certainly accommodate you, but I do not have the document here. I shall arrange to take the deed to my solicitor, Mr. Billings on Worth Street, and he will oversee the sale for that sum."

"Very well, then." The Commodore opened the door to the carriage and squeezed his large body out. "I shall send my own counsel. Make sure it is there at four o'clock tomorrow afternoon," then he slammed it shut behind him. Emma heard him pass by the horse and say to Samuel, "Be off, boy. Use the stable gate."

The carriage veered left into the large stable yard. They sat before the closed gate until a groom came scurrying to lift the latch. The prospect of the Commodore's offer was almost too large to absorb. Emma slumped back in the seat, still rattled by his indignant tone. But was it possible that her worries were finally over? That she could spend the entire summer at her leisure in Saratoga or Newport? She imagined Augusta in a dress styled after the classical manner, with an Empire waist and a blue sash, standing with Ambrose Wicken at the altar in a dove grey suit. What were the fashions in Paris this year?

The groom pulled open the gate that opened onto Seventeenth Street, a street lined with small buildings and stables that served the mansions on Fifth Avenue. As the carriage turned, a servant from the kitchen appeared with a barrel of remains. She dropped a bit of the trash, and the wind picked it up, and twisted it into eddies around the girl's feet, then she poured the barrel into a street receptacle.

Some women were huddled, waiting; they rushed forward, wraithlike, their cheeks sallow and bloated, their eyes lusterless, their teeth discolored, and their hair matted with dirt. The women plunged their arms up to the shoulders in the trash bins and pulled out feathers, bits of fat, bones, and entrails of fowl and ate ravenously from the waste.

A little girl, about ten years of age, pulled out a ham bone still pink with bits of flesh. Upon seeing the carriage moving past, she ran up to the window with a taunting manner and paraded before it, mimicking an actress strutting across the stage. Her face was defiant, and she pulled up her tattered frock to her armpits, exposing her naked body. She laughed at her own impudence and walked up and down before the mansion gate until a group of boys coming along the other side of the street shouted, clapped, then threw sticks at her and the little girl tired of her act. She shouted some half-worded insults, then, with the quickness of a cat, she scurried away.

# CHAPTER TWENTY-FIVE

Emma fished in her purse and jiggled the large key in the front door to unlock the heavy bolt. She could tell by the hat on the hall table that Dr. Burdell had now returned home. The errand boy came forward to take her coat.

"Are there patients waiting?"

"None today, Ma'am. Since it is Friday," he said. "Dr. Burdell has been settling his business and is going out to his bank and other errands."

She rushed past him, upstairs, past the closed door to Dr. Burdell's office where the light above the transom was burning bright. She would take the deed right away, downtown to Mr. Billings, for safekeeping. She hurried to the third floor and closed her bedroom door behind her. She sat on the vanity stool, pulling off her gloves. She opened the drawer, and as her hand entered the space, her fingers grazed the wood at the bottom of the drawer and she moved her hand around inside where it encountered the four sides of the drawer. She moved it again and again before she dared to look down and confirm what she sensed—that the drawer was empty and her document was not there.

She reached around and around, pulled the drawer open wide, but it was empty. Then she yanked the opposite drawer. Bottles and crèmes rattled as she pulled the drawer out too far, causing the contents to spill to the floor.

She was overcome by a sense of alarm. Perhaps she had forgotten and placed the deed inside the closet. She ran to her armoire and began thrashing to get to the shelves, pushing aside her muslins and petticoats. She pulled everything out, causing clothes and fabric to fall in a pile, creating more hiding places and confusion, clawing harder as a surge of panic came rushing over her in waves.

She hadn't put the deed in her armoire or in her closet, nor under the mattress or behind a picture frame. She let out a muffled cry of despair at the certainty of what she had known at the first moment she put her gloves in the drawer—Harvey Burdell had taken her deed.

The minutes passed and Emma fell to the ground defeated, sitting in a pile of scattered clothes and the disorder of her room. Fractures were spreading deep into the most believing parts of her, and the fearful emotions that now began to rise up were mixed with outrage. Harvey Burdell would rue the day that he had the effrontery to enter her room and remove her possession. With her heart still beating heavily, she stood up, tossing the clothing that was in her way. She knocked over the vanity stool as she made her way to her door and headed downstairs. The sight of Dr. Burdell's closed door so invoked her outrage of the theft that she was overcome with the urge to confront him, her anger and agitation rising to a pitch. With one knuckle, she knocked, pounding loudly and insistently.

There was no answer so she put her ear against the door and envisioned papers lying across the desk, and on top of them, her deed. She turned the knob.

"Emma." She jumped back, startled to see Dr. Burdell behind her, coming up the stair.

"I am looking for you," she said defiantly. He stopped at the top stair, facing her. She was blocking his door.

"Step aside, I have work to do," he said dismissively.

"You have taken my deed," she said.

"What? I have done no such thing."

"You have, and you have lied to me about its worth."

"You are mad. I have no interest in something that is valueless. Nor do I intend to pay you for it. You have lost your chance and my offer is withdrawn."

"You have stolen it and are selling it."

"Move away from my door. I am expecting a visitor and I have business to do." Downstairs, the doorbell rang, and John answered it, and then she heard the singsong voice of a woman. Her mind raced with the urge to confront Dr. Burdell—to chastise him for his betrayals, his infidelity, and his scurrilous behavior.

"You have been out every night with another woman, and your treatment of me has been dishonorable!" she declared.

He sighed. "If you say so."

"Did you not promise to marry me and say that after we were to be married that we were going to Europe?" her voice was rising, incredulous.

"Yes, I suppose you are right." His tone was resigned, as if he were talking to someone whose mind was addled.

"And that we would live in this house as husband and wife, or move to Fifth Avenue?"

"Of course, of course."

"Is anything the truth? Do you lie to get your way? Do you believe that my daughters and I are just figurines for you to move about for your own purposes? That I wouldn't see a magistrate and bring a suit against you for breach of promise?"

He glowered, now rising to anger himself. "Will you leave me alone? I have a visitor. She is waiting downstairs," and he pushed

Emma aside and entered the office, shutting the door in her face, and turning the lock.

Rattled, she banged at the door vehemently, repeatedly calling out, loudly, "You will regret this. You have taken my papers, and I will see that they are returned to me."

Her mind raced to the fact that she had nothing to show the Commodore, and if there were any delay in presenting the deed, he would suspect she was a fraud. Then she remembered Mr. Billings—he knew of the transfer of Augusta's dowry and kept slips of paper marking her transactions. He would certainly be able to help her secure her rightful claim to the land. And she thought of Ambrose Wicken. She could appeal to him for advice; as Augusta's suitor he would have an active interest in the matter. She rushed back to her room and went to her desk, where she took out her note paper and still standing, hastily penned a note,

> *Mr. Wicken,*
>
> *I am most grateful for your offer of friendship and advice, and I am now in need of such, but it must be kept in the strictest confidence.*
> *As you know, I have a deed to a parcel of land purchased with proceeds of my daughter Augusta's dowry. I know you are a man of honorable intentions. I am obliged if you would meet me tomorrow to discuss this matter*
> *My daughter Helen will be leaving for school in the morning, and after her departure, I will come with the carriage to your hotel at 1 p.m.*
>
> *E. Cunningham*

She sealed the envelope with a drip of wax and hastily wrote Ambrose Wicken's name on the envelope and then headed downstairs to place it on the hall table. In the foyer, she passed the visitor who had just rung the bell, a plump, middle-aged woman who nodded anxiously and said, "Good morning, Ma'am." Emma rushed by with barely a nod and spoke to John.

"When Mr. Wicken rings to take Augusta for a ride, please see that he has this letter," she told him.

Next, she determined that she would get the keys from Alice so she could use them to examine Dr. Burdell's room, after he had gone out. When she reached the kitchen, Hannah started complaining right off.

"I won't be able to finish the bread, because I have run out of yeast. There is none in the larder, for no one has kept up with the provisions."

"Where is Alice?" snapped Emma.

"Doing the bedrooms, I suppose."

"She is not upstairs, Hannah. She has not been seen since I returned."

Hannah avoided Emma's eyes. "Am I supposed to make bread rise without yeast, and also to keep track of the parlor maid?" she muttered.

"You are insolent! Where is she? Is Alice in the basement?"

"I don't have eyes at the back of my head to see where she goes while I am at the stove." Furious, Emma marched into the pantry, which served as a washing room. There was a door to the back garden and another door to the basement. Emma opened the basement door and stepped onto the rickety stair that descended down into the cold space, feeling her footing on the crooked boards. High windows emitted discreet shafts of murky light, and as she descended, she made out the shadows of iron cranks that served the dumb waiters and deep stalls of inky black coal set against the fortresslike walls. She heard a cough and as her eyes adjusted saw Alice, seated on a crate.

"Alice!" She heard rustling, "Is that you?"

"I came down here because I am feeling poorly," the girl said. "I have a cold in my feet, and needed to rest."

"I am looking for the keys, do you have them?"

"I don't leave 'em around, 'cause I know you're always lookin' for 'em." Alice slurred.

"You are drinking whiskey!" Emma exclaimed. Beside Alice was a barrel, with a bottle of whiskey on top.

"It's a cure for my rheumatism, just as my doctor says." Alice sat with her legs loose in front of her, her skirts askew. She leaned over and stretched her legs out, and as she did so, she became unbalanced and toppled sideways, falling right off the crate.

"Get up, and give me the keys, I say!" ordered Emma. Alice scrambled to her feet and tottered toward Emma at the stairs. Alice clutched her apron and pulled the large ring from its pocket, clasping the key ring to her breast, in a challenge.

"Give them to me!"

"You always wanted these keys, now, didn't you?"

Emma rushed toward her and snatched the keys. She abruptly slapped Alice across the face. Alice shrieked and toppled forward onto the bottom stair. She sat on the stair, holding her hand to her face, mumbling curses. Emma declared, "I am dismissing you immediately, for drunken conduct. You are rude and insubordinate. I want you out of this house."

"Dismiss me? I should speak with the Doctor, first, so I might tell him how you was spying on his meetings, and stepping out of bounds, all over this house."

"Go upstairs!" said Emma. Alice gripped the banister and crawled forward up the rickety staircase with Emma behind her. When they reached the top, Emma opened the back door to the yard and pushed Alice out, who stumbled into the cold. Emma stepped out after her, pointing to the back gate.

Alice stood, shivering in the yard, where the snow was drifted against the fences. She let out a loose, petulant cry and rubbed her face, as if the combination of the cold air and the sting of the slap had stunned her sober.

"Be gone, before I fetch the police."

Alice turned and stumbled toward the back gate, whining, "There's a better place to work than here, I declare. There is many a lady who wants my services. I shall be placed in a finer home than this," she said, staggering toward the alley.

Back inside, Emma closed the door to the yard. She walked into the pantry and was about to enter the kitchen when she heard someone speaking through the door.

"And what about the water?" It was the voice of the lady she had seen upstairs in the hall.

"There is a sink with a pump to the cistern in the back," answered Dr. Burdell, who was in the kitchen as well. What was he doing there? He never entered the kitchen.

"No running pipes from the street? Well, it is a spacious kitchen and I have made do with less. And it's a good cook that keeps a house in shape, I always say."

"Hannah is a formidable cook," replied Dr. Burdell. "She works from five in the morning to ten o'clock at night, except Sunday, when she leaves after a midday meal."

"I do my best, sir," said Hannah. "Even when my provisions are low."

"What about the lady who has the position, now?" asked the woman.

"She will be leaving shortly," said Dr. Burdell.

"Is there any problem?"

"No, no problem. She will be sailing for Europe, any day now, with her daughters."

"Europe! Well, some say it's a superior place, but I don't understand why some folks aren't happy with what they find here at home."

"Mrs. Stansbury, if you are interested in moving here, I have prepared a lease for your use of the upstairs floors, in exchange for your housekeeping duties."

"Now that I have seen the whole house, I am certain I shall be happy here. My husband is getting on in years, and he will be most comfortable. I shall bring him by tomorrow to look over the lease and to sign it."

"Very well," said Dr. Burdell, and Emma heard them exit the kitchen, their footsteps pounding as they went up the stairway above her head. There was no exit from the pantry except through the kitchen, unless she went out to the backyard and followed the alley out to Bond Street, and then reentered the front door. Emma pondered the conversation—she was going to Europe? She let several moments elapse and then stepped through the kitchen door.

Hannah looked up at her, with a mirthful look on her face. "I didn't know you was going on a trip, Mrs. Cunningham," she said.

"Oh, keep your mouth shut, Hannah." Emma took a market basket from the kitchen table, and grabbed her hooded cloak, which hung on a peg. She rushed out of the kitchen and left under the stoop, heading to the Bowery.

# CHAPTER TWENTY-SIX

*May 6, 1857*

Henry Clinton passed through City Hall Park on his way to the courthouse. The cherry blossoms gave off a heady fragrance and the white marble columns on the façade of City Hall glistened through the branches. Clinton stopped next to the fountain to tie his shoe as cool water flowed through lion's head medallions into a sequence of bronze pools. In the sequestered stillness of the early morning, one got the impression that civic life was still conducted in a sylvan glade in Ancient Greece.

At the courthouse steps, he dropped a penny in the hand of a newsboy. Heading inside, he scanned the headlines, all of them about the trial. "Prosecution's case continues with Servants to testify today." Near the bottom of the page, his eye caught a single item: "Abraham Oakey Hall a Mayoral Nominee; Party Leaders shift support from Mayor Wood." Although the mention was small, Clinton was astonished by the brashness of the timing. It was as if the party leaders were anticipating a win by way of a verdict for the prosecution. Clinton snapped the paper shut and dashed up the steps.

In the defendant's room, Emma sat at a table, waiting for the court session to begin. A group of stocky matrons hovered. "Will it be much like yesterday?" she asked Clinton as he arrived, referring to the long day inside the courtroom.

"Today, the servants are at the top of the roster," said Clinton. "This will be more difficult. Try not to show emotion, even if you think they are not telling the truth." It was best that her face was hidden under a veil, for the strain of these months in jail was clearly wearing her down. The jury would be searching for signs of guilt, ready to read into her slightest expression a vision of Lady Macbeth, wringing her hands in blood.

An officer announced it was time to enter the court. Emma carefully positioned the veil over her head and headed to the courtroom with Augusta and Helen. In their seats, they sat with their hands clasped together, each girl in her fashionable garb, a somber veiled figure between them.

Clinton sat at the defense table as the courtroom buzzed with the preparations of spectators anxiously struggling for seats. The preliminaries were delivered and silence descended. The court crier announced the first witness: Hannah Conlon. As she positioned herself into the chair, she looked like a cook, even without an apron. She had a ruddy face and wore a clean gingham dress. Her white fluted collar was the only indication that she was not spending the day in the kitchen. She crossed her palms, as if sitting for a portrait. Uncomfortably elevated in the witness box, she appeared determined to mimic the airs and manners of her superiors.

Oakey Hall slowly led Hannah through the familiar details of the crime, how the servant boy arrived and screamed for her to run upstairs; how Mrs. Cunningham and her daughters ran downstairs at the commotion; how Augusta dropped dead away in a faint; and how no one had the presence of mind to send the boy out to find help, except Hannah herself. She shuddered at the memory, clasping her hand to her heart. "Oh, Lord," she said, crossing herself, "it was the very worst calamity."

"Did Mrs. Cunningham attempt to go to his aid, or to assist him in any way?"

"She didn't weep. There was no move to go near him. I don't know if she expected *me* to go to him, but I could see that his head was nearly unattached. The blood was running ankle deep. There was nothing anyone could do, that was plain to see." Spectators in the gallery gasped.

"Did she appear mournful, or distraught?"

"I recollect her words, she said 'I saw him before suppertime, just last night.'"

"And she stated this calmly?"

"She said it matter of fact, that was all. Like she didn't have a care in the world. She didn't even send the boy to the precinct house." There was the hint of an Irish roll to her r's, but she was straining to suppress them. Clinton listened, glancing at Emma. Her hands were now at her lap, twisting and retwisting a handkerchief.

Oakey Hall continued his interrogation of the cook, and her observations of the household. Hannah was dogged in her presentation, outlining the chores and routines and insisting at every chance that she was overworked, and making her resentment against her mistress plain. Hall swaggered back and forth in his peg trousers, his blond pompadour oiled and waved. He had the habit of patting his cravat, to make sure it was securely tucked into his vest, like a bird puffing his colors. He deftly moved the witness through the sequence of the events and the jury remained alert.

"Did Dr. Burdell bring a visitor into the kitchen, on the day that he died?"

"He did, sir, a lady was coming in to look at the house, Dr. Burdell was showing her all the rooms."

"And where did you see her?"

"She came into the kitchen, and she said that she would be pleased to take the rooms upstairs and to take Mrs. Cunningham's place."

"Did Dr. Burdell or the lady say why she was replacing Mrs. Cunningham?"

"Why, he said she was leaving on a long trip, faraway, to Europe, I believe."

"Would you state Mrs. Cunningham's manner and appearance, later on that night, on the evening of January thirty-first?"

"Well, she appeared regular, but she came down to kitchen earlier than usual and ordered me to go to bed."

"At what time?"

"It was about ten o'clock and I had much work to finish up in the kitchen."

"And did you go up to your room at that time?"

"Well, I had myself the rest of the pork, and I went upstairs at ten thirty."

Hall repeatedly inquired on the point, as to why she was asked to retire early, with Hannah repeating herself, until the Judge finally intervened, saying, "We have heard from the witness sufficiently on this matter." After more questions about Hannah's sleep patterns and her insistence that she heard no noises all night, Hall finally retired the witness.

Clinton stood. He aimed to conduct a swift cross-examination without appearing to be unsympathetic to the cook. He knew that with every question, the jury would be pondering his intent. By questioning less, he caused them to ponder deeper.

"Mrs. Conlon," began Clinton, "did Dr. Burdell discuss his daily plans with you?"

"Why no, sir, he didn't come to the kitchen much at all, that was the housemistress's job."

"Did he discuss his business or his travel with you?"

"No, sir, I was not privy."

"Did he discuss any travel arrangements he was making with Mrs. Cunningham, to go to Europe together, perhaps?"

"Why no, I didn't hear nothing about that."

"Now, you said that Mrs. Cunningham came to the kitchen on the evening of January thirty-first. Was she expecting Dr. Burdell home at his usual time?"

"He usually returned by eleven o'clock, and she told me to fill the water basin."

"She asked you to put fresh water in Dr. Burdell's basin?"

"She asked me to carry up the water, and place it in his water basin on my way to bed. It wasn't my duty, but there was no chambermaid." Hannah sniffed.

"Did you take the fresh water upstairs?"

"I did. I filled a pitcher and I carried it all the way upstairs and placed it in his water closet in the hall."

"Did you see Mrs. Cunningham after that?"

"I saw her in her bedroom as I passed by on my way to the attic. Her door was open, and she was packing some things."

"Did she say anything else to you?"

"No, she just bade me good night. She called out, 'Good night, Hannah.'"

"Thank you, Ma'am, that is all," said Clinton, nodding and turning quickly to his seat; his only intention was to show that a person's actions could be given sinister overtones, or simply be seen as part of an everyday routine.

Next, the chambermaid was called. Alice Donahoe stepped up, wiry, her lanky hair topped by a Sunday hat. As Hall queried the witness, he sprinkled artificial flatteries among his questions with his elongated drawl, appearing to show the housemaid respect. He asked about her duties and about the layout of the house. "During your period working at 31 Bond Street, did you ever have any difficulty with your master?" he asked Alice.

"Never, sir, by any chance," said Alice with emphasis. "Dr. Burdell was a respectable gentleman, one of the finest."

"Did you have difficulties with the housemistress?"

"With Mrs. Cunningham! There wasn't nobody in the house that didn't have trouble with her."

"Objection," said Clinton from his chair.

"I will ask the witness to refrain from speaking for others," said the Judge.

Hall continued. "Madame, to your knowledge, was Mrs. Cunningham married to Dr. Burdell?"

"Objection, Your Honor!" Clinton called out loudly, now raising himself from his seat. "Questions about the marriage are prohibited from this proceeding by prior order and such inquiries are barred from testimony."

The Judge looked squarely at Oakey Hall and stated: "Mr. Hall, I will remind you, the matter about which you speak is being litigated in another courtroom. There will be no questioning on the subject."

"Excuse me, I withdraw," said Hall, fiddling with the architecture of his large cravat.

The Judge spoke to the jury and said, "The jury shall disregard this question, and make no inference from it."

"Let me ask the witness, then," Hall continued, "since you attended to Dr. Burdell's bedroom, did you observe from the bedding, that two persons slept in his bed?"

"Objection!" said Clinton.

"Overruled, the witness may answer that," said Judge Davies.

"Well," hinted Alice coyly, "on certain mornings, I saw that the covers was mussed and the pillows looked used, like two was sleeping there instead of one. I found hairpins on the mattress." Her eyes darted about, and she leaned forward. "What went on in the room, I can only guess," she said.

"Was it a regular occurrence that you found the bedding disheveled?"

"Regular enough," she said. "Up until the month of January. On some nights, the bed wasn't used at all. Dr. Burdell was spending his nights out. He'd come back in the early morning, wearing the same clothes he had on the day before." At this mention, there was a stirring throughout the courtroom, at the implication that Dr. Burdell had a mistress, planting the idea of jealousy as a motive.

"Were others in the house aware of his habits of sleeping away from home?"

"I kept quiet and didn't talk about it because I was worried that I might be compromised if I told tales. I have been a chambermaid in New York for seven years. It was the depth of winter, and I feared to lose my job."

Clinton listened, subdued. He had to be careful. Too many objections might elicit sympathy for the working girl. He hoped that if she spoke long enough, she would hang herself.

Alice gave off a rattling cough and Hall was quick to offer her a glass of water from a tumbler. "Thank you, sir; I'll thank you for it." She drank from the glass.

"Did you ever observe the defendant, Mrs. Cunningham, entering Dr. Burdell's room when he was not at home?"

"Oh, my, she went in there many times. The Doctor always kept his rooms locked. I saw her entering that room when he was away, I cannot tell a lie about it."

"Miss Donahoe, I trust you are telling us the truth, and honoring your oath and your duty."

"I saw her with my own eyes. One time, I even saw her listening at the door to the parlor. Dr. Burdell was inside with a gentleman."

"So would you say she was in the habit of tracking his movements?"

"She certainly kept a watch on him. She had a halter around his neck, that's for sure. I may not be a lady, but I knows about the truth." The room was hushed and Alice's voice was rising.

"And on the day of the murder, was she keeping track of his movements?"

"She was all over the house, checking on everything. When I was downstairs, passing by the stair, there was a big argument."

"Which day was this?"

"Why, Friday, sir, the very day he was slaughtered."

"Can you tell me the nature of the argument?"

"She was at his door, banging. It was about some papers or a paper that was stolen. Then I went about my business. I headed to the basement. That's when she came down looking for the house keys."

"Did you give her your house keys?"

"She grabbed them away from me, just as you please."

"Afterward, what did you do?"

"I tried to prevent her from taking them. I told her, with all due respect, that she could not have them, they were the possession of the Doctor. Then she slapped me just as hard as she pleased, and it sent me reeling." There were faint gasps from the audience. "I told her I would not work in such a place. I told her I was finished, and that I would not suffer in such a way. I went to the back door and left that very day, without even getting my things." Alice appeared distraught and reached for her glass of water. Hall stepped forward with a look of concern and refilled her tumbler from the pitcher. When she finished sipping down the water, she coughed again, and gasped, as if she was having trouble breathing. Hall paced, patiently.

After she had sipped some more water, Hall deliberated and

then said, "Miss Donahoe, I do not want to disturb you any further. That shall be all. I thank you for your testimony." He quickly retreated, for she had served her purpose.

"Does the defense wish to cross-examine this witness?" asked Judge Davies, who looked at Clinton squarely, but the task was to be Thayer's. "Yes, Your Honor," replied Thayer, standing up, pushing his hair out of his eyes.

"Easy," Clinton whispered, sotto voce as Thayer edged behind, approaching the bench. By agreement, Clinton would show deference to witnesses, as he had with Hannah, and allow Thayer to be the one to go on the attack. It seemed insincere to a jury when a lawyer shifted his stance. Thayer had an aggressive nature, which was valuable when impeaching a witness, but untethered, at cross-examination, it could leave the least credible witness looking wounded and sympathetic. Clinton hoped that the young lawyer was up to the task. The workingmen in the jury would have little sympathy if the defense badgered the servants. Alice, however, was hostile to the defendant, and discrediting her testimony would take a certain amount of skill and finesse.

'Miss Donahoe . . . ," Thayer began, his voice trailing off, as if he were still formulating his thoughts in his mind. "Madame . . . ," he began again. Alice pulled herself upright, readying herself, with a look of scorn. "Let me understand something. Did you say there was a halter around Dr. Burdell's neck? Was it a real rope or an artificial rope?" Thayer asked, speaking with a puzzled tone.

"Well, sir, the imaginary kind, the kind a lady holds over a man, to keep him in her command."

"Do you mean the kind of rope a wife might pull to bring her husband home from the taverns?" asked Thayer, bringing laughter from the spectators.

"Dr. Burdell hardly drank," she said emphatically. "I always considered him very refined—a correct gentleman."

"And Mrs. Cunningham? Was she a proper lady?"

"Oh, heavens no! As a mother and a widowed lady, it was most improper for her to be in his room late at night."

"Is it improper for any wife to be in her husband's room at night?"

"Well, if I could look through the keyhole, I could tell you if it was improper or not." Again the room erupted in laughter, and Alice seemed to take pride in her bawdy joke.

"I trust you never did look through your employer's keyhole, did you Miss Donahoe?" and Alice blushed at the insinuation. "On the night of the murder," he continued, "on Friday night, January thirty-first, did you observe any unusual behavior?"

"I was not there in the evening of the occurrence, if you please."

"You did not sleep in your bedroom in the attic with Hannah that night?"

"That was my usual place to sleep, but I was not there, because I gave my dismissal."

"Wasn't it Mrs. Cunningham who dismissed you from your job that very morning?"

"Mrs. Cunningham got it wrong," Alice replied, brashly. "I took leave on my own accord."

"Is it true that Mrs. Cunningham went looking all over the house for you and found you in the basement?"

"After I finished in the bedrooms, I was feeling poorly and got a cold in my feet and felt ill, so I went to the basement to rest."

"Did she find you in the cellar with a whiskey bottle, and you could hardly stand?" The spectators shuffled and murmured. Oakey Hall pursed his lips, listening.

"No, sir, that is not the case," replied Alice, tartly. "I had the rheumatism, and I went down to the cellar for a rest."

"Did you go down into the cold basement to drink whiskey and when you became intoxicated you could not stand up? And did your mistress tell you she would have to let you go because you drank too much?"

"That's not true!" said Alice, indignant. "If she saw me on the ground, it was because I was going down on my knees to say a prayer to God."

"Were you intoxicated on the morning of January thirty-first? Answer the question, yes or no," said Thayer.

"Please allow me, sir," said Alice imploringly, turning to the Judge.

"I asked you, yes or no!" Thayer said loudly.

The Judge interrupted: "Mr. Thayer, let her give her own explanation, in her words."

"Thank you, sir," Alice said, nodding to the Judge. She settled in her seat and continued her tale, now speaking to the Judge. "I had been doing very poorly. I am a poor girl, and I get cold in my feet and my hands get the rheumatism. I feel poorly in the wintertime and I was . . ."

"Witness, you have not answered my question."

"Mr. Thayer, I have asked that she have time to speak without interruption," Judge Davies said. "Miss Donahoe, you must speak to the question of whether or not you were intoxicated during the day of January thirty-first. Please take your time."

"Sir, if I had some liquor, it was but a little bad brandy. In wintertime the cook sometimes adds it to the soup, and it made me ill. I did not ask for it, for I am not accustomed to having it. No, sir, after I had my meal, I went down into the cellar and I took a fainting fit, or a spasm—and I fell to the ground. Mrs. Cunningham came looking for me. She was mistaken, thinking I was in my cups. I was never in the beastly state of intoxication that I have seen Mrs. Cunningham in!"

The room erupted in laughter, which was suppressed by the rapping of the Judge's hammer. "Sir," Alice implored, "I am but a poor person, and I have to depend upon myself," she whined.

As the laughter subsided, Clinton glanced around to see the effect. The jury and spectators had a sneering look. As he swiveled slightly he caught a glance at the door, where he saw Snarky, bobbing urgently, handing something to the court attendant. The attendant came forward and dropped a note before Clinton on the defense table. It was a ripped scrap of paper folded in two and Clinton opened it to see the words: "Stansbury off list. Husband Tammany fixer." Clinton allowed himself a deep breath as the news sank in. Hall had just lost an important witness, slated after the maid. She was the woman who had come to rent rooms in the house from Dr. Burdell the very same day as the murder. Unlike the servants, who carried grudges, this woman had no prior contact with the defendant and had a simple but damning message—that she came to the house to lease the upper floors; that Dr. Burdell intended that Emma's and her daughter's rooms would soon be vacated. Her message, if true, was troubling, for it could be inferred that Dr. Burdell wanted Emma gone. The tip from Snarky meant that the woman's husband had a link to ward politics, and perhaps to payoffs, and the party bosses feared the exposure. Clinton lifted his eyes to focus back on the testimony and kept his facial muscles still, but if he could allow himself a spontaneous response to both the note and Thayer's performance, it would be a smile as broad as a schoolboy's.

"Let me make sure your statement is clear," resumed Thayer carefully, allowing the room to settle and Alice's words to linger in the air. "You witnessed the defendant, Emma Cunningham, in a drunken state?"

"Well I certainly suspected. . . ."

"Do not give me your opinion. Answer me, yes or no? Did you ever witness Mrs. Cunningham heavily intoxicated?"

"Well if you put it so clearly, I was always told to leave the room when she was sneaking the bottle."

"Yes or no!" Thayer was standing next to the jury box and he thumped on the railing for emphasis.

"Please, sir. . . ," she said in a whining voice.

Thayer continued with a soft voice. "Then let me redirect your testimony to the facts of which you can be aware. Let me ask you, then: have you ever been jailed for the habits of intoxication?" he asked quietly.

"Objection," said Hall.

"I have not!" burst the maid before the Judge could answer. "I was only taken to the jailhouse two times, but that is because they thought I was another girl. I have never been known to imbibe in excess."

Thayer nodded and began to speak, but she rambled on.

"I am not addicted! I take but small sips. I have my references here and I will give them to the Judge." She fumbled with some papers in her thin purse.

"There is no need," said Thayer. "The witness is dismissed."

# CHAPTER TWENTY-SEVEN

*January 31, 1857*

At Tompkins market, Emma wandered the stalls while the locksmith finished copying the keys. Her cape was huddled around her and her hood was up, shadowing her face. The locksmith's shop on the Bowery had a forge in the back. He had pressed the two keys into the wax and poured the metal in the impression, but the cooling and filing would take the better part of an hour, so she roamed the maze of the market stalls. Once she had the keys, she could return the key ring to its nail by the pantry cupboard where they belonged.

The bell of St. Mark's in the Bowery tolled and then the bells from the faraway church towers began, each one starting up at a different moment, chiming in a dissonant pattern. The sky was broodingly dark and the canvas on the stalls snapped when a gust came through, but so far there had been no heavy gales or falling snow. She returned to the locksmith and urged him to hurry. He gave her the copied keys, one for Dr. Burdell's office door and one for his bedroom door.

She hurried down the alley behind Bond Street, her cape flapping at her heels as the wind bore down from behind. Her foot twisted on an irregular cobblestone and she nearly stumbled. She slowed—ahead she spotted Samuel leading the horse out of the alley door of the stable, stopping to fit the bit in a horse's mouth. She was almost upon him, so it was not possible to pass without him seeing her.

He looked up at her approach. "Madame," he said, with quick nod. The horse's head hung, obedient and patient.

"Is Dr. Burdell taking the carriage right away?" she asked.

"He will be leaving for the bank and then will use the carriage for the evening. He has bid me to rig her up and meet him at the bank."

"What is his business? Where is he going tonight?"

He looked at her warily, as he had earlier in the morning. "I am the servant, Ma'am, I only drive the horse."

His cryptic answer and his perceived loyalty to his master triggered her fury. She confronted him. "Is he going to a business meeting?"

"Ma'am, please be obliged that he goes many places," he said.

"Or is he going to the hotel to see his mistress?

"That I can't say."

"Samuel," she said in a loud whisper, "surely you know where he is going, and what business he conducts?"

"I don't, Ma'am," he said, looking uncomfortable. She thought she saw the bright whites of his eyes flash under his dark brow. His haunted look made her crazy. She stepped forward, close to him, as if she were going to challenge him, and by reflex he grabbed her by both wrists and held them tight in his fists, so that her skin twisted and it hurt. His eyes bore down on her, and he hissed an angry whisper, *"If therefore the light that is in thee be darkness, how great is that darkness!"*

She gasped. He was close to her body. "Let me go, what has

possessed you?" She wriggled and tried to pull from him, but the steel grip of his muscles only made her small bones feel as if they might snap. And then, just as suddenly as he had grabbed her, he dropped his grip, letting her arms drop. He stepped away from her. It was clear his action had stunned him as much as it stunned her.

"How dare you put your hands on me. You have overstepped all decency. I will see that you are dismissed!"

"Madame, you would do me a service to relieve me of this duty."

She rubbed her wrists furiously. "I shall report that you have tried to brutalize me," she mumbled, sensing now that he was truly afraid.

"I beg your pardon, I am just trying to warn you, Madame. This is no place for a lady," he said and stumbled backward a step.

She regained her sense of urgency. "From now on, you will listen to me. If you know what is good for you, you will follow my orders," she said. "Tomorrow I will need the carriage for the entire day. It is Saturday, and you will do as I say—you will drive Helen to the train. Then you will come back for me. I have a rendezvous at one o'clock." She spoke with an emphatic tone that implied *it is understood.*

"Madame, if your daughter is getting on a train tomorrow, I bid you get on that train with her."

Disturbed by the encounter, she was anxious to get back to the house. "My travel arrangements are my own affair," she stated, hurrying away.

Emma passed though the garden gate, shut the back door quietly, then put the key ring on the hook by the cupboard in the pantry. She entered the kitchen, removing her cloak. Hannah was busy at the stove with her back turned and seemed intent on ignoring her, so Emma headed upstairs. She glanced at the hall table and saw that her envelope to Mr. Wicken was gone.

"Has Augusta been gone with Mr. Wicken?" she asked John, who was sitting on a stool by the door.

"Mr. Wicken has taken her," he said. "They left in his phaeton. It's a fast runner, an open racer with gold lines painted on the side."

"And where is Dr. Burdell? Would I find him in his office?" she asked.

"He has walked to the bank," the boy answered. "And then he goes to supper, he is out for the evening." Confirming what she had heard from Samuel, she went straight up to the second floor. At Dr. Burdell's door, she pulled the new keys out of her pocket and slipped one in the lock. The door creaked open along the carpet and she shut it quickly behind her and locked it from the inside. Alone in the office, she gingerly looked around, hearing only the gentle sizzling of the gas in the burners. The coals in the fireplace were aglow, burning like rubies. The writing table had a ledger laid across it, open. She glanced at the notations of entries next to patients' names. She opened a drawer in the desk. It held inks and instruments for writing. She went over to the washbasin, where the paneling made way for little cupboards. She tapped on a panel, and it swung open, revealing powders in apothecary jars, but no papers. Her hand was shaking so much that she held it to her breast to calm it down, feeling her beating heart under her dress. She needed to calm her nerves.

There was a safe between the desk and the fireplace. She had often seen Dr. Burdell when his office door was open, bent over the low safe, shuffling through it. The safe took a key and not a combination. It must be hidden somewhere nearby, she thought, to give him easy access. She felt behind the ornate gold mirror that hung over the mantel and fingered the edges of the mantel cornices, feeling for anything that might have a small ledge to hide the key. Her heart was still beating fast as she urged herself to focus on finding her deed.

On the top of the mantel were two glass bell jars; inside each one was a specimen of a human jaw on display. She moved them carefully to each side, to look behind them. As she was rearranging them back into position, she spotted a glint of metal. She stood on tiptoe and peering inside one of the jaws from above, she saw it—a small gold key.

She lifted the glass and dipped her fingers into the jawbone behind the row of teeth, and pulled out the tiny key. She quickly knelt down to the level of the safe and fumbled with the latch. Inside the safe was an assortment of business papers placed on the shelves, many rolled and tied. She pulled out a document, on yellow paper. She opened it and saw that it was a lease—made out to Mr. and Mrs. Ezekiel Stansbury. Shocked by the clear evidence that the lady Dr. Burdell had interviewed was to take over her place as housemistress in her rooms, who had come that very morning, she rashly threw the lease in the fireplace, where it caught on the coals and burst into a quick flame. Half of the paper fell forward and sat curled on the firestone, with its ink turning brown. Frightened, Emma grabbed the poker and pushed it back into the coals until it burnt and disintegrated into a feathery ash.

She returned to the safe, now focused on finding her deed. There was another scroll inside, wrapped and tied. As she reached for it, she heard the jingling of bells on a horse's neck, the sound of a horse stopping before the house. Was it Augusta returning or Dr. Burdell? She listened to the faraway sound of the front door opening and closing in the hallway below. She could not take a chance of being discovered, so she grabbed the scroll and stuffed it in her pocket.

She jammed the safe shut and locked it, her heart beating. She lifted the bell jar and dropped the key into the jaw and immediately realized that she had dropped it into the wrong one. She dipped her finger inside the bone, but it slipped out of the grip of her finger until finally she pinched the key and placed it under the next jar. She heard voices muffled, down below.

She rushed into the wardrobe passage that led between the office and the bedroom, her skirts brushing against the cabinets as she passed. It led to the other side, to his bedroom, which was dark, with the velvet drapes drawn and the door to the hall closed and locked. She fumbled in her pocket for the new keys. She found a key and, trembling, slipped it into the lock to let herself out, but before she turned the key, she heard the tread of a footfall on the hall carpet coming up the stair. She froze, listening through the door. Then she heard the key click in the keyhole of the office next door. He was back.

She stood still, not daring to move. Dr. Burdell was bustling around in the office, as if he was looking for something. Her hand held the scroll tight. She tried hard not to breathe. She heard the faint rustle of his movements in the other room. She fumbled again with the key and slipped it into its lock.

Then she froze again at the sound of his heavy step entering the wardrobe passage and the loud tread of his boots on the wooden floorboards where there was no carpet. Terrified, she expected him to appear in the bedroom and see her there, huddled against the door, poised to flee. Then she heard the scraping of a heavy drawer and the sound of wood banging. He was pulling out the drawers of the wardrobe cabinets, which were built solidly into the wall and always stuck. She could hear the wood shriek as he yanked it.

She took advantage of the commotion and turned the key quickly and opened the bedroom door, pulling it softly across the carpet just enough to slip out and then slowly pulled the knob from the other side so that it made hardly any sound. She slipped the key back in, turning it around in the hole until it clicked. Then she turned and ran up the high staircase to the third floor. At the top, she waited just long enough to listen to the sound of her own heart battling inside the cave of her chest: he didn't emerge from either door; he wasn't chasing her; he hadn't heard her after all.

# CHAPTER TWENTY-EIGHT

*May 14, 1857*

S amuel opened his eyes to the spokes of sunbeams dancing through the branches. He had dozed. He was lying on his back on a cool bit of earth in the dappled shade of an oak tree. It was three o'clock in the afternoon, and he listened to the sound of the water at the riverbank as it slapped against the sides of the wooden skiff.

He had left the skiff down near the water. Samuel had a crumpled newspaper page in his hand that he had picked up on the street to check the date. According to the headline, the trial was at day eight and the defense was at the bar. It was still not over.

For the last three days, Samuel had been drifting through the bay. After the trial began, Katuma had said it would be safest for Samuel to take to the river and wait it out afloat. Katuma had borrowed a boat, a little wooden skiff with a rudder and single sail. Katuma and Quietta padded up and down the path from the hut to the water, filling it with provisions: buckets and blankets, string and some tools, as well as bottles of ale. When Samuel was ready to depart, the boy showed up, and seeing them with the boat ready, turned to Katuma first, and then Quietta, appealing to them: "Can I go? Can I go, too?" Quietta laughed and said "Bird, you're not the one they are hunting." And Katuma said, "I promise, I'll take you out fishing later when the shad are running."

It was because John didn't accept no for an answer, and kept jumping up and down pleading, and because Samuel could see that there was a spell of warm weather ahead, mild enough to sleep under the stars, and because the boy was good company and was keen on boats, that Samuel said, finally, "Let him come. We'll go to Canarsie Landing, and I'll bring him back in a few days."

"Is it wise?" asked Quietta, looking at her father.

"It might be a good thing, to get him out of the way of this murderous business. It's no place for a child," Katuma said.

John hollered, "Yahoo!" and scrambled aboard. Now, three days later, Samuel had brought the boy back as he had promised, so that he could visit his mother.

The day they set sail, they got a strong push from Katuma, and the hull scraped against the shallow river bottom and floated them off into the current. Samuel and John navigated the crowded harbor, dodging the schooners and barges, taking turns at the rudder, the other lying low. It was not unusual to see a Negro on the water. Negroes were ideal haulers on the oyster scows that trolled the flats. There were plenty of boys afloat, too, some skipping school on rafts, others running away for good, finding work in the crow's nests of ships. But a Negro and a towheaded boy together on an open boat might be a peculiar sight. In the expanse of the busy waterway, they caught no more notice than the bobbing pieces of timber that floated over the wakes of the tall ships.

The first night was spent at the Sandy Ground on Staten Island, where there was a village of whitewashed cottages made up of slave runaways out of Virginia. Now two generations old, the village had a Negro minister and a Negro doctor and a Negro running the general store. Everyone there had heard about the trial going on in the city. Samuel picked up other news as well, like which ships were slavers and which ships unloaded barrels of rum and rowed them to the wooded inlets before the customs men came aboard to fix a tariff, and which ones were running guns, selling them to the unmarked ships huddled just over the horizon. "Pirates!" exclaimed John, excited by thoughts of treasure.

The following morning, Samuel and John set sail again, drifting past the lighthouse at Robbins Reef, past Swinburne Island, the island that held those quarantined with smallpox, past the full-masted Navy fleet, charging at them from the Lower Bay. They drifted around the Bay Ridge, into Gravesend Bay where the Brooklyn Flatlands emptied into miles of waterways and creeks and sandbars. They found a sandy island in the Canarsie fishing ground and spent the next days fishing in the sunshine and trolling the beaches. John walked around in the shallows with a net, far out in the water, ankle deep, his pants rolled up, as if he were heading right into the iridescent sky, with the sun catching the top of his head like a lighthouse beacon.

At night they dug a fire pit into the sand. They drank cool brown ale in bottles stopped with wax that Samuel placed in the water to chill. The fish roasted until the soft white flesh fell from the bones. They ate slowly and talked late into the evening. Samuel told John about his home in Virginia where he had grown up in a shack near a field of tobacco.

"Where's your pa?" asked John. Samuel told him that he was gone, up to heaven.

"Mine, too," John said looking out at the horizon. "Where's your ma?" and Samuel said she was gone also, taken away when he was a boy, but he didn't tell him about the men that pulled her through the door of the shack as she grabbed for her children, one after another, until they pried her hands off them and took her wailing into the night. He told him instead about the washerwoman, a slave on the plantation who wore a wrapped headdress, and cleaned clothes in big vats, and watched over the children who weren't old enough to work the fields.

"After the sheets were hung wet on the lines between the old oaks, she sat us down with the Bible and taught us to read."

"So that's how you learnt?" asked John.

"That was just the beginning," said Samuel. "After I started, I couldn't stop, and I took that old book and wrote those words over and over. If you do that, you can read anything. That's why I kept practicing."

John nodded, thinking. It was dark now, and John began to talk. He told Samuel about that morning he showed up at 31 Bond Street during the storm and took the tray upstairs and opened up the door to Dr. Burdell's office and saw his neck near cut from his head. He spoke in a hushed tone, the way a boy does when he tries to appear proud and brave.

"I'm sorry you had to be the one," said Samuel. "You're too young to set your eyes upon such bloodshed."

"Wasn't so bad," said John, shrugging, but the boy had a tremor in his lip and a look in his eyes like he had stored this memory down deep. "Samuel, how come you never told me about the buggy ride? Where you went the night before, when you was driving Dr. Burdell?"

"We rode around town, doing business, that's all." Samuel remembered that evening well, a fugue of blasphemy that wasn't fit for a boy's ears. "I can tell you this, when Dr. Burdell got out of the carriage, he was carrying a satchel of money, most of it gold."

"Gold? Where did it go?"

"Disappeared, I guess."

"Stolen? Or maybe stashed away—I always thought he had a treasure hidden somewhere. I know he had a secret place in that wardrobe," said John. "He kept things hidden, that's for sure."

"What kind of secret place?"

"I was cleaning the stove in the bedroom once when he was in the office and I think he forgot I was there. I heard him go in the wardrobe, and he was there one minute and the next he disappeared. I heard him making noises at one of the cabinets, and when I looked up, he had vanished altogether. Then some time went by, and I heard him in the office again."

"What do you mean 'vanished'? Show me which cabinet." Samuel pulled his letter fold out of his rucksack where he kept sheets of paper. Some were already scrawled with the Bible quotes that he gave John to practice. He handed John a piece that had a fragment of writing and turned it over to the blank side and gave him a pencil so he could make a diagram. John drew the office and bedroom as two rectangles, and then another rectangle between them to show the wardrobe passage.

"Here," said John. "There is a long row of cabinets, and this one here is a tall one, with hanging clothes. At the bottom is a drewer," he said, making an x.

"Drawer," corrected Samuel.

"Yes," John said. "Well that's where I heard some noises, like he was pulling it out. When I looked in, he had disappeared, like he vanished inside. Maybe there is a hiding place under."

"Hm," said Samuel, "I don't know about that, because the ceiling space is too shallow for a man to lower himself into. It's the parlor that's directly below."

"I'm just telling you what I saw," said John, and Samuel put the paper away and they started to eat shellfish, breaking open a pile of mollusks. The moon rose in a haze of stars turning the shoreline into a silvery ribbon. They held the shells right over the fire until the fish roasted, then blew to cool it and swallowed it right down.

"I ain't never tasted anything so good," said John, the brine slipping down his chin.

"Have not ever," corrected Samuel.

# CHAPTER TWENTY-NINE

*January 31, 1857*

E mma heard the resounding clatter of hooves outside, and she ran to the window as a sleek pacer pulled to stop. It was Mr. Wicken with Augusta.

Dusk was settling like a dark shroud over an already dark day. Dr. Burdell's carriage was still waiting below. He was still downstairs in his room. Her heart was still irregular, and she still clutched the document she had taken from the safe.

She unrolled the document and fingered it gently. Opening it, she saw right away that it was something she did not recognize, something else altogether. It was not a deed—it was printed with a floral border and was written with penmanship in an overly ornate fashion.

*Certificate of Marriage*
*January 14, 1857*
Dr. Harvey Burdell and
Emma Hempstead Cunningham
Are hereby joined in Holy Matrimony

By all the forces of God,
in the presence of the
Reverend Uriah Marvine

Thoughts were scrambling and turning over in her mind. At first glance, she felt as if she was witnessing a phantom, like a day in the future that was part of a dream. A marriage? With her name and Dr. Burdell's? It was dated in the past, just two weeks earlier. But within seconds she realized that this dislocation was not pleasurable but forebodingly real. A false marriage was not a gift but an omen—the certificate was created so he could sell her property. If the sale was happening soon, the deed must be with him. Her thoughts raced along—to the woman at the hotel and the tickets to Europe, and the lease of the house and the visitor, Mrs. Stansbury. His actions were not random. His plans were rapidly unfolding, and none of them included her. She was in the way, and as long as she was inside this house, she was in danger.

She gripped the paper to her breast and leaned against the wall with her eyes shut. She heard someone enter her room. She jumped with fright.

"Mother." It was Augusta standing at her door, her curls out of place.

Emma tried to make sense of her daughter's presence. "You scared me," she began.

Augusta's mouth trembled. "I dropped my purse and lost my keys. I could have left them in the carriage." She led out a sob. "Mr. Wicken is a terrible man."

"What has happened? Has he hurt you?" asked Emma, alarmed.

"No, but he made advances. I resisted him, and I shall continue to resist him."

Emma turned to the window, where she saw the flash of a cape and Dr. Burdell's carriage pull away. He was gone again. "Get your sister, and come back to my room," she ordered.

"Mother, didn't you hear me? Mr. Wicken says he will marry me, but I will not do it," she stated adamantly. "He is not who you think he is. He took me up the Yorkville Road in his racing chariot, and we stopped at an inn for some ale. Then he took me far into the woods, by the river, and he tore at my dress. He said he is my fiancé."

"Augusta, you should be honored at the prospect. You cannot hold yourself above all mankind, or there will be no marriage and no prospects for your future."

"He forced himself and I fought him. I scratched his face, for he has no right to such brutality. Mother is it true, have you arranged my marriage to him?"

"Do not speak ill of Mr. Wicken," Emma said. She remembered her plan to see him tomorrow, and in her vulnerable state, she certainly needed an ally, with his ability to give advice and protection. "You are a foolish girl to spurn him! He has our best interests in mind." Emma looked strange, her eyes wild. "Go! Go get Helen, and bring your nightclothes with you. We need to be together tonight. We will sleep in this room." She would keep her daughters with her close together in her bedroom tonight, and in the morning Emma would see Helen off, with Samuel driving her to the train, where a chaperone from the school would take Helen north. After the carriage returned, she would make haste to see Ambrose Wicken. She hoped he would help her. He would certainly know how to retrieve her stolen claim.

Augusta stood staring, uncomprehending. She saw the trunks on the floor and the room in an unusual state of disarray.

"Get your sister and come down here! Bring her down!" Emma insisted.

Augusta stood defiantly, with tears at her eyes, and then started for the door. "You will not rule me, Mother. I know my own mind. I won't marry that man against my will. Besides," she said, now lacing her words with controlled venom, "Mr. Wicken despises me and I despise him back."

Dr. Burdell wrapped his cape and placed his satchel on the carriage seat. Samuel drove, at his direction, to Gramercy Square. They reached a residence with a shiny brass plate and the owner's initials next to the house number. Dr. Burdell pounded the knocker and a servant appeared and handed him a packet. He returned to the carriage and told Samuel that the next stop was Union Square. They stopped before the row of political clubs, the street deep with waiting carriages. It was six o'clock, and Samuel hadn't eaten. Dr. Burdell ordered him down. "Come inside with me."

They entered the men's club, passing through the bar, lined with crystal and mirrors. No one looked up at the man and his Negro servant as they passed. Behind the barroom were gaming rooms with tables covered with felt. They were empty, and when they reached a door with smoked glass, Dr. Burdell stopped and took off his cloak. "You will stay close by me all evening, unless I dismiss you," he whispered to Samuel. He lifted the flap of his frock coat, revealing a pistol in a holder at his waist, easily reached by a swift hand. Samuel knew that the gesture was a message that business was going to be discussed and Dr. Burdell wanted to ensure his silence. His presence was required, for his muscle and bulk were a looming protection and a threat to the others, if anything were to go wrong. But if Samuel tried to bolt, Dr. Burdell could easily dispatch him with a hard steel ball ripping through his flesh.

They entered through the door to a smoke-filled room, a private dining room. Men were standing and milling about, talking together. A gentleman looked up as Dr. Burdell entered. "He is here," he said, tapping the next man on the shoulder. Everyone turned toward them. "We were not sure if you would change your mind again. You have gone behind our backs several times now and then returned."

Dr. Burdell simply looked at them without nodding. There were plates of food spread out around an oval table, banquet style, and papers laid out on one end where the table was clear of platters.

"I am here to give you what you have asked for," Dr. Burdell said, handing them the packet of papers he received at Gramercy Square. A man laid them out across the table next to the others.

"Send your manservant to the kitchen where he can eat," said one.

"No, he is to stay here, with me," Dr. Burdell said, glancing at Samuel, who posted himself against the wall of the room, near the door. He carefully observed the men present, for he had been hearing these renegade plans for months. He intended to report back to the Reverend, as he had done before. Samuel eyed everyone in the room carefully, making note of their physical appearance and attire, down to every stitch on their broadcloth suits, memorizing each face like a caricature indelibly etched on a printing plate. He had seen many of them before. Two months earlier, after a late meeting in another smoke-filled room, they discussed slave ships and fugitive rings, and the best way to bypass the customs men in New York Harbor. Afterward, they all piled into Dr. Burdell's carriage. Someone with a Southern accent directed Samuel to Mercer Street, behind Broadway, where carousers in top hats weaved among stage doors and into the darkened entrances of brothels, identified by the glow of a flame in a red-tinted bowl.

At the corner of Prince Street, he was ordered to stop at a house of faded stucco with no markings. It was a large residence, but the patched façade and worn marble steps were a sign of its decline. Dr.

Burdell told Samuel to follow. In the foyer, a woman with a paste of white flour across her face greeted them.

"The beautiful Delia," crooned the Southerner, lifting her hand to kiss it. "I am here to show my Northern friends the finest of Southern virtue." The madam's chest, no longer buoyant, was held upright in a tight corset.

"Come along then," she said, sashaying into the parlor, where divans and fringed ottomans were scattered about. On every seat was a young woman in a billowing skirt, attended by a Negress, a girl kneeling on the floor, fanning her mistress. The offerings were belles or slaves. One by one, the men chose a girl and passed out of the room, headed up the staircase.

The girl assigned to Dr. Burdell insisted she was only fifteen. She was not fifteen, maybe twenty. She wore piles of ringlets that looked silly on a woman her age. As they passed out of the parlor, Dr. Burdell stopped before Samuel and said to the girl, "Never mind. I won't be staying after all." Then he turned to Samuel and said, "Let's get out of here. I have another meeting at Delmonico's."

"But, sir, don't you want to see my bloomers?" protested the girl. "My daddy says I am the naughtiest girl in Louisiana."

"Tell your madam that I'm not impressed." Dr. Burdell put on his hat and walked toward the front door. "And tell your daddy, I think you're just another trollop."

In the clubroom on Union Square, the same men now eyed Dr. Burdell with suspicion. "So you are now interested in our terms. We have conferred among ourselves," said one man, "and come up with a portion for your share of the profits. I think you will be satisfied."

"I am here to finish this up," said Dr. Burdell.

"We are almost finished. These documents come from an advocate at Gramercy Square, who sealed our signatures to this deal. It is only left for you to sign." Samuel recognized the man speaking

as a New Yorker, a party boss, a round man with a tweed coat. And
he had watched carefully when they stopped at the residence of the
advocate, making a note of the brass plate on the door, with the
monogram *A.O.H.*

"I will sign when I am assured that my terms will be met," said
Dr. Burdell.

"Your share of profits shall be a payment of twenty percent." It
was the man in a tweed coat speaking. He pulled aside some of the
papers and directed Dr. Burdell to sign.

Dr. Burdell hesitated and then said, "We spoke of two portions,"
he said abruptly.

"You will be making your commission from every Negro hide
going through this port. At four hundred dollars a head for every
freedman sent back South, that is a quite a bounty."

"What about the guns and munitions?"

"And the same for every rifle shipped out."

"That would suffice, as long as I also receive my full price for the
land." Dr. Burdell started to move to the papers, shuffling through
them.

"We will pay you for the land. It will be the depot for our opera-
tions. One day we will develop it to be the main port connecting the
waterways to the railroad, to control all goods traveling from the
South and across the ocean and the continent. With this sale, I see
we have finally seduced you to the Southern point of view."

"I have no point of view."

Another man spoke. "This is not just business. Many of us are
New Yorkers and we are aligned with the principles of the Southern
Wing. If you sign these papers now, you will assure your share of
profits, and then you will go downtown to meet the emissary from
the syndicate. He will pay you in cash directly for your land. It will
be deeded to the Louisiana Corporation."

"What if there is a change in government, or a blockade or a revolt?" asked Dr. Burdell gruffly. "What are my assurances that I will receive future profits in that event?"

"Once the Corporation has control, there will be no room for revolt. With guns and slaves as our currency, we will operate our business in the underground until our political aims are secured. We will run the Negroes south along the same routes that they flee North. We have set up our men along their trails, who bag them at both ends. When slavery is legalized again in the North, it will be like minting money."

Samuel felt his stomach lurch. For months, he took the information from these meetings back to the church, where it was written down. Then the preacher warned the network of city abolitionists and station agents outside the city, who sent word to the Quaker farmers that transported runaways in their vegetable carts across Pennsylvania and New Jersey. With the inside information, they were able to alter their routes, avoiding the targeted roads, using older cow paths and Indian trails through the swamps. Now, with these papers on this table, there was a larger plan in place that left no place to run.

The men paid Samuel little attention, but as they talked, one or another's eyes would dart around, sometimes alighting on him. Samuel did not know if he could stand by any longer or keep himself from springing at these men like a jackal. He had hoped one day to peer at the bottom of this vile well, but so far no bottom was in sight. His muscles tensed, but he remained motionless against the wall, watching each man's hands, for it was not only Dr. Burdell who carried a pistol.

"Let's finish," said Dr. Burdell. He signed the papers that had the advocate's seal and fancy markings. Dr. Burdell only glanced at them, signing one after another, hurrying to be done. He took a note with an address penned on it, where he was to pick up his cash.

"As for the change in political winds, we find that Mayor Wood has outlived his purpose," said a man, watching Dr. Burdell sign. "We need a stronger grip. Removing him as our candidate is just the beginning. With New York in place, we can determine the next president, who will unite us under the South."

"Gentlemen, lift your glasses," called out another. "I propose a toast—'To a Southern reign. New York and Washington, commerce and cotton, united at last.'" There was a clinking of glassware and chuckling. "To our next president, Jefferson Davis." Everyone sipped except Dr. Burdell, who did not drink. Another man toasted, loudly, "And to our next mayor, a man loyal to our cause, Abraham Oakey Hall."

# CHAPTER THIRTY

*May 14, 1857*

I t was the eighth day of the trial. The prosecution had closed its case after testimony on Emma's first marriage and her compromised financial situation; by shopkeepers who saw her spending lavishly; exhibit boards showing the position of the coal stoves in every room, where she might have burned her bloody clothes; and a neighbor's report of burning wool late on the night of the murder. Now the defense was at the bar. "Did it appear that the person who administered the blows had anatomical knowledge, or are you of the opinion that they were struck at random?" Henry Clinton paced before a medical expert.

"The knife wound severed the carotid artery and the great vessels of the neck," said Dr. Jeremiah Gideon, the doctor and scientific scholar from Columbia University, with degrees and titles in Latin. "The gash wrapped around the front part of the neck, as deep as six or seven inches. The neck wound appeared to be inflicted with skill, much the way a butcher cuts the throat of a calf."

"Was the neck wound the fatal blow?"

"That blow was not instantly fatal, for the victim was still able to stagger forward, as we can see by his footprints in his blood."

Clinton walked to an easel with an exhibit on plasterboard. The board showed Dr. Burdell's office, painted realistically, accurate down to the placement of furniture and the pattern of the wallpaper. The artist had placed the corpse on the floor and used red ink to make the surrounding splatters of blood that splashed up along the door and along the walls.

"Can you estimate how much time elapsed after the neck was cut?"

"Perhaps one or two minutes elapsed. The release of blood from the neck artery made the most profuse expulsion. The heart was pumping rapidly, propelling the blood from the neck like a fountain, which is why we see large masses of blood—as much, I would guess, might have weighed half a pound, to a pound and a half of coagulated blood all over the walls."

Clinton pointed to the easel with a pointer to indicate the blood on the walls. The rendering of the blood had a troubling effect on the jury.

He moved the pointer down. "Is this the spot in the room where the neck was cut?"

"Yes. Dr. Burdell was standing by the cabinet of his washbasin, for that is where we see the blood high up on the wall," Dr. Gideon continued. "The victim then staggered to the center of the room, and as he reeled, the killer thrust the knife again. This time it was expertly aimed into the heart. Those who attack the heart with skill know to start from below the rib cage and strike in an upward motion."

"And was that the fatal blow?"

"Yes. After the victim collapsed, the heart stopped pumping and the blood seeped slowly on the carpet from the lesser veins."

During the course of the questioning, Clinton kept his eye on the jury. With scientific experts, it was a challenge to avoid numbing the jury with technical matters. During the last two days of the defense testimony, Clinton and Thayer had questioned numerous experts about physical evidence, all carefully examined by microscope. There was a nightgown with blood that proved to be menstrual, a knife with red stains that proved to be rust, and remnants from the stove ashes that was a fragment of a discarded apron belonging to the cook. The results of the studies were placed on boards to show the jury. Other boards outlined the crime in intricate detail, including the timeline and execution of the attack.

Today, the jury scrutinized the painting of the office earnestly, their eyes moving back and forth from the picture to the witness. It was only the produce dealer, an elderly man, whose chin nodded into his chest, but he had been plagued by narcolepsy from the beginning. With careful guidance, Clinton knew that a clear story of the events would unfold. With matters of science, one was dealing with the authority of facts.

"Can you tell us anything about the perpetrator from the nature of the wounds?" asked Clinton. Dr. Gideon's expertise was that he had devised a method of determining the physical character of a murderer by looking at the pattern of his blows.

"The person who inflicted the wounds was taller than Dr. Burdell. The first strikes were from behind, with stab wounds to the back and shoulders. I measured the wounds with calipers, and from the measurements I can deduce that the thrusts were downward, penetrating deeply at an angle, determining that the attacker stood several inches taller."

"And what could you say about the strength of the attacker?"

"The attacker had considerable strength. As the victim was repeatedly attacked from behind, the victim cowered forward, covering his head with his arms." Here the doctor demonstrated, bending forward and placing his arms over his head. "This resulted in wounds to the backs of the arms and shoulders. Then, the attacker moved in close, and pulled back the victim's head, making a rapid motion with the knife across the throat, cutting from the right ear, slicing across the neck to the left carotid vein, creating the large neck wound."

"Would you match the stature of this attacker with the diminutive woman that you see in this room?" asked Clinton. Here he pointed to the defendant. In her veil and black garb, Emma Cunningham was nothing more that an outline, the lace covered her head and shoulders entirely. She made no movement as every eye in the room turned to look at her in the box.

"I would infer that the attacker had a very strong musculature, that of a strong man," replied the doctor.

"Madame, would you now stand?" Clinton asked. Emma stood slowly and remained standing as she was studied. "Is her height the same as the height of the presumed intruder?"

"From the way the blows were delivered, I am concluding that the murderer stood taller than Dr. Burdell, who we know to be five foot eleven. This woman is considerably shorter than that."

"Is it your opinion that the assassin and Emma Cunningham are one and the same?"

"It is my conclusion that this deed was perpetrated by a male with a strong and well-developed physique, who was taller than the victim, and able to subdue him with the force and the rapid nature of the blows, so that the victim was unable to flee before the fatal thrust to his heart."

"Thank you, Doctor," Clinton said, in conclusion, returning his seat.

Oakey Hall sprang from his seat to engage in a cross-examination.

"Dr. Gideon," he called out. "Mrs. Cunningham, the defendant, is left-handed. Is it possible to determine whether a left-handed person made these wounds?" he asked.

"The knife used was a double-sided blade, so it is difficult to make a judgment as to which hand was gripping it. We can usually tell the direction of the thrusts from the mark on the flesh by the sharp end of the blade, but when the knife is sharp on both sides, it is difficult to tell."

"So could a left-handed person have inflicted these wounds?"

"It is in the range of possibility, yes."

"Sir, you told the jury that the attacker was taller than Dr. Burdell. Wouldn't it be possible for a shorter person to make the shoulder and neck wounds, if the victim had been crouching? If he had been kneeling at his safe, or perhaps seated at his desk." The stenographers were furiously writing. The produce dealer was alert.

"I might entertain such a scenario."

"Wouldn't that explain how a shorter person could inflict wounds from above?"

"Again it is remote, but in the realm of scientific possibility."

"You said that the attacker was a muscular person who stuck with deliberate force. But since you have studied the character of persons who commit such crimes, you must know that such heinous crimes are often guided by passion. And passion can summon a force not present in a person during regular circumstances. Couldn't one surmise that sixteen wounds randomly inflicted, indicate an attack executed in passion, angry and random?"

"Well, the smaller wounds and stabbings seem randomly inflicted. It was the cutting of the throat and the thrust to the heart that I claim are deliberate."

"Have you heard the expression, 'Heaven has no rage like love to hatred turned, and hell has no fury like a woman scorned?'" Clinton had trouble controlling his expression of disbelief at the invocation of the phrase. That well-worn line had been used at every criminal trial with a female defendant since it was first delivered onstage in 1697.

"Yes, sir, I have."

"When a person is in a state of impassioned fury, even a frail woman, isn't it possible that they could gain the momentum or strength of a much stronger person? Wouldn't you agree that under such circumstances, random and helter-skelter acts may have as deadly and mortal an effect as those perpetuated by strength or co-ercion?"

"Again, the smaller wounds were opportunistic, but the heart wound was the mortal wound, and it appears to have been executed with purpose and skill."

"But do you agree, that when someone is driven by anger or malice or greed, even the one unskilled with a knife can accidentally approximate a deadly skill."

"Well, I can only say to you, that is possible."

With the use of literary devices, Hall had supplanted the defense's picture of a strong male attacker with one of a furious Emma, stabbing randomly and thrusting the knife with wild abandon. The use of such images and devices were the currency of a successful trial. Clinton knew that it would take his remaining hours at the bar, going over the blood splatters one by one, along with further analysis, to eliminate the image of Emma as the certain perpetrator, beyond a reasonable doubt. In the end it would be the use of logic, between jury members, when they were arguing among themselves, that would determine if the defense had been successful painting a picture of another killer in their minds.

At that moment, from the corner of his eye, Clinton caught sight of the door to the Judges' corridor creaking open. A clerk shuffled in, his britches scratching as he moved toward the dais with some papers in hand. He placed the papers before the Judge, who lifted his bifocals to glance at them.

A resigned frown came over the Judge's brow. He hesitated and then lifted the gavel. "Counsel and witness. I must interrupt this testimony. Counselors, would you approach?"

# CHAPTER THIRTY-ONE

*May 14, 1857*

L ying by the riverbank, he had fallen asleep for what must have been a full hour. Samuel dozed off in the warm sun, not expecting John back for a while. When John returned, he planned to fill some jugs with freshwater and head out on the river again for a few more days, for the trial would certainly be finished by next week. He awoke to the whisper of a movement that did not come from the leaves above; it was a rustle of soft earth from back near the bramble and sounded like a squirrel running fast. Then, he heard a crashing sound. White men smashed their way into the woods.

He sat up with a wild look in his eyes. He heard the sound again in the bramble. Horses became confused in overgrowth, and he heard branches breaking, as if a horse was moving erratically. A rider would be kicking the horse, and yanking the reins, while searching for a direction through the bushes, while the horse was trying to retreat.

He heard a whinny in the distance. Any minute he would be in view to the rider. Samuel looked left. He needed to dash through the trees and reach the small strip of sand at the river's edge. His body felt sick with the reality that he was hunted again. He grabbed his rucksack and raised himself up to a crouch, not fully standing, and half crawled across the ground to the hardwood trees closest to the water, shielded by their trunks. He dared to rise up and glance back. In the acre of bramble, still far at a distance, he saw the head of a man, bobbing on top of a horse, with one gloved hand on the reins.

Samuel sprinted through some trees and slid down the soft earthen bank, shoulder high. He was now hidden below the riverbank, so he started to run along the smooth stretch of sand dotted with pebbles, his feet lightly splashing at the edge of the river. He kept going, and after he passed a bend formed by a boulder, he climbed up the bank again. He was in the old orchard where he could run through the apple trees to Greenwich Street. He hoped the old man who tended the chickens would not be sitting by the coops, so there would be no witness to say, *Yes, I saw a Negro dashing by*.

He made it to the street and felt as if he had run for miles, but it had only been a roundabout circle through the woods and out the orchard, maybe the circumference of a city block. The traffic was indifferent in the bright afternoon sun. He leaned against the wall of a factory building in the long shadows created by the brickwork. He stood close to a group of day laborers as they were leaving the warehouse. They were black men, lounging around, ending the day's shift. He could be one of them, except for the terror coursing through his veins.

The men started to disperse, and Samuel snuck through the brick archway of the warehouse and ducked into one of the storerooms piled high with sacks on top of wooden pallets. Shafts of light streamed in from windows high up near the beams. He found a spot and hid deep among the maze of stacks. He would wait here for night to fall and then he would go back again to the river and look for the boy.

He listened in his mind to the sounds he had heard, made by the weight of the horse as it pushed through the bramble. The horse had moved into the thicket with its flank to the branches, as if it was protective of something. By the sound of the twigs breaking, Samuel knew the horse had been rearing, trying to buck its master, acting instinctively. This horse was acting like a mare protective of a foal, or the way horses sidestep in the woods to avoid hurting something delicate.

Samuel settled low, surrounded by high sacks of burlap in the cavernous space. Soon, the sounds of horses and cries filled the streets. It sounded like there was a full brigade out, searching the warehouses. He heard the excited yelps of bloodhounds. *Dogs*, he thought. *This time they are bringing the dogs.*

Alarmed by the nearby sound of footsteps outside on the cobblestones, he glanced to his right and left. There was no exit but the one that lead back to the street. A dog in the stacks would detect his scent in the warehouse in a matter of seconds. He glanced upward. Crates were piled high against the walls, and above, the high boxes met the wooden latticework that held the crossbeams to the roof. His only chance was to get up into the beams.

He pulled off his shirt, which carried the heaviest scent of sweat. He took a little pot out of his rucksack and spread a waxy potion of grease and herbs along his chest and arms. The Indians had given him this vial when he traveled north. They passed the ointment along to runaways, for it masked a man's odor during a manhunt and warded off the dogs. He rifled in his rucksack for his letter fold and pulled out his papers and folded them into his pants pocket, and left the shirt and the rucksack in a pile. Then he took a deep breath and crouched to a leap. He scaled the crates against the wall. At the top of the pile, he jumped from one high stack to another until he could grasp a crossbeam above his head. He pulled himself up and climbed to the highest group of beams, now about thirty feet into the roof, overlooking the entire warehouse from a network aerie. The beams themselves were solid—the width of a man, and he teetered along them until he found a spot where he could wedge himself next to the roof slats, blocked from view by a host of vertical beams. From the vantage of the floor, he was well hidden in the shadows of the cathedrallike ceiling, and he froze as the clamor of dogs and horses on the street became deafening. He heard a voice yell. "In here, inside this warehouse!"

Clinton and Hall stepped close to the Judge's bench. The late sun slanted through the courtroom. Spectators often strained to overhear a Judge's conference, but realizing it was not possible, they murmured among themselves and rearranged themselves in their seats.

"I have before me some papers from the sheriff," whispered Judge Davies. "It appears that the constabulary is in the process of detaining a missing person who is germane to this case. It is the manservant who was present on the evening of the crime. If, indeed, they have detained this missing witness, I want to know if each side needs to prepare new testimony."

Hall smoothed his cravat and whispered. "Absolutely, sir. The prosecution would most certainly want to reopen our case and question this man in the witness box." Clinton was flummoxed at the response. Hall seemed too poised, too relaxed.

"Your Honor," protested Clinton. "To introduce a new witness at this stage in the trial is disruptive and counterproductive. Besides, this witness is a defense witness, not the prosecution's. If he is detained, we are willing to forgo putting him on the stand."

"I have recent information, Your Honor," Hall whispered, "that this witness may have been working in concert with the defendant.

We know that he was in communication with her during the day of the murder and may have knowledge of her various actions and rebut her alibi."

"Preposterous!" hissed Clinton, unable to contain himself.

"Are you saying that he may be an accessory to this crime?" queried Judge Davies.

"Mr. Hall has knowledge of no such thing, Your Honor," interrupted Clinton. "He is grabbing at straws," replied Clinton, disgusted. "There is no reason to bring this man in now, except to sow confusion."

"Mr. Clinton, please! Let me inquire into this matter without your interruption." The Judge said this loudly enough to receive glances from the front row. Lowering his voice again, he said, "This is an important matter. Because it is nearly five o'clock, I suggest that we recess for the day. We will meet in my chambers, and each side can state an offer on this matter." He banged his gavel, receiving immediate attention throughout the room. Judge Davies called out: "The court will be adjourned for the day. I instruct that the jury make no inference from this and be prepared to resume tomorrow morning." He banged his gavel again, dismissing the room. Various people stood and milled about in giddy confusion. Clinton headed swiftly to the defense table, but instead of sitting, he grabbed his papers and nodded at Thayer to follow. Clinton and Thayer left the courtroom, pushing through the set of swinging leather doors.

Clinton found an empty chamber. As he was about to enter, he spotted James Snarky running toward him, practically skidding across the marble floor. He held the door open, and when his two aides were inside, he slammed the door shut.

"I was up in the balcony, watching," said Snarky. "What's happened?"

"A note came through from the sheriff that Samuel has been

located and they are expecting to seize him and bring him in," said Clinton.

"Where did they find him?" asked Thayer.

"No word yet, just that he is about to be detained. This isn't good. If they produce him, the prosecution wants to reopen its case and examine him."

"But the prosecution has no interest in Samuel," protested Thayer. "Why would they want him on the stand? They leave themselves more vulnerable. Any of Dr. Burdell's evening activities could create a scenario of reasonable doubt for Emma Cunningham."

"A new witness will cause delays and confusion in the minds of the jury, and the disruption creates a hole in the trial. Not to mention that the press will pounce on this like dogs to meat." Clinton spoke with resentment, angry that the flow of defense testimony had been interrupted. He had planned so carefully, in control of a progression that the jury would follow, like a chess game, piece by piece, as it moved across the board. He turned to Snarky. "I told you to stay on top of the search for Samuel. How can it be that the sheriff has discovered him now?"

Snarky was jittery and a bit breathless. "Sir, I am as shocked by this turn of events as you are." He wiped his sweating brow. "I've been asking around for news about him but nothing turned up. The only lead I had was the boy. One day I saw John sneaking some food from the basket, and I thought Eureka! He might be taking it to the fugitive, so I decided to tail him."

"You tracked him?"

"Mostly he just goes to see his mum, who lives in a garret down on Rector Street. But once I followed him all the way to the riverfront, in Greenwich Village. He had a sack of food with him. He ran right into some brambles and broken-down boards. Then I saw a little Indian girl go down after him, and I thought, well, he was probably just meeting some kids to go look at the boats, so I left it alone."

"How did we get blindsided by this?" asked Thayer.

"Well, sir, I got something to confess," continued Snarky. "As you may recall I've been playing cards with fellows from the *Herald*; Finnerty was looking for tips. I had a losing streak, and we trade tips when we are short of cash. He asked me about Samuel, if I had any information. I said I didn't have any, but the boy knew him, and how I tailed him, but it didn't ever lead anywhere."

"Where is the boy now?" said Clinton, angry. "You were supposed to keep an eye on him, too."

"He hasn't showed up for a few days," Snarky admitted.

"Is it possible that your tip to Finnerty went straight to the DA's office and they sent someone out to follow the boy to Samuel?"

"Sir, I didn't mean no harm, but it could be that my caper backfired. . . ." Snarky was shaking now. "Honestly, sir, I am sorry if this jeopardizes things, I see now, I'm sorry, sir."

"This is bad," agreed Thayer. "If Samuel is brought in now, he could be frightened enough to testify falsely."

Clinton was not listening; he was pacing the room, strategizing. "Let me think." He moved about with his arms folded tight, pacing and shaking his head.

"We can treat him as a hostile witness," Thayer offered. "I can take him hostile. It shouldn't be hard to find a reason that he carried a grudge against his master—that's easy enough, given what a scoundrel Burdell was. Samuel was the last one to see the victim alive; he had opportunity and motive. If we attack him as a possible suspect, it's a perfect chance to sow reasonable doubt for Mrs. Cunningham."

"No," replied Clinton vehemently, envisioning the sensational headlines if they turned the carriage driver into the prime suspect on the stand. "It won't work. They can just as easily play this the other way—Hall's tactic will be to suggest that he was her accomplice. If Samuel was seen at all with Emma Cunningham in the final days, then the prosecution can assert that she paid him or colluded with him to do her bidding. If a strong man committed the act, in concert with Emma, it unravels our case, as untenable as the claim may be." He thought of his promise to the Reverend to protect Samuel. What seemed like an easy assurance to the minister at the church was about to vanish.

Snarky still had his head in his hands. "Sorry, boss," he muttered again, thinking of Finnerty from the *Herald* easing the information out of him, and him falling for the bait. He was worried about John but dared not voice his concern in the heated moment.

Clinton paced some more, thinking things through. "It's possible that this is a ploy," Clinton said, "to stop the logical progression of the case in its tracks." He kept pacing, glancing at the door. "They don't want this man as their witness; they want an interruption and a distraction. It's just a smoke screen. I always sensed that ultimately they want Samuel out of the way—eliminated."

"You mean they are just buying time?" asked Thayer.

"To allow the jury to forget our scientific testimony. They don't want to have to rebut it. If they have the fugitive in custody, that alone will create an uproar. They could back down and not put him on the stand after all, and still achieve their goal."

There was a knock on the door. "Mr. Clinton, sir, I have a message from the Judge," said a court officer. "He is ready to meet in his chambers."

Clinton took the note. "I'll be there in a moment," he said, then shut the door again. "Here's what I am going to do," he said to Thayer and Snarky. "Today is Thursday. I'll go to the Judge. I'll propose to Hall that we close both cases now. We will offer to drop our remaining testimony. And the prosecution will remain closed, and neither side will use this witness. I have a strong hunch the prosecution will go for it. They may feel that ending the case quickly could serve the same purpose as disrupting it. Everyone stands to risk if we turn this into a circus and prolong the trial into another week of disruption."

"So what does this mean?" asked Snarky.

"It means that if the Judge is in agreement, the trial's over. Tomorrow we close."

## CHAPTER THIRTY-TWO

S amuel could not see the room below from his spot high in the beams. He crouched, his back against a crossbeam, his arms pinned to his side to avoid any exposure. There was commotion outside from the street, as if a battalion of men on horseback was converging on the block, with shouts and iron hooves ringing on the rounded cobblestones. Horses whinnied as men pulled the reins and jumped off. In a matter of seconds he heard the crowd entering the storehouse, and the hounds were loosed among the maze of crates. As Samuel expected, the crescendo of barking dogs scrambled right through the room, straight to where he had been hiding, piling atop his satchel and shirt.

"We got him!" rose a jubilant cry, accompanied by deafening barks and the violent sound of the dogs jawing at his clothes. The men must have believed there was a body under those dogs for there was pandemonium: "We want him alive! Take him alive!" It took a while for the handlers to tease the pack apart by beating them with sticks.

The men hollered and pounded at the animals, and the dogs whimpered, retreating in disappointment. "It's not him, it's just his

things. He must be nearby! Don't let him escape!" Men scattered
to search the storeroom, tossing the sacks and crates, shouting and
cursing, referring to him as the "nigger" and the "fugitive." Samuel
remained pinned against the rafters. His dark skin and dusky pants
aided his camouflage; he dared not move a muscle for his slightest
movement might draw an eye upward. The noises below went on
for an interminable time until someone yelled, "The dogs have another scent. In the next warehouse!" and he heard the dogs run after
the lead, scrambling after the next smell of meat.

Samuel waited in the roof until moonlight shone through the
panes of the high windows. All sounds had subsided, and the
search party had retreated hours ago. Below, it was pitch-black.
He believed that the posse had gone, but he took no chances
and waited long into nightfall. As he crouched in the rafters, he
thought of this long year that he had served the Underground,
by reporting the plans of the men who were doing business with
Dr. Burdell. Besides reporting to the pastor and the abolitionists,
he recounted the comings and goings to Katuma and his Indian
friends, when they sat, grilling fish, around the riverbank. "Why
don't you tell the constabulary?" he recalled one of the Indians
asking, when Samuel told of the illegal business in slave trade that
was underfoot. Katuma scoffed at the comment. "Even if they stop
the slave trade, who will return our kingdom, our sacred land?" It
was the disruption of the marshlands that made Katuma seethe,
for in his mind, his ancestors and their gods had been defiled. But
Samuel knew, as did the pastor, that this business was deadly and
it involved more than the exchange of slaves or land. There was
no authority to turn to—not the Sheriff, or the Police Chief, the
District Attorney or the courts. There was no chance that Samuel
would be safe, for he had seen too much.

The distant bells rang that it was now ten o'clock. He finally
swung his way out of the rafters and crept through the warehouse.

Before stepping out onto Greenwich Street, he listened to the darkness; from the trees near the river he heard owls and other night birds. Far off in the direction of the city, he could hear the cries of newsboys in singsong. The choral was faint, but by straining to hear, he made out some isolated lines: "The trial is over" and "Verdict tomorrow."

On the empty street, he encountered nothing but a soft breeze on his cheek. He crossed to the far side of the avenue to the orchard. Deep in the trees, the river shimmered down the slope.

He would go back and look for the boat that he left on an abandoned stretch of waterfront, so he could set out again across the inky river. If the trial were really over, then he might outlive this manhunt. But first, he'd check to see if there were any signs of the boy. He crept low as he entered the orchard, passing behind the chicken coops, careful not to wake the old man's dog.

When he approached the spot where he had dozed, he saw a flickering farther on, and was drawn by the strangeness of the light. It was a lantern, far into the woods, hanging on the door of Katuma's hut. It tilted and dangled in the gentle night's breeze. It was odd; Katuma slept in his home on Perry Street every night, and none of the Indians hung a lantern on the door. He crept forward, approaching it with foreboding, coming close from the backside of the hut. He made his way closer and crouched low. There was no sound of anyone present, just the lantern swaying. Several feet around the hut, he saw the smashed branches where a horse's bulk had come right up to the hut and then passed again back out of the woods. He saw how the mud had been distressed from the hooves, and the boot prints from a single rider's dismount. The muddy footprints made a scrambled pattern at the entrance, showing that the man had stooped down and entered through the little door.

Samuel stepped around and peered inside, and in an instant all the sounds he had heard when the rider approached added up, the little padding, the horse rearing protectively, even the leaves seemed to have been crying out for a kind of mercy. At the opening to Katuma's hut he saw what he most feared in the world—curled on the floor was the young boy, John, his small limbs turned like the sparrow wings of a fallen bird, his yellow hair matted with mud and his eyes closed, his lids milky. His little neck was snapped, and his body was still warm, dead on the floor.

Samuel heaved himself down on the ground in pain. The stars, the riverbank, even the leaves seemed to be shrieking.

*January 31, 1857*

Helen's nightdress twisted around her leg. Augusta was asleep beside her. Emma had made up the large four-poster bed with a place for both girls and a spot for herself at the bottom with a pillow at the opposite end. The trunks were packed and moved near the door. Emma had locked her door, but if anyone managed to enter, the trunks were close enough to the door to make the intruder stumble. All evening she had felt fearful or agitated. Either way, her mind was never calm.

It was near midnight. When Dr. Burdell had left around six, Emma had sat limply on her bed with the scroll in her hand, in a state of disbelief. The date of the marriage certificate was January 14, two weeks earlier. The certificate was clearly fabricated, and as her mind worked around the strange document, she knew that he kept it as the proof he needed to lay claim to her land and make the sale on his own behalf. But as she thought of the other occurrences—the lady at the hotel, the trip to Europe, leasing away her rooms—she was certain that his intention was that she be thrown out on the street. Her disappearance was now desirable; it was quite possible that he preferred her dead.

Earlier, she had sent Augusta and Helen to the kitchen to have some soup for supper and to bring her meal back on a tray. Then she went to her washbasin and opened a vial that contained powder, a supply of laudanum given to her by Dr. Burdell. She mixed the solution in water and felt the tingle as the drink went down, which calmed her nerves. Augusta and Helen returned to her room after supper. The stretch of nighttime hours dragged on. Augusta was withdrawn and sullen and spent time at the washbasin in her bodice and bloomers, sponging her arms and legs. Emma ordered Helen to finish packing. Helen retreated to the trunks, spooling ribbons onto loose wooden sticks, and packing her clothing in an awkward way, leaving the linens crumpled. Emma was agitated and could not focus. She paced around, straightening up, or picking at a bit of sewing, but everything seemed haphazard. With each noise outside, Emma lifted her head to the dark windows. Finally, at ten, she went down to the kitchen and sent Hannah to bed.

Her daughters were now asleep and hardly breathed. They were still except for the occasional twitch of Helen's dark lashes. The coal in the fireplace gave off a faint glow. Emma slipped carefully out of bed and crept across her room. She lit a taper in a brass holder, and the small light flickered its illumination across the bedroom and across the tableau of her two daughters side by side, their silken hair mingled, dark and light across the pillows. She had had an urge to creep downstairs and reenter Dr. Burdell's room to examine again the contents of his safe, to read his letters and toss the contents in the fire, to destroy the nefarious sequence of his plans, but she restrained herself, biding her time, knowing she must be careful not to do anything rash.

Emma held the taper and sat next to the window, looking out at the houses across the street, where she could make out one or two flickers deep inside, but mostly the houses were dark. The cobblestones glistened under the streetlights, and a paper skittered across the pavement from a sudden gust of wind that also set the streetlamps banging on their hinge.

She wasn't sure of the time, it slowed to a crawl, and she felt as if she'd entered into a trancelike state. She could feel a deep menace inside the house, as if it was sidling up to her in the dark and rubbing against her skin. Then a carriage came along the street. The noises that followed were faint, of a distant door, the house sighing at the presence of an entry. She touched the keys on her table. There was a shriek from outside, like a bird or a crow that echoed through the winter night. The noise resounded through her room, as if it came from another world. She glanced around the bedroom, her knuckles white, gripping the candleholder. The room wavered in patches of moving shadow across the carpet and pillows and soft furniture. The house below was beckoning. Patience, she told herself. She would be mistress of the house, and he would rue the day.

# CHAPTER THIRTY-THREE

*May 14, 1857*

After a closed-door session with the Judge, the trial was over. At the five-o'clock hearing in the Judge's chamber, the prosecution and the defense mutually agreed to rest their cases. Clinton appealed to the Judge that subjecting the trial to the drama of a manhunt would create a fevered chaos. As Clinton had suspected, Hall had plenty to gain by closing swiftly, by not having to cross-examine any additional forensic testimony produced by venerable authorities. After much posturing and bluffing, Hall relented to a deal. Both sides would summarize their cases in the morning, and by the next afternoon, Friday, the jury would return their answer, with a final verdict.

After an hour in the Judge's chambers, Clinton and Thayer left the quiet courthouse for the Tombs to give Emma the news. Snarky appeared, running up Centre Street to intercept them. "They haven't captured Samuel after all," he said breathless. "I just heard. They are saying that they had him cornered, but he 'escaped.'" Clinton shot Thayer an ominous look. "Why am I not surprised," he said.

"Did we just gamble our case away?" asked Thayer.

"No, we did the right thing. We've negotiated a path that is consistent with our aims. We have lost some evidence, but we have a strong enough position to close."

Clinton and Thayer entered the prison and climbed the iron stair to Emma's cell. When the matron let them in, they found Emma sitting with a woolen shawl wrapped tightly around her shoulders. The spring evening was mild, but dampness seeped through, creating a chill. The hardship of confinement was etched all over her face. Her bloodless complexion, which had not seen sunlight in many months, looked strained and weary. She had now been three months in captivity, first at 31 Bond Street, and then in the Tombs. She was much thinner, and her hands and arms showed the sinewy muscle and knobby bones of the joints, as it does with the elderly. Her mouth often hung open, as if she was in a daze. Her eyes looked creased and worn, and her expression was burdened.

When the lawyers entered, she looked up. "Your ordeal is over," said Clinton. "This evening, both sides have agreed that the case is closed. We will not give any more testimony, and tomorrow we will deliver summations to the jury. The verdict will come directly after. Your patience and fortitude have been most admirable."

Her eyes widened and her facial muscles succumbed to involuntary tics. "Will they find me guilty?" she asked. Both men offered her their most level assurances that all had gone favorably, that the prosecution case was weak and riddled with holes, and that the jury was a just and reasonable lot. Despite the very real threat of the gallows, they attempted to reassure her that there was no reason to look toward a guilty verdict. It was their job to bolster her courage for one more night.

She seemed relieved by their optimism and got up and started moving about the room. "Then, I will get ready to go home," she said. "I must be ready for tomorrow." She began laying out her small pile of books and belongings on the cot. Clinton and Thayer glanced at each other. It was not uncommon to see a prisoner, at the crucial hour, alternate between despair and the giddy euphoria that accompanied freedom. Clinton had often seen prisoners shift back and forth between the two moods on the night before a verdict: it was the disorienting effect of legal fatigue. Seeing that she was pre-occupied with her task, they bowed, and with more assurances, they bid her good night.

Clinton returned home and, after supper with Elisabeth, retired to the library. Elisabeth brought in a tray and placed it beside his desk with a teapot, cheese, and biscuits and a decanter of water. He removed his jacket, vest, and collar, and loosened the buttons of his shirt and rolled up his sleeves. He laid the notes and draft of his final speech, penned at intervals over many months, across the desk and placed a stack of fresh paper beside it, lined.

Elisabeth bustled about, readying the room. Clinton glanced at his notes. On one page he had listed the main points that would bind the opposition's case.

"Oakey Hall will say that the defendant had the motive, the means, the ability, and the opportunity to commit this murder. *'And murder she did, in cold blood, in the presence of her children, and of the servants who so reviled her,'*" Clinton said aloud, mimicking Hall's Southern drawl. "*'She resented him for his home and possessions, and resentment can be motive.'*"

"She wasn't physically capable," replied Elisabeth as she pulled shut a window against the night chill, "so, that eliminates the op-portunity. And as for motive, it could have been any of the mil-lion who live within the sound of the fire-bell on the City Hall. It seems a large portion of the population had resentment against him. And," Elisabeth added, "no mother would commit such an act with her own children sleeping in such close proximity."

"Not if she was blinded by greed and the passion of the moment," countered Clinton, adding, *"Heaven has no rage like love to hatred turned, and hell has no fury like a woman scorned."*

"Do you think he will dare repeat that cliché?" asked Elisabeth. "Dr. Burdell was missing for six hours, which opens up the possibility of scores of unknown encounters, all of whom had opportunity, and possibly followed him home. Why hasn't the prosecution brought forth any witnesses to his encounters?" Her hand drifted over his shoulder, and he grabbed it and kissed it.

"You might write this speech for me, darling."

"But I can't deliver it, so one of us should sleep," she said, kissing the top of his head. "I'll leave you, now, to work," she said. "I'm off to bed."

"Good night my dear," he said, burrowing again into his notes. Indeed, there was a mystery surrounding Dr. Burdell's missing hours. Emma had been vague about many things—about whether she heard the carriage return or not. The prosecution had carefully avoided mention of Burdell's various business ventures, for any one of them might raise reasonable doubt. Emma had always remained elusive on that subject. Her own travels on that day were a mystery. Her explanations fell toward a romantic but naïve description of his intentions toward her, but to Clinton, it appeared that she saw beneath his surface. The contradictions gnawed at him. Had she married him? Did they plan to go away to Europe together? Who had entered the locked house that night, and how? Emma stuck to her story about being in her bedroom, and if Clinton believed anything, it was that she did not kill Harvey Burdell. So he kept her focused on her most important task: to convey absolute innocence to the act of murder.

After Elisabeth left the library, he started scratching a revised draft of his closing speech, his pen nib moving over sheet after sheet as the rhythm of the words poured forth in its loopy scrawl, replacing pages that he had written earlier. He wrote in a flow, pausing only to dip the pen in the inkpot.

*We are not before the court to prove who committed the deed. Why would the prosecution charge this woman with this crime any more than any of the million who live within the sound of the fire-bell on the City Hall?*

*There are others that had proximity to the victim during the evening of January 31. Where did Dr. Burdell have supper? Where did he go between the hours of six o'clock and midnight? Why has the prosecution closed this case without calling a single witness to testify to these missing hours? Is it because the seeds of this murder lay elsewhere than inside his own home? Surely he had contact with others during that fateful night, for no man can become invisible in this city, and travel around it unseen.*

He wrote for hours, tearing up pages, and reworking the words on each fresh sheet. The oil lamp cast its unnatural yellow glow, creating a distorted pattern of shadow across the page.

When the pile of discarded pages filled the desk, he paused to crumble them, tossing them on the coals. As the paper caught fire, a burst of flame danced up in the grate and caught its reflection on the velvet black of the windowpane. The leap of the flame appeared menacing, like a wraith in colorful garb, dancing in a pirouette. Then the sputtering firelight faded and the room darkened a shade and Clinton was left with a momentary feeling of sinking doubt, of being up against something ineffable and wrong, as if something surrounded and lurked behind the scrim of this case that could derail even the best-laid plans. First there had been the Coroner, a clownlike character and a sinister menace. And the press, so effective as recorders, had become a rabid force, spinning rumors and false tales. Oakey Hall moved with an oiled efficiency and the slick deception of ambition, between the courts and the gallows and political back rooms, aligning to an unseen heart of power. It was a combustible combination, making even the logic of the law uncertain. Clinton was overcome with the thought that something had been unleashed that would not go away at the end of this trial, and was burrowed down under, like a conspiracy, a dark place, where it would fester, deeper even than the human instinct against murder.

He took the blotter and passed it over the wet spots on his sheet. He shook off his doubt and fatigue and forged ahead with the only tool he had, his reason and his ability to make a clean dissection of the moral and legal points of the case. He continued writing for another hour, cutting the page with the sharp edge of his words until he reached the end of the draft.

*Let us use the cold impartial reason of the law to take the place of heated passion and coarse ignorance. Let evidence be substituted for gossip and fact for scandal. Let every weak link in the chain of circumstantial evidence be dissipated. If that happens, this defendant will be vindicated, and every stain placed upon her name and that of her children by this atrocious prosecution shall be removed.*

# CHAPTER THIRTY-FOUR

*January 31, 1857*

The horse snorted a breath of smoke. The carriage was winding downtown toward the tip of the city, past Wall Street and Exchange Place to the small streets that dotted the edge of the island, ending at the docks and wharves. During the day, Water Street was alive with money changers, sail makers, commission merchants, and cotton agents. Now, long after the dinner hour, the only lights came from the phosphorous lamps dangling from the masts of the ships, a string of beads along the waterline. The streets were empty, except when the door of a lone tavern opened, releasing a raucous blast of laughter as men fell out into the night, their voices fading away along the quays.

The carriage twisted along tiny streets that were only a block or two long, and they circled around, for in the oldest part of town, there was no grid. "Stop here," said Dr. Burdell to Samuel. It was so dark that Dr. Burdell got out to examine the numbers on the doors. In his black cape and hat, he darted left and right, in front of a squat row of buildings hobbled with crooked dormers, looking for the correct entrance. A shadow slithered along the ground, like rippling velvet, a rat scudding through the gutter. From the water, Samuel heard the faint sighing of masts and the clanging of rigging. By the sound of the wind and the lapping waves as they hit the buoys, he could tell which way the sea was running. A fast-rising storm, a squall far out, was headed this way. From out beyond Rockaway Point the ocean sent rolling swells up into the bay. The water lifted the hulls of the boats up high, and then dropped them down against their ropes, pulling against the moorings like ghosts rattling their chains.

"Pull the carriage into this alley," Dr. Burdell ordered, in a hoarse whisper. Samuel led the horse by the reins and squeezed the vehicle into the rutted space between two buildings. "Leave the carriage and come with me." Dr. Burdell pulled his gun from its holster and pointed the muzzle at Samuel as a warning, then returned it to its place under his jacket. Dr. Burdell opened a wooden door and followed behind Samuel up a twisting staircase to a captain's den. The room was lined with cases of bound ship's ledgers and leather chairs that were cracked with years of use. Overhead was a hanging whale oil lamp with polished brass fixtures in the shape of harpoons. It cast an amber glow across a round table. The light beams bounced everywhere like a mirage—for spread across the table were piles of gold, shimmering along the length of the tabletop. And standing on the other side of the table, bathed in the luminous aura, was Ambrose Wicken.

Burdell faced him across the table, mesmerized before the jumble of gold, arranged in different heights, like a miniature city. The effect of such abundance was hypnotic. "The syndicate has been most generous, don't you agree?" said Wicken, lifting his hand and passing it through the air like a benediction across the columns of coins.

"I will count it later," said Dr. Burdell, placing his satchel on a chair and unlatching the straps. He reached for some drawstring bags that he had brought to carry the money, and he opened them with the thirsty look of a man who had been denied his liquor too long.

"Not so fast," said Wicken.

"Let's be done. I am here to take the money." Dr. Burdell started to lift some of the coins to drop them in his bag. Wicken slapped away his hand. Burdell stopped short, shooting a glance at Samuel, standing by the door.

"I see you have brought your Negro watchdog." Wicken's grin turned nasty, with a slight curl of his lip. "In the South, we use Negroes to procure life's illicit pleasures: women, guns, intoxicants. They are our go-betweens, and their silence is assured because the law never comes down on their side. As our shadows, they will always take the fall." Wicken picked up a few of the gold coins and threw them at Samuel. "But if they are rewarded, they become most helpful." The coins fell under the table and rolled to a stop at his feet. Samuel did not bend to pick them up. "Now, Dr. Burdell, before we continue, I must inform you that I feel entitled to share this bounty with you."

Burdell shot an incredulous look at Wicken. "There is nothing that gives you a share. This is my money for the sale of the land. Your commission was paid by the syndicate, and you should be satisfied with that."

Wicken picked up a stack of coins and let them fall through his fingers like poker chips. "You swindled an unsuspecting widow into buying a worthless piece of swampland. Afterward, you discovered it had value. I happen to know the deed is still in her title, and it seems that by selling it, you are committing another swindle."

"She will do as I say, for her main interest is marriage. That gives me control of her property. She has every intention of following my course."

Wicken laughed, half scornful, half incredulous. "Is that so? On the night you abandoned me at the opera with your lady friends, I discovered you feasted at Delmonico's with Commodore Vanderkirk. You were going behind our back and double-crossing the syndicate as an attempt to raise the price. I am sure you saw your maneuver as beneficial to yourself. However, while doing so, I had the opportunity to become intimate with the ladies and gain their confidence and trust."

Dr. Burdell growled, clearly unnerved by the silky delivery of Wicken's message. "There are no more obstacles to this sale," Burdell said. "The men from the party have signed the papers, their advocate's mark is upon them, this deal is done. Give me my money."

"I agree that the deal should not be undone. That is why I am proposing that we join forces, to avoid it unraveling. I suggest we become partners, and as partners we will split this pot, and everything else, half and half. I am aware that the title of the deed is not yours, nor is it Emma Cunningham's to sell. The property is rightfully her daughter's, as it was purchased with the girl's dowry. As her fiancé, I have an active interest in it."

"This is madness! You are a fortune hunter."

"Do you take me for a rogue? The impression I made on Madame Cunningham was most favorable, and her daughter is as much as delivered to my lap," said Wicken with a gracious smirk. "And I have taken the proper measures to secure my prize. I took her for a buggy ride, if you know what I mean," he cackled.

"Even Emma has more sense than to marry her daughter to a blackguard like you," Dr. Burdell hissed, and then paused to comprehend the meaning of Wicken's insinuations. He shot Samuel a glance. Samuel tensed. "Don't threaten me," Burdell said. "Or this game is over." Wicken saw Dr. Burdell's glance toward Samuel, and now the three men silently stared at one another. Samuel dodged his eyes downward, his muscles taught, while the two men eyed each other, as if at a duel. Whichever man reached for his revolver first, he would shoot the other, and Samuel would be shot next.

"It would be quite an arrangement! If I married the daughter, and you married the mother, you would be my father-in-law." Wicken laughed again, his head rolling back, as if drunk on his own mirth. And in that split second he missed Dr. Burdell's hand flashing to his waist, so quickly that it seemed merely a second before the gunmetal clicked and burst, pointing and sending a bullet downward toward the table, in such a loud rupture that the room was filled with the explosive sound. The table was solid oak and the bullet simply disappeared into it, sunken and caught inside the thick meat of the wooden surface, but before it got there, it passed directly through the white flesh of Ambrose Wicken's right hand.

Wicken gaped at his hand on the table, swollen and bloodied, disabled and broken. The room was encased in the sickening smell of gunpowder, and smoke hung in the silent aftershock. Dr. Burdell hastened around the table and placed his Colt revolver at Wicken's head. "I am leaving now. Don't make me shatter your skull, too." He patted down Wicken at his waist and retrieved his pearl-handled revolver, a delicate ladylike instrument, fashionably lethal.

With one hand pointing a revolver at Wicken, and the other revolver pointed at Samuel, he waved to Samuel to drop the stacks of coins into the money bags. Samuel complied, and soon they were filled. Then he indicated that Samuel was to place them in the satchel. With the revolver still pointed at Wicken's temple, he said to Wicken, "I am leaving. Don't follow us. And get rid of any attachment you have to that girl or this money." He started to walk carefully toward the door, both guns still lifted, inching out of the room. Burdell hurried Samuel out of the building. In the alley, Dr. Burdell climbed onto the coachman's seat, instead of into the cab, and sat next to Samuel, with the gun clutched in his hand, and the barrel pressed into Samuel's side, into the fleshy area at his waist. Samuel snapped the reins and the horses moved forward, and Dr. Burdell said, "Get me home, fast."

# CHAPTER THIRTY-FIVE

*May 14, 1857*

Clinton put down his pen, extinguished the last light, and climbed the stairs. In his bedroom, he moved across the carpet in his slippers. He took off his clothes and put a nightshirt over his head. Elisabeth was asleep in the high feather bed with her arm bent behind her head. He thought of Emma Cunningham's story about the night of the murder, her girls, together, all asleep in one bed, and he thought of the boy, John, and the bed Elisabeth had made for him in the room off the pantry, with its pile of bedding, and he thought of the boy's mother, who could no longer sew, ensconced in a tiny garret. And he thought that it would be a long time before the law could protect those soft places.

He slipped into the sheets next to Elisabeth. Even when she was sleeping, he could feel her love, for she loved in the largest way. He lay his head down on the pillow. As a way to quiet his mind after a clamorous day in court, he often repeated verse in his head to keep his own words from revolving in his mind. Elisabeth had introduced him to poetry early in their marriage, carrying slender volumes along on their country walks. They would stop somewhere and sit, and she would read from the Romantics, introducing him to Shelley and Byron and Wordsworth. They both enjoyed memorizing verses, and he often recalled these poems in bed, to ease himself to sleep before a big day at trial.

> *Render thou up thy half-devoured babes,*
> *And from the cradles of eternity,*
> *Where millions lie lulled to their portioned sleep*
> *By the deep murmuring stream of passing things.*

The stanza came from *The Daemon of the World*, a long poem by Percy Bysshe Shelley, and Elisabeth had read it aloud, years ago, tackling the hundreds of lines over many sittings. They sparred at a competition to see who could commit the most lines to memory. She labored over it and won, by walking around the house as she performed her chores, singing out large portions. But he knew that the poem held her fascination because of a later stanza. When she had first discovered it, it spoke to her, not of the universal, but the personal, as if it had been written for them alone.

> *She looked around in wonder and beheld*
> *Henry, who kneeled in silence by her couch,*
> *Watching her sleep with looks of speechless love,*
> *And the bright beaming stars*
> *That through the casement shone.*

*January 31, 1857*

The dropping of the horse's hooves made a hollow ring. A sharp gust lifted the horse's mane. The brick walls and iron fences along Bond Street were covered with tangled twigs from the leafless vines that twisted and scraped in the wind. Samuel pulled the reins to halt the horse in front of 31 Bond Street. He winced when he heard the metal click again, but it was from the release of the gun cock as Dr. Burdell returned the gun to his waist.

Dr. Burdell descended without a word and paused under the lamplight for his key. He pulled a heavy key ring from his cloak and slid the largest iron key into the door, then turned and snarled: "Be off to the stable." Samuel trembled at his release, and then plodded the horse along the block to the stable door, his rage returning, for the Bible says: *There shall be no reward to the evil man; the candle of the wicked shall be put out.*

Inside the house, the lamps were left low, with just enough light to illuminate the way up the stairs. The key to his office door fit into the lock with a smooth and noiseless turn. He moved across his office and threw some coals on top of the dying embers of the grate. After turning up a lamp, he took off his cloak and folded it on the sofa. He took off his overshoes and placed them next to the fire. He checked the contents of the satchel, opening a drawstring bag and sifting his hand pleasurably through the gold. He took the satchel into the wardrobe passage and closed the door. He pulled out the single drawer under the hanging clothes, near the floor, and lifted the shelf that covered the low drawer. It revealed a hatch. Inside the hole was a ladder that descended, and he lowered himself down, descending fourteen feet, deep into a hiding space inside the thick parlor wall that contained the massive sliding door that separated the two parlors. He brought the satchel down with him. He enjoyed the descent. It was dark; it was silent. He deposited the satchel and the two pistols at the bottom and climbed back up.

He stepped back into his office and looked at the clock on the mantel. It was ten minutes past midnight. He noticed that the ledger on his desk was open with pale lines and inked entries, with orderly dollar signs in correct columns. There was no need to share. Not with Wicken, and not with Emma. Control was of the essence, and if necessary, control was the ability to silence, exerted at incremental moments. Such a moment had arrived. Emma would be in bed. Should he pull the cord for her to come downstairs, or should he go up with a rag and a cloth to place over her face? He stood up and walked over to the sliding panel under his washbasin and bent down to look at the powders in the hidden cabinet, lined up in glass bottles. Laudanum and ether and cocaine. And behind a crystal bottle of strychnine.

As he crouched down low, reaching into the cabinet, he did not hear the movement on the carpet until the shadow was at his back. From behind, a sharp sliver of ice descended into the side of his neck, deep and swift. Colors flashed across his eyes. He cowered, lowering his head into his arms and covering his face against the dark blows that now penetrated into his back, in and out. He was overcome by the sensation of his own tearing skin and muscle. He choked back dark air as an arm grabbed him from behind, yanking his hair, exposing his throat. The blade sliced the thin membrane of his neck, and fluid filled his mouth. He stood up, blinded by the flow of blood, staggering like a bull, and turned toward his attacker, who prevented his escape, as the dagger hit him, again and again, now from the front, thrusting into his torso and pushing him against the shaft of steel. A carrion of birds ripped into his flesh. He slipped to the ground as if into a spiral, floating and twirling, becoming smaller and smaller, diminishing into a bottomless abyss.

"Damn you," said a voice at his ear. "Damn you."

# CHAPTER THIRTY-SIX

*May 15, 1857*

The entire city had come out for the last day. People arrived in droves, filling up the courtroom until the bailiffs threw open the sliding doors to the Marine Court room next to the Supreme Court, so that entire room filled as well. So dense was the crowd on the stairways and in front of the buildings and in the adjoining rooms, that the courthouse seemed packed with half of the population of the city. A file of people climbed up the tight spiral stair to the balcony so that there was not an inch of standing room unoccupied, with men squeezed tight between one another's elbows. James Snarky found a spot on the floor at the railing and sat with his legs dangling over.

The anticipation ended when the Judge's gavel dropped, introducing the final speeches, with the prosecution having the advantage of closing last. Henry Clinton placed his notes on a small podium and walked away from them as he launched into his speech from memory, facing the twelve jurors, speaking with passion and conviction, pausing only for emphasis and effect. He asked the jury to be as certain of Emma Cunningham's innocence as he was, and as were her daughters sitting beside her. He asked them to entertain all of the scientific certainties that eliminated her participation in this murder: notably the lack of a murder weapon and the brutality of the attack. She had no means to dispose of the weapon, nor of the bloody clothes. And he asked them to entertain the inconsistency of the motive: if she murdered from passion or greed to obtain the Doctor's wealth and possessions, why would she do it in the very home she hoped to acquire, in the presence of her children?

Clinton had no doubt that the twelve men were attending to his words carefully, for this is when juries listen most deeply, and he knew to appeal to their strong intuition and principle. After an hour-long speech, he asked them to seek truth with the best of their ability, and he knew by the scrutiny and resolve on their faces as he took his seat, that they would give it their very best try.

When it was the prosecution's turn, Hall stood close to the jury box. He spoke intimately with his silky voice, his delivery more modulated than his thunderous opening. He laid out the complexities and irregularities of the facts of the night, and those of the relationship between Emma Cunningham and Dr. Burdell. "Do not be fooled into believing that motherhood is intrinsically sacred," he intoned softly, with both hands on the jury's bar as he played upon the mysterious idea that motive lies far under the surface of things. "Even a frail woman, a mother, can be led to engage in the most base human actions." Hall's skill had an impact, and the jury was rapt. Hall knew that for simple, God-fearing men, there was nothing more painful than to reconcile a divided point of view.

Mrs. Cunningham wept during the Attorney General's summing up, and she sat bowed under the weight of her veil, as if her physical system had become prostrate. After the summaries were completed, Judge Davies gave his charge to the jury:

"Gentleman of the jury, you will now retire to deliberate amongst yourselves, and form a decision in the case of *People versus Cunning-*

*ham.* The prisoner at the bar stands charged with one of the highest crimes known to the law, that of taking the life of a human being—Harvey Burdell—on the night of the thirty-first of January last." His words seemed to reverberate beyond the courtroom, throughout the silent city. "For those members of the jury who have read this story in the newspapers before this trial began, do not be misled by anything but what you have heard in this courtroom. I must emphasize that the jury may not discuss any evidence or testimonies besides what was presented to you here."

He clarified his instructions with regard to the points of law for malice aforethought, premeditated design to kill, and circumstantial evidence. "The circumstances all taken together must be of a conclusive nature and tendency, and producing a reasonable and moral certainty that the accused, and no one else, committed the offense charged. In the case of doubt, it is imperative to acquit than to condemn."

It was precisely four o'clock when the jury returned. It was generally believed that the jury would arrive at a conclusion that afternoon, and after having been out for three hours, they returned to the courtroom and announced that they were in agreement. The folding doors to the adjoining Marine Court room were closed, to keep any massive outpouring of feeling at the rendition of the verdict. Thus, some hundreds of people, who had been in attendance earlier in the day, were deprived of witnessing the most important scene of all.

James Snarky sat in the balcony, mashed up against the railing, his legs dangling over the side, watching the swirl of activity below. The bailiff rushed over to the jury room door and opened it with a flourish. Judge Davies tugged on his robes, Oakey Hall stared solemnly at his notes before him, and shifted the weight of his crossed legs. Barnaby Thayer ran his hand through his unruly dark hair.

The jurymen filed in, each one walking with the peculiar gait and personality of the man's age and occupation. The room was deadly quiet, and yet it was a ballet of anticipation.

After the jurors took their seats, the jury foreman called upon them to answer to their names. When this was done, the Judge asked:

"Gentlemen of the jury, have you agreed upon your verdict?"

The foreman replied, "We have."

An officer of the court asked Mrs. Cunningham to stand up, remove her veil, and turn her unveiled face to the jury box. She stood, stooped forward, her hands gripping the railing in front of her box. Helen and Augusta sat on either side of her. Augusta's eyes were trained at a spot upward at the ceiling biting her lip, whereas Helen's eyes were trained on her mother, as if ready to catch her if she were to drop. Then the clerk said: "Prisoner, look upon the jurors; jurors look upon the prisoner. How say you, gentlemen? Do you find Emma Cunningham, otherwise called Burdell, guilty or not guilty?"

The foreman said, in a not very distinct voice, "Not guilty." Mrs. Cunningham appeared not to hear the foreman's reply. She stooped down and asked Helen what the verdict was, and on being told, fell back into her daughter's arms. There were some attempts at applause that were immediately suppressed.

Judge Davies said, "Gentlemen of the jury, you say that you find Emma Cunningham, otherwise called Burdell, not guilty of the murder and felony of which she stands indicted, so say you all?

One after another, each jury member read the verdict of "not guilty."

There were no cheers, as often trials become like cockfights, with spectators picking a winning team, but there was excitement in the room as the conclusion was repeated from man to man. The

Judge then thanked the jury for the attention that they had bestowed upon the trial during each stage of its progress, and discharged them from further attendance.

Emma was supported out of the court and taken to one of the judge's chambers, where a crowd immediately hastened to swarm around her, curious to see her response to her sudden acquittal, but she was hurried inside, with her daughters and her legal team. She was kept behind closed doors until much later, when she was hustled to a back entrance where a shiny black carriage had been brought up. Across the city, the newsboys crowed. The newspapers had kept the presses stoked, and within minutes, had printed up flyers with the verdict, and the boys ran around town screaming the news, tossing the flyers. "Buy your paper tomorrow and read all about it," they wailed. The stealthy exit was successful, for the carriage pulled away from the courthouse unnoticed. Emma sat next to her daughters, her veil lifted up as she looked out the window with stunned confusion at the passing lights and buildings, the city blurring through her tears. She was heading back home, finally free.

Late into the night, small knots of people gathered in front of 31 Bond Street with the expectation that Mrs. Cunningham might appear at the windows. They were disappointed. Occasionally they would raise a feeble cheer, with the intent to draw her forth. The shutters and curtains remained closed, and she did not make herself visible, and after the dusk had darkened into night, the last disappointed straggler departed.

# Part IV

---

# CHAPTER THIRTY-SEVEN

*July 29, 1857*

H enry Clinton crossed the large open room, surrounded by tall windows at the level of the treetops. There were planks of wood laid across sawhorses and workmen's boxes filled with tools. Just outside the window, a flag drooped on its pole. The room was empty of workmen, who had taken off for lunch. Sawdust hung in a yellow haze, suspended in the sultry summer air. He opened one of the windows wide, heaving it up to the level of the top sash, but the air outside was still and offered no relief. His new office on Astor Place was just a jumble of construction, but by the beginning of September it would have room for a junior staff and twenty clerks. With the success of the verdict, a deluge of cases had come his way. Criminals love a sensational trial, and they flock like gamblers to a winning firm. There were enough clients flocking to him, so that he could pick and choose his cases, and expand the firm as large as he would like. And he had chosen the location on Astor Place because he had promised Elisabeth that the new firm of *Clinton and Thayer* would be within walking distance of home.

He placed a pile of papers on a makeshift desk on a plank of wood. That morning, he had been to a brief session at Surrogate's Court for a hearing on the estate of Harvey Burdell. The Burdell family was litigating Emma's claim as his spouse to receive his property, and the unfinished business had droned along during summer sessions as various members of the bar vanished from the city, escaping the heat. Bit by bit, presentations were made. The newspapers followed the proceedings on back pages, but the interest in the murder case had not entirely dissipated. The papers ran readers' letters with sharp opinions about the verdict, and opinions on Emma's guilt or innocence. Many New Yorkers believed she had escaped prosecution through the cunning of her lawyers, escaping punishment for her infamous deed. Others believed the verdict to be entirely justified. Occasionally, in an effort to drum up circulation, the *Herald* or the *Tribune* ran a front-page headline: "Who killed Dr. Burdell?"

At home, Elisabeth set to work putting the household back in order. Maids had been rehired, and Mrs. Fullerton was cooking around the clock. When the trial ended in May, Elisabeth had wistfully waited for John to return. "When will he pay me a visit?" she asked. When he never appeared, she decided to contact his mother to inquire after him. Clinton had Snarky find the address. Elisabeth sent a letter to the address Snarky provided, 25 Rector Street. When the letter was returned with a red pen scratched across the address, "No longer in Residence," she became even more determined, so she went down to Rector Street herself. The landlord of the little house said that John's mother had moved away, but he didn't know where. He hadn't seen her son in a long while, but the woman was doing poorly with rheumatism, and a relative had come and taken her away.

Clinton tugged at his collar, which chafed in the heat. He was sweating in a linen suit. A vest had been necessary for the morning appearance before the Judge. The final papers had been submitted, and if successful, Emma would be granted a share of Dr. Burdell's estate. The Judge himself was about to take a holiday and would return with his decision in mid-August, so Clinton planned to leave now for a week at a cottage in Hastings-on-Hudson. At the house in Hastings, there were rocking chairs on the porch and gingerbread along the cornices and roses that climbed the porch pillars. Stiff breezes came up the hill from the Hudson and flapped all the curtains. Clinton and Elisabeth sat on the porch at night long after the fireflies and the moon came out.

The workmen reappeared and took up their tools. Saws started to grind away, blending in with noises from the street. Clinton directed the men to various tasks that needed to be completed while he was gone, and then he gathered up his files. First he would stop at Bond Street to see how Emma was doing before he left the city and to give her the latest news.

As he made his way down Bond Street, the arcade of lindens and Dutch elms drooped in the still air. He arrived at the house and lifted the latch on the iron gate that hung crooked on its hinge. One of the stoop ornaments was missing, and the black paint on the front door was worn and scuffed. The bell pull was broken, so he rapped the knocker against the door. After rapping and pausing several times, he heard footsteps. Emma opened the heavy door, looking smaller than he remembered. She wore a dress that seemed dusty and slightly soiled. Her hair was pulled back, but there were pieces that were adrift across her face. She pushed them away.

"Henry, it's very nice to see you. I am so pleased that you have dropped by."

"I sent a note over earlier, to let you know I was coming," he said.

"A note? Oh, yes. There are so many calling cards, that they get buried in the pile." She opened the door wide and stepped aside.

"Come in." He walked into the hall and looked for a place to put his hat. He seemed to remember that there had been a hat rack, but now there was no furniture in the hall, except the tall clock, its pendulum still, so he kept his hat in his hand and went into the parlor. The room was warm and airless in the July heat. He wondered how she was managing.

"Please sit down," she said in her most engaging voice. She pulled her skirt aside delicately and sat on one of the parlor chairs. He placed his hat on a table and looked around. The parlor looked as if Emma had tried to clean it. There was a dustbin abandoned in the corner, with scraps, and a rag on the mantel with a bar of lye soap. The wool weave of the carpet was worn through in large patches from the hundreds of feet that had trampled it during the winter months of the inquest. In some places, the floorboards were bare. Smoke stains left cloudy trails along the top of the walls, leaving the plasterwork mottled and grey. The windows facing the garden were streaked; it seemed that Emma had begun cleaning them, and abandoned the job, half-finished.

"How are Augusta and Helen? Are they well?" he asked. In the cavernous silence of the upper floors, there was no sign that anyone else was home.

"Oh, quite well. Augusta has a beau. I try to have her entertain at home, but she is always invited everywhere."

"Really? I am pleased," he said, though he could hardly imagine Augusta, who had been the most damaged by events, entertaining anyone, especially a suitor.

"Can I get you some tea?" she asked.

"Is it iced?" The minute he asked, he regretted it. Ice delivery would be a luxury she could hardly afford.

"Well, perhaps," she said thoughtfully. "I have been drinking hot tea all day long." She grinned broadly, as if something were funny or amusing. "I shall ask if I can get you ice for the tea. Perhaps I can just ring." She started to get up from her chair, but as she rose, she appeared to be having difficulty, and she swayed slightly.

"Please, never mind. I am fine without tea, hot or cold," said Clinton. "I would rather concentrate on the business at hand. I will be leaving for a week, and I want to let you know how things stand."

"Are you going to Saratoga?" she asked, pleasantly.

"No, we go to Hastings, along the Hudson."

"Oh, that must be lovely."

"Well, it will be, for Elisabeth. She loves roses, and there are a profusion of them. She spends all morning cutting away, and then more bloom overnight."

"Pink or red?" asked Emma, as if nothing delighted her more.

"Pink, I think." He was surprised at her composure. She looked haggard, but her spirits seemed gay.

"You might want to get away yourself. You are looking tired, and the country air is the best tonic."

"I am afraid I cannot leave. I have some pressing social engagements involving my daughters. I have lost so much time." There could be little in the city in the way of social engagements, and he doubted she had much to occupy her besides the household, which was crumbling around her. "I will be back next week," he said, "and that is when the magistrate shall determine the decision on the house and possessions, so perhaps I can convince you to take a trip then." It seemed as if the windows hadn't been opened since January. Dust motes floated weightless in the rays of flat yellow light that managed to come through the blinds. An oily film sat on top of everything. "The Surrogate's Court has nearly finished hearing the case," he told her. "But there has been no judgment because the judge will take a holiday, but when he returns, he shall deliver his verdict. Fortunately for us, Dr. Burdell's family did not present much of a case."

"Harvey had no use for his brothers," said Emma, solicitously. She spoke of Dr. Burdell as she always did lately, as if he were about to walk into the room any moment and enter into familiar banter.

"Nor they for him. I think their feuds dismiss the claim that he desired his estate to go to his family. There is no proof that he ever made a will at all."

"For someone who was so businesslike, Harvey was often careless about personal matters," said Emma, primly.

"It is a good chance the judge will rule in your favor. A widow without heirs inherits one half the property. The other half will go to the family. I want to warn you, unless we uncover some of the other assets, perhaps the house will need to be sold to make payments to the family."

"Well, he did want to sell the house," said Emma, seeming tired and confused, "so we could move to Fifth Avenue."

"There is no need to worry about a sale yet, I am sure you will be here a while—as a matter of fact, it is best that you keep the house occupied so that others do not take liberties. I hope it is not too difficult for you, staying in this large house." She looked thin and did not seem to be eating well. It was too hot to use the ovens. He wondered how often she was getting out.

"Oh no, not at all. I have plenty of company, and I occasionally go to the market myself." She wearily moved the stray hairs from her face again, and he saw a streak of dirt across one of her cheeks. Was she trying to convince him of her fortitude? It was a folly to think that she could maintain this house without servants.

"Do people still notice you, at the market, or along the streets? I should think they would have tired of you by now."

"All the neighbors are so kind to me." She touched her fingers to her temple, as if she had a sudden headache. Her isolation must be complete, he thought. Almost every house on Bond Street was shuttered for the summer, and those few remaining would hardly be embracing their infamous neighbor.

Emma touched her forehead again, and Clinton sensed that he was wearying her.

"Well, I should be off." He stood up. Rivulets of sweat had formed along his neck and into his collar. "I am glad to find you managing. I will be back next week. We shall know the decision by then." He made a slight bow, and she stood to follow him out.

On the stoop, he placed his hat on his head. The house at 31 Bond Street would be difficult to sell. It would most likely stand empty for many months, a tarnished blight on this polished block, a house of infamy, causing the neighbors great concern. After a while, the stigma of the murder would lessen and a buyer would come along who would restore the insides with fresh paint and finally purge the house of its notoriety. With the sale of the house, there would be enough to see that Emma would be taken care of. Depending on what remained, he might be able to shave off some for his costs, although the success of the trial made a fee unnecessary. But first, he was glad to be departing for the country. He greatly needed the rest and the time alone with Elisabeth.

# CHAPTER THIRTY-EIGHT

*August 4, 1857*

When Emma awoke, the shutters of the bedroom were shut and the full glare of the morning sun came through the slats. She slipped on some house shoes and knocked over an empty glass with a white film around the edge off of the night table. She picked the glass up from the floor and placed it on her vanity, which was piling up with odds and ends. Ever since she had returned, she had done nothing but walk up and down the tall staircases, making note of items that were missing or out of place. Eventually, she believed the house would return to its previous state, the way a dial on a clock worked the day back to the beginning.

What time was it? The tall clock in the hall no longer chimed. One day she had opened the glass and used the key to wind it up. The brass pendulums began to swing, and she heard the ticking sound and saw the minute hand jump on the dial. She set the time, satisfied that it was synchronized correctly. Later that day, when she passed by again, she saw that the clock had stilled. She gave it repeated windings, and the clock would tick on for a random amount of time, and then peter out, for no reason that she could discern. She even pushed it away from the wall to look at the gears in the shaft, but the intricate placement of the machinery left her puzzled.

It seemed that everything in the house was run-down. While she was in jail, Dr. Burdell's family had sold some furniture, unjustly it appears, for the ownership of the house and its contents were as yet unresolved. Mr. Clinton saw that she was awarded a sum of money for the missing furniture. She put the money in a drawer. Each day she would dip into the box and walk to the markets with her basket, and then return to her chores and meals, but as the weeks ticked by, she barely seemed to make headway on the overall improvement of the house.

She opened the bedroom shutters and put on a housecoat. From the energy of the traffic, it seemed to be well past ten in the morning. Although most of her neighbors had left for the summer, there were a few who still remained in the city during the week, along with servants who served the houses and stables. By afternoon it seemed that everyone had retreated far from the heat, and the leaves hung limp in the direct sun.

She descended the stairs. The door to Doctor Burdell's office was slightly ajar. The wall had been whitewashed over the wallpaper where the blood had splattered, and the carpet had been removed leaving the floorboards bare. Emma descended to the kitchen, and as she entered, she heard the scurrying sounds of mice in the brick oven. The furnaces smelled of old coal and the house had a lingering odor of rotting eggs from leaking gas. Today she would buy some beeswax and mix some citrus into the wax as she polished, to freshen the stale air in the parlor.

There was a loaf of bread in the pie cabinet, but it was hard. She felt light-headed, so she sat down at the kitchen table. She couldn't remember if she had eaten the night before, only that she had mixed a drink with laudanum and lay down on her bed, listening to the house creak and settle in the dark. She would send a note to Augusta to stop by the apothecary for more powder. Augusta was living with the old woman named Nellie, who had once cared for her and Helen when they were younger. After the acquittal, Augusta had chosen to remain there. Helen was still living with the relation, on Second Avenue. Both girls had resisted moving back to Bond Street because the house made them uncomfortable. Emma assured them that when the fall season arrived, everything would be fixed and they would all live together, and the girls would have piano lessons and pretty new wallpaper in their bedroom. But the summer dragged on, the only visits were from her daughters, and from Mr. Clinton, who stopped by with reports on legal matters.

Today she would dress and go to the market. Every day she made this plan. There was no hurry. As she headed up the kitchen stairs, she noticed an envelope sitting inside the vestibule, dropped through the slot of the front door. When had it come? Usually a messenger left an abrupt set of rings to alert the owner of the house to a delivery. Had she slept through the bell, or was it out of order?

She took it into the parlor and sat before a table that she used as a makeshift desk. She opened it smoothly with a letter opener that she had salvaged from Dr. Burdell's desk set. It was on dusty grey stationery, with a blue crest.

*My dear Mrs. Cunningham,*

> *I hope that you and your daughters are well acclimated to Bond Street. I have hesitated calling on you until you have fully settled in.*
>
> *I regret not being in touch with you during the length of your ordeal, but I have spent most of the past months at my plantation in Louisiana. I am now in New York, and wish to extend my congratulations on the success of your legal proceedings.*
>
> *Rather than put you to the trouble of returning my note,*

*I will call on you at home at noon tomorrow to extend my solicitations.*
  *I hope I find you well,*

  *With affection,*
  *Ambrose Wicken.*


She anxiously searched the top of the letter, but it wasn't dated. She wasn't even sure what day it was, or if the letter had come yesterday or this morning. There was no food or refreshments in the house. She put down the letter, thinking she had just enough time to dress and get to the market before noon. She dressed quickly, but with care. Had he returned for Augusta?

She headed for the market at the Bowery, and as she crossed the busy intersection, she was startled by the dangerous approach of a stagecoach. Suddenly, a hand was at her elbow. "Allow me," said Ambrose Wicken, guiding her across.

"Why, Mr. Wicken, you have given me a start." She turned to look up at him, so tall that his hair seemed to burnish in the sun.

"It was not my intention to frighten you, but to offer you aid," he said, leading her firmly to the opposite curb. "Are you headed to the market?"

"I was going to do some shopping, but I had no idea the trip was such treachery," she said, laughing, as if the crossing had endangered her, and he had saved her life. She stood on the sidewalk and patted at her hair.

He eyed her with concern. "I admire a lady who can prevail through great hardship, and come away from it lovelier than ever." She had no idea what to think about his flattery. It had been a long time since she had basked in the reflected glow of an appreciative man, so she smiled but chose not to answer. "I have been meaning to come and call on you," he said, "but I wanted to be considerate of your need for privacy. I imagined that you and your daughters needed time alone for a reunion."

"There has been so much to do. I have the household to manage and there will be new servants that will need to be trained."

They were at the other side of the avenue, now moving among the market stalls. She had never noticed how gnarled and small the ordinary class of humanity was until she saw them in contrast to Ambrose Wicken.

"Are these fresh? I fear not," he said lifting a bruised peach and dropping it back, at the displeasure of the man behind the stall. He wore a glove on his right hand, and kept that hand limply at his side. Seeing her notice it, he lifted it and said, "A carriage accident, while I was racing in Louisiana. Most unfortunate, for otherwise I would have won the race. How is the fair Augusta? I assume your girls are making the rounds at the spas this summer."

"Oh, I hardly see them for all of their comings and goings. They are often away from home, so I have to keep their suitors at bay." She suddenly felt dizzy, as though she was caught in the crush of every vendor and pushcart.

"Are you all right?" he asked, taking her elbow again.

"It is a spell of nerves. I have been much afflicted by it lately," she replied, feeling faint. He led her to a small bench near the lorries. She sat for a moment, waiting for the dizziness to pass.

"This is no place for a lady," he said, offering her his hand. "Let me escort you home." They crossed the busy avenue and walked down Bond Street, past the hushed townhouses. As they neared the house, Mr. Wicken said, "Do you remember, we were to meet, on that fateful day? The death of Dr. Burdell was a most terrible shock."

"Yes, poor Harvey."

"I remember you wrote me about a matter. It was concerning

some land. Dr. Burdell was a careful man. Did you resolve that matter of the land for you and your daughters?"

"It's all so confusing. There are many papers missing. Even the deed to the house is in question."

"Perhaps I can still be of help to you."

"Why thank you, but my lawyer will sort it all out." They were on the sidewalk in front of the house. She thought he was expecting to come inside but she was hesitant to invite him into the house and see it in its sorry state. "I am afraid that this afternoon I need some rest."

"I shall leave you, then," he said. "But I will come back on Sunday, and will take you out for some fresh air and entertainment. A day of pleasure, how does that sound?"

"I am not sure if Augusta is available."

"Then it shall be just the two of us. I shall come in the morning."

"Where shall we go, in the heat of the summer?"

"You shall see, the summer has endless surprises."

# CHAPTER THIRTY-NINE

There was a note on the front table from her mother, asking her to pick up an elixir at the apothecary on Sixth Avenue. It had scientific words and notations on it, to show the pharmacist. Augusta lived on Bedford Street, where she lived with Old Nellie, once her nursemaid. The woman's tidy little house had a garden and fruit trees, and breezes from the river, and seemed far away from the nightmare days of the trial. Helen went back to visit their mother more often than Augusta did, but neither of them wanted to return to Bond Street to live in that haunted shell of a house.

The letter sat on the table for two days. Both afternoons had brought thundershowers—the thunder cracked, and the rain came down so hard that it bounced back up a foot and then streamed off the paving stones, leaving puddles so deep she needed to pin her dress up to the shins just to pass along the road. There were no city storm drains in Greenwich Village, so the water pooled into little rivers and flowed under the trees in the orchard that bordered the church garden. Finally, on Thursday, the sun came back out, and the Hudson glimmered through the apple trees.

Augusta had no desire to leave Bedford Street, where the long summer days washed away the accumulated trauma of the last months. She could walk barefoot in the yard, getting mud between her toes, and spend mornings pinching roses off the back fence, filling up little vases with fragrant buds, still tightly closed. The front door was painted blue, and hollyhocks leaned against the sunny side of the house. Augusta and Nellie cleaned the house together in old linen dresses and used candles instead of gas. Augusta loved the house because of its simplicity, and knew that it was exactly its simplicity that would make it unacceptable to her mother. She felt possessive about it, and realized her possessiveness must be the same feeling her mother had for Bond Street.

Nellie was well into her seventies and had lived there since she was a girl and British troops had camped out in the fields. While Nellie combed Augusta's long blond hair she told stories about the handsome soldiers and wove tales about Augusta's future that conjured images of a house like this one, with a kitchen garden and little babies in the yard.

Augusta resisted going back into the heart of the city to do her mother's errand, especially now, because the day was becoming very hot. The walk east to Bond Street meant putting on stockings and shoes. She changed her thin dress, and rolled her hair up into two twists, to lift it off her shoulders. She found a basket and put in some vegetables from the garden to give to her mother. Her mother was getting thin, and she didn't know how she was managing without a cook.

Augusta lifted the latch of the gate. Vines wound up the front of the house with thick trunks the width of her wrist. As she walked east on Christopher Street, she passed Greenwich Lane and Factory Street. The streets gave way to small wooden houses, well kept, but modest, with doors just steps off the street. She crossed

Sixth Avenue and entered the apothecary with its high cases of jars with colorful liquids, lined up behind glass. Mr. Bigelow prepared a bottle of elixir to match her mother's order and stopped up the glass bottle and sealed it with wax.

"Careful now with this concoction," he said. "It's not for everyday consumption." She put the bottle in her basket and continued on her way, past the Gothic buildings on University Place. She thought of stopping into one of the cool churches to pray but was no longer sure that piety could comfort her. This part of the city seemed empty in the middle of summer. There were no prams or children minding their nurses at Washington Square, or students from the university, just the still buildings and a tangy smell of rotting food where refuse was piled in boxes, abandoned at the curbside.

When she reached the long block of Bond Street, the sight of the house filled her with dread. She walked up the stoop and rang the bell, but the pull was rusted and loose and she could hear that it did not ring. She turned the knob on the large oak door, and it pushed open to the vestibule. Her mother was getting absent-minded, with the large house to care for, that she was not even remembering to lock the front door. She went up two flights and found her mother in her bedroom, walking around, as if she were looking for something.

"Mother, I came from the apothecary. Mr. Bigelow said to be careful of this mixture."

"Thank you. I need it to give me strength. I have had a series of nervous jolts, but I feel better now. Did you tell the pharmacist about my condition?"

"I didn't know what to tell him," replied Augusta, hesitant to sit and stay.

Her mother sat down in the armchair. She had a strange look on her face. There was a glass in her hand.

"Mother, there are no servants here and no one to look after you. You don't look as if you are eating well."

"I will be fine, now that I have more medicine."

"There is no need to be alone in this big house. It is foolish to remain here."

"It's my home," Emma insisted. "I will fix up the house and make it lovely again. For you and Helen. You will see."

"Helen is staying with Cousin Matilda, and I am not coming back. You know I prefer staying with Old Nellie. I do not want to be in this house."

"Of course you do, it will be perfect for us."

"Mother, when will you abandon this folly?"

"In September, we can get a season's box at the symphony, and the seamstress will come to make some new dresses." Her mother lifted her hand to reach for one of Augusta's curls, and Augusta dodged her hand away. "There will be suitors, and parties, in the fall."

"I won't return to that charade, with you trying to sell us to the highest bidder."

"Sell you?" Emma said.

"Yes, you have trotted Helen and I around in circles, in finery and jewels, for years. I will not suffer it any longer."

Her mother's face contorted to reveal teeth that had yellowed from the cheap tea in prison. "You mock me," she said with vehemence. "I struggled to make sure you had decent surroundings. You and Helen had what every girl needs and desires—frocks and hats and music lessons!"

"You did everything to make sure we had decent surroundings, but nothing to surround us with decent people," Augusta snapped.

"It is time you were married—where will you be without that? You board with an old woman, and when she passes away, then what will you have? Will you live in a shanty? A shack? When a woman keeps going backward, it's a bottomless hole—there's nothing but degradation. Why would you choose such a life, when I have worked so hard to lift you above it?"

"I find degradation here, in this house," said Augusta.

"You ungrateful girl! This is an elegant home, and it will be beautiful again. It will be yours and your husband's. Certainly a woman has to make small bargains, but they are always for the good."

"What kind of bargains have you made? You made bargains with our father, and with Dr. Burdell. You brought us here to Bond Street, and the next thing we were all sitting in a murderer's box, waiting to see if you would hang!"

Emma slumped back in her chair, as if fatigued by the fight and the oppressive heat of the house. "Augusta," she said, imploringly, "he is back."

"Who?

"Mr. Wicken—"

"Stop, I refuse to hear any more." Augusta slammed the apothecary bottle on the vanity, and picked up her basket. "I am leaving."

"I will order you a wedding dress from Hartbelle's," insisted Emma softly, smiling with her cracked smile, as if there was nothing wrong with her outlandish plans.

"Are you mad? Is there no way to bring you back to your senses? Can't you look around and see the circumstances?"

"We will all live here together. You'll have a baby. It's a fine home for a family." The air in the room was close and stale. Augusta felt the old feeling of desperation roll through her so fiercely that she could hardly breathe. It was a physical sensation, like having a revolver pointed to one's head, waiting indefinitely for the flint to click.

"Good-bye, mother," she said, with determination. She turned from the room.

"Come back, listen to me! Ambrose Wicken has a fine plantation in Louisiana, and he will be living here, in New York, half the
year."

"You have mentioned that man's name for the last time in my
presence." As she walked out, she heard her mother call after her.
Augusta continued quickly down the staircase, past Dr. Burdell's
office, its door slightly ajar. She knew the room had been cleaned
and emptied long ago, but she imagined blood on the floors, turned
foul and rancid in the summer heat. She rushed faster, down the
final staircase to the vestibule.

Emma was calling now, down the well of the stairway from the
third floor. "Darling, will you be back in time for supper? We will
all eat here tonight in the dining room. When you have a baby, I
will have a nurse come over and care for it." Her voice sounded odd
and plaintive.

Augusta turned the knob of the front door and screamed with
all her strength, "I am leaving and I am not coming back. You are
mad and I won't listen to this lunacy," and she turned the knob and
ran down the stoop.

# CHAPTER FORTY

Emma went down to the kitchen and fixed herself a tray with tea. She carried it upstairs to the office on the second floor. Dr. Burdell was so good at hiding things, she thought. She patted one of the panels in the recessed area where there was a cabinet with a washbasin. The panel slid away, revealing a cubbyhole with apothecary jars, filled with powders he mixed for the patients before surgery. There was still a small amount at the bottom of these bottles. Harvey would bring her some laudanum in quinine on the nights he desired her in his bed. She would sip it until it made her loose and sleepy. He kept the jars well hidden from the servants behind these secret panels, and no one had removed them, even after the house had been thoroughly searched during the inquest.

She dropped several spoonfuls of the snowy substance into the elixir that Augusta had brought. Then she poured some into her teacup and poured the tea on top. The herbs of the tea seemed to swirl in ornate patterns as she drank. After a while she didn't remember which room she was in or which one she went to next.

She found herself in the parlor, not knowing how much time had passed, but the house was getting dark.

She went to light some candles on the mantel. Her hand trembled as she struck the match on a piece of hearthstone. Did the servant boy take the flints? She stepped across the carpet to a table by the window. She lifted the crystal globe of a lamp and inspected the interior. It was covered with sticky black soot, and the glass bulb showed a small amount of yellowed whale oil that barely reached the bottom of the wick. She shook the lamp to wet the rope and put the match against it until a flame sputtered.

Whale oil is so expensive, who is wasting it? She sat down next to the lamp and picked up her sewing basket. The windows to the street held some of the evening glow, but the back parlor and the hallway were dark.

She started sewing along the edge of a nightdress that needed embroidery. Augusta's trousseau demanded extra touches. Emma struggled with the stitches. Her rings glistened as she pulled the needle back and forth, fingers trembling, worn and thin.

"Hello, my dear."

Emma looked up, startled. She saw a shadow through the arched doorway between the two parlors. The heavy pocket doors were halfway open, and a figure stood in the back room, framed by the archway and the heavy white molding that soared up to the plasterwork ceiling.

"Oh, Harvey, you startled me," said Emma.

"What has happened to the carpet in my office?" he asked.

"It was soiled and it's being cleaned. It will be back next week, I think." He was obscured, so that she saw only his outline.

"What are you doing, Emma?"

"I am preparing Augusta's wedding clothes. I have so little time during the day, so I must finish this embroidery in the evening.

I hope you don't mind." She pricked her finger, and a small dot of blood appeared on the tip. She stared at the small red orb, swelling up.

"Do you need some laudanum? I am going up to the office, and I can bring you some," he asked. His voice was strange, as if it were being channeled through a long pipe.

"Oh no—this is just a little prick, it's not painful at all. You are thoughtful to ask, though."

"Well, I just want to take care of you."

She laughed. "Oh, Harvey. You always take care of me. And I am such a boring wife, trying to accomplish these fancy stitches, when I should be tending to you."

"You're a wonderful wife, and a wonderful mother. And I am grateful for that." His voice now sounded more muffled, as though he was trying to talk underwater.

"Harvey, are you all right? I hope you are not ill?" She squinted, trying to make out his features. He stepped forward under the archway, his face slowly emerging into the half-light. His sideburns spread across his cheeks, and then she saw dark smears of purple, clotted in his whiskers, and there were black bruises across his forehead. He smiled, and his mouth spouted a foul, dark substance. He tilted his head back slightly, and the skin on his neck separated, with pieces of loosely flapping skin, until a gash widened, revealing crimson sinews and pink tendons, releasing more viscous fluid.

"Harvey!" she gasped. Then a sound came across the room in waves, and she was not sure whether the sound was in her head, or in the room, or if it was silent, or loud, for the pitch was so high, it was like the end of a nerve, screaming.

"I must go now, dear—I am in the middle of doing a tooth extraction," said Dr. Burdell. "Mind you, I am not in pain—but if you are alarmed, I will get you some laudanum." He receded into the back parlor, and she heard him, from the other room, distinctly now, "You have made our house so beautiful and I am proud of you. I am so proud that you are my wife."

The ringing pitch in her ears increased to such a degree that her energy drained away. Her hands slackened and the sewing fell from her lap. Her head nodded into her chin. "I love you, I love you, I love you, and we will sail to Europe!" Now it was her own voice she heard, singing. "And when we come back from Europe, we shall be so happy!" She lifted her head. The carpets looked so clean, now that the lamps were full and the gas flames were dancing along the walls of the room. The upholstery was fresh with bright colors that she had picked out herself. There was music; Augusta was playing the piano in the back parlor. Through the archway, all the crystal and silver on the sideboard was buffed and shiny. Ambrose Wicken was standing behind the piano bench, with his hands resting on Augusta's shoulders, leaning over her, looking intently at the sheet music, smiling and solicitous. As her fingers rippled across the keys, Augusta's body swayed from side to side to give her hands wider reach. It's so silly of him to love her so much, thought Emma, fixing the knot on the thread and clipping it with her gold scissors. Helen sailed by in the hall and rushed upstairs. The girl was always in such a hurry. Three maids filed down, having fixed the coal in the bedrooms. They were headed to the kitchen to help Hannah clear the dinner dishes and lay out the breakfast china for the morning.

"Mama, Ambrose and I are going for a walk," said Augusta, appearing before her mother in a white billowing dress, with gold billowing hair. Ambrose Wicken had his arm around her waist.

"Take your cape, dear," said Emma. "It is still winter, isn't it?" She suddenly wondered what season it was.

"I am not sure, Mother. I am confused." Augusta suddenly looked puzzled. She turned pale and her legs began to buckle. Alarmed, Ambrose grabbed and caught her.

"Augusta!" he cried, alarmed. He caught her in his arms.

Augusta's eyes blinked open and she smiled. "You have that effect on me, Ambrose. When I am near you, I am always swooning." He helped her upright.

"Let's go, you silly goose, let's get some air." Looking relieved, he smiled, showing her his pearly teeth. The door shut, and Emma heard their laughter, and their steps across the paving stones.

# CHAPTER FORTY-ONE

*August 7, 1857*

Everything seemed encased in a sticky yellow haze. When she woke, the gauze of her nightgown and the filmy cotton of the sheets were tangled up, and her room was hot.

"Is it already noon?" she wondered. By now, she was sitting at her vanity, unsure what to wear for a day on the town on a Sunday in August. Mr. Wicken was already in the house, chiding her about how long it took her to get ready. He had brought her a bouquet of summer pansies and a bottle of dark liquid that he said would soothe her nerves. As she dressed, watching in the mirror, the colors of her clothing became more vivid and iridescent. She changed her mind about what to wear, again and again, searching the closet to find a different dress. It was like being in dreamtime, when one repeats a simple routine, over and over, but never finishes.

How had Ambrose Wicken entered the house? Had she gone downstairs in her nightdress to let him in? How strange. But he was here, on the third floor, talking to her from outside her bedroom door, teasing her about taking so long to dress and laughing and joking. Sometimes he would go downstairs and stay for a while, and she would hear him rustling around in the rooms below. He must have gone into Harvey's office, for there were noises and banging from that part of the empty house.

Finally, she had on a dress of deep vermillion. She was trying to find ornaments—a bracelet, a sash, or colored bits to put in her hair. Wicken spoke again from outside her door, and when she told him to wait just a little longer, he said, "Hurry, now, it's been long enough."

"I am finished," she said finally, teetering as she got up from her vanity.

"Let's be off, the day is half gone."

Then they were sailing, or at least the carriage seemed to be sailing, as if the wheels would pick right up off the ground and jump over the uneven spots in the pavement. He was driving his open phaeton and the wind was in her hair. They passed the brown geometry of St. Paul's Church, but she couldn't tell how long they had been riding—minutes? Hours? It seemed like a long journey, yet with so little traffic on lower Broadway, and the city empty on a summer Sunday afternoon, they were still only a short distance away, a clear shot from Bond Street.

At the tip of the island, there were breezes at the Battery. They stood looking out at the pleasure boats darting around the harbor. Wicken led her to a boat slip where the fancy yachts moored.

"There is nothing like a racer," he said, pointing at the sleek vessels, "don't you think?"

"Too much wind," she protested, holding her hair. A yacht was bobbing at the slip. It had a sinister beauty, with brass fittings on a jet-black hull. The sails had black markings, with a jib that was being readied for a sail. The boat belonged to an actor, famous from the stage, and it was often seen slicing across the harbor like a sharp knife.

The actor spotted them and yelled from the deck, "Ambrose! Come aboard, we'll take her to Sandy Hook and back."

Wicken called, "Isn't it time you started to earn an honest living? Only a pirate would own a boat like that." Then Wicken laughed, and agreed to come along, and urged Emma, but she protested until she realized it would be rude to decline. The actor reached out to take her arm, and she made an unsteady jump from the dock to the deck. The actor looked dashing with his shirtsleeves rolled and his arms brown from the sun. She felt as if she were leaping from a theatre box onto the stage boards to run off with the leading man.

She sat down at the stern, on the broad cushions of seating for the passengers. Ropes were pulled and the sails filled up with a stiff breeze that seemed to come out of nowhere, filling the canvas until it snapped tight, then the inky water rushed past. The men called over the spray, yelling at each other with exuberance, pulling and ducking at the boom. Clouds followed them, competing with the boat, like fluffy yachts, racing to beat them to an imaginary mark in the open water.

There was a group of men, all of them young, some were the actor's brothers. Wicken stayed by the bow, and occasionally he came back to where she was sitting, holding on to the railing to make his way as the deck tilted. He would sit next to her and make some comments about the passing scenery, but it was difficult to hear him, so she would laugh into the wind, holding back the strands of hair that were whipping in her face. The boat tacked with broad sweeps, changing angles, so that different masses of land loomed ahead of them, first Brooklyn and then Staten Island, each dropping away as they tacked to the other side

At the end of the harbor, they passed through the Narrows, and at the sight of the open ocean, she felt queasy when the rougher water rose up over the bow, spraying the salt water high into the air. The vastness of the ocean seemed to swallow the boat, or was it her unsteady nerves? She decided to go down into the hold. Below, there were small dark staterooms with polished wood and brass. She moved through them, the floor unsteady beneath her feet. She sat on a berth that was nestled in an alcove, and then she lay down as if in a tomb, to calm herself.

Sometime later, maybe it was hours, they pulled back to a different pier, and docked along a wooden slip on the East River. Back in the sheltered waters, the wind was dead, and without the river motion, the air was stagnant and unmoving. The clock on the Custom House tolled six bells, the time of evening when the sun sweats with a flat light and the August twilight is still many hours away. The group disembarked while wharf hands coiled the ropes around the long piles.

A pleasure steamer pulled up to the opposite side of the pier and a crowd rushed off the boat. They had been out to picnic at Rockaway and they staggered down the boat ramp, with red burns on their faces, carrying buckets of clams and oysters and warm bottles of lager, dropping papers and debris on the ground. Emma was suddenly disoriented by the swarming crowd, and Wicken grabbed her arm and led her away from the wharf.

The group from the sailboat wandered aimlessly along the downtown streets until Wicken suggested that they see the Chinaman. They ducked under a low door, past dusty curtains, into a dark room that had the appearance of a men's saloon. "Drinks for everyone," Wicken called to the barkeeper. There was another room behind the bar, and everyone sat close in a spread of settees around a low table. A man with a long coat and a pigtail down his back padded in and out of the room. The actor instructed her on the funny arms of a brass water bottle. When it lit up on top, Wicken told her to breathe in softly.

"When you said the Chinaman—I thought we were going shopping for crockery," Emma said, laughing, as she relaxed at the inhalation of the delicate smoke. Wicken told her it would settle her stomach after the boat trip, and it did, smoothing out the roughness until her insides were like silk. The smoke was everywhere in the room, swirling around, making her think of her daughters, and how precious they were, such beauties. All her sensations were vivid. There were high cushions everywhere, pillows and fringe and lots of oriental patterns mixed up with brocade. Did someone lift her legs up so that they were stretched out on the divan?

"There is no need to be coy." The voice had the velvet undertone of a man of the stage. The actor from the sailboat was now dressed for dinner, or was it one of his handsome brothers? She wanted to go home, but she couldn't remember where she lived.

"The evening is young," said Wicken, but it had gotten dark. Next, they were walking toward the lights of the amusements at the Bowery. Her shoes tapped along the sidewalks. She thought she saw Samuel glowering from a doorway. Then she saw Helen floating down the Bowery, hoisted to the crook of a young man's arm, her hoops sailing her along, as if her feet barely touched the ground. It was Sunday night and the street was lit like a carnival. Was it really Helen?

A girl lamplighter perched on a ladder and struck a match that burst at the wick. Suddenly they were in the thick of it: dime museums with midgets and deformities; flashy goods; ladies with squeaky voices calling out for a séance; men with hand organs and a monkey tied to a rope, with a tin cup for coins. Every sort of novelty was spread around, and the lantern lights were twinkling along the street. The brassy notes of a tuba swelled from the door of a German lager saloon.

"We are stopping here—this is Claxton's," someone said, and they entered a music hall. Emma was handed a colored drink that had an acrid taste of fruit and kerosene, leaving a slow burn.

"Drink up!" Everyone was standing up or sitting at chairs scattered around small wooden tables. Many young men were well dressed and handsome like the actors, and there were lots of bawdy girls in low dresses.

"Personally," said a man next to her, slurring his words during a conversation about the books of the transcendentalists, "I have no use for religion or philosophy."

There was a stage up front, and a young man lifted up a banjo and placed a strap over his head. He turned to watch the other boys playing, studying their beat. His face was blackened with burnt cork, so that all that was left was a ring of white skin around his eyes. He swooped his head down, his blond curls flopping into his eyes. He was dressed in a cutaway coat and tan flared pants; his boots had a tooled wooden heel. A red silk kerchief was knotted at his throat.

He tapped his foot and picked at the strings, plucking faster and faster, in a giddy rhythm that roused the crowd, who clapped and stomped their feet. Music pulsed from his fingers. The other players sang along, chorus after chorus, until they finished the song with a rousing flourish. The boy with the banjo jumped down off the stage and put his arms around the waist of a girl in big hoops. Was that Helen? Was that her daughter, with the bee-stung lips, and too much rouge? The boy grabbed the girl by the arm and led her away. "Let's sail," he said.

Then Emma was outside again. Giants, Siamese twins, ventriloquists, jugglers, rope-dancers, panoramas, gypsies, pawnbrokers, lottery dealers. The street was filled with smoke, and she heard the hiss and crackle of roman candles and then a cascade of fireworks fell from the sky.

She was being led down a long alley—the rough cobblestones were treacherous in the dark, and Emma was staggering now.

"Why, Harvey has not joined us, because he is always doing

business," she whispered to Wicken. "He'll meet us at Bond Street," and she thought yes, Dr. Burdell shall be waiting at home.

The next place was a building at the end of the alley with wooden stairs, and inside were tables for cards and lots of cigar smoke. "Out back there's a pit where I bet on the cockfights," said Wicken. The air was sticky again. Was everything a dream?

Suddenly she felt faint. "Do you mind? I need to rest." There were funny rooms, like stalls, with little cots, and she was lying on one, swaying, the way she had in the berth of the boat. Everything floated in a pleasurable way when she closed her eyes, and she nodded into a sea of warm sensations.

She heard screams and was not sure where they came from, but she tried to sit up. "It's a raid!" There were crashing sounds and screeching cries. "Get out, hurry," she heard someone say as footsteps crashed along the wooden floorboards outside the room until it sounded like everyone was gone. What was she to do when she was so limp and tired?

Then there was a stomping of feet. The door burst open. A group of officers burst into the room she was in. "Fancy seeing her here," said the Police Captain.

In shock, she saw the District Attorney, and now she screamed. He stood over her, pointing down at the bed, and the officers rushed toward her with iron cuffs. She screamed again, louder this time: "Don't take me away. My daughters need me. My beautiful girls."

And then they lifted her up and led her out to a police wagon; it was like the final act of a melodrama she had once seen on Broadway.

# CHAPTER FORTY-TWO

*August 8, 1857*

The newspaper was folded next to his breakfast plate. The birds sang in the leafy vines at the open casement windows. The garden was filled with glorious sunshine, and he was well rested from his trip to the cottage. Elisabeth came into the dining room, and she stood nervously, before pulling out her chair. She eyed him warily as she placed her napkin in her lap. Mrs. Fullerton deposited a plate of morning biscuits, and there were new maids upstairs, who helped keep the dust at bay.

As he unfolded the newspaper, he noticed that it had already been opened and the creases were not fresh. Now, Elisabeth was eyeing the paper as his eyes fell on the front-page headline.

"My lord, what the devil!" He rapidly scanned the page, and then pulled the pages open to see the story as it followed inside.

"This can't be! I am astonished. Utterly astonished. I just saw her before we left. Elisabeth, why didn't you call me downstairs when you saw this? How long have you known?"

"I just saw it a moment ago."

"This is preposterous. It says Emma was arrested in a gambling den. How absurd. The last time I saw her, she was sequestered in that house, foolishly washing the windows."

"Well," said Elisabeth, "the cook has the *Herald* downstairs, and I'm sorry to say the story gets much worse. The gambling parlor was filled with women of ill repute, and Emma was found sleeping in one of the prostitute's rooms."

"Oh, Good Lord Jesus," he said, throwing his napkin on the table.

"It seems Emma was carried away from the gambling den in a drugged stupor. The Police Captain and Oakey Hall took her into custody in a raid. And the paper reports that the daughter, Helen, has been seen with a boy in a minstrel band. The *Herald* is trumpeting moral degradation."

He pushed his chair back. "I've got to get down to the Tombs. I have absolutely no doubt that Oakey Hall is behind this. This is a setup, a sting." He hurriedly put on his suit jacket, which was draped on the back of his chair.

Elisabeth reached over and pulled the newspaper across to her side of the table, and started scanning the *Times*. "It says that everyone is wondering anew if she was the murderess, after all."

At the jail, he followed the matron's footsteps across the stone floors, down a long corridor of the dankest cells, dimly lit by sparse fixtures, giving it the atmosphere of a dungeon. The female warden separated an iron key from her ring and banged it into its hole. He had visited the prison countless times, but the Tombs had never felt so tomblike.

Emma Cunningham was sitting on a bare mattress, wearing a

stained prison gown. She was leaning against the wall, her mouth open and her jaw slack so that a trickle of saliva glistened along the side of her chin.

"Emma, I just got back to town, and heard the news. I have come to help you." He went up to her and bent down, close to her, but she showed little reaction to his presence.

She gazed at him without answering, as if she had no powers of comprehension. She stared mutely. She sat with her limbs askew and her hair matted and tangled, her very being fractured and crumpled on the mattress. "Emma, do you recognize me? Do you know who I am?" Clinton wondered how she had fallen into this alarming condition. In his drive to push the case to its successful conclusion, he had created an image of her at odds with the woman before him. The strength and fortitude he believed she had possessed were merely an illusion. He now realized that he had committed a fallacy greater than any legal miscalculation: by collaborating in his fantasy of who she was, he had collaborated in her decline.

Humbled, he pulled a wooden stool close. "Emma, do you know why you are here?" he asked. "Do you know what happened?" He watched her, searching for answers in the strange dislocation of her face. She rolled her head. Her mouth curled up at the corner, to which he assigned a flash of cleverness, only to realize it was only an involuntary twitch. Then her jaw dropped, and she let out a sudden howl that blasted through the chamber; it was a cry of such anguish that Clinton was propelled to his feet and backward a step or two. The sound repelled him, cutting past his reserves of compassion. How many times had he heard cries of agony as he moved through the jails to the magistrate? He had believed that the power of law could make a difference, yet the fragile network of reason and logic stretched and cracked like a thin parchment over an unknowable and unreachable chasm.

"I will act as your counsel," Clinton said, uttering the few words that were necessary. "I promise, I will see that the charges against you are dropped. You have not committed any crime. I believe this is a case of entrapment, and Mr. Thayer and I will present that position before Judge Thomas. I am fairly certain you will be released within the week."

Emma stared, uncomprehending, taking no notice of his words. Clinton moved to the door and gestured through the bars for the matron. She reappeared with the keys swinging from the hoop on her hip. She pulled open the barred door, and Clinton stepped out of the cell, hesitating a step. The door shut, and as he walked away he heard her moan, her cries rising and lowering in pitch, like a series of soft wails that trailed behind him as he headed down the corridor. "Don't leave me, don't leave me, don't leave me," he thought he heard her say. Was she calling him back? Or was it his imagination in the echoes in the Tombs? He did not turn back, lest he attach a meaning that wasn't there.

# CHAPTER FORTY-THREE

*August 22, 1857*

S amuel and Katuma leaned against the wall, under the awning of a shop front on the Bowery. In front of the shop, hats were piled high on tables—stovepipe hats, flat caps, and cheap bowlers that the boys on the Bowery wore with their colored kerchiefs and flared pants when they strolled for amusement. Vendor boards lined the pavement, advertising trinkets and penny entertainments, propped out in the middle of the sidewalk, so that pedestrians collided into them. The street was alive on a summer Saturday at noontime—young men had giggling girls on their arms and a week of pay in their pockets, strolling on the cheap.

Samuel stood behind the hat table, in shadow, under the shade of the shop's awning, brooding. Quietta stood near Samuel, tracing a finger along the feather of a fedora on the hat man's table. "He followed the boy, like a bloodhound after his scent. I saw him on the horse; he tracked him to the woods, looking for me." He said, his furrowed brow obscuring the yellow glare of his eyes.

"I have kept my eye on him as well," said Katuma. "He follows a path, like everyone. He will stop today at the séance parlor, where the Gypsy sells cocaine on Saturday morning to the swells who come round to buy for the weekend." Katuma moved out onto the sidewalk, in the glare of the noonday sun, scanning the broad intersection as traffic flowed past from every direction. "There he is," said Katuma, looking up the avenue. "I see him now."

Across the street and up a block, he spotted the tailored garb and flaxen hair of Ambrose Wicken, striding tall.

Katuma turned to Samuel, who slid back deeper in the shadow of the awning. "Get ready. Watch me closely, then wait five minutes and follow us into the alley." Katuma gestured for his daughter. She was wearing a fringed and beaded dress, with bare legs and moccasins. Her black hair was slicked back in a braid down her back, thick as an arm. In her Indian costume, she looked like the daughter of one of the painted wooden Indians that stood before the cigar stores, instead of Katuma, whose faded workmen's clothes hung loosely from his powerful frame.

Wicken had crossed the street and was nearing the shop front. Katuma took Quietta's hand and led her a few paces, into a bright blast of sunlight in the middle of the sidewalk, where they stood and waited as Wicken approached. Samuel receded farther back into the shade behind the tables, his muscles tightening, and his blood pulsing through his body in a red rage, bracing against the instinct to attack.

As Wicken saw them, his pace slowed at the sight of Quietta standing in her beaded costume. An inquisitive look crossed his face, as if he were amused by one of the colorful signboards that beckoned with pleasurable trinkets for sale. Katuma whispered a phrase to Wicken; it was a quiet offer, muttered in an undertone. "Take my daughter, only ten dollars," he was saying, with Wicken close enough to feel Katuma's breath, and smell the musky allure of the girl's skin.

Wicken's eyes darted about at the pedestrians passing, not because he feared exposure, but because a busy man always had to weigh his pleasures before he alters his schedule. He patted his breast pocket, and cocked his head, indicating that he had money, but like a savvy buyer, he was not willing to part with it until the wares were in hand. Katuma led his daughter by the arm, with Wicken, now grinning, following beside them, looking down, not at Quietta's face, but at her firm breasts, which rose visibly under the smooth suede dress. When they passed by the hat vendor's table, Wicken was too preoccupied with his prey to notice Samuel lurking in the shadows.

Samuel watched them pass, and waited under the awning, measuring the time. He calculated a minute passing, but it felt like an hour. The rays of summer sun seemed carved in stone. A street car clanged along the Bowery, and when the sounds of the bell finally faded away, he told himself to get moving. It was difficult for him not to break into a run.

A block and a half south was an alley, overrun with wooden shacks, sagging rooftops, and broken stairways with missing boards. The alley was so narrow that very little sun filtered through, keeping it cool and dim, even in the middle of the day. Samuel was neither too early nor too late. Wicken was holding Quietta's hand, and his other was on his breast pocket, hesitating, this time to indicate that now that the tawdry wares were his, surely they were not worth ten dollars. Katuma was staring at his daughter's hand, being fondled by Wicken. She was behaving with silent poise.

Samuel saw the men before Wicken noticed them. The two men were on a low rooftop, silent as alley cats. Even in the dim light, Samuel could make out that they were the friends of Katuma, Indians, dressed in black clothes. They rose from a prone position, and sprung off the roof, flying down as Wicken looked up, too late, until they were upon him, and he recoiled, as if warding off a blow from above. The men landed at his feet, one on each side, grabbing Wicken from behind, and another flinging his arm around his throat and clamping his mouth, stifling a cry. Samuel saw the stricken look in Wicken's eyes as he struggled. Then one Indian pulled a rag and a bottle from a burlap bag and soaked the rag with chloroform, smothering it across Wicken's face, pressing hard. Wicken gagged in an effort to bring air to his lungs, sucking in the fumes. Quietta slipped back a few paces, and Katuma stood very close to her. Wicken tried to kick, but the motion made him unstable, and he lost his footing. When Wicken's knees sagged, the man with the rag held it on for several more seconds until he was sure that the body had gone limp.

The Indian with the chloroform pulled the burlap bag over Wicken's head and tied the drawstring at his feet. Then, like a dockworker, he hoisted it onto his shoulders, and tossed the bag into an open wooden cart that the men had brought to the alley.

"Run home, now," Katuma said to Quietta, who swiftly turned and ran, her moccasins silent, dashing away like an Algonquian girl on a path through the woods. Samuel positioned himself at the barrow handles. The four men pulled the wagon down the alley and turned onto a walkway that led behind the buildings to Broome Street. From the side streets, they could make their way to the river. No one would even glance at three Indians and a Negro pulling a load of cargo through the city, for men did this every day, for a quarter, handed out by a foreman, at the end of a day of labor.

They arrived at the riverbank in half an hour. It was not yet one o'clock. The afternoon sun bounced off the blue river, shimmering through the trees. An abandoned glass factory sat on the bank, grown over with weeds and underbrush. One of the men dragged a flat panel of hammered boards away from the building, a raft they had constructed to carry the heavy load out into the river. They placed the bag on the raft and slid it to the river's edge. Then they pulled a rowboat beside the raft—the boat was small, a sturdier version of the dugout canoes that the Lenape still used to navigate and fish.

They stepped into the water, glistening with brown pebbles and minnows, swarming, a few inches deep. The water lapped against the wood of the boat. "Thank you," Katuma said, with a nod. The two Indians gave a soft salute and left without a word, climbing back up the bank. Katuma tied a rope at the prow, and looped it through an iron ring on the raft. Samuel lay flat on the raft. Katuma used his oars to push into the current while Samuel helped with a long paddle. They floated into the Hudson, tethered together, using the oars as rudders to steer themselves. In a matter of minutes, they were heading south, reaching the quiet space in the center of the broad river, where the current ran strongest, while the buildings of the city receded into specks along the island's ring. Even the tall schooners clustered at the ports and the ferries darting in the distance seemed like tiny toys. Two men on a small craft were as indistinguishable as workmen pulling a wagon on a city street.

They floated along for a time, sometimes rowing, sometimes drifting, toward Staten Island. Reaching the river mouth where it opened into the wide harbor, the water was often choppy, but on this August afternoon, it was still, with a breeze soft enough to cool the sun on their cheeks but barely able to ripple the skin of the water's surface. White gulls swung above, their wingspan suspended, gliding on shafts of air, cawing and swooping for shellfish. Samuel and Katuma floated to the west of Staten Island, where the harbor seeped into miles of marsh.

"This land is sacred," said Katuma as the marshes swelled out in a gentle fringe, edging the harbor for miles. "My father is buried here, in one of those mounds, and his great-grandfather, before him, who was the chief. They lived in peace in these parts."

"This same marsh was to be the scene of infamy," Samuel said.

The raft made its way, slowly lapping closer into the reeds. "There isn't a bobwhite within a hundred miles of Manhattan in January, but when I heard the whistle, I knew it was you, for you had taught me well."

"City people don't know the sounds of birds, certainly no one on Bond Street." That cold night after the carriage had dropped off Dr. Burdell, Katuma had made the long bird whistle, as a signal to Samuel. Then Samuel had taken the horse back to the stable, and pulled the rigging off, and removed his boots and britches, and changed into work pants and a warm jacket that was lined with sheep fur. Inside the stable he lit a lantern and kept it low on the floor. About twenty minutes passed, and Katuma appeared at the alley door. He stood there, holding his hands before him—the grey pants and shirt were covered with dark stains, and when Samuel brought the lantern over close to him, the stains turned crimson, for he was covered from neck to cuff with blood.

"Stand there, don't come in," said Samuel, who placed a sheet at Katuma's feet. He stepped on top of it and gingerly began to remove his clothing and let it drop piece by bloody piece. Then he stepped off the sheet, naked, and began to put on fresh clothes that were waiting in a pile. Katuma wrapped the sheet around the clothes and carefully tucked the ends of the sheet together and then pried loose the floorboards and dropped the sheet into the dark hole. Before putting the boards back, Katuma asked Samuel to bring him a bucket of water. He dipped his hands into the bucket and then rinsed his hands over the hole, the soiled water falling deep into the chasm.

"You have done it, so let's be gone," Samuel said. "I wish there was another way, but I could not stop this myself."

"There was no other way," said Katuma. And then he went to the doorway and retrieved the dagger he had left on the ground. He returned to the bucket and washed it over the hole, and emptied the remaining water, and placed the knife in the loop of his trousers. "No use losing a good knife."

Samuel extinguished the lantern, and they saw the horse's eyes in the dark, its breath smoky from the cold, and the restless movements of its tail. "The deed is done," Katuma said. And Samuel remembered the uneasy feeling of dread at the plan Katuma had spoken of when he heard the conspiracies that were afoot. "Those swamps were the kingdom of my ancestors and the shells were our currency," he had told Samuel. "The rivers and streams were our highways connecting to all the tribes. My spirit is Manitou, who speaks to me through my dead great-grandfather, once chief of the Lenni Lenape. The Dutchmen did not steal our land, for the land was there for all to share. They blocked our trade. Now the spirits have bidden me to stop theirs."

It was with ease that Katuma had climbed to the second story, using a rainspout that had provided a grip as he scaled the wall. Then he had used a burglar's wedge to unhinge the catch on the office window, and refastened it once he was inside. He had waited hidden, in the house, then had slain the beast and made his way out again with the stealth of a cat, locking the street door with a key Samuel had given him, after he exited. And the two of them, warmly dressed, made their way from the stable quietly down the alley to the Bowery, and slid around the corner without attracting any notice.

The sack lay motionless on the raft beside them. Katuma pointed to a rivulet that made a passage through the marsh, and they paddled into the reeds, with marsh grass forming a soft green wall on either side. "Bloody money," said Katuma. Samuel and Katuma had retrieved the gold just a week earlier, going back to 31 Bond Street in the dead of an August night, near midnight. This time, Katuma used a knife to jimmy the lock of the kitchen door.

Once sprung, they left it broken and walked right in. To Samuel's nose, the rooms were weighted down with death and decay. They went up the main stairs, and passed through the office, to the wardrobe passage. They pulled at the drawer—it had warped from the summer heat but, once removed, revealed a cool hole, and Katuma lowered himself inside, feeling his way down the ladder without a candle. He pulled up the contents of the cache, which consisted of the satchel Dr. Burdell carried that night and some rolled-up deeds for this marsh, and others for empty lands, some faraway, out in the West.

They left the house the same way and walked the mile west under a white moon, until they heard the sound of a screech owl and stopped near the graveyard on Greenwich Street. "This money is unclean," Katuma had said, wiping his brow. "We'll bury it here," pointing to a spot between the roots of a very old oak. Katuma took a long sip from a bottle of rum he carried in his pack. Increasingly, Samuel had seen him swig from it to quell the spirits that raged inside of him.

"What about the girl?" Samuel reminded him.

"I'll take her a portion," said Katuma, and Samuel told him where she lived with the old woman, in the house, not far from the river, with the blue door. In the morning, Augusta would find a sack of gold and some papers sitting by the kitchen steps, like a bottle of fresh milk.

Samuel said good night and left Katuma to the task, for he was more adept at these shadowy jobs. They would hide the money for now, for possession of even a few gold coins was enough to damn a Negro or Indian. Then they could siphon it out in bits and funnel it to the church and the Underground workers, who helped to keep the slavers at bay. To Samuel, the money was fuel for the abolitionist cause. For Katuma, the shining coins represented a foul currency destined to suppress his ancestor's legacy, and it needed to be put under the earth, as if to purify it. Money was not a balm that could slake his anger. Samuel left Katuma resting under the oak tree, with the faraway squint of a man with a rifle site before his eye, still focused on revenge with a phantom target.

When the water became shallow, they used the oars to push against the bottom. The stream forked and bent, heading west, into the wetland. Clusters of firm ground appeared, here and there, where trees sprouted in clumps.

"I can see the railroad now," said Samuel. Across the expanse, the tracks bisected the marsh, running north along a spine of dry land that the Passaic Indians had used as a roadway north and south. The raised ridge had iron rails running along the top and was widened with stone and earth, landfill hauled on barges from the city, by laboring gangs.

"This is a good spot," said Samuel, when they were in full view of the railroad tracks.

"What should we do? Should we dump him?" asked Katuma, about Wicken's limp body. Samuel did not answer but stepped off the raft, hopping to a tiny island of solid ground amid the high reeds, where some trees had died and fallen, their trunks in a pile. Samuel picked up a tree trunk that was weathered and smooth as a post. He pushed the post into the mud, where it sank then settled into the firmer sand at the bottom, standing it upright. "Do you want to kill him?" asked Katuma.

"Not kill him," said Samuel. "You know that is not part of my teaching. God did not give me the power to do that."

"I will kill him," said Katuma. "I wasn't bred with the same teaching as you, and I wouldn't feel dishonored to commit the act. This man was searching for you that afternoon, and he took the boy's life to send you a message, and seal your lips. This man and this mud are the same, and I would be putting things back to their natural order by burying him here, alive."

"I want to lash him up," said Samuel, untying the burlap sack and pulling it off Wicken, who was curled, still unconscious, his fancy clothes wrinkled and twisted. Samuel took a rope that was coiled at the bottom of the boat. "Prop him against the post, and I'll tie him on."

Katuma pulled Wicken off the raft and heaved him upright, holding him against the piling. The limp body sagged heavily. Saliva fell from his drooping lips, though his heart was still beating. Samuel wrapped the rope round and round, so that Wicken hung tightly to the pole. In the distance, from the south, came the whistle of a locomotive.

"Leaving him here is the same as killing him," said Katuma.

"Perhaps, but I'll leave his punishment to God and the mosquitoes," said Samuel.

Wicken hung, with his jacket fallen around his shoulders and his linen shirt torn open, revealing the fair skin of his chest. His head was slumped forward, and his flaxen hair matted with sweat covering his eyes.

Samuel and Katuma got into the rowboat, leaving the raft behind, bobbing in the marsh. They used the oars to turn the boat, and started to row, with small strokes, to the east. The train came upon them, coursing along the ridge in a thunderous roar of iron pistons and steam. The windows of the train flickered past with the silhouettes of passengers, some reading, some talking, ladies with large hats, and men in suits, dressed for travel. Some would certainly be gazing absently at the scenery and would spot a white man, half naked, hanging in the middle of the marsh, tied to a tree. The flashing scene would be etched in their minds, perhaps dismissed as a mirage or a trick of the eye. In an instant the clattering train was gone.

"We all deserved to be saved," said Samuel as the boat slid through deep reeds. "Every man stands a chance to be redeemed."

# CHAPTER FORTY-FOUR

*November 12, 1857*

A flag snapped in the wind, just outside the window. A sign painter with a tiny brush was painting his name in gold, HENRY LAUREN CLINTON, ESQ, on the milky glass of his office door. The new office on Astor Place smelled of new paint and shellac. The outer room had twenty desks for clerks, who were already grumbling under the caseload. He had two trial lawyers to keep him from having to appear downtown daily at the court. Despite Emma's notorious arrest, which hit the papers like a firestorm in the doldrums of August, he and Thayer had successfully gotten her released, for she had not committed any crime. As for her actions that night, he had learned that she was enticed to a night of entertainment by a man she had met earlier. Snarky uncovered word that there had been a tip-off to the DA, for her presence at the gambling den had all the earmarks of a trap, and a sting set up by Oakey Hall.

The adverse outcome was that the Surrogate Judge delayed his decision on the estate. The incident had clearly prejudiced him, and he had reversed his thinking on the matter. His final decision gave everything to the family, so by the time Emma was freed again, she was left with no money and few possessions, and was sent to a charity house for infirm women, where she was cared for by a group of Mission ladies. She regained some coherence, but at times her mind remained addled. She alternated between a docile belief that she was returning to 31 Bond Street and an angered understanding of her circumstances. The firm of Clinton and Thayer became busier and busier, attracting hordes of new clients.

By the fall, New York had taken another turn. A flurry of bank failures had rippled through the city in October. In the short period of a single month, the city's exuberant expansion had been reversed, and New Yorkers, many rich and more poor, had lost everything. The city was reeling from the panic as it settled in for a colorless period like the depression of '37, when the hungry wandered down kitchen alleys, scavenging for scraps of food, and slept, burrowed under the stoops of private homes.

A wiry young clerk appeared at the door of Clinton's office. "Someone is here to see you, sir. It's curious—he's an Indian. I thought he was begging, but he said he has a parcel to give you."

"For me?"

"Yes, he says you will understand when you see it. I tried to take it from him, but he held on to it steady, like it was filled with gold."

"You can send him in."

"Are you sure? He hardly says a word."

"Yes, go ahead and bring him to me." The sign painter had paint buckets everywhere, disrupting his concentration. He saw the Indian being led through the maze of desks; he wasn't wearing hard soles, so his steps padded softly. At closer view, Clinton could see that he was not a derelict. His clothes were worn but were not dirty. He had no sores; his skin was smooth and clean. His black hair was pulled back in a ponytail; he no more belonged in a law office than did a bobcat, muscular and sleek.

"How do you do, sir? How can I help you?" said Clinton. The

man ignored his question. He placed a packet on Clinton's desk. It was a small parcel wrapped with waxy brown paper that didn't fold neatly but crumpled into a boxy shape and was tied together with a fine string.

"For me?" he asked warily. The Indian only nodded. Clinton's fingers fumbled with the tiny knots, and he wondered if perhaps he should have delegated such minutiae to a clerk. He felt foolish pulling at the tiny string when there were so many pressing things to be done. Finally, the string fell away and the paper opened to a small pile of trinkets, tiny bits of debris, jumbled together like the sweepings of a dustbin. There was an old penny, with a hole pierced above the flying eagle. Twine was threaded through the hole—at closer glance the thread was a jute fiber carefully braided together with a mosaic of delicate bits of ceramic beads. Next to the penny was a feather, downy and yellow, finch colored. When Clinton touched it, it fragmented, and he realized that it was a lock of hair, as silky as the finest filaments in nature. He lifted the golden tuft onto his palm, and he was suddenly stricken by the significance of the offering.

"It was the Negro that sent you?"

The man nodded. What Clinton's instincts told him was too horrifying to fully acknowledge. As the summer had turned to fall, and he had become preoccupied with the new office, he had denied his suspicions and buried them in a deep trench, and once buried, he felt the constellation of his life flowing smoothly again along the surface. The enormity of his emotions now came welling up. His throat was tight, and it was difficult to talk.

"The boy's death—was it painful?"

The man pointed to a scrap in the pile, a paper folded in half. Clinton opened it and saw a tiny inked script with a few lines, written by the hand of someone who had labored hard at the effort. *But he shall let go the living bird out of the city into the open*

*fields, and make an atonement for the house: and it shall be clean. Le-*
*viticus 14:53*

The tragedy stabbed him now with the full force of its invisible grief. Clinton had never voiced his fears about John's absence
to Elisabeth, and did not know if he could tell her now, for she
would certainly hold him responsible for steering this boy closer to
the cruelty that led to his death. Yet, if he kept a secret from her, it
would be his only deception in all their years of marriage. And he
thought back at the long trial, and the stresses and sacrifices, and
he wondered, had this case advanced justice? Were all of his actions
actually callous and vain? Were his own motives, as Armstrong had
insisted, more about successfully winning a duel with Oakey Hall?

"Samuel, is he safe?" he asked.

"He is alive," the man answered.

The trinkets glimmered before him, more precious than any
gem. "Thank you," said Clinton. He looked up—hoping to find a
hint of absolution in the Indian's coal black eyes, but the man had
gone. He was already in the outer office, padding past the desks,
and without the notice of a single clerk, he let himself out the door.

From the window, Clinton saw the man on the street below,
heading through Astor Place, blending in with the crowd that was
scattering in all directions. As a child, he had been told that Astor
Place was the spot where several Indian highways came together,
the center of a web of paths that forked across the continent. At
this convergence, a tribe had buried their chief's heart beside an
acorn, and an oak grew with twinned trunks, with ancestors' spirits
dangling from the boughs like silent totems.

Thayer came to the door, peering into the office. Seeing him
distracted, he rapped on the glass, to get his attention. "Henry, you
have a court session later this afternoon, do you remember?" He
stepped in and leaned against the wall, folding his arms, waiting to
catch him up on the docket.

Clinton looked up, not hearing anything. "It's a strange thing, freedom. It doesn't mean much when there is so much bondage and pain," he said.

"I'm sorry . . . I don't follow you," said Thayer. "Are you speaking about the South? Slavery?" Thayer was perplexed by the direction of the conversation. "Henry," he said, trying to bring his partner back on course. "You asked me to brief you on the Matthews case for the hearing with Judge Thomas this afternoon."

"I'm sorry, I need you to take care of that for me, I am going home," Clinton answered.

Thayer looked confused. "Are you well, Henry? Is everything all right?"

Clinton stared at the trinkets on his desk. "I will be. I just need to see my wife."

# Author's Note

This book is a work of fiction. It draws from accounts of the murder of Harvey Burdell as described in the newspapers and testimonies of the time. The characters who figured in the actual case and have lent their names to this tale are: Henry Clinton and Abraham Oakey Hall, who tried the case of Emma Cunningham; Doctor Burdell and his brothers; Edward Connery, who conducted the Coroner's inquest; Hannah Conlon, the cook who testified on the stand; and John Burchell, the houseboy who discovered the body and ran to the precinct to fetch the police. Barnaby Thayer was the name of a lawyer whose name was borrowed. Elizabeth Clinton Clinton (spelled with a z) was the granddaughter of New York politician DeWitt Clinton, but she met and married Henry Clinton after this case had ended. The Elisabeth Clinton in the book is an invention.

The story departs from the record by eliminating a number of real people: in fact, Augusta and Helen Cunningham figured prominently in the case, and captured the public's attention, but they had three siblings, two boys and an older girl. Also, Emma Cunningham rented rooms in the upper floor at 31 Bond Street to some boarders who were eliminated from this fictional drama, even though they played a role during the investigation and inquest.

The characters of Samuel, Katuma, Quietta, Ambrose Wicken, James Snarky, and Commodore Vanderkirk are figments of the imagination, as are the inner thoughts and personal dialogue of everyone in the book.

The *New York Times*, founded in 1851, was then called the *New-York Daily Times*. The common usage was to hyphenate New York, and although much of that earlier city has vanished, New York itself is a central character of the book, as vibrant and alive then, as it is today.

The following is a brief summary of the lives of the three main characters after the trial ended:

**Abraham Oakey Hall:** Hall was elected mayor of New York in 1868. In 1871, the *New York Times* broke a story alleging massive corruption by members of the "Tweed Ring." Over six million dollars were removed from city coffers under the direction of Tammany boss, William Marcy Tweed, and every check to city contractors for inflated charges was signed by Mayor A. Oakey Hall.

Mayor Hall was indicted for corrupt neglect of official duty and tried three times. The first case was declared a mistrial when a juror died before the verdict; the second ended with a hung jury; and in the third case, in 1873, Hall defended himself and was acquitted. He claimed no knowledge of the frauds perpetrated and that he never benefited financially from them. He resumed the practice of law in New York but encountered serious financial difficulties. On March 21, 1877, the *New York Times* ran the front-page headline:

ABRAHAM OAKEY HALL; HE MYSTERIOUSLY DISAPPEARS.
BELIEF THAT HE HAS EITHER GONE TO EUROPE OR COM-
MITTED SUICIDE—NOTHING SEEN OR HEARD OF HIM
SINCE LAST FRIDAY—

HIS IRREGULAR HABITS —EVIDENCES OF MENTAL
DERANGEMENT—ANXIETY OF HIS FRIENDS.

Hall vanished from the city, and after much conjecture was discovered to be living in London, where he took up another calling as a writer and a playwright for the stage. He spent his remaining career between London and New York, where he worked as a journalist, newspaper publisher, actor, playwright, and again returned to the law. He entered into a lawsuit for libel against him by an author that noted his role in the Tweed frauds. The case was dropped, but the pursuit was costly, and when he died, his wife turned to his friends for financial aid.

**Henry Lauren Clinton:** Henry Clinton had an illustrious and prominent career in New York City, and his obituary in 1899 stated that he had earned the highest fees of any lawyer in the century. He wrote two books, *Extraordinary Cases* and *Celebrated Trials,* that became best sellers of their time. In them, he detailed his legal strategies in the Cunningham-Burdell murder case as well as his role in another celebrated case: in 1872 Henry Clinton was a prosecuting attorney in the trials against Mayor Abraham Oakey Hall. Henry Clinton made the opening statements:

"May it please the Court—Gentlemen of the Jury :
Sad and mournful is the spectacle this day presented.

"... With me this day begins the most painful duty of my life. Since I first met the defendant at this bar, ... more than twenty years have rolled by. Since then, when we were both young, often have we crossed forensic swords.

"Many have been the trials of deep and absorbing interest in which we have been opposed, not a few of them equalling, if not surpassing, the present."

*Celebrated Trials*, p. 387

When he died at his home on Park Avenue, his wife, Elizabeth Clinton Clinton, was at his side.

**Emma Cunningham:** Emma Cunningham was listed in the 1860 city directory as working in a liquor store on Spring Street. Later newspaper items reported that she had left for the West Coast, presumed to be in San Francisco. In the post-Civil War decades, interest in Emma Cunningham or her whereabouts waned and the murder trial was long forgotten. In 1887, an obituary appeared in the *New York Times*:

> *Mrs. Emma A. Williams died Tuesday in this City. Few persons would suspect that this woman was the conspicuous figure of one of the most celebrated murder trials that ever took place in this city or country.*
>
> *Soon after being acquitted for the murder of Doctor Harvey Burdell, Mrs. Williams, known as Mrs. Cunningham, left this city for San Francisco where she married William Williams. She lived for many years in California with her two daughters, where she claimed to be the owner of extensive copper lands in Lower California known as the "Muleje Copper Mines."*
>
> *According to her niece, Mrs. Phoebe Morrell, Mr. and Mrs. Williams visited New York City around a year ago. During this visit, Mr. Williams tried to have her adjudged as a lunatic,*

*and when he was not successful at this, abstracted 192 bonds
and cash from her trunk, leaving her destitute.*

*She wandered about from place to place, friendless and
alone, whereupon her niece invited her into her home, where
she died after a brief illness.*

*The New York Times,* SEPTEMBER 16, 1887

# Acknowledgments

I am deeply indebted to my gracious and talented agent, Marly Rusoff, and her partner, Michael Radulescu, for taking on this book. Thanks to my brilliant editor and publisher, Claire Wachtel and Jonathan Burnham, it found a home at Harper, where the dedicated team of editors, marketing, publicity, and sales have skillfully guided it to publication.

This book is based on a true story and made the transition from nonfiction to a fictional narrative over many years. During the long incubation of the novel, I had the good fortune to be included in a fiction workshop. Each member had a unique talent and perspective that greatly enriched this book, and I am immensely grateful for their ongoing dialogue and input: Martha Chang, Caren Chesler, Catherine Greenman, Brendan Kiely, Esther Noe, Rob Weisberg, and the novelist Jonathan Rabb, who hosted the workshop.

I would like to give special thanks to a group of readers who offered a fresh eye and intelligent feedback as well as many years of deep friendship and loyal support: Josephine Wallace, Deborah

Newmyer, Sian Evans, Claudia Thomas, Jed Brickner, and Wendy Weitman.

The author Beverly Swerling was a generous source of experience and professional advice. Other professionals offered insight and encouragement as I struggled to make this book happen, and for each contribution, the book came closer to reality: Alexia Paul, Marika Kyrimis, Shula Rosenblum, Hyeri An, Sarah Horan, Alexander Black, and Christine Brown.

Finally, I would like to thank my wealth of friends and extended family, especially my daughter, Ji Tan Haines, for being an endless source of spirit, humor, and creative inspiration. I dedicate the book to my late father, Hubert J. Horan, who had a special knowledge of politics, history, and the Civil War. He offered passionate discourse, friendship, and a guiding hand.

# Illustration Credits

Page 1: *Frank Leslie's Illustrated Newspaper*, August 22, 1857.

Page 83: *New York Times*, February 13, 1857.

Page 179: *Harper's Weekly*, May 9, 1857.

Page 291: "City of New York," sketched and drawn on stone by C. Parsons. Published by N. Currier, 1856. Library of Congress.